# THE CHILDREN'S
# GOLDEN TREASURE BOOK

# THE CHILDREN'S

No treasure chest ever contained a hoard of greater riches than will be found between the covers of this entrancing volume. On the magic wings of imagination the charmed reader is conducted from one end of the earth to the other, back into the past and into the present. Now with gypsies, with knights of old, fairy folk and grumbling giants. There is never a moment of boredom. Here is a book of rare delight, a book that will quickly become a well-beloved friend.

ODHAMS PRESS LTD.

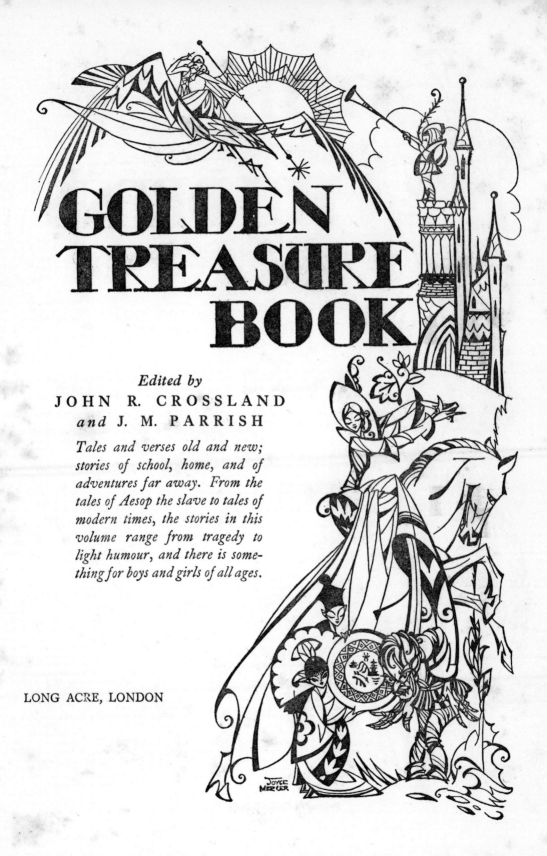

# GOLDEN TREASURE BOOK

Edited by

### JOHN R. CROSSLAND
### and J. M. PARRISH

*Tales and verses old and new;
stories of school, home, and of
adventures far away. From the
tales of Aesop the slave to tales of
modern times, the stories in this
volume range from tragedy to
light humour, and there is something for boys and girls of all ages.*

LONG ACRE, LONDON

Copyright, 1935

*Printed in Great Britain*

# Contents

# ILLUSTRATIONS
## IN COLOUR

# ACKNOWLEDGMENTS

THE Publishers and Editors desire to express their gratitude to the under-mentioned Authors and Publishers for their courteous permission to include the copyright extracts and poems named below.

Lloyd Osbourne, Esq., for " Travel " by R. L. Stevenson.

Miss Pamela Hinkson for " A Wandering Cat " and " Lighting-up Time " by Katharine Tynan.

Messrs. Martyns & Gane for " The Children in the Moon " by Robert Buchanan.

Messrs. Macmillan & Co., Ltd., and the Author's Executors for " The White Knight's Song " by Lewis Carroll.

Mr. Louey Chisholm for " The Pink Vest."

If, in spite of the great pains taken to trace ownership of copyright matter, there still remains some item for which due permission has not been sought, the Publishers trust that the matter will be brought to their notice, so that due acknowledgment may be made in future editions.

# Candida's
# First School

*by*

### KATHARINE L. OLDMEADOW

## CHAPTER I

### ENTER CANDIDA

THE Dresden china clock on the mantelshelf struck three little silvery strokes, and Miss Elizabeth Wymer put down her pen with a sigh of relief, for at three o'clock she had promised herself a cosy rest near the fire before tea, with a new number of *Punch* as a companion.

The room in which she sat was oddly unlike the usual sanctum of a busy schoolmistress.

It was more like the ante-chamber of some stately drawing-room. The walls were lofty, and painted with the flowery garlands beloved in the time of the Regency, and the firelight flickered on the beautiful, graceful lines of Heppelwhite and Sheraton furniture, corner cupboards containing treasures of old china, quaint fire-screens of old tapestry, and high-backed chairs that might once have been sat upon by Jane Austen herself.

There was nothing modern in the room except the big, comfortable chair drawn up to the fire, covered with quaint and flowery chintz ; a few exquisite little water-colours painted by an old pupil of Miss Wymer— and Miss Elizabeth Wymer herself.

She had an old-world air, for the soft brown dress she wore was slightly high-waisted, and her wavy hair was decorously swept back by an old silver comb.

The little clock struck three and Miss Wymer laid down her pen and looked out of the window. A drearier January afternoon could hardly be imagined. Rain and sleet had been falling since early morning, reducing everything underfoot to a murky slushiness ; and a noisy north-east wind was cruelly bending and twisting the trees and garden shrubs with icy, relentless fingers.

Miss Wymer shivered and drew up the gay chintz chair cosily to the fire for the little rest she had promised herself ; thinking, with a sigh of relief, that nobody could possibly call on such an afternoon.

She felt more inclined for *Punch* than visitors ; but before she had time to stretch out her chilly fingers to reach it, a clamouring peal at the door-bell rang through the house.

Her first thought was not her own annoyance, but that Eliza would be annoyed.

Eliza was her staid old parlourmaid, a privileged person who had lived with Miss Wymer's mother when the head mistress was a schoolgirl herself, and she was the mainstay of Magnolia House.

Eliza resented loud ringings of door-bells, arguing that nobody had any right to make a clamour at private front-doors except the Queen of England; and, as the Queen of England was hardly likely to call on Miss Wymer then, or at any other time, Eliza would, of course, be horribly annoyed; especially as before she could cross the hall loud and fresh peals were pulled at the bell.

" Ill-bred—that's what I call it ! " Miss Wymer heard Eliza mutter as she passed the door, and she hoped devoutly once more that it was not a visitor ; for it was what Eliza called " plate-basket day," and she knew how she hated to be called away from her rubbing and polishing.

She heard the door open and the north-east wind, who had been clamouring at doors and windows in his ill-bred, noisy way all day, rushed along the hall, rattling china and pictures and snorting his icy breath under doors as he passed. She heard the whir of a taxi, and a man's voice talking rather loudly ; then came a small unknown voice, drowned by Eliza's indignant tones.

Nearly five minutes passed in argument, then something heavy was thrown into the hall, and the front door was slammed against the wind and intruders.

In another moment Eliza appeared, bristling with indignation.

" Whoever is it, Eliza ? "

" It's a young lady, Miss—she won't tell me her business, but she's a schoolgirl, any one can see, and it wouldn't have been amiss, I'm sure, Miss Elizabeth, to tell me that you expected a new pupil, seeing that I've got to make things ready for her and all." Eliza put on her martyred look and proceeded before Miss Wymer could protest—" But don't you go and be soft-'earted now, and have her cluttering up the place a week before her time—she's been packed off here in a hurry, any one can see—most likely because there's measles or scarlet fever broke out in the house——"

" My dear Eliza, do leave off being dismal about scarlet fever, and fetch the child in—whoever she is—immediately ! I don't expect any new pupil, nor mean to have one. She has evidently come to the wrong house and all we can do is to put her in the right one at once."

" Very well, miss, I'll fetch her in ; but I'll ask you to remember, if you please, that it's plate-basket day, and not keep her too long, for it'll put me out nicely with all I've got to do, if I can't get the tea off my mind at four o'clock as usual."

" Perhaps she would like some tea, too, on a wretched day like this," said Miss Wymer bravely, and Eliza bristled again and said severely, " You're rucking up that clean chair-cover something awful, Miss Elizabeth."

Rebuked into silence, Miss Wymer began to smooth out the crushed chair cover like a guilty schoolgirl, and Eliza departed.

In a few minutes she appeared again, and, mumbling a name, she withdrew, leaving the unwelcome guest to face her hostess.

For the first moment Miss Wymer felt amazement, and then pitying consternation for the child before her ; for an odder, more pathetic figure could hardly be imagined.

She looked about fourteen, and tall for her age, and was extremely thin. Her little oval face was very pale, her eyes were so darkly blue they seemed almost black, and deep shadows of weariness lay beneath them. Masses of thick, black silky hair, unconfined by ribbon or plait, hung to her waist in a dark cloud.

She wore a fur travelling-coat, which had very evidently been made originally for somebody more than twice her age, for it reached to her feet and hung round her slender figure in voluminous folds. The fur was magnificent, of dark Russian sable, matching the big granny muff she carried.

Her shoes were ill-cut and clumsily made; her hands were covered with thin, black cotton gloves, and she wore a cheap, unbecoming little black felt hat.

*" Well, child, I don't know who you are in the least."*

Miss Wymer, trained to observe quickly, took all these things in at a glance; then she rose hastily and said briskly but kindly : " Well, child, I don't know who you are in the least, but I am afraid you are lost and very tired and cold. So you must tell me all about it at once and let me help you to put things right."

The child looked at her with grave, sad eyes.

" Tell me, if you please, Madame, is this Magnolia House ? "

" Certainly it is." Miss Wymer's heart sank, for she saw difficulties ahead.

" Permit me, then, if you please, Madame, to see Miss Wymer."

" I *am* Miss Wymer."

A look of relief came over the pale face and the child said gravely, " Then, Mademoiselle, all is now correct. I wish, if you please, to enter your school at once."

Immediately a thought flashed through Miss Wymer's brain—" This girl has run away, and thinks a small school will be a good hiding-place." Aloud, she said severely : " But, my child, I *never* take new pupils in this extraordinary way."

No sooner had she made this remark than she regretted it, for a look of utter dismay and consternation came over the pale little face before her, and her guest said quietly : " You mean, Mademoiselle, that it is unusual— you find me an inconvenience ? "

It was at this moment that Miss Wymer began to grow what Eliza called " soft-'earted " towards the oddly-dressed, pathetic figure before her, and she said gently : " Well, it *is* unusual, and it would be rather inconvenient, too, if I took any one who came to my door into the school. You see, it is a very small one—I never have *more* than twenty pupils, and I always know a great deal about my girls."

If this were a runaway, it was wiser to speak plainly.

" But, Mademoiselle—that is my desire. Permit me to explain myself, if you please."

The eagerness in the tired face so touched Miss Wymer's heart again that she moved towards the bell and rang it bravely. " Plate-basket day " or not, this poor, weary traveller must be warmed and fed. Turning to her guest she said kindly : " You must tell me everything, my dear, while you have some tea—but first take off that heavy coat and then sit down and be cosy."

" I thank you, Mademoiselle."

The visitor slipped off the fur coat and laid it carefully on a chair with her muff, gloves, and queer ugly hat on the top of it.

Then Miss Wymer received another surprise.

Her guest was clad in a very short white dress of fine embroidery ; much more suitable for a Christmas party than a first appearance at school on a bitter January afternoon. Her long, slim legs were encased in thin black silk stockings, exquisitely darned, and looking oddly out of place with the strong, clumsy shoes. Round her neck there hung a black, wooden crucifix.

As Miss Wymer drew the child near the fire she touched this gently and said : " My dear, are you a Catholic ? "

" No, Mademoiselle—it is the crucifix of Lisette ; she wished that I should wear it across the sea and until I am arrived in safety at Magnolia House."

" Across the sea ? "

" Yes, Mademoiselle—I am departed from Calais this morning."

" Alone ? "

" But yes, Mademoiselle—but all was correct, I can assure you, for Lisette had the happy idea of asking a *dame Anglaise*, who crossed also, to permit me to be near her. She was *très gentille* with me and has advised me with my *bagages*, and found the carriage for me to travel to your house."

" And who is Lisette ? "

" She was *bonne-à-tout-faire* to Maman and to me, Mademoiselle."

At that moment Eliza entered with the tea tray, nearly dropping it with horror when she saw the white-clad figure, probably sickening for measles or scarlet fever at that very moment, installed comfortably before the fire without hat or coat.

She drew up the table in front of Miss Wymer and said sharply : " It's getting darker every minute, Miss Elizabeth—and a real nasty night too ! It won't do to keep the young lady too long, and with her way to find and all."

The " young lady " shivered, and Miss Wymer said sweetly : " Thank you, Eliza—I'll remember. Please draw the curtains ; it makes the fire-light more cosy."

Eliza withdrew, frowning severely, and Miss Wymer pressed her guest to drink the hot tea and eat well after her journey. But she seemed too disturbed and anxious to eat at all, and just crumbled a biscuit nervously while she waited for her hostess to question her.

" What is your name, my dear ? "

" Candida."

Candida ! Miss Wymer smiled. Never had she heard a name so absolutely right for its owner, she thought, as she looked into the deep, truthful eyes before her. Whatever the story was that she was about to hear, she felt sure that it would be as true as the face of the teller.

" Candida what ? "

" Candida Dumanoir."

" French ? "

" My father was French, Mademoiselle—my mother was English."

" *Was !* " It was that sad little word that made Candida's face so sorrowful, Miss Wymer felt sure, and she said gently : " But why did you leave Calais this morning and come to me ? "

Candida spoke with a foreign accent and very slowly. It was as though she thought in French all the time, and then strove to express herself very literally and correctly in English.

" It is because Maman had desired me to come, Mademoiselle."

" But did she know me ? " Miss Wymer felt bewildered.

Candida shook her head. " No, Mademoiselle, but she had heard of you, and when she was a *jeune fille* in England she—she knew this house. During two years she has said continually : ' It is the wish of my heart that you go to England to this school, *petite*.' We were then in the Breton village where I was born—and it is not a month since we left it, Mademoiselle, to come to Calais in order to cross to England. Maman, she was suffering then, and each day she said : ' I shall be well to-morrow,'—but she grew worse, Mademoiselle, and—and, as you see, I am now alone."

Miss Wymer nodded gently. She knew if she offered the sympathy she felt that the over-wrought nerves of the child would break down, and, until the tale was ended, it was wiser to keep her calm.

" Lisette desired me to return to our village and allow Monsieur le Curé there, who was our good friend, to place me in a convent ; but Maman did not desire that, I knew, and we were at Calais even then for the purpose of crossing to the English school. So I have decided to come to you at once, Mademoiselle, though I find myself all despair that it has made such a great inconvenience for you."

" Not so much inconvenient as unusual, my dear. You see, this is not quite an ordinary school. I have never allowed myself to be persuaded to increase my number of pupils, and it would hardly do now to admit a complete stranger ; and there are other difficulties, too, that you are too young to understand."

Miss Wymer was thinking of all the perplexities connected with taking a pupil into the school of whom she knew so little ; but Candida imagined something quite different.

" Mademoiselle," she said shyly, " Maman has told me many times that these English schools are very costly, but I can assure you that all that is correct also. We were not rich, and when all was finished in Calais and I had given our good Lisette all she needed, there was not much left, as Maman's illness was very expensive. But she had often told me that a good education would be more valuable to me than jewels, and it was her intention when she reached England to sell all she had for that purpose.

" I do not know much about selling, Mademoiselle, naturally ; but you yourself, of course, are wiser, and if you will do me the kindness to accept them in payment for the education I receive, everything will be as Maman desired."

Then, to Miss Wymer's amazement, this quaint child rose from her chair and lifted up the skirt of her white frock. Underneath it she wore a petticoat as dainty and finely embroidered as the dress itself, and round her waist was tied a quaint pocket of quilted purple and gold brocade.

As she unfastened the many tapes and pins that secured it, her eyes filled with tears, and she said gravely, " The good Lisette had great fear of robbers, as you see, Mademoiselle."

She opened the pocket and took out a square leather case, but here the good Lisette had shown her wisdom again ; for the tiny key belonging to it hung round Candida's neck underneath her frock, on a slender gold chain.

The key was fitted into the lock and the leather case unfastened, then Candida crossed the room and calmly poured its contents on to Miss Wymer's lap. For a moment her hostess was speechless. She was equal to most situations ; but, to use Candida's own words, this one was so " unusual and inconvenient " that she was unable to think quite clearly.

Candida stood before her, her tragic little face saying plainly : " Surely, Mademoiselle, all is now correct—you have the jewels. Permit me to stay in your house and receive the education Maman wished for me in return."

Miss Wymer looked at the shining heap on her knees curiously. She knew something about gems as well as old china and schoolgirls, and it was very easy to see that this medley of necklaces, bracelets, rings, and pendants was valuable, especially a row of beautiful pearls. She wondered if Eliza were listening at the keyhole, for there was certainly nothing else to be done at the moment than to be " soft-'earted."

She put the jewels back into the case and said, " I will certainly keep all these pretty things, Candida, for you to-night. It makes me shiver to think of your carrying them all day in that casual way, in spite of your good Lisette's pins and tapes. As for you, I should like you to give me the address of that old curé you spoke about, and any other friend you have, and I will write to them to-night.

" In the meanwhile you must be my guest for a day or two, and I hope

*Candida stood in the doorway while Miss Wymer lit two candles.*

you are a very tidy person, for Eliza is very busy, and if she had her way the holidays would last from January to December."

"Lisette has taught me to make the *ménage*, Mademoiselle, and I could help your *bonne* to make the beds."

"Very well, we will make you useful, and you must be happy here until we hear from your friends. You mustn't worry about schools. I know of a very nice one not far from here where I feel sure you would be happy."

"But, Mademoiselle—it was *this* school that Maman wished me to attend."

Candida's face became so tragic again that Miss Wymer said hastily, "We can decide nothing yet, of course—now we will lock up these jewels in my safe, and let me see—I think *you* will have to be tucked away in the little Bird Room."

Candida's pale cheeks suddenly flashed and her eyes shone like stars.

"Why, she is *pretty*," thought Miss Wymer, and pleased to see her interested, she went on, "The Bird Room is a little room opening out of one of the large ones upstairs—I think it must have been a powdering-closet in the old days, and long afterwards it must have been given over to some one who knew how to make things look pretty. A young cousin of mine who went to a school in Paris this morning has been sleeping in it for a night or two, so it is all ready, and we need not upset Eliza at all. Bring your coat and hat and I will show it to you."

"Thank you, Mademoiselle."

Candida gathered up her possessions and followed Miss Wymer. She looked curiously round the old hall. It was very wide, and the floor was polished and bare except for two beautiful old faded rugs.

The wide, shallow staircase of shining black oak led to a long, lofty corridor with doors on each side of it. Miss Wymer walked to the end of this and threw open a door on the right.

The dusk had fallen so rapidly it was almost dark, and Candida stood still in the doorway while Miss Wymer crossed the room and lit candles in two china candlesticks on the dressing-table ; then, turning to her guest she said : " Here we are in the Bird Room. What do you think of it ? "

The walls of the Bird Room were of a soft grey, and the ceiling was the pale, misty blue of an April sky. Right round the room some one had painted a frieze of delicate peach blossom of the palest pink, and perching among the blossoms were gay little woodland birds. Candida stood still for a moment, then she said very quietly, " I find your Bird Room beautiful, Mademoiselle, and I thank you for permitting me to occupy it and for all your great kindness towards me."

Miss Wymer felt embarrassed. She was not used to having schoolgirls make prim little speeches to her, but she said kindly, " I am so glad you like it.—I believe it was done by some daughter of the house years ago, and it is wonderful how careful it has been kept.

" I will leave you now and send up your lighter luggage, and tell Eliza you are staying here for a few days." Miss Wymer's knees rather trembled at the thought of breaking this news to Eliza. " I am going to be very busy until supper-time," she continued, " but when you are ready you can amuse yourself in the drawing-room which is next to my room downstairs. Eliza put a fire in it to-day, it felt so chilly."

She smiled at the little figure once more and left Candida alone.

## CHAPTER II

### SILK ATTIRE

EARLY the next morning Eliza discovered that French ways were decidedly " inconvenient."

Entering Candida's room at half-past seven with hot water, she found the guest already up, wrapped in a gorgeous dressing-gown, just finishing her task of stripping the bed.

Two chairs were pushed as near the windows as possible, and the sheets and blankets were spread out over them. The mattress was thrown over the rail of the bed, and the pillows were arranged neatly along the wide window-seat.

" Well, I never ! " ejaculated Eliza surveying these arrangements with dismay. " I'm sure there was no call to have a spring-cleaning with the bedclothes, miss."

Candida looked perplexed.

" But I have only put the bed to air, as Lisette has taught me."

" Air ! " cried Eliza tartly. " I'm sure, miss, you'll find me as particular in my ways as most folks, and I turn the mattresses regular every other day, and the beds air till nine o'clock—after the breakfast's cleared away. If you'll excuse me, miss, I don't hold with dragging bedclothes about like that—making fluff all over my clean room—whatever ' Lizzie ' taught you about it."

She put the water down and bounced out. Candida's face grew tragic again, for evidently *ces fous Anglais* as Lisette called them, did not air their beds, and instead of helping, she had offended the stiff and disapproving Eliza.

She dressed and descended to the West room shyly. It was empty, and the warm scent of the hyacinths, and the pine-logs burning on the hearth, brought comfort to her chilled fingers as well as her lonely heart. The curtains were drawn back from the high window, and three stone steps outside it led to the garden. Snow had fallen thickly again in the night and the contour of every bush, tree and plant was hidden under its heavy burden.

Miss Wymer gave a shiver when she came in a few minutes later and saw the slender figure near the fire, clad in the white muslin frock. She at once rang the bell for Emma and sent her upstairs to fetch a gray woolly coat from her wardrobe.

" There, my dear, put that on. I can't have you catching cold, and we are in for a cold spell of weather, I fear. After breakfast I want you to bring the key of your big box, which Eliza has put in the garden-room and we will hunt in it for a warmer frock."

It was at this moment that Miss Wymer realised the firmness of Candida's chin.

The child answered politely but firmly in an " all-that-has-already-been-arranged " kind of way—" I fear that is quite impossible, Mademoiselle."

" *Impossible*, Candida ! " Miss Wymer had a firm chin, too, and she was not used to schoolgirls questioning her commands.

" Yes, Mademoiselle. It is true that there are a great many robes in my *malle*, but they are all in colours. I cannot wear those, Mademoiselle, as Lisette has said—it would not show a respect for Maman."

Miss Wymer's face softened. Evidently " the good Lisette," with her peasant idea of heavy mourning, was responsible for the child's odd appearance.

" My dear, I never knew your mother, but I feel sure I am right in saying that she would not like to think that you show your grief for her by making yourself ill through wearing thin, unsuitable clothes."

" But, Mademoiselle——"

" One moment, Candida. How old are you ? "

" I shall have fourteen years in eleven months, Mademoiselle."

" And I shall be an old lady of seventy in twenty-five years and two months, Candida, if I put it as quaintly as you do ! Well, even if you *are* getting on for such a big age as fourteen, remember I am approaching *seventy*, so it stands to reason that I am wiser than you, and must be allowed to judge what is best for you ; also, I think you forget that when you place yourself at school, obedience is the first thing to learn, and while you stay with me I am your guardian, you know."

" I wished to say only, Mademoiselle, that I have a little money in my purse, and Lisette had told me that you will be so kind as to advise me about a dress of black."

" Of course I will advise you, Candida ; but I want to see your frocks ; because you *must* wear something warmer. If you have finished your breakfast, you may get the key at once."

Candida's eyes went very bright, but she said nothing ; only slipped from her chair, raised her frock, and displayed the big, brocaded pocket round her waist once more.

" What a wonderful pocket that is ! "

" It was the pocket of my great-grandmother, Mademoiselle. She carried keys in it, and books of receipts, her diary, and *bonbons* for good children. Maman received it when she had twelve years, and she gave it to me when I had that age also."

She drew out a small, gold chain purse and abstracted a key from it, which she handed to Miss Wymer, who received it with a smile, saying, " That's right, now come along with me and let us see what we can do."

She took Candida to a small room with a glass door opening into the garden, evidently a room used by her pupils as a place for their out-door things. Wooden pegs hung round the walls, with lockers beneath them, and croquet-sets were stacked in the corner.

" Now, I will unlock your box, and you can show me your frocks, Candida —leave everything else as it is."

Miss Wymer unlocked the box and threw back the lid. The top tray was filled with more white muslin frocks, and piles of beautifully laundered and folded underclothes.

Candida, with her mouth set firmly and her eyes full of unshed tears, lifted out the tray, and several sheets of tissue paper which covered the dresses that " the good Lisette " had decreed should not be worn until the days of her mourning were over. As she took them out one by one, and laid them across a chair for inspection, Miss Wymer's astonishment and consternation grew greater every moment.

First came a green velvet, with a voluminous box-pleated skirt, and a detached bodice, linen-boned and buckramed. The next was a fine terra-cotta cloth, satiny in appearance, made with a panel of plush down the front, and with the yoke and high-boned neckband covered with cream lace. Then came a bright blue, shiny alpaca, with a full skirt edged with little frills, a cross-over bodice, and immense " leg-of-mutton " sleeves.

This was followed by a red dress trimmed lavishly with black military braid ; a tartan skirt, very narrow at the top and enormously wide round the bottom ; a red silk blouse fastening down the back with rows of smoked-pearl buttons, and a pink satin party dress trimmed with white swansdown.

When the last of these glories was laid before Miss Wymer's astonished eyes, Candida surveyed them affectionately, but doubtfully.

" Those are all the robes I have, Mademoiselle, but there are several more blouses in silk and velvet. They are not quite *à la mode*, it is true, for they belonged to Maman before she was married. She wore them little when she arrived in France, and they were laid away for me until I should come to the English school ; then Maman and Lisette they have made them to fit me."

Miss Wymer drew a deep breath and said gently, " My dear, when was your mother married ? "

"In 1896, Mademoiselle—twenty-four years ago."

Candida's face began to grow tragic.

It was plain to see the English Mademoiselle did not approve of the glories before her, for she was arching her fine brows with the same puzzled expression she had worn when she first saw the muslin frock.

"You do not find these dresses correct then, Mademoiselle?" she asked gravely.

"I'm afraid I do not, Candida. They are very handsome, of course, and when your mother was married they would have been considered pretty and suitable for a bride; but even then I do not think a schoolgirl would have worn them. You see, very simple 'unspoilable' things are more comfortable and healthier, too.

"I allow my girls to wear what they like on some occasions; but I always insist upon plain blue serge coats and skirts and simple blouses for everyday wear; and if they appeared in unsuitable clothes at any time, I should object most decidedly.

"Now tell me, child—did your mother ever go to school?"

"But no, Mademoiselle—Maman was an only child and very much indulged. She had a German governess until she was seventeen, then until her marriage she had masters for music, painting, and languages."

"Then that explains it all, my dear; your mother would naturally know nothing at all about school and school outfits. Did she speak English with you or French?"

"Always French, Mademoiselle, until I had ten years. As a child I was indulged by Lisette and had much wickedness. I screamed when Maman spoke the English to me, for Lisette had told me that the English never laughed on account of the ugliness and largeness of their teeth, and that the food they ate was as heavy as the cannon-ball in the garden of old Père Bois. But when Maman heard that she said it was all foolishness, and she insisted that I should speak and read English with her every day. Then she told me of her old home—she loved England—and I came to love it too, and wish to be English as Maman was, though she said continually that I speak it as if my tongue was of rust."

"I wonder why your mother did not bring you to England before this, Candida?"

"It was impossible, Mademoiselle. My father died when I was a baby, and Maman was very poor, and she has said often that it cost little to live in a Breton village."

"And you were her only child?"

"Yes, Mademoiselle, but there were five before I came—a girl and four boys, who all died before they were six months old. Then I was born and my father died, and Maman had much grief, and suffered so much from the shock to the nerves, that she allowed Lisette to indulge me whilst she wrote her stories and taught Mademoiselle Duprès to play the harp."

"It is all very sad, Candida, and I confess I am perplexed about you; but we must come back to the frocks—what did you wear in Calais—not these, I feel sure?"

"No, Mademoiselle, but my frocks were all outgrown, and extremely *passées*, and Lisette gave away all to the little girl of the *blanchisseuse*."

Miss Wymer sighed with dismay. It was bad enough to have a homeless child thrust upon her at her business time ; and a homeless child possessing a wardrobe of velvet, silk, and pink satin atrocities was almost worse than one without any clothes at all. She took hold of the green velvet dress.

"Well, Candida, I do not wish to seem cruel and misunderstanding, but I have decided that I cannot take you to buy new clothes in this weather, unless you wear something warmer, and this is the darkest and quietest of all the dresses. I think if we cut off this stiff neckband and find you a white collar, it will look passable until you have something else.

"But first tell me—have you any other coat in your box ? "

"Only this, Mademoiselle."

Candida took from the box a long coat of vivid scarlet, admirably suited to her dark hair. It was cut well, and made quaintly and becomingly, and three little " highwayman " capes on the shoulders.

"The tailor of the village has made this for me out of a cloak of Maman's last year. It is a pity that it is so bright in colour, Mademoiselle," said Candida, looking at Miss Wymer anxiously.

"Yes, Candida, it is—but it is such beautiful cloth, it will dye well. A very dark grey would be nice—don't you think so ? You are too young to wear all black, my dear, and I am sure your mother would not wish it."

"It will be as you advise, Mademoiselle, of course," said Candida with a sigh—it seemed useless to rebel against English people.

She searched in the big box carefully, and then took out a quaint apron of blue check, a yellow duster, and a pair of white cotton gloves, which she put aside on the floor before proceeding to put everything else away except the green velvet dress and the scarlet coat.

"What are those for, Candida ? "

"If Mademoiselle will permit me, I will put my room in order before I unpick those stitches."

"I don't think there is any need for that, child—Eliza will see to it."

"But the good Eliza has anger because I have made so much disorder. I should prefer to make all correct again if it is not inconvenient, Mademoiselle."

"Very well then, it is nice to have such a tidy person about ! But don't be long, it is so cold upstairs."

Miss Wymer left the room carrying the frock and coat over her arm, and Candida tied on the apron, drew the white gloves over her chilly fingers, and stole upstairs carrying the yellow duster.

In twenty minutes the Bird Room was a miracle of neatness ; sheets, blankets, pillows and coverlet were spread on the bed with a preciseness which would have pleased even the most fidgety, and the fluff on the carpet caused by the bed's upheaval, and so upsetting to Eliza's peace of mind, was all picked up with laborious care. Every chair and ledge was carefully dusted, and even the toes of the brown and pink bedroom slippers were arranged to meet the carpet with exquisite orderliness.

When Eliza arrived with an indignant bounce, loaded with dust-pans, brooms and dusters, she surveyed the room with amazement.

"You see that the bed and the coverings have all been to the air, which Lisette has said is very necessary, and yet now all is in order again," Candida said to Eliza severely, removing her apron as though it had been a princess's robe.

But instead of being pleased Eliza was offended. " You'll excuse me, Miss, but if you'll be so kind as to leave my work alone, I shall be greatly obliged."

Candida gave up *ces fous Anglais* in despair, and went downstairs to wrestle with the green velvet dress. She sat on a high-backed chair near the fire unpicking tiny stitches with conscientious care, and from time to time Miss Wymer watched her curiously. She felt oddly attracted towards this old-fashioned child with her stiff ways, amazing wardrobe and delicate prettiness. She seemed to belong to Magnolia House, just as the quaint old flowery china in the cabinets did ; and, try as she would, Miss Wymer found it impossible to imagine her banished to the large school she had mentioned the night before—amongst a crowd of critical schoolgirls.

## CHAPTER III

### PRINCESS CANDIDA

BEFORE another day was over, Candida was the possessor of a short, black serge skirt, and two white woollen blouses with deep collars turned over a soft, black silk bow.

The green velvet dress was buried in tissue paper at the bottom of the big box, and Miss Wymer, at least, was resolved that if the matter rested with her, it should never make its ugly appearance again.

*She flitted in and out of the gilded furniture as happily as a butterfly among flowers.*

Candida attracted her strangely, apart from the pity she felt for her loneliness. During the four snowy days which followed her arrival, she was so quietly unobtrusive she disturbed nobody ; and at the same time she had enough personality to make her presence felt by everybody.

She advised cook on the correct way of making an omelette, taught the cat to jump, and gave such a French touch to Emma's best hat that even Eliza was forced to admire it.

Although always courteous, she had rather a haughty little way with her, which was admired by all the maids except Eliza, who resented haughtiness in a person who apparently came from nowhere.

She requested to be allowed to dust the saloon, and after a moment's hesitation Miss Wymer consented ; and she flitted in and out of the gilded furniture in her blue check apron with a feather brush and duster, as happily as a butterfly among flowers, to Miss Wymer's amusement and Eliza's disgust.

" Well, miss, you've only yourself to blame when there's a smash," she prophesied, and Miss Wymer answered, " There won't be any smash, Eliza—see how lightly she touches everything—she has French fingers."

" And when is she going, I'd like to know ? " answered Eliza. " There's the other young ladies back in three days, and if you'll take my advice, miss, you'll pack her off before they arrive ; it won't do the school any good if anything nasty happens."

She marched out of the room, and Miss Wymer called in Candida.

" Candida, I have not yet had any reply from your friends in France, as you know."

" Yes, Mademoiselle."

" But I have been thinking a great deal about you, and I have decided not to send you to another school—not at the present at least—but to keep you here for a few weeks until you get more used to school life and English girls."

Such an expression of happiness and relief came over Candida's face that Miss Wymer's heart became softer than ever towards her—she had not quite realised what banishment meant to this lonely child.

" Mademoiselle, you have given me much joy of the heart, for it was Maman's wish, and mine also that I should come to school at Magnolia House."

" Very well, now you have your wish, and you must not look such a sad little person, for it depends quite upon yourself how long you remain here. You will find it difficult at first, when school begins perhaps—a new girl is always outside things, and as you are not entirely English the girls will very likely be rather slow in making friends with you.

" There are a few more things I want to say to you. First, I do not wish you to say too much to the girls about the way you came here—you know, Candida, it *was* a little unusual, and schoolgirls are terrible creatures for scenting a mystery that does not exist ! Also, do not speak about the jewels you have.

" The next thing is about your bedroom—only the senior girls have rooms to themselves, the others sleep in the dormitories, and I am rather afraid it will be called unfair if I let you have a senior privilege. I think that while your stay here is indefinite, I shall let you sleep in the Bird Room, which is really a small guest chamber. That will explain matters, and it will be nicer for you to be alone until you know English girls better. Now you may call Emma to help you unpack your box and put all the things away in the big tallboy in your room."

It was nice to see the tragic look almost disappear from Candida's face, and Miss Wymer was rewarded, that very afternoon, for her kindness to the lonely child who had nobody to pay her school bills. Mademoiselle Souvestre, who was spending her holiday in Paris, wrote to say she was ill, and the doctor would not permit her to return to her work at Magnolia House for some weeks.

This was distinctly annoying, as Miss Wymer made a great point of French with her pupils, and it was difficult to find any one to take Mademoiselle's place at so short a notice. She felt that it was immensely lucky that Candida was in the house ; for she had soon discovered that the child's French was perfect, in spite of the fact that she had been brought up in a Breton village, and " the good Lisette " probably spoke a *patois*.

" She can read with Isobel and the older girls, and chatter a little with the others," she thought with satisfaction.

On the day the pupils of Magnolia House were expected to return, Miss Wymer had a letter from Candida's friend, Monsieur le Curé. It was a rambling sort of letter, and it was easy to see that he was a very old man. He told Miss Wymer that he had known Madame Dumanoir for many years—a widow lady with one little girl who lived quietly in part of an old farmhouse with one maid. In fact, he told the same story that Candida had told herself, except that the curé added that he knew nothing of Madame Dumanoir's death until Lisette returned from Calais alone ; and he had scolded her severely for not letting him or the English parson arrange the affairs of Mademoiselle *Candide*.

All the same he knew well that it was Madame's wish that the child should be educated in England, so all was no doubt done for the best. He sent his *amitiés sincères* to Mademoiselle *Candide*, and hoped to hear occasionally of her welfare.

The day before school began again, a very tall, capable person named Miss Browne arrived at Magnolia House, and Candida learned that she held the post of matron and lady-housekeeper there.

She exerted her authority over Candida at once, greatly to that young lady's dismay ; for in spite of her gentleness she liked her own way.

" My dear child, *what* a mane ! " She caught hold of Candida's cloud of hair. " You must have it put into a nice tidy plait at once."

" But, Mademoiselle——"

" Don't call *me* Mademoiselle, for goodness' sake ; I'm only plain English Miss Browne."

" I want only to say, Mees Browne, that Maman liked my hair always to be loose."

" But not at school ; it would be wretchedly uncomfortable, always in ink-pots and tickling somebody else's nose. Besides, it's against the rules."

" But, Mademoiselle—I mean to say Mees Browne—Mees Wymer has not said it must be in a plait so ugly and unbecoming."

" My dear child, you don't suppose, surely, that Miss Wymer has time to bother about all the hair in this establishment ? *I* do that—so come upstairs at once and I'll show you how it is to be worn for the future."

It was no good Candida showing a firm chin. Miss Browne escorted her to the Bird Room, and plaited the long, silky hair into a pigtail, a style she was informed was to be adopted altogether except on festive occasions.

To Candida's indignation Miss Browne then calmly opened all the drawers and examined the arrangement of them critically.

" They look very neat now," she said. " But I expect to find them like that every Saturday morning when I inspect, and remember I know all about tidy top layers and a jumble of underclothes, ties, blouses and stockings underneath."

" Mademoiselle——"

" Miss Browne, *please*. But now that I see you have nothing to do but raise objections to my rules, you can come and make yourself useful in the linen-closet."

When the linen had all been carried to the bedrooms and dormitories, Miss Browne ordered Candida into the garden to gather holly and ivy for the bowls on the dining-tables ; a task that she enjoyed in spite of chilly fingers, for the snow had all disappeared and she was able to tread the green alleys, between the twelve quaint yew trees, peacocks and ships, in the formal garden, for the first time since she came.

One of the windows in the library upstairs looked over the drive of Magnolia House, and early that afternoon Candida took up her position on the window-seat, to watch the arrival of those long-looked-for schoolgirls, who were expected to return in time for tea.

For nearly two hours she watched taxis whirl up to the door, and heard clear young voices greeting each other with a friendliness and comradeship which made her feel more lonely than ever. Footsteps rushed along the corridor, doors were banged, and once the door of the library was thrown open and a tall girl with a thick plait of red hair and very merry grey eyes, looked in for no reason at all as far as Candida could see.

She looked at the new girl with astonishment and then said hastily, " Oh, I say ; awfully sorry, but I hadn't a notion any one was here," and she pulled the door to with a bang, but not enough to prevent Candida from hearing her say to her companions, " Didn't you see that awfully queer girl ? Looks like Lady Macbeth. Who on earth can she be ? I thought the Potteries was full up ! "

Just before half-past four Eliza came up and requested Candida to go to Miss Wymer's room at once, and she went with trembling knees down the staircase.

Miss Browne was in the hall, and looked at Candida with amusement.

" Well, Candida. When did Miss Wymer elect you head girl of the school ? "

" Mees Browne, I do not understand that."

" Well, remember this—only the head girl is allowed the privilege of sauntering down the front staircase. Go upstairs this minute, and come down again by the back stairs, or the rest of them will be saying before evening that you are a favourite."

*" When did Miss Wymer elect you head girl of the school ? "*

Candida mounted the stairs again a little haughtily. She was beginning to realise that being a schoolgirl in Magnolia House was not quite the same as being a guest ; and she was not sure she liked this new Mademoiselle.

She descended the back stairs, and, after knocking at Miss Wymer's door, entered shyly.

Near the fire, warming her toes, was a lady in a big, dark blue travelling coat and silver fox furs ; she was little and pensive looking.

Sitting by Miss Wymer's writing-table was another lady, wearing a short, tweed coat and skirt and looking rather formidable. A tall girl of about seventeen, with quantities of light hair and a slightly indolent expression, was standing near the table, too, talking to Miss Wymer.

They all looked at Candida a little curiously as she entered.

" Well, Candida, I want to introduce you to Miss Budd and Miss Prior —and this is Isobel, our head girl. You must go to her if you feel puzzled about anything, and she will advise you ; she is most anxious to practise her French, of course ! "

Isobel flashed a charming smile at Candida, as she shyly shook hands with everybody.

At the same moment the tea-bell rang, and Isobel said, with another pretty smile, " Come along ; we'll go in together, shall we ? "

Candida followed her, grateful for her protection on her first appearance among so many strange girls. She had been in the dining-room several times before, a long room with ample Georgian windows, and dark panelling hung with portraits of the Twelvetrees family.

The dining-room seemed a cheerful place that afternoon ; for it was lighted up and the tapestry curtains were drawn cosily.

Miss Browne stood at the end of the table, very busy with cups and saucers, and two rather small girls, with very long legs and very short skirts, stood one on each side of her.

There seemed to Candida to be a hundred girls present instead of twenty, and every one of them appeared to be talking to somebody else.

Isobel, with another friendly nod, left her to herself, saying : " Ask Brownie where you are to sit—that's my table over there," and she sauntered along to a small table in the window and began an animated conversation with a tall girl she called Kathleen.

Candida was terrified of taking somebody else's place, and she approached Miss Browne timidly and said, " Mad—I mean to say Mees Browne—where is it that I sit, if you please ? "

" Oh, it's you ; well, go over there, between Sylvia Lee and Bettine Carr—Doris is taking their tea now and will show you. Now, Doris, if you spill a drop, you know what to expect ! "

She gave two cups of tea to the little fag, and Candida followed her round the table.

Sylvia Lee was the darkest girl Candida had ever seen, and her gipsy colouring was made more noticeable by the row of deep pink coral beads which she wore round her neck.

Bettine Carr, a rather petulant-looking girl, was feverishly knitting away at a woollen scarf half hidden under the table away from Miss Browne's sharp eyes. On the unoccupied chair between the two girls there was a satin work-bag, a ball of wool and a pile of letters. Both girls were talking rapidly, and did not see Candida.

" Mademoiselle, pardon me, but will you permit me to sit down ! "

Candida spoke in a low, clear voice, with more of a foreign accent than usual in her nervousness, and every girl in the room left off chattering and looked at her, and there was a stifled giggle from the long-legged Doris.

Then every one looked away, and Sylvia said : " Oh, I beg your pardon, I didn't see you. Bettine, do shove that everlasting knitting out of the way."

Bettine obeyed, with a stare at Candida, and the new girl sat down, thankful to hear the chattering around her begin again.

The girl with the red plait, at the other side of the table, arched her eyebrows and murmured : " French ! what an awful bore, and how mean of Miss Wymer to take in a new kid when my aunt begged her to make room for my cousin."

Next to the red-haired girl there was a girl with a silky mass of honey-coloured bobbed hair, very long lashes veiling dark, greeny-grey eyes, and a mouth which tilted up at the corners in an enchantingly attractive way. She seemed to be a great favourite, for half the girls were listening to her with intense interest, and " Lorraine " was called from all sides.

All down the long table were white baskets full of cut bread, and plates of very plain, home-made cakes. In front of each girl was a small, china saucer divided into two, containing a portion of butter on one side and jam on the other.

Miss Browne suddenly rapped on the table, and the smaller of the long-legged little girls near her said grace ; then the chatter began again, and the bread baskets began to empty.

Candida took a slice of bread and began to crumble it nervously, for she was far too much excited to eat, and felt that twenty pairs of eyes were criticising her.

A rather heavy, fat girl, wearing spectacles, sat on the other side of Bettine, and suddenly she leaned forward and said to Candida anxiously, " I say, you haven't eaten your butter and jam."

Candida, thinking this concern about her appetite extremely kind, said nervously, " Thank you, Mademoiselle ; but I do not wish to eat."

" Well, it's a pity to waste it, and I'm ravenous ; so if you really cannot eat it, you might pass it over here."

" But certainly, Mademoiselle." Candida pushed the saucer across the table, and from all sides came a murmur of " Oh, Laura—you *pig* ! "

*Every girl in the room left off chattering and looked at her*

" Well, it *is* a pity to waste it," answered Laura calmly, and she proceeded to help herself to more bread and enjoy her purloined ration, while Candida gasped with shocked surprise that these English *jeunes filles* should use the insulting term *cochon* so lightly to a comrade.

No sooner was tea over than everybody filed into the back hall, which was piled to overflowing with boxes, and every one made a rush at Miss Browne to give up their keys.

Candida watched the scene with curiosity. Miss Browne, Isobel, and the girl named Kathleen each unlocked a box and piled the contents into the arms of its owner to carry upstairs to arrange in her own particular drawers.

Other things besides clothes came out of the boxes—cakes, sweets, and boxes of biscuits—all confiscated by Miss Browne and put on one side to be eaten on some suitable occasion.

" Very clever of you, Lorraine, to fill the toes of your dancing slippers with cocoa-nut ice," she said calmly ; " but I once read an interesting book on the duties of Custom-House officials, so I am afraid you will find it rather hard to deceive me."

She took out the offending sweets, very ingeniously wrapped up in crumpled tissue paper in the toes of the slippers, and put it with the other confectionery; and Lorraine, instead of dropping to the ground with shame and mortification, as Candida supposed she would, said, " Oh, I say, Miss Browne, what rotten luck ! It was only the weeniest scrap to keep me from dying of home-sickness to-night."

" What sort of luck did you say it was, Lorraine ? " asked Isobel severely.

" Oh, Isobel, you know what I said well enough ; don't preach the first night."

" I asked you what sort of luck you said it was ? " repeated Isobel with a frown.

" Well, I said ' rotten ' if you want to know."

" Well, you can bring me twenty lines of Macaulay before bedtime to-morrow, and remember, all of you, I'm simply not going to have that horrible word used in the school."

" Lorraine," said Miss Browne sarcastically, " you seem to be beginning well—two rules broken already, and I suppose that's *your* mackintosh thrown down in the hall, instead of hanging up on its own peg. Go and put it away at once, and then carry the rest of these things upstairs."

There was now an orderly procession going up and down stairs with armfuls of clothing, although Candida could hear peals of laughter coming from the dormitories.

" That will do, Lorraine, you can't carry any more," said Miss Browne to the girl with the honey-coloured hair, who carried an armful of clothes reaching to her chin, a sponge-bag between her teeth, and two sandal-slippers suspended by their elastics from her ears.

" Oh, no, Miss Browne, do give me something else ; look, I've got two empty teeth, a little finger, and my chin not carrying a thing ! I say, Doris, just stick my red woolly on the top, there's a duck ! "

The long-legged Doris obligingly helped to break the camel's back, and the red woolly proved to be the last straw, for Lorraine tripped on the bottom stair and fell full length, scattering her wardrobe in all directions.

To Candida's surprise this accident caused peals of laughter to every-body except Miss Browne, who said : " I told you so. Well, you've got your work cut out to-night, Lorraine, folding up all your things again properly."

Lorraine sat among the wreck of her wardrobe ruefully, and nobody attempted to help her pick up the things until Candida went forward shyly and offered her services. Lorraine looked at her through her silky, long lashes and said, " Thanks *awfully*, it's jolly of you to offer, but really I can manage, thanks." Then, seeing Candida's look of disappointment, she added, " Well, if you will give a hand with these petticoats it will be fright-fully decent of you."

Candida's clever French fingers began to fold up the petticoats with a nimbleness which astonished Lorraine, and soon they were both mounting the stairs carrying the load between them.

"Sarah's my billet," said Lorraine ; but this information was Greek to Candida until she followed her leader into the Siddons dormitory. The girl with the red plait—called Alix, she had discovered—Sylvia Lee, and the fat girl who had appropriated her butter and jam allowance, were all in the room arranging drawers, and they seemed surprised to see Candida enter.

"Thanks most awfully," said Lorraine, as Candida put her load carefully down on the bed. "I haven't a notion what your name is, you know."

"Candida."

"Candida !—how rummy—I mean how jolly. My name's Lorraine, and that's Alix Rowe, Sylvia Lee, and Laura Piggot." She waved her hand towards the other girls, who gave Candida rather stony smiles. "Where are you sleeping ?"

"In the Bird Room."

"The *Bird* Room !" The four girls exchanged glances and Lorraine said hastily : "Pretty ripping, having a room to yourself, I should think. Well, I'll have to have these beastly things put away, I suppose," and Candida felt that she was dismissed.

No sooner had she gone than Sylvia threw herself on the bed and cried, "Well, what do you think of *that* ? A new girl green enough for C, any one can see, swanking it in the Bird Room, while *we* have to stuff ourselves in cubicles ! Why, even those swelly seniors, Nancy and Joyce, have to share a room. If you ask *me*, there's some mystery about this girl."

"What mystery could there be ?" asked Laura curiously.

"Mesdemoiselles, pardon me, but is it permitted for me to speak?"

*Candida went forward shyly and offered her services*

cried Alix, so exactly imitating Candida's French accent and precise little voice that there was instant applause.

"No, it's my turn first," broke in Sylvia. "And you may all be interested to hear that the second sight I inherited from my grandmother tells me that she *is* a mystery. You must confess that she's got an 'air,' and she looks so tragic. I believe she's really some princess or grand duchess or somebody like that escaped from Russia after seeing unspeakable horrors !— Perhaps her family was murdered before her eyes by the Bolshevists ! "

Laura shuddered and said, " But she *can't* be—I thought the Russians were starving—and *she* can't be very hungry if she'll leave all her butter and jam."

"Oh, Laura, you *were* a pig about that," cried the others, and Lorraine said, " Well, she seems a decent kid whoever she is, but it's my opinion that Miss Wymer has imported her here on purpose to worry us about French ; it won't do to be too chummy with her ; Mademoiselle's bad enough. Look here, what do you think of the Custom-House official not spotting this ? "

She took a big sponge from her sponge bag, and then a good-sized bag of peppermint creams.

"Give them to the Russian princess to keep," said Sylvia. " Brownie won't be likely to rummage in her drawers to-night, and Russians are splendid about plots and secrets."

"Well, perhaps I will later," promised Lorraine. " And meanwhile they must go and live with my sponge again. What a bore ! There's the bell, and I haven't half finished, and of course I've put my blouse under every blessed thing ! "

When the bell rang Candida changed into her new black frock with its plain muslin collar ; but when she saw the girls trooping downstairs in pretty, simple blouses and light frocks, she realised with dismay that Maman and Lisette had been wrong, and that the velvets and silks in her big box were, as Mademoiselle said, " Impossible."

Miss Wymer presided at supper, and Miss Prior, Miss Budd and the peppermint-hunting Miss Browne were there also. Afterwards, the girls gathered round the fire in the big billiard room, which had been turned into a schoolroom, and talked about the holidays and made plans for the term.

Candida only was silent, and she would have been miserable, too, if she had not received every now and then one of Lorraine's attractive smiles. At half-past eight the junior girls trooped off to bed, and, for the first time since she had occupied it, the Bird Room seemed lonely.

Candida wrapped her gorgeous dressing-gown around her and opened her diary ; but although the day had been eventful, her entry in it was short, only :—" All the girls have returned to school. I like very much the one they call Lorraine, and I *wish*—I *wish* she would like me, too." She lay for some time in the darkness, thinking, and sat up with a start when a tiny knock came at the door.

"*Entrez.*"

The handle turned softly and Lorraine came in, holding a night-light carefully in one hand, and in the other a paper bag. She was dressed in a long, pale blue dressing-gown, and her honey-coloured hair looked like

*" I thought I'd just pop in and say good-night "*

a silky mop. She gave her most attractive smile, and sitting on the bed, she said sweetly : " I thought I'd just pop in and say good-night."

Candida's eyes shone like stars ; it seemed as if Lorraine *did* like her.

" The fact is," continued the visitor, " that I wanted to ask you to do me a favour, too ; you were so frightfully decent about picking up my togs."

Candida wondered which of the garments were " togs," but she clasped her hands over her knees in such ecstasy, that Lorraine decided that the new girl was decidedly pretty.

" But of course, Mad—Lorraine—I will do anything."

" That *is* jolly of you ; you see, it's this way. Brownie's dead against our bringing back any grub, and simply *can't* understand that we eat sweets all day in the holidays and never die. Of course, I suppose there must be such a rule because of pigs like Laura."

" Laura—she is really a *cochon*, then—yes ? " asked Candida, horribly shocked at the schoolgirl's opinion of her room-mate.

" *Rather* ! She'd stuff anything, and she's always pouring over books, too ; that's why we call her the ' Learned Pig '—L.P., you know."

" Oh ! " gasped Candida.

" Well, we *do* smuggle in grub sometimes—everybody does—and this time our cook's made me some most heavenly peppermint creams,"—she produced the bag—" and wherever I put them, Brownie'll sniff them out and kick up no end of a row."

" I do not think Mees Browne *gentille* myself."

" Oh, she isn't bad as matrons go. *Do* be an angel and keep the creams in one of your drawers till to-morrow ; she'll never come rummaging here, and it's perfectly safe, or I shouldn't ask you, of course."

Most of these explanations were Greek to Candida, and she regretted Maman had never mentioned such words as " grub " and " ripping," as they seemed to be used so often ; but she understood what Lorraine wanted, and said : " But of course, Mademoiselle ; it will give me much happiness to permit them to remain in my bureau."

" How jolly of you—shall I put them in ? "

Lorraine hopped across the room, and hid the bag in Candida's drawer, well covered with the embroidered scarf. Then, saying good-night sweetly, she disappeared.

Candida had hardly recovered from the excitement of Lorraine's visit before the door opened again, and Miss Browne appeared. She had been to the dormitories, and now meant to include the Bird Room in her nightly round, for who knew what the new girl might be up to with candles, etc. ?

No sooner did she put her foot inside the door than she trod on a peppermint.

It was like Lorraine to have a hole in the bag !

Her sharp eyes instantly saw another by the tallboy, and she strode across the room and pulled out the top drawer and sniffed suspiciously, and in another moment the " heavenly creams " were in her hands.

She turned to the indignant Candida, who considered it extremely shocking for even an authoritative person like Miss Browne to open another person's drawers.

" Are these things yours ? "

" No, Mad—I mean to say Mees Browne."

" Whose are they, then ? "

" They are to be kept for a friend."

" Do not be impertinent, Candida. Who gave you these things to keep ? I mean to know, for I simply will not have this constant sweet-eating going on under my very nose ? Well, do you hear ? "

" Mademoiselle, it is not polite to take things from the bureau of another."

Miss Browne, who was naturally good-tempered but blunt, went crimson with indignation at Candida's daring to criticise her way of fulfilling her duties, and she said severely : " Very well, if you are determined to be impertinent and refuse to answer my question, we will ask Miss Wymer what she thinks about the matter. Now, once more—who gave you those sweets ? "

Miss Wymer brought upstairs !—Candida trembled. It was Miss Wymer who had said so plainly that one came to school to obey. Poor, inexperienced Candida knew nothing of the school law which decrees that one must never betray a school friend, and although she was indignant at Miss Browne's impolite curiosity, she said : " I think you should not ask that, Miss Browne, but if it is necessary to obey you, it was Lorraine who has given me her confidence and those *crèmes de menthe.*"

" Oh, I thought so ; well, for *your* part in the affair, you can go without jam for a week."

She left the room with the bag of peppermints, and Candida was left to fret herself for hours about Lorraine's punishment.

Miss Browne visited " Sarah Siddons " while her blood was hot, and before ten o'clock that night, by some mysterious means which only Alix could have explained, the inmates of the other three dormitories were made aware that the new girl was "a horrid little sneak," and had already got Lorraine Somerset into an awful row!

# CHAPTER IV

### CANDIDA BEGINS HER EDUCATION

TO Candida's grief and dismay Lorraine looked upon her with cold politeness the next morning, and her example was followed by every girl in the school except the four seniors, who did not trouble to notice the new girl at all.

She had no idea that every one of them would have tried her utmost to have wriggled out of the affair; but if that proved impossible, would have remained silent and accepted the punishment rather than betray the real culprit.

"Always speak the truth, and everything will come right, little Candida," Maman had said continually, and now Candida had followed Maman's advice, and sixteen pairs of eyes held coldly aloof in consequence.

Then followed a week of bewilderment. Miss Wymer thought it wiser to let her new pupil make friends her own way, and saw little of her except during meals and in the schoolroom. Isobel smiled at Candida whenever she came across her, and always addressed her in French; but the other senior girls only surveyed her curiously, while the juniors continued to ignore her, treating her with courtesy, but without one touch of friendliness.

*Lorraine looked upon her with cold politeness the next morning*

She found the school was divided into three classes : A, B, and C. The senior girls were " A," and were taught almost entirely by Miss Wymer, and " B " consisted of a class of eight about Candida's age or older. " C " was the class of the long-legged Doris and five other girls younger than those in " B."

After a satisfactory test paper Candida was placed in " B "; only to realise sadly once more that poor Maman had known nothing at all of all the strange ways of English schools. Miss Prior, fresh from Girton, ruled " B," and before Candida had been her pupil for a day her exasperation over the new girl's slowness began.

" We are all waiting for *you*, Candida. It is *your* question, *please*, Candida. Kindly read your answer out *quickly*, Candida," were the sentences that Miss Prior uttered all day ; and the eyes of eight strange girls seemed to rest upon her in continual impatient amusement.

Maman's motto had been " slow and sure," and the first fable she had given Candida to learn by heart had been that of the hare and the tortoise.

Miss Prior seemed to have no sympathy with tortoises, and said " swift and sure " was best in a world which had changed very much since a tortoise won the race.

The class could not wait while Candida wrote her notes in small, exquisite writing as she wished to do ; looking upon the untidy, scribbled hieroglyphics of the other girls with horror ; for she believed that a note-book should be as tidy as the essay written for Miss Wymer once a week.

" But *every one* scribbles in note-books, that's what they're for," argued Alix in despair one day when Candida held up the whole class with what the girls called " her old maid's ways."

" *I* do not scribble in mine," answered Candida firmly, and her chin went up in a way the whole school was beginning to know and understand, which added to her unpopularity.

Visiting masters and mistresses came to Magnolia House daily to hold classes for languages, music, painting, and dancing ; but Candida's queer little stiff way, which was sometimes almost autocratic, made her unpopular with all of them except Madame Verrier.

On these afternoons the whole school wore their prettiest frocks, and plaits were not compulsory. Miss Browne approved of Candida's fine, white muslin for this occasion, and when she appeared with her long, cloudy hair only loosely tied back with a wide, black silk ribbon, the girls agreed with one accord that although she was queer she was " frightfully pretty."

Madame Verrier was one of the most famous teachers of dancing in London, but she was not exactly loved by her pupils, except by those who won her approval by showing more than ordinary talent.

The girls of Magnolia House detested the dancing-lessons, for Madame's sharp tongue, eagle eye, and determination that even the largest and the clumsiest should benefit from every movement of the two hours' lesson, gave them a strenuous afternoon.

Madame Verrier possessed the happy gift of being able to do three things well at once.

She brought no accompanist with her, but sat at the piano on the raised daïs at the end of the room, playing lightly and brilliantly, while all the time she watched every movement of her pupils and criticised them with her biting tongue.

At the very first class that Candida attended, Madame picked her out before the hated " exercises " had proceeded ten minutes. New girls, little girls, and stupid girls always stood in the front row, regardless of height and age, and Candida, always the " odd one," was placed right in front and a little in advance of the others.

Suddenly, Madame leaned forward from the piano majestically, and addressed Candida, who was dreaming ; for she found the eagerly-looked-for dancing-lesson dull, and the piano hard and uninspiring after the music of Maman's harp and the wind playing in the beechwood.

" What is your name, child ? "

Candida continued to dream of the old Breton farmhouse, with its walled garden full of fig-trees, cherries, plums, apples and medlar trees, where she had danced in the sunshine like a yellow butterfly.

Doris awoke her by a thump in the back, and whispered : " Oh, do buck up and answer, silly ! "

Then Candida gave a jump and realised that the elegant lady in the ravishingly *chic* frock was speaking to *her*.

" Candida Dumanoir, Madame."

" Then, Candida Dumanoir, perhaps you will kindly tell me why you don't dance when you *can* ? "

Every girl became interested at once, for it was unusual for Madame to tell her pupils they could dance, she usually spent her time informing them that they *couldn't*.

Candida looked at Madame thoughtfully. She might have replied that she *was* dancing, for she had certainly been moving through the exercises, while she dreamed dreams ; but she knew at once what the dancing-mistress meant, and she answered : " I do not dance to the piano, Madame."

" And why not, if you please ? "

Candida made a little gesture of disapproval, and said : " It does not make the heart sing, Madame ; I dance to the harp—that is as soft and sweet as the voices of fairies, and sometimes I dance to the wind that makes the music so wild and beautiful ; but the piano, Madame "—she gave another shrug—" it is but tum-tum-tum."

The " C's " began to titter, and the " B's " hugged themselves with enjoyment. The new girl might be a sneak, and it was sickening that she kept the arithmetic lesson dragging ; but it was impossible for Madame, with her endless engagements, to keep the class over time, and if Candida was going to talk bosh about harps, and fairies, and beautiful wild wind, it would pleasantly shorten the lesson.

The " A's " looked uncomfortable, and if Candida had turned round she would have seen Isobel frowning at her horribly. The idea of this French chit calling Madame Verrier's brilliant playing a *tum-tum* !

" Oh, you do not feel inspired, that is it, *hein* ? " Madame gave her a sarcastic smile. " Well, perhaps that is why the others move as though one has dropped pennies inside them and then turned a handle round and round, so "—she made a movement like an automatic machine—" we will play them a different *tum-tum* before we take the waltz, and see what that can do. The girls in the front row will kindly sit down, and the others will please show me a little *impromptu* solo-dancing to this *tum-tum*."

The front row sat down with alacrity, ready to enjoy the entertainment provided by their unfortunate friends, and the back row stood looking extremely foolish, and once more blamed Candida for making trouble.

Madame sat down to the piano, and poising her hands for just one moment over the keys, she began to play the wild and passionate music of Grieg's " Anitra's Dance," never taking her eyes for a moment off the ten reluctant, capering girls before her.

Before she was half-way through the dance, she rose again with the well-known smile fluttering round her lips.

" Thank you, girls, that will do ; it is nice to know that we have so many ready to step into the divine Pavlova's shoes ! Sit down now, and we will see what the others can do."

Consternation among the new victims, and triumph amidst the panting Pavlovas of the future ! They sat down to enjoy *their* turn of being severely critical.

While Madame Verrier had been playing Candida's face had changed. Soft rose-colour flushed her pale cheeks, and her eyes became dark and bright. Unconsciously she pulled off the ribbon which held her masses of hair, and as she stood up it fell round her like a black cloud.

At the first note she swayed slightly, looking like a slender, white blossom shaken by a rough wind. Then suddenly she began to dance with wild, passionate sadness, her dark hair floating round her, her slender feet hardly touching the floor. The antics of the others were unnoticed by any one except Madame after all, for the eyes of the watching girls were all fixed on Candida, and Sylvia said triumphantly : " There, I told you so ! Russians always dance ! "

Isobel, a little piqued, murmured to Kathleen : " No wonder Madame thinks *we* are clumsy idiots ! "

At the last note the dancers stood still, all panting except Candida, and she, still flushed and bright-eyed, went slowly up to the daïs where Madame sat at the piano, and held out her hand.

" Madame," she said in a low voice, " permit me to thank you for the music. It does not make the heart sing, it is true, it makes it ache and the feet fly to a home perhaps one will never see again."

And Madame, who had a passionate love for her art, and was growing tired of disappointing pupils, embraced her fervently on both cheeks in the French way. Candida was a darling child, and a born dancer, and from that moment she was to be her favourite. Unlike the English teachers, she did not care one jot what the other girls thought of favouritism.

" *Ma chérie* ! " she said, " you are going to work hard, and make me proud of you—*hein* ! You are right about the piano, it is *tum-tum*, and not half so inspiring to dance to as the harp or that little wind playing in the trees. Some day, *petite*, I will compose a dance for you alone—the dance of the south wind, and we will not play a *vilain* tum-tum for it—we will borrow a harp from the fairies. Now go and rest, little one."

Then Madame stood up and addressed her astonished and slightly jealous pupils, who were all dying to hear what she was saying to Candida.

" Young ladies," she said, " to-day I have made a very interesting discovery. This should be called the natural history class, for in it there is one elephant, three kangaroos, a dancing bear, a dozen frisky goats, a duck, a long-legged colt, a bird that hops—and *one little butterfly.*"

As the days passed Miss Wymer noticed that Candida grew paler and more tragic-looking, and she guessed that she was not quite a success with the girls. She sent for her one day and said : " Well, Candida, have you been making friends with the girls, and chattering in French to them sometimes, so that they do not miss Mademoiselle too badly ? "

Candida threw out her hands with a gesture of despair. " But no, Mademoiselle, it is impossible. If I speak French they melt away from me

*She began to dance with a wild, passionate sadness*

like the snow, and when I speak English it is easy to see that they are amused. One must be dumb in these days, Mademoiselle."

She shrugged her shoulders and her eyes filled with tears.

" But, my dear, that is foolish ; you must *try* to be bright. It is no good brooding over past troubles, dear. Make friends with them, and you will see how much happier you will be."

She dismissed Candida, and sent for Isobel, and asked her why the new girl was so unpopular.

" I really don't know, Miss Wymer. There is some story among the juniors, I believe, that she got Lorraine into trouble with Miss Browne through telling tales."

" Remember, she has had an odd bringing-up, and has never been to school before. She probably did it innocently."

" Y—yes," answered Isobel doubtfully. " Well, anyway, Miss Wymer,

I'll look after her. It's my *salon* next week. How would it do to invite her, and give her a sort of welcome to Magnolia House ? "

" Just as you like, dear ; but remember, I don't want her to appear as a favourite ; she is one of the youngest and a new-comer, and it may cause some grumbling."

" Oh, I don't think that will matter, Miss Wymer," said Isobel, who, having been behind the scenes, knew better than Miss Wymer that invitations to drawing-room teas were not very much coveted by the juniors.

It was a custom in Magnolia House for the senior girls to hold an occasional *salon* in the big drawing-room, each taking it in turn to act as hostess under Miss Wymer's critical eyes. The seniors were always present and a few girls from a well-known school in the neighbourhood, as well as six girls from the junior classes chosen by the hostess. The invitations were sent by post, and acceptances and refusals were also thoroughly criticised by Miss Wymer.

Afternoon tea was served in wonderful china cups, and it was the duty of the hostess to keep the conversation interesting and amusing, which was a decided strain, as school subjects were not encouraged, and the guests were supposed to be keenly interested in books, celebrated people, places and current events.

But it is to be feared that the juniors, at least, came more for the hot cakes, always made by cook for the occasion, than to enjoy the intellectual conversation.

Candida received her invitation, and was rather puzzled. It seemed odd to be invited out to tea by a person in the same house, but with Miss Budd's help she sent a precise little note of thanks and acceptance.

It was not long before she gathered from the conversation around her that Lorraine, Alix, Laura Piggot, Sylvia and a girl named Norah Hastings were also to be amongst the guests.

She knew nothing about English tea-parties. Maman and she had never gone to them or given them ; in fact, they seldom drank tea at all, and she was terribly afraid of doing the wrong thing once more, so she approached Lorraine timidly.

" Lorraine, will you tell me, if you please, what is it one would wear at the *salon* of Isobel ? "

" I say—I mean, *are* you going ? "

Lorraine stifled a whistle, and the rest of the girls listened eagerly. Drawing-room parties were dull things, but if the Russian princess were going to be present there might be a chance of some fun.

" Oh, we wear our best bibs and tuckers, of course."

" And what are they, if you please ? "

Lorraine flashed her slow smile at the other girls—here was a glorious chance for a rag ! Then she answered : " Oh, hats with feathers and things like that, you know, and hand-bags containing fans and smelling-salts, in case we feel faint ; the bread and butter *is* frightfully thin, and it's a sort of ' grown-up ' party, you see, so it's only polite to Isobel to dress up a bit."

" But do you wear *hats* ? " inquired Candida.

" Of course ; we ring at the front door bell, too, and Eliza lets us in one by one and takes our coats and umbrellas. She then conducts us to the drawing-room and announces us just as though each of us was the Duchess of Somewhere."

" I have never been to a tea-party," said Candida, turning pale at the ordeal before her.

" Oh, you'll get on all right," promised Alix so kindly that Candida thought she was making friends at last. " All you have to remember," continued Alix, " is that these *salons* are rather rummy things—lots of ceremony and all that, you know, not a bit like an ordinary tea-party. It's to teach us how to behave if the Queen asks us to tea. You mustn't shake hands with Isobel, just sweep her a curtsey, like this "—Alix swept a magnificent Court curtsey—" and, of course, as Miss Wymer will be the principal guest, and rather a swell, you must kiss her hand."

She exchanged looks with the other girls when Candida thanked her for this information.

" And Mademoiselle Wymer, she goes to this *salon* also ? " asked Candida in consternation.

" And when you sit down," broke in Sylvia, " you mustn't forget to take off your gloves, and blow well into the fingers before you spread them out on the arm of your chair—and also it's the polite thing to spread your handkerchief over your lap before Isobel passes you the grub, in case it's anything sticky."

Candida had no idea what " grub " was, but she thanked Sylvia for her contribution towards her social education.

" You mustn't forget either," added Laura Piggot, " to take a piece of everything when the cake-stand comes round—it saves the hostess lots of trouble, of course."

Candida looked horrified at this idea, and if the faces of the rest had not remained so immovable, she would have suspected that this was a social custom of a " learned pig " more than of a polite guest at a tea-party ; but as nothing was said she put it down as another peculiarity of *ces fous Anglais*, as Lisette so continually called them.

" Oh, and if the tea is too hot—it usually is—you must, of course, drink it out of your saucer," said Norah Hastings sweetly.

But this was too much ; Candida, in her horror, forgot all her English, and threw up her hands, crying : " *Mais non, Mesdemoiselles, quel horreur ! c'est impossible !* "

Seeing they had gone too far, Lorraine said hastily : " No, Norah, I believe the Queen just blows her tea if it is too hot, and that's what I advise Candida to do."

Then they melted away, for it was the recreation hour, and a wet day ; and Candida was left to prepare for her first appearance in English society.

She went into the Bird Room and pulled out the deep bottom drawer of the old tallboy, which contained all her mother's treasures. Lorraine had said that it would be impolite to Isobel not to dress up, and, of course, all those lucky girls downstairs would have everything correct. She could not very well wear her muslin frock if it was a grown-up party as Lorraine had said ; it was too short, and so was the new black dress.

At the bottom of the drawer there was a grey alpaca skirt trimmed with black velvet, which Miss Wymer had not seen, and a very gorgeous white satin blouse with black velvet butterfly bows all down the front. She tried on the skirt; it had never been altered, and reached down to her ankles. The stiff sleeves of the satin blouse came up almost to her ears; but there was no doubt that she looked splendidly " grown-up." In the drawer, too, there was a box containing three long, white ostrich feathers, which she tried on her hat and felt very much pleased with the effect; although she regretted she did not possess a large hat of black velvet.

She found a satin hand-bag, too, and a beautiful fan, as well as an old Venetian scent-bottle, which had belonged to her great-grandmother.

The collar of the blouse was very high, and mindful of Miss Wymer's dislike of the stiff ones on her dresses, she unpicked it patiently and stitched in a cascade of lace instead.

The next day, at half-past four, when afternoon school was dismissed, Isobel's guests went to their rooms to array themselves, and twenty minutes later, Lorraine, in her best hat, and a long coat of cream serge over a pretty frock, crossed over to " Maria " for a gossip with Norah, just as the door of the Bird Room opened and Candida emerged.

For a moment Lorraine stood transfixed in horror and amazement, then, seeing Candida's look of surprise, she forced a smile and said :

" Oh, I say, how absolutely topping you look ! *Do* come in last ; you will make such a ripping sensation. *We* are going now."

She flew back to her own dormitory and collapsed on the bed in shrieks of laughter.

" What on earth's the matter ? " Alix, putting on a fluffy beaver hat, asked indignantly, for Lorraine had fallen on *her* bed.

*She passed her fur coat to Eliza with the air of a princess*

" Oh, girls—she's *done* it ! Candida—she's dressed up like a " grown-up," as she calls it. You never, never saw such a guy in all your life—she's like a picture in an old Volume of *Punch*, or a photograph in one of those rummy old albums aunts always have ! "

When Eliza answered Candida's loud peal at the front door bell, you could have literally knocked her down with a feather smaller than the one in the guest's hat.

If it had been one of the other girls, she would have expostulated with them, realising that it was a practical joke ; but she at once put down Candida's extraordinary appearance as another proof of her " foreign ways," and set her lips in a tight line of disapproval.

" We'll see what Miss Elizabeth has got to say," she thought almost with satisfaction. " It's not *my* business to see that she's properly dressed and all, and if I *do* tell her she looks like a guy, like enough she'll begin to tell me that ' Lizzie ' knows more about dress than I do."

Eliza had not forgiven the bed-airing episode.

Candida slipped off her fur coat, and passed it to Eliza with the air of a princess, and stood upright in all her " grown-up " elegance.

The grey alpaca skirt clung round her ankles, and the white satin blouse had as many wrinkles in the back as black velvet bows in front. She had done up her heavy hair with a huge tortoise-shell comb, and the feathers in her small hat rested on this gracefully. She wore white cotton gloves, and the hand-bag containing fan, smelling-salts and embroidered handkerchief hung over her wrist.

Eliza flung open the drawing-room door and announced " Miss Candida Dumanoir," and the guest swept in magnificently.


## CHAPTER V

### ISOBEL'S SALON

A BRIGHT wood fire was burning on the hearth in the long drawing-room, and there were bowls of fragrant spring flowers set on the slender gilded tables and on the tops of the cabinets of gaily painted old china. Isobel had bought them and arranged them herself ; and the deep colours of the violets and the clusters of cream and purple anemones harmonised well with the soft blue of her own pretty frock ; for Isobel prided herself on being the most artistic, as well as the best, of the Magnolia House hostesses.

Miss Wymer sat near the tea table, which was drawn up to the fire, talking to one of Isobel's guests, Evelyn Russell, who was the head girl of the neighbouring school, " Heathlands." Evelyn was eighteen, wore her hair up, and was known to be " frightfully clever." She was going to Girton the following term, and was always a little bit patronising to Isobel, who was not going to College at all, and was only the head of what Evelyn and her friends rather contemptuously called " a potty little school in a private house."

The rest of the guests, wearing pretty, simple hats and afternoon frocks or coats and skirts, were sitting about in groups, wishing devoutly that Isobel could give a tea-party without the presence of Miss Wymer, and that the cups and saucers and cakes could be laid on a nice, solid table instead of being balanced on one's knees.

As Candida swept into the room everybody looked up, and Isobel, rising to come forward, gazed at her in speechless amazement. Her first thought was that the French girl was not so innocent as she looked, and that she was attempting to carry out a very daring practical joke.

" The *insolence* of it," she thought wrathfully, " and that stuck-up Evelyn Russell, sitting there simply dying to get back to school and tell all the seniors there that the juniors at Magnolia House have no respect at all for *me*."

Miss Wymer, also overwhelmed at the appearance of Candida, thought rapidly but differently ; for she knew at once that somebody had taken advantage of Candida's entire ignorance of English ways to get some fun out of Isobel's *salon*.

Very angry, she glanced at the five junior girls present—four of them were looking at Candida in horrified amazement, and Lorraine was pale, but wore her usual expression of calm innocence.

Isobel gave Miss Wymer a rapid despairing glance—surely this impertinent child, who looked more ready to take part in some absurd charade than in her select tea-party, should be instantly dismissed !

Miss Wymer's face remained immovable, and Isobel realised that this was a test for her as hostess and that at the end of this trying afternoon Miss Wymer would give her so many " points " for her method of dealing with the situation. The correct attitude, of course, for a hostess, was to be surprised at nothing. And though, as the outraged head of the school, Isobel felt inclined to box Candida's ears soundly, she did nothing of the sort, but advanced with outstretched hand and greeted her, smiling sweetly if coldly.

" *Bon jour, Mesdemoiselles*," said Candida, and swept the whole company as magnificent a curtsey as had ever been seen, even in that old Georgian drawing-room that had witnessed so much ceremonious curtseying.

Candida then crossed the room and kissed the fingers of Miss Wymer with charming gracefulness, greatly to that lady's astonishment and chagrin.

She then sat down on the chair Isobel offered to her and glanced round, beginning to feel slightly nervous, for nobody, except the girl talking to Miss Wymer, wore a long skirt, and hers could hardly be called that either —and worse still, there was not a *feather* to be seen.

Surely it seemed strange that not one of the guests had found time to dress suitably for the occasion !

All the same, she *must* be all right, for Isobel had smiled politely, and so had Miss Wymer, and every one seemed pleased to see her. The only one behaving oddly was a fat girl of about fifteen on the sofa, who seemed to be choking, and no wonder, considering the foolish way she was stuffing a handkerchief into her mouth !

Feeling quite satisfied, she gave another sweet smile to Isobel, took off her gloves delicately, blew into the fingers as Alix had instructed her, and spread them out on the arm of her chair.

Isobel, blushing furiously, and more indignant than ever, began to pour out the tea and talk rather feverishly about a new song. What *would* Evelyn Russell think of the new girl at Magnolia House ?

Candida then drew forth a wisp of handkerchief and spread it over her grey alpaca knee with old-maidish precision.

This was too much for Miss Wymer, and she leaned forward and said gently : " There is a table near you, dear, all ready for your cup and saucer and plate—a knee makes an uncomfortable table, doesn't it ? "

Candida surveyed her gravely, then said : " I thank you very much, Mademoiselle, the table will be a great convenience ; but the handkerchief is necessary, too, for one never knows if the grub will be sticky."

The fat girl on the sofa choked violently, and brought utter disgrace on Evelyn and her own school by upsetting her tea into her lap in her wild efforts to suppress her giggles.

Lorraine cast up her eyes to the ceiling and said : " Oh, my aunt ! " so loudly that Isobel heard her and decided that there would be more than one junior to deal with after her duties as hostess were over, and the rest of the guilty girls began to talk so loudly and wildly about the " Heath-lands " hockey match, that Miss Wymer raised her eyebrows.

" What have you been reading lately ? " Evelyn Russell asked Isobel, fixing a cold and glittering eye on the fat girl, who was now purple in the face and fast becoming hysterical, while she made vain efforts to mop up the tea with her handkerchief.

" What *do* you think—*The Scarlet Pimpernel*—for the fourth time, too. I love it, don't you ? " answered Isobel nervously.

" Yes, it's quite good ; all the same, one gets rather bored with so many books about the French Revolution," drawled the cultured Evelyn.

Candida, who had been blowing her hot tea, to Miss Wymer's horror and indignation, and the terror of her five mentors, put down her cup and said to Evelyn : " Mademoiselle, my grand-père was guillotined during the French Revolution, for he was a very great aris—I mean, ' a big swell '— one *must* be English—and I have heard that even on the scaffold he had no fear, but showed the greatest—*swank*, even as the knife fell."

" Well, anyhow, she's putting in a bit on her own," murmured Alix to Sylvia. " I believe I shall burst in a moment."

" How fearfully interesting ! " Evelyn smiled at Candida sweetly. She believed with Isobel that this was a daring prank, and she could not help admiring the pluck of this pretty French girl.

" I believe *The Scarlet Pimpernel* brought some of his refugees to Magnolia House," said Miss Wymer hastily. " There are one or two old books belonging to them in the library."

Candida's eyes began to shine, and she put down her plate, on which, to Isobel's horror and disgust, she had piled bread and butter, hot cake and raspberry sandwich, anxious to " save the hostess trouble," as Laura had advised.

Then she crossed over to Miss Wymer, her long skirt trailing behind her, and said : " Mademoiselle, to me what you have said is very, very interesting—permit me, if you please, to examine those little books."

" Some other time, Candida," said Miss Wymer, a little impatiently, for really things were getting a little too much. One never knew what the child would say next, and she was certainly finding her new pupil, to use Candida's own words, both " unusual and inconvenient," at that moment. " Go back and finish your tea, my dear," she added quietly.

Candida retired and was silent for the next ten minutes, fanning herself elegantly, while the others chattered gaily about the coming bazaar at " Heathlands," new books, new music, and games. Then the conversation came round to old furniture and china, until Evelyn stood up to go.

Candida was the last to leave—the other five thought it wiser to escape —and she swept another curtsey to Isobel and Miss Wymer with the regal bearing of her aristocratic French ancestor, which hardly went with her appearance, for the grey skirt—too small in the waist—had burst from its fastenings, and had to be held on, although Candida never betrayed her embarrassment about it. One of the long white feathers had also escaped from its pins, and waved above her small head with such ridiculous effect that the fat girl's cold had grown rapidly worse before she left, and the five guilty guests just departed were rolling on their beds in speechless laughter at the thought of it. But Candida, unconscious and happy, said to Isobel : " Mademoiselle, I thank you very much for the afternoon so amusing." (" Impertinent little monkey ! " thought Isobel. " ' Heathlands ' will certainly be amused to-night, thanks to *you*.")

" Do not think that because I have not quite eaten the grub on my plate that it is that I have not liked it—I can assure you that it is excellent, but " —she made her little gesture—" when the conversation is interesting one has no hunger, as you know. *Bon jour, Mademoiselle. Bon jour, Isobel.*"

She swept another magnificent curtsey, and departed, clutching her skirt desperately ; for the last curtsey had almost caused it to come off entirely.

Isobel sank on to a chair helplessly, saying indignantly : " Miss Wymer, pardon me, but is it permitted to call her back and box her ears ? I have been dying to do it ever since the little wretch entered the room."

Miss Wymer smiled. " I know you have, Isobel, and I was pleased to see how well you hid your real feelings. But the ears that deserve boxing do not belong to Candida at all ; though I must confess that two or three times this afternoon I should have enjoyed giving her a nice old-fashioned slap myself."

" But, Miss Wymer, you *surely* can't believe that Candida was not doing it all on purpose ? Kathleen and I have suspected several times that she is not so innocent as she looks, and she seems to be pretty well up in *slang*."

Isobel was almost tearful.

" Candida *is* innocent, but woefully ignorant," Miss Wymer said. " She has been brought up in the strangest way in a Breton village, seeing nobody but an old-fashioned mother—who was an invalid, I believe—and a French peasant maid. She is an odd mixture of a prim English mother and a very French father ; and the French part of her is so childish and candid it has been very easy for some one to persuade her that all these foolish things she did this afternoon were English customs—and I happen to know she is very anxious to be English in her ways."

" I wonder how that ' somebody ' *dare* ! " cried Isobel, more wrathfully than ever.

"My dear, they naturally would never believe that Candida would take their advice so literally—when the poor child filled her plate with bread and butter and cake I saw Laura turn quite pale."

"It was like that greedy little wretch to teach her *that*," cried Isobel. "Miss Wymer, what will you do about it?"

"I would rather you decided that, Isobel; it will be a nice problem for you to solve, and I want to see how you do it. I am just as angry as you are, and of course the delinquents must be punished. But when you are dealing with Candida, don't forget that she is just a little ignoramus in some things,"—she smiled—"though very fond of giving advice to others."

*She swept another curtsey to Isobel and Miss Wymer*
*with the regal bearing of her aristocratic French ancestor*

"As for the rest of them, try to make them realise what a serious lack of good manners *they* showed in putting such ideas into Candida's head; and if you can, let the punishment fit the crime."

That evening Candida sat down and wrote a note to Miss Wymer with her usual exquisite neatness and a great deal of reference to the worn English Dictionary.

"DEAR MADEMOISELLE,—I you ask for forgiveness for my conduct so outrageous this afternoon. I had not known of it until Isobel has told it to me.

"It is my hope sincere that you no longer feel sick with disgust at my shocking allusion to the 'grub' on my plate; but, alas, Mademoiselle, I have little English, as you know, and was ignorant that 'grub' meant a worm so revolting.

" For all my behaviour so shocking, Mademoiselle, I express my profound regret, and remain,

"Your pupil sincere,

"CANDIDA M. DUMANOIR."

This note was delivered by Eliza, who had already told her mistress what she thought of the new girl's latest exploit.

Miss Wymer read it with a smile, and passed it to Miss Prior and Miss Budd, who were in her room listening to her account of Candida's social blunders.

"She is an odd mixture of a baby and a prim old lady," said Miss Prior.

"But rather a darling child, all the same," laughed Miss Budd.

---

# UNDER THE GREENWOOD TREE

### TRADITIONAL

IN summer time, when flowers do spring,
And birds sit on each tree,
Let lords and knights say what they will,
  There's none so merry as we.
There's Tom with Nell, who bears the bell,
  And Willy with pretty Betty,
Oh how they skip it, caper and trip it,
  Under the greenwood tree.

In summer time when flowers do spring,
  And birds sit on each tree,
  Let lords and knights say what they will,
    There's none so merry as we.

Our music is a little pipe,
  That can so sweetly play,
We hire Old Hal from Whitsuntide
  Till latter Lammas day :
On high days and on holy days
  After evening prayer comes he,
And then we do skip it, caper and trip it,
  Under the greenwood tree.

In summer time when flowers do spring,
  And birds sit on each tree,
  Let lords and knights say what they will,
    There's none so merry as we.

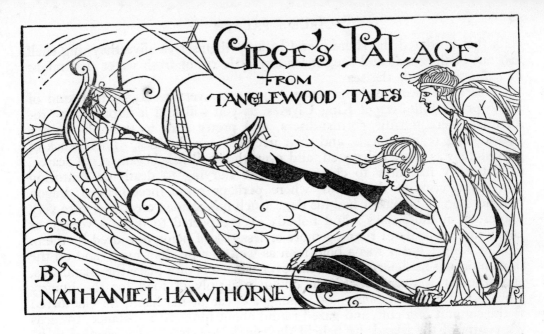

# CIRCE'S PALACE
## FROM TANGLEWOOD TALES

### BY NATHANIEL HAWTHORNE

SOME of you have heard, no doubt, of the wise King Ulysses, and how he went to the siege of Troy, and how, after that famous city was taken, and burned, he spent ten long years in trying to get back again to his own little kingdom of Ithaca. At one time in the course of this weary voyage, he arrived at an island that looked very green and pleasant, but the name of which was unknown to him. For, only a little while before he came hither, he had met with a terrible hurricane, or rather a great many hurricanes at once, which drove his fleet of vessels into a strange part of the sea, where neither himself nor any of his mariners had ever sailed. This misfortune was entirely owing to the foolish curiosity of his shipmates who, while Ulysses lay asleep, had untied some very bulky leathern bags, in which they supposed a very valuable treasure to be concealed. But in each of these stout bags, King Æolus, the ruler of the winds, had tied up a tempest and had given it to Ulysses to keep, in order that he might be sure of a favourable passage homeward to Ithaca ; and when the strings were loosened, forth rushed the whistling blasts, like air out of a blown bladder, whitening the sea with foam, and scattering the vessels nobody could tell whither.

Immediately after escaping from this peril, a still greater one had befallen him. Scudding before the hurricane, he reached a place which, as he afterwards found, was called Laestrygonia, where some monstrous giants had eaten up many of his companions, and had sunk every one of his vessels, except that in which he himself sailed, by flinging great masses of rock at them from the cliffs along the shore. After going through such troubles as these, you cannot wonder that King Ulysses was glad to moor his tempest-beaten bark in a quiet cove of the green island, which I began to tell you about. But he had encountered so many dangers from giants, and one-eyed Cyclopes, and monsters of the sea and land, that he could not help dreading some mischief, even in this pleasant and seemingly solitary spot. For two days, therefore, the poor weather-worn voyagers kept quiet, and either stayed on board of their vessel, or merely crept along under the cliffs that bordered the shore ; and to keep themselves alive they dug shell fish out of the sand, and sought for any little rill of fresh water that might be running towards the sea.

Before the two days were spent, they grew very weary of this kind of life ; for the followers of King Ulysses, as you will find it important to remember, were terrible gormandisers, and pretty sure to grumble if they missed their regular meals, and their irregular ones besides. Their stock of provisions was quite exhausted, and even the shell fish began to get scarce, so that they had now to choose between starving to death or venturing into the interior of the island, where perhaps some three-headed dragon or other horrible monster had his den. Such mis-shapen creatures were very numerous in those days ; and nobody ever expected to make a voyage or take a journey without running more or less risk of being devoured by them.

But King Ulysses was a bold man as well as a prudent one ; and on the third morning he determined to discover what sort of a place the island was, and whether it were possible to obtain a supply of food for the hungry mouths of his companions. So, taking a spear in his hand, he clambered to the summit of a cliff, and gazed round about him. At a distance, towards the centre of the island, he beheld the stately towers of what seemed to be a palace, built of snow-white marble, and rising in the midst of a grove of lofty trees. The thick branches of these trees stretched across the front of the edifice, and more than half concealed it, although, from the portion which he saw, Ulysses judged it to be spacious and exceedingly beautiful, and probably the residence of some great nobleman or prince. A blue smoke went curling up from a chimney, and was almost the pleasantest part of the spectacle to Ulysses. For, from the abundance of this smoke, it was reasonable to conclude that there was a good fire in the kitchen, and that, at dinner time, a plentiful banquet would be served up to the inhabitants of the palace, and to whatever guests might happen to drop in.

With so agreeable a prospect before him, Ulysses fancied that he could not do better than go straight to the palace gate, and tell the master of it that there was a crew of poor shipwrecked mariners not far off who had eaten nothing for a day or two, save a few clams and oysters, and would therefore be thankful for a little food. And the prince or nobleman must be a very stingy curmudgeon, to be sure, if at least, when his own dinner was over, he would not bid them welcome to the broken victuals from the table.

Pleasing himself with this idea, King Ulysses had made a few steps in the direction of the palace, when there was a great twittering and chirping from the branch of a neighbouring tree. A moment afterwards a bird came flying towards him, and hovered in the air, so as to almost brush his face with its wings. It was a very pretty little bird, with purple wings and body, and yellow legs, and a circle of golden feathers round its neck, and on its head a golden tuft, which looked like a king's crown in miniature. Ulysses tried to catch the bird, but it fluttered nimbly out of his reach, still chirping in a piteous tone, as if it could have told a lamentable story, had it only been gifted with human language. And, when he attempted to drive it away, the bird flew no farther than the bough of the next tree, and again came fluttering about his head with its doleful chirp, as soon as he showed a purpose of going forward.

"Have you anything to tell me, little bird?" asked Ulysses.

And he was ready to listen attentively to whatever the bird might communicate; for, at the siege of Troy and elsewhere, he had known such odd things to happen that he would not have considered it much out of the common run had this little feathered creature talked as plainly as himself.

"Peep!" said the bird. "Peep, peep, pe—weep!" And nothing else would it say, but only: "Peep, peep, pe—weep!" in a melancholy cadence, and over and over and over again. As often as Ulysses moved forward, however, the bird showed the greatest alarm, and did its best to drive him back, with the anxious flutter of its purple wings. Its unaccountable behaviour made him conclude, at last, that the bird knew of some danger that awaited him, and which must needs be very terrible, beyond all question,

*"Have you anything to tell me, little bird?" asked Ulysses*

since it moved even a little fowl to feel compassion for a human being. So he resolved, for the present, to return to the vessel, and tell his companions what he had seen.

This appeared to satisfy the bird. As soon as Ulysses turned back, it ran up the trunk of a tree, and began to pick insects out of the bark with its long, sharp bill; for it was a kind of woodpecker, you must know, and had to get its living in the same manner as other birds of that species. But every little while, as it pecked at the bark of the tree, the purple bird bethought itself of some secret sorrow, and repeated its plaintive note of "Peep, peep, pe—weep!"

On his way to the shore, Ulysses had the good luck to kill a large stag. Taking it on his shoulders (for he was a remarkably strong man), he lugged it along with him, and flung it down before his hungry companions. A dish of venison was no unacceptable meal to them, especially after feeding so long on oysters and clams. So, beholding the dead stag, they felt of its ribs in a knowing way, and lost no time in kindling a fire of driftwood to cook it. The rest of the day was spent in feasting.

The next morning their appetites were as sharp as ever. They looked at Ulysses, as if they expected him to clamber up the cliff again, and come back with another fat deer upon his shoulders. Instead of setting out, however, he summoned the whole crew together, and told them it was in vain to hope that he could kill a stag every day for their dinner, and therefore it was advisable to think of some other mode of satisfying their hunger.

"Now," said he, "when I was on the cliff yesterday, I discovered that this island is inhabited. At a considerable distance from the shore stood a marble palace, which appeared to be very spacious, and had a great deal of smoke curling out of one of its chimneys."

"Aha!" muttered some of his companions, smacking their lips. "That smoke must have come from the kitchen fire. There was a good dinner on the spit; and no doubt there will be as good a one to-day."

"But," continued the wise Ulysses, "you must remember, my good friends, our misadventure in the cavern of one-eyed Polyphemus, the Cyclops. Instead of his ordinary milk diet did he not eat up two of our comrades for his supper, and a couple more for breakfast, and two at his supper again? Methinks I see him yet, the hideous monster, scanning us with that great red eye, in the middle of his forehead, to single out the fattest. And then, again, only a few days ago did we not fall into the hands of the king of the Laestrygons and those other horrible giants, his subjects, who devoured a great many more of us than are now left? To tell you the truth, if we go to yonder palace there can be no question that we shall make our appearance at the dinner-table; but whether seated as guests, or served up as food, is a point to be seriously considered."

"Either way," muttered some of the hungriest of the crew, "it will be better than starvation."

"That is a matter of taste," said King Ulysses. "My proposal is that we divide ourselves into two equal parties, and ascertain, by drawing lots, which of the two shall go to the palace and beg for food and assistance. If these can be obtained, all is well. If not, and if the inhabitants prove as inhospitable as Polyphemus, or the Laestrygons, then there will be but half of us perish, and the remainder may set sail and escape."

As nobody objected to this scheme, Ulysses proceeded to count the whole band, and found that there were forty-six men, including himself. He then numbered off twenty-two of them, and put Eurylochus (who was one of his chief officers, and second only to himself in sagacity) at their head.

Ulysses took command of the remaining twenty-two men in person. Then, taking off his helmet, he put two shells into it, on one of which was written "Go," and on the other "Stay." Another person now held the helmet, while Ulysses and Eurylochus drew out each a shell; and the word "Go" was found written on that which Eurylochus had drawn. In this manner it was decided that Ulysses and his twenty-two men were to remain at the seaside until the other party should have found out what sort of treatment they might expect at the mysterious palace. As there was no help for it, Eurylochus immediately set forth at the head of his twenty-two followers, who went off in a very melancholy state of mind, leaving their friends in hardly better spirits than themselves.

No sooner had they clambered up the cliff, than they discerned the tall marble towers of the palace, ascending, as white as snow, out of the lovely green shadow of the trees which surrounded it. A gush of smoke came from a chimney in the rear of the edifice. This vapour rose high in the air, and, meeting with a breeze, was wafted seaward, and made to pass over the heads of the hungry mariners. When people's appetites are keen, they have a very quick scent for anything savoury in the wind.

" That smoke comes from the kitchen ! " cried one of them, turning up his nose as high as he could, and snuffing eagerly. " And, as sure as I'm a half-starved vagabond, I smell roast meat in it ! "

" Pig ! Roast pig ! " said another. " Ah, the dainty little porker ! My mouth waters for him ! "

" Let us make haste ! " cried the others, " or we shall be too late for the good cheer ! "

But hardly had they made half-a-dozen steps from the edge of the cliff, when a bird came fluttering to meet them. It was the same pretty little bird, with the purple wings and body, the yellow legs, the golden collar round its neck, and the crown-like tuft upon its head, whose behaviour had so much surprised Ulysses. It hovered about Eurylochus, and almost brushed his face with its wings.

" Peep, peep, pe—weep ! " chirped the bird.

So plaintively intelligent was the sound, that it seemed as if the little creature was going to break its heart with some mighty secret that it had to tell, and only this one poor note to tell it with.

" My pretty bird," said Eurylochus—for he was a wary person, and let no token of harm escape his notice—" my pretty bird, who sent you hither ? And what is the message which you bring ? "

" Peep, peep, pe—weep ! " replied the bird, very sorrowfully.

Then it flew towards the edge of the cliff, and looked round at them, as if exceedingly anxious that they should return whence they came. Eurylochus and a few of the others were inclined to turn back. They could not help suspecting that the purple bird must be aware of something mischievous that would befall them at the palace, and the knowledge of which affected its airy spirit with a human sympathy and sorrow. But the rest of the voyagers, snuffing up the smoke from the palace kitchen, ridiculed the idea of returning to the vessel. One of them (more brutal than his fellows, and the most notorious gormandiser in the crew) said such a cruel and wicked thing that I wonder the mere thought did not turn him into a wild beast, in shape, as he already was in his nature.

" This troublesome and impertinent little fowl," said he, " would make a delicate tit-bit to begin dinner with. Just one plump morsel, melting away between the teeth. If he comes within my reach, I'll catch him, and give him to the palace cook to be roasted on a skewer."

The words were hardly out of his mouth, before the purple bird flew away, crying " Peep, peep, pe—weep ! " more dolorously than ever.

" That bird," remarked Eurylochus, " knows more than we do about what awaits us at the palace."

" Come on, then," cried his comrades, " and we'll soon know as much as he does ! "

The party, accordingly, went onward through the green and pleasant wood. Every little while they caught new glimpses of the marble palace, which looked more and more beautiful the nearer they approached it. They soon entered a broad pathway, which seemed to be very neatly kept, and which went winding along, with streaks of sunshine falling across it and specks of light quivering among the deepest shadows that fell from the lofty trees. It was bordered, too, with a great many sweet-smelling flowers, such as the mariners had never seen before. So rich and beautiful they were, that, if the shrubs grew wild here, and were native in the soil, then this island was surely the flower garden of the whole earth ; or, if transplanted from some other clime, it must have been from the Happy Islands that lay towards the golden sunset.

" There has been a great deal of pains foolishly wasted on these flowers," observed one of the company. " For my part, if I were the owner of the palace, I would bid my gardener cultivate nothing but savoury pot herbs to make a stuffing for roast meat, or to flavour a stew with."

" Well said ! " cried the others. " But I'll warrant you there's a kitchen garden in the rear of the palace."

At one place they came to a crystal spring, and paused to drink at it for want of liquor which they liked better. Looking into its bosom, they beheld their own faces dimly reflected, but so extravagantly distorted by the gush and motion of the water that each one of them appeared to be laughing at himself and all his companions. So ridiculous were these images of themselves, indeed, that they did really laugh aloud, and could hardly be grave again as soon as they wished. And after they had drunk, they grew still merrier than before.

" It has a twang of the wine cask in it," said one, smacking his lips.

" Make haste ! " cried his fellows ; " We'll find the wine cask itself at the palace ; and that will be better than a hundred crystal fountains."

Then they quickened their pace, and capered for joy at the thought of the savoury banquet at which they hoped to be guests. But Eurylochus told them that he felt as if he were walking in a dream.

" If I am really awake," continued he, " then in my opinion, we are on the point of meeting with some stranger adventure than any that befell us in the cave of Polyphemus, or among the gigantic man-eating Laestrygons, or in the windy palace of King Æolus, which stands on a brazen-walled island. This kind of dreamy feeling always comes over me before any wonderful occurrence. If you take my advice, you will turn back."

" No, no," answered his comrades, snuffing the air, in which the scent from the palace kitchen was now very perceptible. " We would not turn back, though we were certain that the king of the Laestrygons, as big as a mountain, would sit at the head of the table, and huge Polyphemus, the one-eyed Cyclops, at its foot."

At length they came within full sight of the palace, which proved to be very large and lofty, with a great number of airy pinnacles upon its roof. Though it was now midday, and the sun shone brightly over the marble front, yet its snowy whiteness, and its fantastic style of architecture, made it look unreal, like the frost work on a window pane, or like the shapes of castles which one sees among the clouds by moonlight. But, just then, a puff of wind brought down the smoke of the kitchen chimney among them, and caused each man to smell the odour of the dish that he liked best; and, after scenting it, they thought everything else moonshine, and nothing real save this palace, and save the banquet that was evidently ready to be served up in it.

So they hastened their steps towards the portal, but had not got half-way across the wide lawn when a pack of lions, tigers and wolves came bounding to meet them. The terrified mariners started back, expecting no better fate than to be torn to pieces and devoured. To their surprise and joy, however, these wild beasts merely capered around them, wagging their tails, offering their heads to be stroked and patted, and behaving just like so many well-bred house dogs, when they wish to express their delight at meeting their master, or their master's friends. The biggest lion licked the feet of Eurylochus; and every other lion, and every wolf and tiger, singled out one of his two and twenty followers, whom the beast fondled as if he loved him better than a beef bone.

But, for all that, Eurylochus imagined that he saw something fierce and savage in their eyes; nor would he have been surprised, at any moment, to feel the big lion's terrible claws, or to see each of the tigers make a deadly spring, or each wolf leap at the throat of the man whom he had fondled. Their mildness seemed unreal, and a mere freak; but their savage nature was as true as their teeth and claws.

Nevertheless, the men went safely across the lawn with the wild beasts frisking about them, and doing no manner of harm; although, as they mounted the steps of the palace, you might possibly have heard a low growl, particularly from the wolves; as if they thought it a pity, after all, to let the strangers pass without so much as tasting what they were made of.

*A pack of lions, tigers and wolves came bounding to meet them*

Eurylochus and his followers now passed under a lofty portal, and looked through the open doorway into the interior of the palace. The first thing that they saw was a spacious hall, and a fountain in the middle of it, gushing up towards the ceiling out of a marble basin, and falling back into it with a continual splash. The water of this fountain, as it spouted upwards, was constantly taking new shapes, not very distinctly, but plainly enough for a nimble fancy to recognise what they were. Now it was the shape of a man in a long robe, the fleecy whiteness of which was made out of the fountain's spray ; now it was a lion, or a tiger, or a wolf, or an ass, or, as often as anything else, a hog, wallowing in the marble basin as if it were his sty. It was either magic or some very curious machinery that caused the gushing waterspout to assume all these forms. But, before the strangers had time to look closely at this wonderful sight, their attention was drawn off by a very sweet and agreeable sound. A woman's voice was singing melodiously in another room of the palace, and with her voice was mingled the noise of a loom, at which she was probably seated, weaving a rich texture of cloth, and intertwining the high and low sweetness of her voice into a rich tissue of harmony.

By-and-by the song came to an end ; and then, all at once, there were several feminine voices, talking airily and cheerfully, with now and then a merry burst of laughter, such as you may always hear when three or four young women sit at work together.

"What a sweet song that was !" exclaimed one of the voyagers.

"Too sweet, indeed," said Eurylochus, shaking his head. "Yet it was not so sweet as the song of the Sirens, those bird-like damsels who wanted to tempt us on the rocks, so that our vessel might be wrecked, and our bones left whitening along the shore."

"But just listen to the pleasant voices of those maidens, and that buzz of the loom, as the shuttle passes to and fro," said another comrade. "What a domestic, household, home-like sound it is ! Ah, before that weary siege of Troy, I used to hear the buzzing loom, and the women's voices, under my own roof. Shall I never hear them again ? nor taste those nice little savoury dishes which my dearest wife knew how to serve up ?"

"Tush ! we shall fare better here," said another. "But how innocently those women are babbling together, without guessing that we overhear them ! And mark that richest voice of all, so pleasant and so familiar, but which yet seems to have the authority of a mistress among them. Let us show ourselves at once. What harm can the lady of the palace and her maidens do to mariners and warriors like us ?"

"Remember," said Eurylochus, "that it was a young maiden who beguiled three of our friends into the palace of the king of the Laestrygons, who ate up one of them in the twinkling of an eye."

No warning or persuasion, however, had any effect on his companions. They went up to a pair of folding doors, at the farther end of the hall, and throwing them wide open passed into the next room. Eurylochus, meanwhile, had stepped behind a pillar. In the short moment while the folding doors opened and closed again, he caught a glimpse of a very beautiful woman rising from the loom, and coming to meet the poor, weather-beaten wanderers, with a hospitable smile, and her hand stretched out in wel-

*It was often a hog, wallowing in the marble basin as if it were his sty*

come. There were four other young women, who joined their hands and danced merrily forward, making gestures of obeisance to the strangers. They were only less beautiful than the lady who seemed to be their mistress. Yet Eurylochus fancied that one of them had sea-green hair, and that the close-fitting bodice of a second looked like the bark of a tree, and that both the others had something odd in their aspect, although he could not quite determine what it was, in the little while that he had to examine them.

The folding doors swung quickly back, and left him standing behind the pillar, in the solitude of the outer hall. There Eurylochus waited until he was quite weary, and listened eagerly to every sound, but without hearing anything that could help him to guess what had become of his friends. Footsteps, it is true, seemed to be passing and repassing in other parts of the palace. Then there was a clatter of silver dishes or golden ones, which made him imagine a rich feast in a splendid banqueting hall. But by-and-by he heard a tremendous grunting and squealing, and then a sudden scampering, like that of small, hard hoofs over a marble floor, while the voices of the mistress and her four handmaidens were screaming all together, in tones of anger and derision. Eurylochus could not conceive what had happened, unless a drove of swine had broken into the palace, attracted by the smell of the feast. Chancing to cast his eyes at the fountain, he saw that it did not shift its shape, as formerly, nor looked either like a long-robed man, or a lion, a tiger, a wolf, or an ass. It looked like nothing but a hog, which lay wallowing in the marble basin, and filled it from brim to brim.

But we must leave the prudent Eurylochus waiting in the outer hall, and follow his friends into the inner secrecy of the palace. As soon as the beautiful woman saw them, she arose from the loom, as I have told you, and came forward, smiling and stretching out her hand. She took the hand of the foremost among them, and bade him and the whole party welcome.

"You have been long expected, my good friends," said she. "I and my maidens are well acquainted with you, although you do not appear to recognise us. Look at this piece of tapestry, and judge if your faces must not have been familiar to us."

So the voyagers examined the web of cloth, which the beautiful woman had been weaving in her loom ; and, to their vast astonishment, they saw their own figures perfectly represented in different coloured threads. It was a life-like picture of their recent adventures, showing them in the cave of Polyphemus, and how they had put out his one great moony eye ; while in another part of the tapestry they were untying the leathern bags, puffed out with contrary winds ; and, farther on, they beheld themselves scampering away from the gigantic king of the Laestrygons, who had caught one of them by the leg. Lastly, there they were, sitting on the desolate shore of this very island, hungry and downcast, and looking ruefully at the bare bones of the stag which they devoured yesterday. This was as far as the work had yet proceeded ; but when the beautiful woman should again sit down at her loom, she would probably make a picture of what had since happened to the strangers, and of what was now going to happen.

"You see," she said, "that I know all about your troubles ; and you cannot doubt that I desire to make you happy for as long a time as you may remain with me. For this purpose, my honoured guests, I have ordered a banquet to be prepared. Fish, fowl, and flesh, roasted, and in luscious stews, and seasoned, I trust, to all your tastes, are ready to be served up. If your appetites tell you it is dinner time, then come with me to the festal saloon."

At this kind invitation the hungry mariners were quite overjoyed ; and one of them, taking upon himself to be spokesman, assured their hospitable hostess that any hour of the day was dinner time with them, whenever they could get flesh to put in the pot, and fire to boil it with. So the beautiful woman led the way ; and the four maidens (one of them had sea-green hair, another a bodice of oak bark, a third sprinkled a shower of water drops from her fingers' ends, and the fourth had some other oddity, which I have forgotten) all these followed behind, and hurried the guests along, until they entered a magnificent saloon. It was built in a perfect oval, and lighted from a crystal dome above. Around the walls were ranged two and twenty thrones, overhung by canopies of crimson and gold, and provided with the softest of cushions, which were tasselled and fringed with gold cord. Each of the strangers was invited to sit down ; and there they were, two and twenty storm-beaten mariners, in worn and tattered garb, sitting on two and twenty cushioned and canopied thrones, so rich and gorgeous that the proudest monarch had nothing more splendid in his stateliest hall.

Then you might have seen the guests nodding, winking with one eye, and leaning from one throne to another, to communicate their satisfaction in hoarse whispers.

"Our good hostess has made kings of us all," said one. "Ha ! do you smell the feast ? I'll engage it will be fit to set before two and twenty kings."

"I hope," said another, "it will be, mainly good substantial joints, sirloins, spare-ribs, and hinder-quarters, without too many kickshaws. If I thought the good lady would not take it amiss, I should call for a fat slice of fried bacon to begin with."

Ah, the gluttons and gormandisers! You see how it was with them.
In the loftiest seats of dignity, on royal thrones, they could think of nothing
but their greedy appetite, which was the portion of their nature that they
shared with wolves and swine; so that they resembled those vilest of
animals far more than they did kings—if, indeed, kings were what they
ought to be.

But the beautiful woman now clapped her hands; and immediately
there entered a train of two and twenty serving men, bringing dishes of
the richest food, all hot from the kitchen fire, and sending up such a steam
that it hung like a cloud below the crystal dome of the saloon. An equal
number of attendants brought great flagons of wine of various kinds, some
of which sparkled as it was poured out, and went bubbling down the throat;

*The servants might be seen to grin and sneer while the guests were
helping themselves*

while, of other sorts, the purple liquor was so clear that you could see the
wrought figures at the bottom of the goblet. While the servants supplied
the two and twenty guests with food and drink, the hostess and her four
maidens went from one throne to another, exhorting them to eat their fill,
and to quaff wine abundantly, and thus to recompense themselves, at this
one banquet, for the many days when they had gone without a dinner. But,
whenever the mariners were not looking at them (which was pretty often,
as they looked chiefly into the basins and platters), the beautiful woman
and her damsels turned aside and laughed. Even the servants, as they knelt
down to present the dishes, might be seen to grin and sneer, while the guests
were helping themselves to the offered dainties.

And, once in a while, the strangers seemed to taste something that they
did not like.

" Here is an odd kind of spice in this dish," said one. " I can't say it
quite suits my palate. Down it goes, however."

"Send a good draught of wine down your throat," said his comrade on the next throne. "That is the stuff to make this sort of cookery relish well. Though I must needs say the wine has a queer taste, too. But the more I drink of it, the better I like the flavour."

Whatever little fault they might find with the dishes, they sat at dinner a prodigiously long while ; and it would really have made you ashamed to see how they swilled down the liquor and gobbled up the food. They sat on golden thrones, to be sure ; but they behaved like pigs in a sty ; and, if they had had their wits about them, they might have guessed that this was the opinion of their beautiful hostess and her maidens. It brings a blush into my face to reckon up, in my own mind, what mountains of meat and pudding, and what gallons of wine, these two and twenty guzzlers and gormandisers ate and drank. They forgot all about their homes, and their wives and children, and all about Ulysses, and everything else except this banquet, at which they wanted to keep feasting for ever. But at length they began to give over, from mere incapacity to hold any more.

"That last bit of fat is too much for me," said one.

"And I have not room for another morsel," said his next neighbour, heaving a sigh. "What a pity! My appetite is as sharp as ever."

In short, they all left off eating, and leaned back on their thrones, with such a stupid and helpless aspect as made them ridiculous to behold. When their hostess saw this she laughed aloud ; so did her four damsels ; so did the two and twenty serving men that bore the dishes, and their two and twenty fellows that poured out the wine. And the louder they all laughed, the more stupid and helpless did the two and twenty gormandisers look. Then the beautiful woman took her stand in the middle of the saloon, and stretching out a slender rod (it had been all the while in her hand, although they never noticed it till this moment), she turned it from one guest to another, until each had felt it pointed at himself. Beautiful as her face was, and though there was a smile on it, it looked just as wicked and mischievous as the ugliest serpent that ever was seen ; and fat-witted as the voyagers had made themselves, they began to suspect that they had fallen into the power of an evil-minded enchantress.

"Wretches," cried she, "you have abused a lady's hospitality ; and in this princely saloon your behaviour has been suited to a hog-pen. You are already swine in everything but the human form, which you disgrace, and which I myself should be ashamed to keep a moment longer, were you to share it with me. But it will require only the slight exercise of magic to make the exterior conform to the hoggish disposition. Assume your proper shapes, gormandisers, and begone to the sty !"

Uttering these last words, she waved her wand ; and stamping her foot imperiously, each of the guests was struck aghast at beholding instead of his comrades in human shape, one and twenty hogs sitting on the same number of golden thrones. Each man (as he still supposed himself to be) essayed to give a cry of surprise, but found that he could merely grunt, and that, in a word, he was just such another beast as his companions. It looked so intolerably absurd to see hogs on cushioned thrones, that they made haste to wallow down upon all fours, like other swine. They tried to groan and beg for mercy, but forthwith emitted the most awful grunting and squealing that ever came out of swinish throats. They would have wrung their hands in despair, but, attempting to do so, grew all the more desperate for seeing themselves squatted on their hams, and pawing the air with their fore trotters. Dear me ! what pendulous ears they had ! what little red eyes, half buried in fat ! and what long snouts instead of Grecian noses !

But brutes as they certainly were, they yet had enough of human nature in them to be shocked at their own hideousness ; and still intending to groan, they uttered a viler grunt and squeal than before. So harsh and ear-piercing it was that you would have fancied that somebody was pulling every hog by his funny little twist of a tail.

" Begone to your sty ! " cried the enchantress, giving them some smart strokes with her wand ; and then she turned to the serving men—" Drive out these swine, and throw down some acorns for them to eat."

The door of the saloon being flung open, the drove of hogs ran in all directions save the right one, in accordance with their hoggish perversity, but were finally driven into the back yard of the palace. It was a sight to bring tears into one's eyes (and I hope none of you will be cruel enough to laugh at it), to see the poor creatures go snuffing along, picking up here a cabbage leaf and there a turnip top, and rooting their noses in the earth for whatever they could find. In their sty, moreover, they behaved more piggishly than the pigs that had been born so ; for they bit and snorted at one another, put their feet in the trough, and gobbled up their victuals in a ridiculous hurry ; and, when there was nothing more to be had, they made a great pile of themselves among some unclean straw, and fell fast asleep.

*" Begone to your sty," cried the enchantress, giving them smart strokes with her wand*

Meanwhile, as I told you before, Eurylochus had waited, and waited, and waited, in the entrance hall of the palace, without being able to comprehend what had befallen his friends. At last, when the swinish uproar resounded through the palace, and when he saw the image of a hog in the marble basin, he thought it best to hasten back to the vessel, and inform the wise Ulysses of these marvellous occurrences. So he ran as fast as he could down the steps, and never stopped to draw breath till he reached the shore.

"Why do you come alone?" asked King Ulysses, as soon as he saw him. "Where are your two and twenty comrades?"

At these questions, Eurylochus burst into tears.

"Alas!" he cried, "I greatly fear that we shall never see one of their faces again."

Then he told Ulysses all that had happened, as far as he knew it, and added that he suspected the beautiful woman to be a vile enchantress, and the marble palace, magnificent as it looked, to be only a dismal cavern in reality. As for his companions, he could not imagine what had become of them, unless they had been given to the swine to be devoured alive. At this intelligence all the voyagers were greatly affrighted. But Ulysses lost no time in girding on his sword, and hanging his bow and quiver over his shoulders, and taking a spear in his right hand. When his followers saw their wise leader making these preparations, they inquired whither he was going, and earnestly besought him not to leave them.

"You are our king," cried they; "and what is more, you are the wisest man in the whole world, and nothing but your wisdom and courage can get us out of this danger. If you desert us, and go to the enchanted palace, you will suffer the same fate as our poor companions, and not a soul of us will ever see our dear Ithaca again."

"As I am your king," answered Ulysses, "and wiser than any of you, it is therefore the more my duty to see what has befallen our comrades, and whether anything can yet be done to rescue them. Wait for me here until to-morrow. If I do not then return, you must hoist sail, and endeavour to find your way to our native land. For my part, I am answerable for the fate of these poor mariners, who have stood by my side in battle, and been so often drenched to the skin, along with me, by the same tempestuous surges. I will either bring them back with me, or perish."

Had his followers dared, they would have detained him by force. But King Ulysses frowned sternly on them and shook his spear, and bade them stop him at their peril. Seeing him so determined, they let him go and sat down on the sand, as disconsolate a set of people as could be, waiting and praying for his return.

It happened to Ulysses, just as before, that, when he had gone a few steps from the edge of the cliff, the purple bird came fluttering towards him, crying, "Peep, peep, pe—weep!" and using all the art it could to persuade him to go no farther.

"What mean you, little bird?" cried Ulysses. "You are arrayed like a king in purple and gold, and wear a golden crown upon your head. Is it because I too am a king that you desire so earnestly to speak with me? If you can talk in human language, say what you would have me do."

" Peep ! " answered the purple bird, very dolorously, " Peep, peep, pe—we—ep ! "

Certainly there lay some heavy anguish at the little bird's heart ; and it was a sorrowful predicament that he could not, at least, have the consolation of telling what it was. But Ulysses had no time to waste in trying to get at the mystery. He therefore quickened his pace, and had gone a good way along the pleasant wood path, when he met a young man of very brisk and intelligent aspect, clad in a rather singular garb. He wore a short cloak and a sort of cap that seemed to be furnished with a pair of wings ; and from the lightness of his step you would have supposed that there might likewise be wings on his feet. To enable him to walk still better (for he was always on one journey or another) he carried a winged staff, around which two serpents were wriggling and twisting. In short, I have said enough to make you guess that it was Quicksilver ; and Ulysses (who knew him of old, and had learned a great deal of his wisdom from him) recognised him in a moment.

" Whither are you going in such a hurry, wise Ulysses ? " asked Quicksilver. " Do you not know that this island is enchanted ? The wicked enchantress (whose name is Circe, the sister of King Æetes) dwells in the marble palace which you see yonder among the trees. By her magic arts she changes every human being into the brute beast or fowl whom he happens most to resemble."

" That little bird, which met me at the edge of the cliff," exclaimed Ulysses ; " was he a human being once ? "

" Yes," answered Quicksilver. " He was once a king, named Picus, and a pretty good sort of a king too, only rather too proud of his purple robe, and his crown, and the golden chain about his neck ; so he was forced to take the shape of a gaudy-feathered bird. The lions, and wolves, and tigers, who will come running to meet you in front of the palace, were formerly fierce and cruel men, resembling in their dispositions the wild beasts whose forms they now rightfully wear."

" And my poor companions," said Ulysses. " Have they undergone a similar change, through the arts of this wicked Circe ? "

" You well know what gormandisers they were," replied Quicksilver ; and rogue that he was, he could not help laughing at the joke. " So you will not be surprised to hear that they have all taken the shapes of swine ! If Circe had never done anything worse, I really should not think her so very much to blame."

" But can I do nothing to help them ? " inquired Ulysses.

" It will require all your wisdom," said Quicksilver, " and a little of my own into the bargain, to keep your royal and sagacious self from being transformed into a fox. But do as I bid you ; and the matter may end better than it has begun."

While he was speaking, Quicksilver seemed to be in search of something ; he went stooping along the ground, and soon laid his hand on a little plant with a snow-white flower, which he plucked and smelt of. Ulysses had been looking at that very spot only just before ; and it appeared to him that the plant had burst into full flower the instant when Quicksilver touched it with his fingers.

"Take this flower, King Ulysses," said he. "Guard it as you do your eyesight; for I can assure you it is exceedingly rare and precious, and you might seek the whole earth over without ever finding another like it. Keep it in your hand, and smell of it frequently after you enter the palace, and while you are talking with the enchantress. Especially when she offers you food, or a draught of wine out of her goblet, be careful to fill your nostrils with the flower's fragrance. Follow these directions, and you may defy her magic arts to change you into a fox."

Quicksilver then gave him some further advice how to behave, and, bidding him be bold and prudent, again assured him that, powerful as Circe was, he would have a fair prospect of coming safely out of her enchanted palace. After listening attentively, Ulysses thanked his good friend, and resumed his way. But he had taken only a few steps, when, recollecting some other questions which he wished to ask, he turned round again, and beheld nobody on the spot where Quicksilver had stood; for that winged cap of his, and those winged shoes, with the help of the winged staff, had carried him quickly out of sight.

When Ulysses reached the lawn in front of the palace, the lions and other savage animals came bounding to meet him, and would have fawned upon him and licked his feet. But the wise king struck at them with his long spear, and sternly bade them begone out of his path; for he knew that they had once been blood-thirsty men, and would now tear him limb from limb, instead of fawning upon him, could they do the mischief that was in their hearts. The wild beasts yelped and glared at him, and stood at a distance, while he ascended the palace steps.

On entering the hall, Ulysses saw the magic fountain in the centre of it. The up-gushing water had now again taken the shape of a man in a long, white, fleecy robe, who appeared to be making gestures of welcome. The king likewise heard the noise of the shuttle in the loom, and the sweet melody of the beautiful woman's song, and then the pleasant voices of herself and the four maidens talking together, with peals of merry laughter intermixed. But Ulysses did not waste much time in listening to the laughter or the song. He leaned his spear against one of the pillars of the hall, and then, after loosening his sword in the scabbard, stepped boldly forward, and threw the folding doors wide open. The moment she beheld his stately figure standing in the doorway, the beautiful woman rose from the loom, and ran to meet him with a glad smile throwing its sunshine over her face, and both her hands extended.

"Welcome, brave stranger!" cried she. "We were expecting you."

And the nymph with the sea-green hair made a curtsey down to the ground, and likewise bade him welcome; so did her sister with the bodice of oaken bark, and she that sprinkled dew-drops from her fingers' ends, and the fourth one with some oddity which I cannot remember. And Circe, as the beautiful enchantress was called (who had deluded so many persons that she did not doubt of being able to delude Ulysses, not imagining how wise he was), again addressed him :—

"Your companions," she said, "have already been received into my palace, and have enjoyed the hospitable treatment to which the propriety of their behaviour so well entitles them. If such be your pleasure, you shall

*" Guard this flower as you do your eyesight," said Quicksilver*

first take some refreshment, and then join them in the elegant apartment which they now occupy. See, I and my maidens have been weaving their figures into this piece of tapestry."

She pointed to the web of beautifully-woven cloth in the loom. Circe and the four nymphs must have been very diligently at work since the arrival of the mariners ; for a great many yards of tapestry had now been wrought, in addition to what I previously described. In this new part, Ulysses saw his two and twenty friends represented as sitting on cushions and canopied thrones, greedily devouring dainties, and quaffing deep draughts of wine. The work had not yet gone any further. Oh, no, indeed. The enchantress was far too cunning to let Ulysses see the mischief which her magic arts had since brought upon the gormandisers.

" As for yourself, valiant sir," cried Circe ; " judging by the dignity of your aspect I take you to be nothing less than a king. Deign to follow me, and you shall be treated as befits your rank."

So Ulysses followed her into the oval saloon, where his two and twenty comrades had devoured the banquet which ended so disastrously for themselves. But, all this while, he had held the snow-white flower in his hand, and had constantly smelt of it while Circe was speaking ; and as he crossed the threshold of the saloon, he took good care to inhale several long and deep snuffs of its fragrance. Instead of two and twenty thrones, which had before been arranged around the wall, there was now only a single throne, in the centre of the apartment. But this was surely the most magnificent seat that ever a king or an emperor reposed himself upon, all made of chased gold, studded with precious stones, with a cushion that looked like a soft heap of living roses, and overhung by a canopy of sunlight which Circe knew how to weave into drapery. The enchantress took Ulysses by the hand and made him sit down upon this dazzling throne. Then, clapping her hands, she summoned the chief butler.

" Bring hither," she said, " the goblet that is set apart for kings to drink out of. And fill it with the same delicious wine which my royal brother, King Æetes, praised so highly, when he last visited me with my fair daughter Medea. That good and amiable child ! Were she now here, it would delight her to see me offering this wine to my honoured guest."

But Ulysses, while the butler was gone for the wine, held the snow-white flower to his nose.

" Is it a wholesome wine ? " he asked.

At this the four maidens tittered ; whereupon the enchantress looked round at them with an aspect of severity.

" It is the wholesomest juice that ever was squeezed out of the grape," said she ; " for instead of disguising a man, as other liquor is apt to do, it brings him to his true self, and shows him as he ought to be."

The chief butler liked nothing better than to see people turned into swine, or making any kind of a beast of themselves ; so he made haste to bring the royal goblet, filled with a liquid as bright as gold, and which kept sparkling upward, and throwing a sunny spray over the brim. But, delightfully as the wine looked, it was mingled with the most potent enchantments that Circe knew how to concoct. For every drop of the pure grape juice there were two drops of the pure mischief ; and the danger of the thing was that the mischief made it taste all the better. The mere smell of the bubbles, which effervesced at the brim, was enough to turn a man's beard into pig's bristles, or make a lion's claws grow out of his fingers, or a fox's brush behind him.

" Drink, my noble guest," said Circe, smiling, as she presented him with the goblet. " You will find in this draught a solace for all your troubles."

King Ulysses took the goblet with his right hand, while with his left he held the snow-white flower to his nostrils, and drew in so long a breath that his lungs were quite filled with its pure and simple fragrance. Then, drinking off all the wine, he looked the enchantress calmly in the face.

" Wretch," cried Circe, giving him a smart stroke with her wand, " how dare you keep your human shape a moment longer ! Take the form of the brute whom you most resemble. If a hog, go join your fellow-swine in the sty ; if a lion, a wolf, a tiger, go howl with the wild beasts on the lawn ; if a fox, go exercise your craft in stealing poultry. Thou hast quaffed off my wine, and canst be man no longer."

But such was the virtue of the snow-white flower, instead of wallowing down from his throne in swinish shape, or taking any other brutal form, Ulysses looked even more manly and king-like than before. He gave the magic goblet a toss, and sent it clashing over the marble floor to the farthest end of the saloon. Then, drawing his sword, he seized the enchantress by her beautiful ringlets, and made a gesture as if he meant to strike off her head at one blow.

" Wicked Circe," cried he, in a terrible voice, " this sword shall put an end to thy enchantments. Thou shalt die, vile wretch, and do no more mischief in the world, by tempting human beings into the vices which make beasts of them."

The tone and countenance of Ulysses were so awful, and his sword gleamed so brightly, and seemed to have so intolerably keen an edge that

CIRCE'S PALACE

Circe waved her wand and repeated a few magic words, at the sound of which the two and twenty hogs picked up their ears  (*Page 66*)

LEO, THE SLAVE

His fetters were sometimes taken off so that he might divert the villagers by his dances and strange antics while his master played the guitar  (*Page* 75)

Circe was almost killed by the mere fright, without waiting for a blow. The chief butler scrambled out of the saloon, picking up the golden goblet as he went ; and the enchantress and the four maidens fell on their knees, wringing their hands, and screaming for mercy.

"Spare me !" cried Circe. "Spare me, royal and wise Ulysses. For now I know that thou art he of whom Quicksilver forewarned me, the most prudent of mortals, against whom no enchantments can prevail. Thou only couldst have conquered Circe. Spare me, wisest of men. I will show thee true hospitality, and even give myself to be thy slave, and this magnificent palace to be henceforth thy home."

*Drawing his sword, he seized the enchantress by her beautiful ringlets*

The four nymphs, meanwhile, were making a most piteous ado ; and especially the ocean nymph with the sea-green hair wept a great deal of salt water, and the fountain nymph, besides scattering dewdrops from her fingers' ends, nearly melted away into tears. But Ulysses would not be pacified until Circe had taken a solemn oath to change back his companions, and as many others as he should direct, from their present forms of beast or bird into their former shapes of men.

"On these conditions," said he, "I consent to spare your life. Otherwise you must die upon the spot."

With a drawn sword hanging over her, the enchantress would readily have consented to do as much good as she had hitherto done mischief, however little she might like such employment. She therefore led Ulysses out of the back entrance of the palace, and showed him the swine in their sty. There were about fifty of these unclean beasts in the whole herd ; and though the greater part were hogs by birth and education, there was wonderfully little difference to be seen betwixt them and their new brethren, who had so recently worn the human shape.

The comrades of Ulysses, however, had not quite lost the remembrance of having formerly stood erect. When he approached the sty, two and twenty enormous swine separated themselves from the herd, and scampered towards him, with such a chorus of horrible squealing as made him clap both hands to his ears. And yet they did not seem to know what they wanted, nor whether they were merely hungry, or miserable from some other cause. It was curious, in the midst of their distress, to observe them thrusting their noses into the mire, in quest of something to eat. The nymph with the bodice of oaken bark (she was the hamadryad of an oak) threw a handful of acorns among them ; and the two and twenty hogs scrambled and fought for the prize, as if they had tasted not so much as a noggin of sour milk for a twelvemonth.

" These must certainly be my comrades," said Ulysses. " I recognise their dispositions. They are hardly worth the trouble of changing them into the human form again. Nevertheless, we will have it done, lest their bad example should corrupt the other hogs. Let them take their original shapes, therefore, Dame Circe, if your skill is equal to the task. It will require greater magic, I trow, than it did to make swine of them."

So Circe waved her hand again, and repeated a few magic words, at the sound of which the two and twenty hogs pricked up their pendulous ears. It was a wonder to behold how their snouts grew shorter and shorter, and their mouths smaller and smaller, and how one and another began to stand upon his hind legs, and scratch his nose with his fore trotters. At first the spectators hardly knew whether to call them hogs or men, but by-and-by came to the conclusion that they rather resembled the latter. Finally, there stood the twenty-two comrades of Ulysses, looking pretty much the same as when they left the vessel.

You must not imagine, however, that the swinish quality had entirely gone out of them. When once it fastens itself into a person's character, it is very difficult getting rid of it. This was proved by the hamadryad, who, being exceedingly fond of mischief, threw another handful of acorns before the twenty-two newly-restored people ; whereupon down they wallowed in a moment, and gobbled them up in a very shameful way. Then, recollecting themselves, they scrambled to their feet, and looked more than commonly foolish.

" Thanks, noble Ulysses ! " they cried. " From brute beasts you have restored us to the condition of men again."

" Do not put yourselves to the trouble of thanking me," said the wise king. " I fear I have done but little for you."

To say the truth, there was a suspicious kind of a grunt in their voices, and, for a long time afterwards, they spoke gruffly, and were apt to set up a squeal.

" It must depend on your own future behaviour," added Ulysses, " whether you do not find your way back to the sty."

At this moment, the note of a bird sounded from the branch of a neighbouring tree.

" Peep, peep, pe—wee—ep ! "

It was the purple bird, who, all this while, had been sitting over their heads, watching what was going forward, and hoping that Ulysses would remember how he had done his utmost to keep him and his followers out of harm's way. Ulysses ordered Circe instantly to make a king of this good little fowl, and leave him exactly as she found him. Hardly were the words spoken, and before the bird had time to utter another " pe—weep," King Picus leaped down from the bough of a tree, as majestic a sovereign as any in the world, dressed in a long purple robe and gorgeous yellow stockings, with a splendidly wrought collar about his neck, and a golden crown upon his head. He and King Ulysses exchanged with one another the courtesies which belong to their elevated rank. But, from that time forth, King Picus was no longer proud of his crown and his trappings of royalty, nor of the fact of his being a king ; he felt himself merely the upper servant of his people, and that it must be his life-long labour to make them better and happier.

As for the lions, tigers, and wolves (though Circe would have restored them to their former shapes at his slightest word), Ulysses thought it advisable that they should remain as they now were, and thus give warning of their cruel dispositions, instead of going about under the guise of men, and pretending to human sympathies, while their hearts had the blood-thirstiness of wild beasts. And, when everything was settled according to his pleasure, he sent to summon the remainder of his comrades, whom he had left at the sea-shore. When these arrived, with the prudent Eury-lochus at their head, they all made themselves comfortable in Circe's enchanted palace, until quite rested and refreshed from the toils and hardships of their voyage.

---

# A MAN OF WORDS

### ANON.

A MAN of words and not of deeds,
  Is like a garden full of weeds ;
And when the weeds begin to grow,
It's like a garden full of snow ;
And when the snow begins to fall,
It's like a bird upon the wall ;
And when the bird away does fly,
It's like an eagle in the sky ;
And when the sky begins to roar,
It's like a lion at the door ;
And when the door begins to crack,
It's like a stick across your back ;
And when your back begins to smart,
It's like a penknife in your heart ;
And when your heart begins to bleed,
  You 're dead, and dead, and dead, indeed.

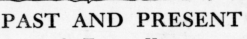

# PAST AND PRESENT

*by* THOMAS HOOD

I REMEMBER, I remember
The house where I was born,
The little window where the sun
Came peeping in at morn;
He never came a wink too soon
Nor brought too long a day;
But now, I often wish the night
Had borne my breath away.

I remember, I remember
The roses, red and white,
The violets, and the lily-cups
Those flowers made of light!
The lilacs where the robin built,
And where my brother set
The laburnum on his birthday.—
The tree is living yet!

I remember, I remember
Where I was used to swing,
And thought the air must rush as fresh
To swallows on the wing;
My spirit flew in feathers then
That is so heavy now,
And summer pools could hardly cool
The fever on my brow.

I remember, I remember
The fir trees dark and high;
I used to think their slender tops
Were close against the sky:
It was a childish ignorance,
But now 'tis little joy
To know I'm farther off from
  Heaven
Than when I was a boy.

# Leo, the Slave

### by
### CHARLOTTE M. YONGE

THE Franks had fully gained possession of all the north of Gaul, except Brittany. Chlodweh had made them Christians in name, but they still remained horribly savage—and the life of the Gauls under them was wretched. The Burgundians and Visigoths who had peopled the southern and eastern provinces were far from being equally violent. They had entered on their settlements on friendly terms, and even showed considerable respect for the Roman-Gallic senators, magistrates, and higher clergy, who all remained unmolested in their dignities and riches. Thus it was that Gregory, Bishop of Langres, was a man of high rank and consideration in the Burgundian kingdom, whence the Christian Queen Clotilda had come ; and even after the Burgundians had been subdued by the four sons of Chlodweh, he continued a rich and prosperous man.

After one of the many quarrels and reconciliations between these fierce brethren, there was an exchange of hostages for the observance of the terms of the treaty. These were not taken from among the Franks, who were too proud to submit to captivity, but from among the Gaulish nobles, a much more convenient arrangement to the Frankish kings, who cared for the life of a " Roman " infinitely less than even for the life of a Frank. Thus many young men of senatorial families were exchanged between the domains of Theodrik to the south, and of Hildebert to the northward, and quartered among Frankish chiefs, with whom at first they had nothing more to endure than the discomfort of living as guests with such rude and coarse barbarians.

But ere long fresh quarrels broke out between Theodrik and Hildebert, and the unfortunate hostages were at once turned into slaves. Some of them ran away if they were near the frontier, but Bishop Gregory was in the utmost anxiety about his young nephew Attalus, who had been last heard of as being placed under the charge of a Frank who lived between Trèves and Metz. The Bishop sent emissaries to make secret inquiries, and they brought word that the unfortunate youth had indeed been reduced to slavery, and was made to keep his master's herds of horses. Upon this the uncle again sent off his messengers, with presents for the ransom of Attalus, but the Frank rejected them, saying, " One of such high race can only be redeemed for ten pounds weight of gold."

This was beyond the Bishop's means, and while he was considering how to raise the sum, the slaves were all lamenting for their young lord, to whom they were much attached, till one of them, named Leo, the cook to the household, came to the Bishop, saying to him, " If thou wilt give me leave to go, I will deliver him from captivity." The Bishop replied that he gave free permission, and the slave set off for Trèves, and there watched anxiously for an opportunity of gaining access to Attalus ; but though the poor young man—no longer daintily dressed, bathed, and perfumed, but ragged and squalid—might be seen following his herds of horses, he was too well watched for any communication to be held with him. Then Leo went to a person, probably of Gallic birth, and said, " Come with me to this barbarian's house, and there sell me for a slave. Thou shalt have the money, I only ask thee to help me thus far."

Both repaired to the Frank's abode, the chief among a confused collection of clay and timber huts intended for shelter during eating and sleeping. The Frank looked at the slave, and asked him what he could do.

" I can dress whatever is eaten at lordly tables," replied Leo. " I am afraid of no rival ; I only tell thee the truth when I say that if thou wouldst give a feast to the king, I could send it up in the neatest manner."

" Ha ! " said the barbarian, " the Sun's day is coming—I shall invite my kinsmen and friends. Cook me such a dinner as may amaze them, and make them say, ' We saw nothing better in the king's house.' "

" Let me have plenty of poultry, and I will do according to my master's bidding," returned Leo.

Accordingly, he was purchased for twelve gold pieces, and on the Sunday (as Bishop Gregory of Tours, who tells the story, explains that the barbarians called the Lord's day), he produced a banquet after the most approved Roman fashion, much to the surprise and delight of the Franks, who had never tasted such delicacies before, and complimented their host upon them all the evening. Leo gradually became a great favourite, and was placed in authority over the other slaves, to whom he gave out their daily portions of broth and meat ; but from the first he had not shown any recognition of Attalus, and had signed to him that they must be strangers to one another.

A whole year had passed away in this manner, when one day Leo wandered, as if for pastime, into the plain where Attalus was watching the horses, and sitting down on the ground at some paces off, and with his back towards his young master, so that they might not be seen talking together, he said, " This is the time for thoughts of home ! When thou hast led the horses to the stable to-night, sleep not. Be ready at the first call ! "

That day the Frank lord was entertaining a large number of guests, among them his daughter's husband, a jovial young man, given to jesting. On going to rest he fancied he should be thirsty at night, and called Leo to set a pitcher of hydromel by his bedside. As the slave was setting it down, the Frank looked slyly from under his eyelids, and said in joke, " Tell me, my father-in-law's trusty man, wilt not thou some night take one of those horses, and run away to thine own home ? "

" Please God, it is what I mean to do this very night," answered the Gaul, so undauntedly that the Frank took it as a jest, and answered, " I

shall look out then that thou dost not carry off anything of mine," and then
Leo left him, both laughing.

All were soon asleep, and the cook crept out to the stable, where Attalus
usually slept among the horses. He was wide awake now, and ready to
saddle the two swiftest ; but he had no weapon except a small lance, so Leo
boldly went back to his master's sleeping-hut, and took down his sword
and shield, but not without awaking him enough to ask who was moving.
" It is I—Leo," was the answer. " I have been to call Attalus to take out the
horses early. He sleeps as hard as a drunkard." The Frank went to sleep
again, quite satisfied, and Leo, carrying out the weapons, soon made Attalus
feel like a free man and a noble once more. They passed unseen out of the
enclosure, mounted their horses, and rode along the great Roman road from

*They rode along the great Roman road from Trèves*

Trèves as far as the Meuse. But they found the bridge guarded and were
obliged to wait till night, when they cast their horses loose and swam the
river, supporting themselves on boards that they found on the bank. They
had as yet had no food since the supper at their master's, and were thankful
to find a plum-tree in the wood, with fruit, to refresh them in some degree,
before they lay down for the night.

The next morning they went on in the direction of Rheims, carefully
listening whether there were any sounds behind, until, on the broad hard-
paved causeway they actually heard the trampling of horses. Happily a bush
was near, behind which they crept, with their naked swords before them,
and here the riders actually halted for a few moments to arrange their harness.
Men and horses were both those they feared, and they trembled at hearing
one say, " Woe is me that those rogues have made off, and have not been
caught ! On my salvation, if I catch him, I will have one hung, and the
other chopped into little bits." It was no small comfort to hear the trot of

the horses resumed, and soon dying away in the distance. That same night the two faint, hungry, weary travellers, footsore and exhausted, came stumbling into Rheims, looking about for some person still awake to tell them the way to the house of the Priest Paul, a friend of Attalus's uncle. They found it just as the church bell was ringing for matins, a sound that must have seemed very like home to these members of an episcopal household. They knocked, and in the morning twilight met the Priest going to his earliest Sunday morning service.

Leo told his young master's name, and how they had escaped, and the Priest's first exclamation was a strange one : " My dream is true. This very night I saw two doves, one white and one black, who came and perched on my hand."

The good man was overjoyed, but he scrupled to give them any food, as it was contrary to the Church's rules for the fast to be broken before mass ; but the travellers were half dead with hunger, and could only say, " The good Lord pardon us, for, saving the respect due to His day, we must eat something, since this is the fourth day since we have touched bread or meat." The Priest upon this gave them some bread and wine, and after hiding them carefully, went to church, hoping to avert suspicion ; but their master was already at Rheims, making strict search for them, and learning that Paul the priest was a friend of the Bishop of Langres, he went to church, and there questioned him closely. But the priest succeeded in guarding his secret, and though he incurred much danger, as the Salic law was very severe against concealers of runaway slaves, he kept Attalus and Leo for two days till the search was blown over and their strength was restored, so that they might proceed to Langres. There they were welcomed like men risen from the dead ; the Bishop wept on the neck of Attalus, and was ready to receive Leo as a slave no more, but as a friend and deliverer.

A few days after Leo was solemnly led to the church. Every door was set open as a sign that he might henceforth go whithersoever he would. Bishop Gregorius took him by the hand, and, standing before the Archdeacon, declared that for the sake of the good services rendered by his slave, Leo, he set him free, and created him a Roman citizen.

Then the Archdeacon read a writing of manumission. " Whatever is done according to the Roman law is irrevocable. According to the constitution of the Emperor Constantine, of happy memory, and the edict that declares that whosoever is manumitted in Church, in the presence of the bishops, priests and deacons, shall become a Roman citizen under protection of the Church : from this day Leo becomes a member of the city, free to go and come where he will as if he had been born of free parents. From this day forward, he is exempt from all subjection of servitude, of all duty of a freed-man, all bound of clientship. He is and shall be free, with full and entire freedom, and shall never cease to belong to the body of Roman citizens."

At the same time Leo was endowed with lands which raised him to the rank of what the Franks called a Roman proprietor—the highest reward in the Bishop's power for the faithful devotion that had incurred such dangers in order to rescue the young Attalus from his miserable bondage.

· · · · · · · · · · · · ·

Somewhat of the same kind of faithfulness was shown early in the present century by Ivan Simonoff, a soldier servant belonging to Major Kascambo, an officer in the Russian army, who was made prisoner by one of the wild tribes of the Caucasus. But though the soldier's attachment to his master was quite as brave and disinterested as that of the Gallic slave, yet he was far from being equally blameless in the means he employed, and if his were a golden deed at all, it was mixed with much of iron.

Major Kascambo, with a guard of fifty Cossacks, was going to take command of the Russian outpost of Lars, one of the forts by which the Russian Czars had slowly been carrying on the aggressive warfare that had nearly absorbed into their vast dominions all the mountains between the Caspian and Black Seas. On his way he was set upon by seven hundred horsemen of the savage and independent tribe of Tchetchenges. There was a sharp fight, more than half his men were killed, and he with the rest were making a last, desperate stand, when the Tchetchenges made a Russian deserter call out to the Cossacks that they would let them all escape provided they would give up their officer. Kascambo on this came forward and delivered himself into their hands ; while the remainder of the troops galloped off. His servant, Ivan, with a mule carrying his baggage, had been hidden in a ravine, and now, instead of retreating with the Cossacks, came to join his master. All the baggage was, however, instantly seized and divided among the Tchetchenges ; nothing was left but a guitar, which they threw scornfully to the Major. He would have let it lie, but Ivan picked it up, and insisted on keeping it. " Why be dispirited ? " he said ; " the God of the Russians is great, it is the interest of the robbers to save you, they will do you no harm."

*Scouts brought word that the Russian outposts were alarmed*

Scouts brought word that the Russian outposts were alarmed, and that troops were assembling to rescue the officer. Upon this the seven hundred broke up into small parties, leaving only ten men on foot to conduct the prisoners, whom they forced to walk, till the Major was utterly exhausted.

After a terrible journey the prisoners were placed in a remote village, where the Major was heavily chained and made to sleep on the bare ground of the hut in which he was lodged. The hut belonged to a huge, fierce old man of sixty, named Ibrahim, whose son had been killed in a skirmish with the Russians. This man, together with his son's widow, were continually trying to revenge themselves on their captive. The only person that showed him any kindness was the little grandson, a child of seven years old, called Mamet, who often caressed him, and brought him food by stealth. Ivan was also in the same hut, but less heavily ironed than his master, and able to attempt a few alleviations for his wretched condition. An interpreter brought the Major a sheet of paper and a reed pen, and commanded him to write to his friends that he might be ransomed for 10,000 roubles, but that if the whole sum were not paid, he would be put to death. He obeyed, but he knew that his friends could not possibly raise such a sum, and his only hope was in the Government, which had once ransomed a colonel who had fallen into the hands of the same tribe.

These Tchetchenges professed to be Mohammedans, but their religion sat very loose upon them, and they were utter barbarians. One piece of respect they paid the Major's superior education was curious—they made him judge in all the disputes that arose. The houses in the village were hollowed out underground, and the walls only raised three or four feet, and then covered by a flat roof, formed of beaten clay, where the inhabitants spent much of their time. Kascambo was every now and then brought, in all his chains, to the roof of the hut, which served as a tribunal whence he was expected to dispense justice.

For instance, a man had commissioned his neighbour to pay five roubles to a person in another valley, but the messenger's horse having died by the way, a claim was set upon the roubles to make up for it. Both parties collected all their friends, and a fierce quarrel was about to take place, when they agreed to refer the question to the prisoner, who was accordingly set upon his judgment seat.

" Pray," said he, " if, instead of giving you five roubles, your comrade had desired you to carry his greetings to his creditor, would not your horse have died all the same ? "

" Most likely."

" Then what should you have done with the greetings ? Should you have kept them in compensation ? My sentence is that you give back the roubles, and that your comrade gives you a greeting."

The whole assembly approved the decision, and the man only grumbled out, as he gave back the money, " I knew I should lose it if that dog of a Christian meddled with it."

All this respect, however, did not avail to procure any better usage for the unfortunate judge, whose health was suffering severely under his privations. Ivan, however, had recommended himself in the same way as Leo, by his perfections as a cook, and moreover he was a capital buffoon. His

fetters were sometimes taken off that he might divert the villagers by his
dances and strange antics while his master played the guitar. Sometimes
they sang Russian songs together to the instrument, and on these occasions
the Major's hands were released that he might play on it ; but one day he
was unfortunately heard playing in his chains for his own amusement, and
from that time he was never released from his fetters.

In the course of a year, three urgent letters had been sent; but no notice
was taken of them, and Ivan began to despair of aid from home, and set
himself to work. His first step was to profess himself a Mohammedan.
He durst not tell his master till the deed was done, and then Kascambo was
infinitely shocked ; but the act did not procure Ivan so much freedom as

*The major was heavily chained in a hut belonging to a huge, fierce old man*

he had hoped. He was, indeed, no longer in chains, but he was evidently
distrusted, and was so closely watched that the only way in which he could
communicate with his master was when they were set to sing together,
chanting out question and answer in Russian, unsuspected, to the tune
of their national airs. He was taken on an expedition against the Russians, and very nearly killed by the suspicious Tchetchenges on one side
and by the Cossacks on the other, as a deserter. He saved a young man of
the tribe from drowning ; but though he thus earned the friendship of the
family the rest of the villagers hated and dreaded him all the more, since
he had not been able to help proving himself a man of courage, instead of
the feeble buffoon he had tried to appear.

Three months after this expedition, another took place ; but Ivan was
not allowed even to know of it. He saw preparations making, but nothing

was said to him ; only one morning he found the village entirely deserted
by all the younger men, and as he wandered round it, the aged ones would
not speak to him.  A child told him that his father meant to kill him, and
on the roof of the house stood the sister of the man he had saved, making
signals of great terror, and pointing towards Russia.  Home he went, and
found that, besides old Ibrahim, his master was watched by a warrior, who
had been prevented by an intermitting fever from joining the expedition.
He was convinced that if the tribe returned unsuccessful, the murder of
both himself and his master was certain ;  but he resolved not to fly alone,
and as he busied himself in preparing the meal, he sang the burden of a
Russian ballad, intermingled with words of encouragement for his master :—

> " The time is come ;
>     Hai Luli !
> The time is come,
>     Hai Luli !
> Our woe is at end,
>     Hai Luli !
> Or we die at once !
>     Hai Luli !
> To-morrow, to-morrow,
>     Hai Luli !
> We are off for a town,
>     Hai Luli !
> For a fine, fine town,
>     Hai Luli !
> But I name no names,
>     Hai Luli !
> Courage, courage, master dear,
>     Hai Luli !
> Never, never, despair,
>     Hai Luli !
> For the God of the Russians is great,
>     Hai Luli !"

Poor Kascambo, broken down, sick, and despairing, only muttered,
" Do as you please, only hold your peace."

Ivan's cookery incited the additional guard to eat so much supper
that he brought on a severe attack of his fever, and was obliged to go home ;
but old Ibrahim, instead of going to bed, sat down on a log of wood opposite the prisoner, and seemed resolved to watch him all night.  The woman
and child went to bed in the inner room, and Ivan signed to his master
to take the guitar and began to dance.  The old man's stick was in an open
cupboard at the other end of the room, and after many gambols and contortions, during which the Major could hardly control his fingers to touch
the strings, Ivan succeeded in laying his hands upon it, just when the old
man was bending over the fire to mend it.  Then, as Ibrahim desired that
the music should cease, he gave him such a blow that he fell down upon the
hearth.  And when the daughter-in-law came out to see what had happened,
he struck her with the same weapon.  Kascambo, utterly helpless, fell almost

fainting upon the floor, and did not cease to reproach Ivan, who was search-ing the old man's pockets for the key of the fetters. But it was not there, nor anywhere else in the hut, and the irons were so heavy that escape was impossible in them. Ivan at last knocked off the clog and the chains on the wrist with an axe, but he could not break the chains round the legs, and could only fasten them as close as he could to hinder them clanking. Then, securing all the provisions he could carry, and putting his master into his military cloak, obtaining also a pistol and dagger, they crept out.

It was February, and the ground was covered with snow. All night they walked easily, but at noon the sun so softened it that they sank in at every step, and the Major's chains rendered each motion terrible labour. It was only on the second night that Ivan, with his axe, succeeded in breaking through the fastenings, and by that time the Major's legs were so swollen and stiffened that he could not move without extreme pain. They soon were on the confines of another tribe of Tchetchenges, who were overawed by Russia, and in a sort of unwilling alliance. Here, however, a sharp storm, and a fall into the water, completely finished Kascambo's strength, and he sank down on the snow, telling Ivan to go home and explain his fate, and give his last message to his mother.

" If you perish here," said Ivan, " trust me, neither your mother nor mine will ever see me."

He covered his master with his cloak, gave him the pistol and walked on to a hut, where he found a Tchetchenge man, and told him that here was a means of obtaining two hundred roubles. He had only to shelter the Major as a guest for three days, whilst Ivan himself went on to Mosdok to procure the money and bring back help for his master. Ivan prevailed, and Kascambo was carried into the village nearly dying.

Ivan set off for the nearest Russian station, where he found some of the Cossacks who had been present when the Major was taken. All eagerly subscribed to raise the two hundred roubles, but the Colonel would not let Ivan go back alone, as he had engaged to do, and sent a guard of Cossacks. This had nearly been fatal to the Major, for as soon as his host saw the lances, he suspected treachery, and dragging his poor sick guest to the roof of the house, he tied him to a stake, and stood over him with a pistol, shout-ing to Ivan, " If you come nearer, I shall blow his brains out, and I have fifty cartridges more for my enemies, and the traitor who leads them."

" No traitor ! " cried Ivan. " Here are the roubles. I have kept my word ! "

" Let the Cossacks go back, or I shall fire."

Kascambo himself begged the officer to retire, and Ivan went back with the detachment, and returned alone. Even then the suspicious host made him count out the roubles at a hundred paces from the house, and at once ordered him out of sight ; but then went up to the roof and asked the Major's pardon for all this rough usage.

" I shall only recollect that you were my host, and kept your word."

In a few hours more, Kascambo was in safety among his brother-officers. Ivan was made a non-commissioned officer, and some months after was seen by the traveller who told the story, whistling the air of Hai Luli at his former master's wedding-feast. He was even then scarcely twenty years old, and peculiarly quiet and soft in manners.

# BALLAD OF
# EARL HALDAN'S DAUGHTER

*by* CHARLES KINGSLEY

IT was Earl Haldan's daughter,
    She looked across the sea ;
She looked across the water ;
    And long and loud laughed she :
" The locks of six princesses
    Must be my marriage fee,
So hey bonny boat, and ho bonny boat !
    Who comes a-wooing me ? "

It was Earl Haldan's daughter,
    She walked along the sand ;
When she was aware of a knight so fair,
    Come sailing to the land.
His sails were all of velvet,
    His mast of beaten gold,
And " Hey bonny boat, and ho bonny boat !
    Who saileth here so bold ? "

" The locks of five princesses
    I won beyond the sea ;
I clipt their golden tresses,
    To fringe a cloak for thee.
One handful yet is wanting,
    But one of all the tale ;
So hey bonny boat, and ho bonny boat !
    Furl up thy velvet sail ! "

He leapt into the water,
    That rover young and bold ;
He gript Earl Haldan's daughter,
    He clipt her locks of gold :
" Go weep, go weep, proud maiden,
    The tale is full to-day,
Now hey bonny boat, and ho bonny boat !
    Sail Westward Ho ! away ! "

# Adventures of Robert the Bruce

*by*

SIR WALTER SCOTT

## THREE TRAITORS

HAVING determined to renew his efforts to obtain possession of Scotland, notwithstanding the smallness of the means which he had for accomplishing so great a purpose, the Bruce removed himself and his followers from Rachrin to the island of Arran, which lies in the mouth of the Clyde. The king landed, and inquired of the first woman he met what armed men were in the island. She returned for answer that there had arrived there very lately a body of armed strangers, who had defeated an English officer, the governor of the castle of Brathwick, had killed him and most of his men, and were now amusing themselves with hunting about the island. The king, having caused himself to be guided to the woods which these strangers most frequented, there blew his horn repeatedly.

Now the chief of the strangers who had taken the castle was James Douglas, one of the best of Bruce's friends, and he was accompanied by some of the bravest of that patriotic band. When he heard Robert Bruce's horn he knew the sound well, and cried out that yonder was the king, he knew by his manner of blowing. So he and his companions hastened to meet King Robert, and there was great joy on both sides; whilst at the same time they could not help weeping when they considered their own forlorn condition, and the great loss that had taken place among their friends since they had last parted. But they were stout-hearted men, and looked forward to freeing their country in spite of all that had yet happened.

The Bruce was now within sight of Scotland, and not distant from his own family possessions, where the people were most likely to be attached to him. He began immediately to form plans with Douglas how they might best renew their enterprise against the English. The Douglas resolved to go disguised to his own country, and raise his followers, in order to begin their undertaking by taking revenge on an English nobleman called Lord

Clifford, upon whom Edward had conferred his estates, and who had taken up his residence in the castle of Douglas.

Bruce, on his part, opened a communication with the opposite coast of Carrick by means of one of his followers called Cuthbert. This person had directions that if he should find the countrymen in Carrick disposed to take up arms against the English he was to make a fire on a headland, or lofty cape called Turnberry, on the coast of Ayrshire, opposite to the island of Arran. The appearance of a fire on this place was to be a signal for Bruce to put to sea with such men as he had, who were not more than three hundred in number, for the purpose of landing in Carrick and joining the insurgents.

Bruce and his men watched eagerly for the signal, but for some time in vain. At length a fire on Turnberry Head became visible, and the king and his followers merrily betook themselves to their ships and galleys, concluding that their Carrick friends were all in arms and ready to join with them. They landed on the beach at midnight, where they found their spy Cuthbert alone in waiting for them with very bad news. Lord Percy, he said, was in the country with two or three hundred Englishmen, and had terrified the people so much, both by actions and threats, that none of them dared to think of rebelling against King Edward.

" Traitor ! " said Bruce, " why, then, did you make the signal ? "

" Alas," replied Cuthbert, " the fire was not made by me, but by some other person, for what purpose I know not ; but as soon as I saw it burning I knew that you would come over, thinking it my signal, and therefore I came down to wait for you on the beach, to tell you how the matter stood."

King Robert's first idea was to return to Arran after his disappointment ; but his brother Edward refused to go back. He was a man daring even to rashness. " I will not leave my native land," he said, " now that I am so unexpectedly restored to it. I will give freedom to Scotland, or leave my carcase on the surface of the land which gave me birth."

Bruce also, after some hesitation, determined that since he had been thus brought to the mainland of Scotland, he would remain there, and take such adventure and fortune as Heaven should send.

Accordingly he began to skirmish with the English so successfully as obliged the Lord Percy to quit Carrick. Bruce then dispersed his men on various adventures against the enemy, in which they were generally successful. But then, on the other hand, the king, being left with small attendance, or sometimes almost alone, ran great risk of losing his life by treachery or by open violence. Several of these incidents are very interesting.

At one time a near relation of Bruce's, in whom he entirely confided, was induced by the bribes of the English to attempt to put him to death. This villain, with his two sons, watched the king one morning till he saw him separated from all his men, excepting a little boy, who waited on him as a page. The father had a sword in his hand, one of the sons had a sword and a spear, and the other had a sword and a battle-axe. Now, when the king saw them so well armed, when there were no enemies near, he began to call to mind some hints which had been given to him that these men intended to murder him. He had no weapons excepting his sword ; but his page had a bow and arrow. He took them both from the little boy, and bade him stand at a distance ; " for," said the king, " if I overcome these traitors thou shalt have enough of weapons ; but if I am slain by them you may make your escape, and tell Douglas and my brother to revenge my death." The boy was very sorry, for he loved his master ; but he was obliged to do as he was bidden.

In the meantime the traitors came forward upon Bruce, that they might assault him at once. The king called out to them, and commanded them to come no nearer, upon peril of their lives ; but the father answered with flattering words, pretending great kindness, and still continuing to approach his person. Then the king again called to them to stand. " Traitors," said he, " ye have sold my life for English gold ; but you shall die if you come

*He shot the arrow, aiming so well that it hit the father in the eye*

one foot nearer to me." With that he bent the page's bow, and as the old conspirator continued to advance, he shot the arrow, aiming so well that it hit the father in the eye. The other two he despatched with his sword.

Then the little page came running, very joyful of his master's victory ; and the king looking upon them said, " These might have been reputed three gallant men if they could have resisted the temptation of covetousness."

## THE DEFENCE OF THE FORD

After the death of these three traitors, Robert the Bruce continued to keep himself concealed in his own earldom of Carrick, and in the neighbouring country of Galloway, until he should have matters ready for a general attack upon the English. He was obliged, in the meantime, to keep very few men with him, both for the sake of secrecy and from the difficulty of finding provisions. Now many of the people of Galloway were unfriendly to Bruce. They lived under the government of one McDougall, related to the Lord of Lorn, who had defeated Bruce at Dalry, and very nearly killed or made him prisoner. These Galloway men had heard that Bruce was in their country, having no more than sixty men with him ; so they resolved to attack him by surprise, and for this purpose they got two hundred men together, and brought with them two or three bloodhounds.

These animals were trained to chase a man by the scent of his footsteps, as foxhounds chase a fox, or as beagles and harriers chase a hare. Although the dog does not see the person whose trace he is put upon, he follows him over every step he has taken. At that time these bloodhounds, or sleuth-hounds (so called from *slot*, or *sleut*, a word which signifies the scent left by an animal of chase), were used for the purpose of pursuing great criminals. The men of Galloway thought themselves secure that if they missed taking Bruce or killing him at the first onset, and if he should escape into the woods, they would find him out by means of these bloodhounds.

The good King Robert Bruce, who was always watchful and vigilant, had received some information of the intention of this party to come upon him suddenly and by night. Accordingly he quartered his little troop of sixty men on the side of a deep and swift-running river that had very steep and rocky banks. There was but one ford by which this river could be crossed in that neighbourhood, and that ford was deep and narrow, so that two men could scarcely get through abreast ; the ground on which they were to land on the side where the king stood was steep, and the path which led upwards from the water's edge to the top of the bank extremely narrow and difficult.

Bruce caused his men to lie down to take some sleep at a place about half a mile distant from the river, while he himself, with two attendants went down to watch the ford, through which the enemy must needs pass before they could come to the place where King Robert's men were lying. He stood for some time looking at the ford, and thinking how easily the enemy might be kept from passing there, provided it was bravely defended, when he heard at a distance the baying of a hound, which was always coming nearer and nearer. This was the bloodhound which was tracing the king's steps to the ford where he had crossed, and the two hundred Galloway men were along with the animal and guided by it.

Bruce at first thought of going back to awaken his men ; but then he reflected that it might be only some shepherd's dog. " My men," he said to himself, " are sorely tired ; I will not disturb their sleep for the yelping of a cur until I know something more of the matter." So he stood and listened ; and by-and-by, as the cry of the hound came nearer, he began to hear a trampling of horses, and the voices of men, and the ringing and clattering of armour, and then he was sure the enemy were coming to the river-side.

Then the king thought, " If I go back to give my men the alarm, these Galloway men will get through the ford without opposition ; and that would be a pity, since it is a place so advantageous to make defence against them." So he looked again to the steep path and deep river, and he thought that they gave him so much advantage that he himself could defend the passage with his own hand until his men came to assist him. His armour was so good and strong that he had no fear of arrows, and therefore the combat was not so very unequal as it must have otherwise been. He there-

*He killed the foremost man with a thrust of his long spear*

fore sent his followers to waken his men, and remained alone by the bank of the river.

In the meantime the noise and trampling of the horses increased ; and the moon being bright, Bruce beheld the glancing arms of about two hundred men, who came down to the opposite bank of the river. The men of Galloway, on their part, saw but one solitary figure guarding the ford, and the foremost of them plunged into the river without minding him. But as they could only pass the ford one by one, the Bruce, who stood high above them on the bank where they were to land, killed the foremost man with a thrust of his long spear, and with a second thrust stabbed the horse, which fell down on the narrow path, and so prevented the others who were following from getting out of the river. Bruce had thus an opportunity of dealing his blows at pleasure among them, while they could not strike at him again. In the confusion five or six of the enemy were slain, or, having been borne down the current, were drowned in the river. The rest were terrified, and drew back.

But when the Galloway men looked again, and saw they were opposed by only one man, they themselves being so many, they cried out that their honour would be lost for ever if they did not force their way, and encouraged each other with loud cries to plunge through and assault him. But by this time the king's soldiers came up to his assistance, and the Galloway men retreated and gave up their enterprise.

## TRACKED BY BLOODHOUNDS

I will tell you another story of this brave Robert Bruce during his wanderings. His adventures are as curious and entertaining as those which men invent for story books, with this advantage, that they are all true.

About the time when the Bruce was yet at the head of but few men, Sir Aymer de Valence, who was Earl of Pembroke, together with John of Lorn, came into Galloway, each of them being at the head of a large body of men. John of Lorn had a bloodhound with him which it was said had formerly belonged to Robert Bruce himself ; and having been fed by the king with his own hands, it became attached to him, and would follow his footsteps anywhere, as dogs are well known to trace their master's steps, whether they be bloodhounds or not. By means of this hound John of Lorn thought he should certainly find out Bruce, and take revenge on him for the death of his relation, Comyn.

When these two armies advanced upon King Robert, he at first thought of fighting the English Earl; but becoming aware that John of Lorn was moving round with another large body to attack him in the rear, he resolved to avoid fighting at that time, lest he should be oppressed by numbers. For this purpose the king divided the men he had with him into three bodies, and commanded them to retreat by three different ways, thinking the enemy would not know which party to pursue. He also appointed a place at which they were to assemble again.

But when John of Lorn came to the place where the army of Bruce had been thus divided, the bloodhound took his course after one of these divisions, neglecting the other two, and then John of Lorn knew that the king must be in that party; so he also made no pursuit after the two other divisions of the Scots, but followed that which the dog pointed out, with all his men.

The king again saw that he was followed by a large body, and, being determined to escape from them if possible, he made all the people who were with him disperse themselves different ways, thinking thus that the enemy must needs lose trace of him. He kept only one man along with him, and that was his own foster-brother, or the son of his nurse.

When John of Lorn came to the place where Bruce's companions had dispersed themselves, the bloodhound, after it had snuffed up and down for a little, quitted the footsteps of all the other fugitives, and ran barking upon the track of two men out of the whole number. Then John of Lorn knew that one of these two must needs be King Robert. Accordingly he com-

*So these two turned on the five men of John of Lorn, and killed them all*

manded five of his men that were speedy of foot to chase after him, and either make him prisoner or slay him. The Highlanders started off accordingly, and ran so fast that they gained sight of Robert and his foster-brother. The king asked his companion what help he could give him, and his foster-brother answered he was ready to do his best. So these two turned on the five men of John of Lorn, and killed them all. It is to be supposed they were better armed than the others were, as well as stronger and more desperate.

But by this time Bruce was very much fatigued, and yet they dared not sit down to take any rest; for whenever they stopped for an instant they heard the cry of the bloodhound behind them, and knew by this that their enemies were coming up fast after them. At length they came to a wood through which ran a small river. Then Bruce said to his foster-brother, " Let us wade down this stream for a great way, instead of going straight across, and so this unhappy hound will lose the scent; for if we were once clear of him, I should not be afraid of getting away from the pursuers." Accordingly the king and his attendant walked a great way down the stream, taking care to keep their feet in the water, which could not retain any scent where they had stepped.

Then they came ashore on the farther side from the enemy, and went deep into the wood before they stopped to rest themselves. In the meanwhile the hound led John of Lorn straight to the place where the king went into the water, but there the dog began to be puzzled, not knowing where to go next; for you are well aware that the running water could not retain the scent of a man's foot like that which remains on turf. So John of Lorn seeing the dog was at fault, as it is called,—that is, had lost the track of that which he pursued—gave up the chase, and returned to join with Aymer de Valence.

## BRUCE REJOINS DOUGLAS

But King Robert's adventures were not yet ended. His foster-brother and he had rested themselves in the wood, but they had got no food, and were becoming extremely hungry. They walked on, however, in hopes of coming to some habitation. At length, in the midst of the forest, they met with three men who looked like thieves or ruffians. They were well armed, and one of them bore a sheep on his back, which it seemed as if they had just stolen.

They saluted the king civilly; and he, replying to their salutation, asked them where they were going. The men answered they were seeking for Robert Bruce, for that they intended to join with him. The king answered that if they would go with him he would conduct them where they would find the Scottish King. Then the man who had spoken changed countenance, and Bruce, who looked sharply at him, began to suspect that the ruffian guessed who he was, and that he and his companions had some design against his person, in order to gain the reward which had been offered for his life.

So he said to them, " My good friends, as we are not well acquainted with each other, you must go before us, and we will follow near to you."

" You have no occasion to suspect any harm from us," answered the man.

" Neither do I suspect any," said Bruce ; " but this is the way in which I choose to travel."

The men did as he commanded, and thus they travelled till they came together to a waste and ruinous cottage, where the men proposed to dress some part of the sheep which their companion was carrying. The king was glad to hear of food ; but he insisted that there should be two fires kindled, one for himself and his foster-brother at one end of the house, the other at the other end for their three companions. The men did as he desired. They broiled a quarter of mutton for themselves, and gave another to the king and his attendant. They were obliged to eat it without bread or salt ; but as they were very hungry, they were glad to get food in any shape, and partook of it very heartily.

Then so heavy a drowsiness fell on King Robert that, for all the danger he was in, he could not resist an inclination to sleep. But first he desired his foster-brother to watch while he slept, for he had great suspicion of their new acquaintances. His foster-brother promised to keep awake, and did his best to keep his word.

But the king had not been long asleep ere his foster-brother fell into a deep slumber also, for he had undergone as much fatigue as the king. When the three villains saw the king and his attendant asleep, they made signs to each other, and rising up at once, drew their swords with the purpose to kill them both.

But the king slept lightly, and for as little noise as the traitors made in rising, he was awakened by it, and starting up, drew his sword, and went to meet them. At the same moment he pushed his foster-brother with his foot to awaken him, and he too got on his feet ; but ere he got his eyes cleared to see what was about to happen, one of the ruffians that were advancing to slay the king killed him with a stroke of his sword. The king was now alone, one man against three, and in the greatest danger of his life ; but his amazing strength, and the good armour which he wore, freed him once more from this great peril, and he killed the three men, one after another.

He then left the cottage, very sorrowful for the death of his faithful foster-brother, and took his direction towards the place where he had appointed his men to assemble after their dispersion. It was now near night, and the place of meeting being a farmhouse, he went boldly into it, where he found the mistress, an old, true-hearted Scotswoman, sitting alone. Upon seeing a stranger enter, she asked who and what he was. The king answered that he was a traveller who was journeying through the country.

" All travellers," answered the good woman, " are welcome here for the sake of one."

" And who is that one," said the king, " for whose sake you make all travellers welcome ? "

" It is our rightful king, Robert the Bruce," answered the mistress, " who is the lawful lord of this country ; and although he is now pursued and hunted after with hounds and horns, I hope to live to see him king over all Scotland."

" Since you love him so well, dame," said the king, " know that you see him before you. I am Robert the Bruce."

" You ! " said the good woman in great surprise ; " and wherefore are you thus alone ? Where are all your men ? "

" I have none with me at this moment," answered Bruce, " and therefore I must travel alone."

" But that shall not be," said the brave old dame, " for I have two stout sons, gallant and trusty men, who shall be your servants for life and death."

So she brought her two sons, and though she well knew the dangers to which she exposed them, she made them swear fidelity to the king ; and they afterwards became high officers in his service.

Now the loyal old woman was getting everything ready for the king's supper, when suddenly there was a great trampling of horses heard round

*She brought her two sons and made them swear fidelity to the king*

the house. They thought it must be some of the English or John of Lorn's men, and the good wife called upon her sons to fight to the last for King Robert. But shortly after they heard the voice of the Good Lord James of Douglas and of Edward Bruce, the king's brother, who had come with a hundred and fifty horsemen to this farmhouse, according to the instructions that the king had left with them at parting.

Robert the Bruce was indeed joyful to meet his brother and his faithful friend Lord James, and had no sooner found himself once more at the head of such a considerable body of followers than, forgetting hunger and weariness, he began to inquire where the enemy who had pursued them so long had taken up their abode for the night ; " for," said he, " as they must suppose us totally scattered and fled, it is likely that they will think themselves quite secure, and disperse themselves into distant quarters, and keep careless watch."

" That is very true," answered James of Douglas, " for I passed a village where there are two hundred of them quartered, who had placed no sentinels ; and if you have a mind to make haste, we may surprise them this very night, and do them more mischief than they have been able to do us during all this day's chase."

Then there was nothing but mount and ride ; and as the Scots came by surprise on the body of English whom Douglas had mentioned, and rushed suddenly into the village where they were quartered, they easily dispersed them ; thus, as Douglas had said, doing their pursuers more injury than they themselves had received during the long and severe pursuit of the preceding day.

The consequence of these successes of King Robert was that soldiers came to join him on all sides, and that he obtained several victories over Sir Aymer de Valence, Lord Clifford, and other English commanders, until at length the English were afraid to venture into the open country, as formerly, unless when they could assemble themselves in considerable bodies.  They thought it safer to lie still in the towns and castles which they had garrisoned, and wait till the King of England should once more come to their assistance with a powerful army.

# A WANDERING CAT

*by* KATHARINE TYNAN

I KNOW a cat that roams the streets.
  Her name is Squibbs.   She likes the air,
And talks to every one she meets.
    She is well known in street and square.
She has no fear of dogs or men.
    She wears a pretty tiger fur.
Whether there's sun or snow or rain,
    The weather's all the same to her.
Through crowded streets this Squibbs she roams,
    And from an island looks to see
What way the roaring traffic comes,
    Because a London cat is she.
But oh, puss Squibbs, in Winter storms
    Have you a friend to make your bed ?
A fire to sit by and be warm ?
    A roof above your sleepy head ?
Come in, poor Squibbs : here you will find
    Saucers of milk to make you fat,
A fireside basket to your mind,
    Come in, and be a proper cat.

# Chiswick Mall

### by W. M. THACKERAY

WHILE the present century was in its teens, and on one sunshiny morning in June, there drove up to the great iron gate of Miss Pinkerton's academy for young ladies, on Chiswick Mall, a large family coach, with two fat horses in blazing harness, driven by a fat coachman in a three-cornered hat and wig, at the rate of four miles an hour. A black servant, who reposed on the box beside the fat coachman, uncurled his bandy legs as soon as the equipage drew up opposite Miss Pinkerton's shining brass plate, and, as he pulled the bell, at least a score of young heads were seen peering out of the narrow windows of the stately old brick house. Nay, the acute observer might have recognised the little red nose of good-natured Miss Jemima Pinkerton herself, rising over some geranium-pots in the window of that lady's own drawing-room.

" It is Mrs. Sedley's coach, sister," said Miss Jemima. " Sambo, the black servant, has just rung the bell ; and the coachman has a new red waistcoat."

" Have you completed all the necessary preparations incident to Miss Sedley's departure, Miss Jemima ? " asked Miss Pinkerton herself, that majestic lady—the Semiramis of Hammersmith, the friend of Doctor Johnson, the correspondent of Mrs. Chapone herself.

" The girls were up at four this morning, packing her trunks, sister," replied Miss Jemima ; " we have made her a bow-pot."

" Say a bouquet, sister Jemima ; 'tis more genteel."

" Well, a booky as big almost as a haystack ; I have put up two bottles of the gillyflower-water for Mrs. Sedley, and the receipt for making it, in Amelia's box."

" And I trust, Miss Jemima, you have made a copy of Miss Sedley's account. This is it, is it? Very good—ninety-three pounds, four shillings. Be kind enough to address it to John Sedley, Esquire, and to seal this billet which I have written to his lady."

In Miss Jemima's eyes an autograph letter of her sister, Miss Pinkerton, was an object of as deep veneration as would have been a letter from a sovereign. Only when her pupils quitted the establishment, or when they were about to be married, and once, when poor Miss Birch died of scarlet fever, was Miss Pinkerton known to write personally to the parents of her pupils; and it was Jemima's opinion that if anything *could* console Mrs. Birch for her daughter's loss, it would be that pious and eloquent composition in which Miss Pinkerton announced the event.

In the present instance Miss Pinkerton's " billet " was to the following effect :—

" THE MALL, CHISWICK,

" *June*, 15, 18—.

" MADAM,—After her six years' residence at the Mall, I have the honour and happiness of presenting Miss Amelia Sedley to her parents, as a young lady not unworthy to occupy a fitting position in their polished and refined circle. Those virtues which characterise the young English gentlewoman, those accomplishments which become her birth and station will not be found wanting in the amiable Miss Sedley, whose *industry* and *obedience* have endeared her to her instructors, and whose delightful sweetness of temper has charmed her *aged* and her *youthful* companions.

" In music, in dancing, in orthography, in every variety of embroidery and needlework, she will be found to have realised her friends' *fondest wishes*. In geography there is still much to be desired; and a careful and undeviating use of the back-board, for four hours daily during the next three years, is recommended as necessary to the acquirement of that dignified *deportment* and *carriage* so requisite for every young lady of *fashion*.

" In the principles of religion and morality, Miss Sedley will be found worthy of an establishment which has been honoured by the presence of *The Great Lexicographer*, and the patronage of the admirable Mrs. Chapone.

" In leaving the Mall, Miss Amelia carries with her the hearts of her companions, and the affectionate regards of her mistress, who has the honour to subscribe herself,

" Madam,

" Your most obliged humble servant,

" BARBARA PINKERTON."

" *P.S.*—Miss Sharp accompanies Miss Sedley. It is particularly requested that Miss Sharp's stay in Russell Square may not exceed ten days. The family of distinction with whom she is engaged desire to avail themselves of her services as soon as possible."

This letter completed, Miss Pinkerton proceeded to write her own name and Miss Sedley's in the fly-leaf of a Johnson's Dictionary—the interesting work which she invariably presented to her scholars on their departure from the Mall. On the cover was inserted a copy of "Lines addressed to a young lady on quitting Miss Pinkerton's school, at the Mall; by the late reverend Doctor Samuel Johnson." In fact, the Lexicographer's name was always on the lips of this majestic woman, and a visit he had paid to her was the cause of her reputation and her fortune.

Being commanded by her elder sister to get "the Dictionary" from the cupboard, Miss Jemima had extracted two copies of the book from the receptacle in question. When Miss Pinkerton had finished the inscription in the first, Jemima, with a rather dubious and timid air, handed her the second.

"For whom is this, Miss Jemima?" said Miss Pinkerton, with awful coldness.

*"For whom is this, Miss Jemima?" said Miss Pinkerton, with awful coldness*

"For Becky Sharp," answered Jemima, trembling very much, and blushing over her withered face and neck, as she turned her back on her sister—"for Becky Sharp: she's going too."

"MISS JEMIMA!" exclaimed Miss Pinkerton, in the largest capitals. "Are you in your senses? Replace the Dictionary in the closet, and never venture to take such a liberty in future."

"Well, sister, it's only two-and-ninepence, and poor Becky will be miserable if she don't get one."

"Send Miss Sedley instantly to me," said Miss Pinkerton. And so not venturing to say another word, poor Jemima trotted off, exceedingly flurried and nervous.

Miss Sedley's papa was a merchant in London, and a man of some wealth; whereas Miss Sharp was an articled pupil, for whom Miss Pinkerton had done, as she thought, quite enough, without conferring upon her at parting the high honour of the Dictionary.

Although Schoolmistresses' letters are to be trusted no more nor less than churchyard epitaphs; yet, as it sometimes happens that a person departs this life who is really deserving of all the praises the stone-cutter carves over his bones; who *is* a good Christian, a good parent, child, wife, or husband, who actually *does* leave a disconsolate family to mourn his loss; so in academies of the male and female sex it occurs every now and then that the pupil is fully worthy of the praises bestowed by the disinterested instructor. Now, Miss Amelia Sedley was a young lady of this singular species, and deserved not only all that Miss Pinkerton said in her praise, but had many charming qualities which that pompous old Minerva of a woman could not see, from the difference of rank and age between her pupil and herself.

For she could not only sing like a lark, or a Mrs. Billington, and dance like Hillisberg or Parisot, and embroider beautifully, and spell as well as the Dictionary itself, but she had such a kindly, smiling, tender, gentle, generous heart of her own, as won the love of everybody who came near her, from Minerva herself down to the poor girl in the scullery, and the one-eyed tart-woman's daughter, who was permitted to vend her wares once a week to the young ladies in the Mall.

She had twelve intimate and bosom friends out of the twenty-four young ladies. Even envious Miss Briggs never spoke ill of her; high and mighty Miss Saltire (Lord Dexter's grand-daughter) allowed that her figure was genteel; and as for Miss Swartz, the rich, woolly-haired mulatto from St. Kitts, on the day Amelia went away, she was in such a passion of tears that they were obliged to send for Dr. Floss, and half tipsify her with sal-volatile.

Miss Pinkerton's attachment was, as may be supposed, from the high position and eminent virtues of that lady, calm and dignified; but Miss Jemima had already blubbered several times at the idea of Amelia's departure, and, but for fear of her sister, would have gone off in downright hysterics, like the heiress (who paid double) of St. Kitts. Such luxury of grief, however, is only allowed to parlour-boarders. Honest Jemima had all the bills, and the washing, and the mending, and the puddings, and the plate and crockery, and the servants to superintend.

Amelia was one of the best and dearest creatures that ever lived.

As she is not a heroine, there is no need to describe her person; indeed I am afraid that her nose was rather short than otherwise, and her cheeks a great deal too round and red for a heroine; but her face blushed with rosy health, and her lips with the freshest of smiles, and she had a pair of eyes, which sparkled with the brightest and honestest good-humour, except indeed when they filled with tears, and that was a great deal too often; for the silly thing would cry over a dead canary-bird, or over a mouse, that the cat haply had seized upon, or over the end of a novel, were it ever so stupid; and as for saying an unkind word to her, were any one hard-hearted enough to do so—why, so much the worse for them. Even Miss Pinkerton, that austere and god-like woman, ceased scolding her after the first time, and though she no more comprehended sensibility than she did Algebra, gave all masters and teachers particular orders to treat Miss Sedley with the utmost gentleness, as harsh treatment was injurious to her.

So that when the day of departure came, between her two customs of laughing and crying, Miss Sedley was greatly puzzled how to act. She was glad to go home, and yet most woefully sad at leaving school. For three days before, little Laura Martin, the orphan, followed her about, like a little dog. She had to make and receive at least fourteen presents, to make fourteen solemn promises of writing every week : " Send my letters under cover to my grandpapa, the Earl of Dexter," said Miss Saltire (who, by the way, was rather shabby) : " Never mind the postage, but write every day, you dear darling," said the impetuous and woolly-headed, but generous and affectionate Miss Swartz ; and little Laura Martin (who was just in round hand) took her friend's hand and said, looking up in her face wistfully, " Amelia, when I write to you I shall call you Mamma."

Well then. The flowers, and the presents, and the trunks, and bonnet-boxes of Miss Sedley having been arranged by Mr. Sambo in the carriage, together with a very small and weather-beaten old cow's-skin trunk with Miss Sharp's card neatly nailed upon it, which was delivered by Sambo with a grin, and packed by the coachman with a corresponding sneer—the hour for parting came ; and the grief of that moment was considerably lessened by the admirable discourse which Miss Pinkerton addressed to her pupil. Not that the parting speech caused Amelia to philosophise or that it armed her in any way with a calmness, the result of argument ; but it was intolerably dull, pompous, and tedious ; and, having the fear of her schoolmistress greatly before her eyes, Miss Sedley did not venture, in her

*" You'll go in and say good-bye to Miss Pinkerton, Becky ? "*

presence, to give way to any ebullitions of private grief. A seed-cake and a bottle of wine were produced in the drawing room, as on the solemn occasions of the visit of parents and these refreshments being partaken of, Miss Sedley was at liberty to depart.

"You'll go in and say good-bye to Miss Pinkerton, Becky?" said Miss Jemima to a young lady of whom nobody took any notice, and who was coming down stairs with her own band-box.

"I suppose I must," said Miss Sharp calmly, and much to the wonder of Miss Jemima; and the latter having knocked at the door, and receiving permission to come in, Miss Sharp advanced and said in French, and with a perfect accent, "Mademoiselle, je viens vous faire mes adieux."

Miss Pinkerton did not understand French; she only directed those who did: but biting her lips and throwing up her venerable and Roman-nosed head (on the top of which figured a large and solemn turban), she said, "Miss Sharp, I wish you a good morning." As the Hammersmith Semiramis spoke, she waved one hand both by way of adieu, and to give Miss Sharp an opportunity of shaking one of the fingers of the hand which was left out for that purpose.

Miss Sharp only folded her own hands with a very frigid smile and bow, and quite declined to accept the proferred honour; on which Semiramis tossed up her turban more indignantly than ever. In fact, it was a little battle between the young lady and the old one, and the latter was worsted. "Heaven bless you, my child," said she, embracing Amelia, and scowling the while over the girl's shoulder at Miss Sharp.

"Come away, Becky," said Miss Jemima, pulling the young woman away in great alarm, and the drawing-room door closed upon them for ever.

Then came the struggle and parting blow. Words refuse to tell it. All the servants were there in the hall—all the dear friends—all the young ladies—the dancing master who had just arrived; and there was such a scuffling, and hugging, and kissing, and crying, with the hysterical *yoops* of Miss Swartz, the parlour-boarder, from her room, as no pen can depict, and as the tender heart would fain pass over. The embracing was over; Miss Sedley parted from her friends. Miss Sharp had demurely entered the carriage some minutes before. Nobody cried for leaving *her*.

Sambo of the bandy legs slammed the carriage-door on his young weeping mistress. He sprang up behind the carriage. "Stop!" cried Miss Jemima, rushing to the gate with a parcel.

"It's some sandwiches, my dear," said she to Amelia. "You may be hungry, you know; and Becky, Becky Sharp, here's a book for you that my sister—that is, I,—Johnson's Dictionary, you know; you mustn't leave us without that. Good-bye. Drive on, coachman. God bless you!"

And the kind creature retreated into the garden, overcome with emotions.

But, lo! and just as the coach drove off, Miss Sharp put her pale face out of the window, and actually flung the book back into the garden.

This caused almost Jemima to faint with terror.

"Well, I never," said she; "what an audacious——" Emotion prevented her from completing either sentence. The carriage rolled away; the great gates were closed; the bell rang for the dancing lesson. The world is before the two young ladies; and so farewell to Chiswick Mall.

# THE PLAINT OF THE CAMEL

### *by* C. E. Carryl

CANARY-BIRDS feed on sugar and seed,
  Parrots have crackers to crunch ;
And as for the poodles, they tell me the noodles
  Have chicken and cream for their lunch.
But there's never a question
About *my* digestion,
  *Anything* does for me.

Cats, you're aware, can repose on a chair,
  Chickens can roost upon rails ;
Puppies are able to sleep in a stable,
  And oysters can slumber in pails.
But no one supposes
A poor camel dozes,
  *Any place* does for me.

Lambs are enclosed where it's never exposed,
  Coops are constructed for hens ;
Kittens are treated to houses well heated,
  And pigs are protected by pens.
But a camel comes handy
Wherever it's sandy.
  *Anywhere* does for me.

People would laugh if you rode a giraffe,
  Or mounted the back of an ox ;
It's nobody's habit to ride on a rabbit,
  Or try to bestraddle a fox.
But as for the camel, he's
Ridden by families,
  *Any load* does for me.

A snake is as round as a hole in the ground ;
  Weasels are wavy and sleek ;
And no alligator could ever be straighter
  Than lizards that live in a creek.
But a camel's all lumpy.
And bumpy, and humpy,
  *Any shape* does for me.

# THE WITCH'S CAVE

### by John R. Crossland

CREEPING down the galleries the tall pines make,
   In the wood by the Ogre's Rock,
Come the little children as their way they take
   At the midnight stroke of the clock.

Parents are a-sleeping snugly in their beds,
   No one knows the children prowl ;
Through the ghostly pinewood where the pale moon sheds
   Glimmerings for bat and owl.

Treading down the pine cones to the Witch's cave,
   Ears a-cock, and eyes all wide,
Creep the wee ones, fairy led, so curious and brave
   To see the cave and peep inside.

Coming to the clearing there they spy a crackling fire;
   A cat of black with eyes of green ;
While crouching o'er the blazing wood where flames mount
      ever higher,
   The wicked witch herself is seen.

Still she is and queer she is a-sitting there alone,
   White of face, with crooked nose and chin ;
Watching all the puffs of smoke as though she's made of
      stone,
   So marble-like her wrinkled skin.

Suddenly she starts, and looks around into the night,
   Snatches up her broomstick from the ground ;
Mounts it as a huntsman strides his horse, and out of sight
   Vanishes without the slightest sound.
.    .    .    .    .    .    .    .    .    .    .

Dawn is bringing colour to the greying sky of night,
   Rays of sunshine strike a little bed ;
Sheets and blankets rustle and upon the morning light
   Breaks a sleepy, tousled little head.

Sitting up and rubbing at a pair of sleepy eyes,
   Dazzled with the sunlight's beam,
There's a little fellow who looks round in great surprise
   And murmurs " So it's all a dream ! "

THE WITCH'S CAVE

Crouching o'er the blazing flames the witch herself is seen, with a cat sitting by her side  (*Page* 96)

## THE WILLOW-PATTERN PLATE

A servant told his master that Kong-Shee was running away with Chang. The nobleman ran after them carrying a whip, but they managed to get away  (*Page* 98)

# The Willow-Pattern Plate

EVERY child, I think, looks very often at the willow-pattern plate, and wonders what the picture on it means.

We have all asked ourselves what kind of people lived in the funny little houses, with the strange trees growing beside them, and who were the three figures crossing the bridge.

We wonder where the odd little boat, without either sail or oar, is going, and why the two doves, high above the lake and the islands, are always kissing each other.

The story which this picture tells is thousands of years old. It comes from China, and is said to be true.

Long, long ago, a great nobleman lived in China. He held high rank at Court, but, when his wife died, he asked the Emperor to let him go to live on his own lands.

The house, which you see on the right of the picture, is his country house. To us, it does not seem large, but for China, long ago, it was very splendid indeed. It was two stories high, which was thought very grand.

You can see the fine roof, and, in front, with the path leading up to it, a tent, where the nobleman sat and drank his tea in the hot weather.

Fine trees grew all round the dwelling. The tall one is an orange tree loaded with fruit. There were, also, peach and almond trees, a fir tree, and a willow growing by the water's edge, near the bridge.

To this beautiful home the nobleman came to live, bringing with him his only daughter Koong-Shee, and a young man called Chang, who had helped him when he was at Court.

After a while, the nobleman did not need Chang any more, and he told him that he might go back to his own home. Chang had no wish to leave. He had fallen in love with his master's daughter, who loved him, and was willing to marry him.

One day they met under the orange tree, and the nobleman heard them saying they would marry only one another. This made him very angry, and he told his daughter she must never see Chang again. The young man was sent away, and told never to enter the house.

Now Koong-Shee had a maid, who helped her to see Chang sometimes. This being found out by her father, he was more angry than ever. He would not let Koong-Shee go outside unless with him, and, to keep Chang from coming in, he built a high wall of wood round the house, reaching to the water's edge. This is the paling which you see in the picture.

Koong-Shee and Chang were full of sorrow, but worse was still to come. The nobleman told his daughter she was to marry a rich prince. He was many years older than the bride, being, indeed, the same age as her father.

In vain Koong-Shee wept, and begged not to be forced to marry this old man. Her father would not listen, but said the wedding must take place, " when the peach tree should blossom in the spring."

It was still early in the year, and the willow was covered with gold and silver catkins, but the buds were hardly yet formed on the peach tree. Day after day went by, however, and no help came.

Poor Koong-Shee wept, as she watched the buds of the peach tree, whose branches grew just outside the window of her room. They were growing larger and larger, and, when they opened into flower, her wedding was to take place.

One day, her father came to her room, looking very pleased. In his hands he had a case of jewels, which he said was a wedding present from the prince. Then he told Koong-Shee to put on her grandest dress, for the bridegroom was coming the next day.

At this Koong-Shee lost all hope, and could only shed tears, thinking she would never see Chang again.

Next day, the prince came with many servants, and Koong-Shee's father made a grand feast. Many people came to the wedding, but among them was one who had not been asked. A poor beggar came into the hall, and all the people looked at him in surprise, whilst the servants laughed at his rags.

The nobleman, who was too pleased to be angry, told his servants to take the beggar away, and to give him some food. But what would he and the prince have said, had they seen the man steal away to Koong-Shee's rooms, and throw off his rags. The beggar was Chang!

You may think how glad the two were, to meet once more. They vowed they would never part, and, when the feast was at its height, they ran away. They took with them all Koong-Shee's jewels, except three which the prince had given her as a wedding present.

They had reached the part of the bridge by the willow, before any one found out what had taken place. Then, a servant told his master that the lady Koong-Shee was running away with Chang. Starting from his seat, the angry father set out to catch them, and to bring them back.

In the picture you can see them crossing the bridge. First comes Koong-Shee, bearing a distaff, with which to spin clothing for Chang, then Chang himself, with the box of jewels. Last comes the nobleman carrying a whip, with which he means to beat them both, if he can catch them.

Koong-Shee and Chang, being young and strong, ran faster than the nobleman, and hid in a gardener's cottage. This is the house you see near the farther end of the bridge, with a fir tree growing by it. Here they found Chang's sister waiting for them, and the gardener's wife, who was none other than Koong-Shee's maid.

In this house, Chang and Koong-Shee were married, and they lived here very happily, until they were found by the prince's soldiers.

The soldiers would have taken them away, had not a boat without oars drifted by. They jumped into it from the window, and the boat was carried a long, long way down the river.

In the picture you can see the boat, with Chang standing in it. For many days and nights they drifted, until the boat came near a small island. Here they stopped, hoping to spend the rest of their lives in peace. The jewels were sold, and, with the money, Chang was able to buy the island, and to build a little house upon it.

This island you see high up on the left of the picture, with the house in which Koong-Shee and Chang lived for several years. The young trees were planted by Chang, who worked hard, and turned the whole place into a beautiful garden.

Many friends came to visit them in their pretty home, and every one talked about the beauty of Koong-Shee, and the wisdom of her husband. After a while, Chang wrote a book upon gardening, which won him great fame.

But alas! the wicked prince was still very angry. He still had soldiers going about the country, in search of the man who had robbed him of his bride. One day, they learned that Chang and the writer of the famous book were one and the same person.

At this news the prince came to the island with a band of armed men. Chang fought very bravely, but was slain. Then his beautiful wife ran into the house, set it on fire, and died in the flames.

Thus ended the lives of the two lovers; but the gods, so runs the tale, taking pity upon them, changed them into the pair of turtle doves seen in the picture.

# THE SNUFF-BOXES

### ANON

A VILLAGE pedagogue announced one day
Unto his pupils, that Inspector A.
Was coming to examine them. Quoth he:
" If he should try you in Geography,
Most likely he will ask—" What's the earth's shape ? "
Then, if you feel as stupid as an ape,
Just look at me ; my snuff-box I will show,
Which will remind you it is round, you know."
Now, the sagacious master, I declare,
Had two snuff-boxes—one round, t'other square ;
The square he carried through the week, the round
On Sundays only.
           Hark ! a footstep's sound :
'Tis the Inspector. " What's the earth's shape, lad ? "
Addressing one by name. The latter, glad
To have his memory helped, looked at the master ;
When, piteous to relate, O, sad disaster !
The pupil without hesitation says :
" Round, sir, on Sundays, square on other days."

# POLLY PERKINS

*by* THOMAS HOOD

I'M a broken-hearted milkman, in grief I'm arrayed,
Through the keeping of company with a young servant-maid
Who lived on board wages to keep the house clean
In a gentleman's family at Paddington Green.

At the sound of my milk-cans when I'd cry " Milk below ! "
Her face at the window in a moment she'd show,
With a smile upon her countenance and a laugh in her eye—
If I thought she didn't love me I'd lay down and die.

Her eyes were as black as the pips of the pear ;
No rose in the garden with her cheeks could compare ;
Her hair hung in ringlets so beautiful and long—
I thought that she loved me but I found I was wrong.

When I asked her to marry me she said, " Oh, what stuff ! "
And she told me to drop it for she'd had quite enough
Of my nonsense ; at the same time I had been very kind,
But to marry a milkman she didn't feel inclined.

The man that has me must have silver and gold,
A chariot to ride in, and be handsome and bold ;
His hair must be curly as any watch-spring,
And his whiskers as long as a brush for clothing."

In six months she married, this hard-hearted girl,
And it was not a viscount and it was not an earl ;
It was not a baronet but a shade or two wuss,
T'was the bow-legged conductor of a twopenny 'bus.

*Refrain :*

She was as beautiful as a butterfly and as proud as a queen,
Was pretty little Polly Perkins of Paddington Green.

# Maggie and the Gipsies

## *by* GEORGE ELIOT

AT the next bend in the lane, Maggie actually saw the little semi-circular black tent with the blue smoke rising before it, which was to be her refuge from all the blighting obloquy that had pursued her in civilised life. She even saw a tall female figure by the column of smoke —doubtless the gipsy-mother, who provided the tea and other groceries ; it was astonishing to herself that she did not feel more delighted. But it was startling to find the gipsies in a lane after all, and not on a common—indeed, it was rather disappointing ; for a mysterious, illimitable common, where there were sandpits to hide in, and one was out of everybody's reach, had always made part of Maggie's picture of gipsy life. She went on, however, and thought with some comfort that gipsies most likely knew nothing about idiots, so there was no danger of their falling into the mistake of setting her down at the first glance as an idiot. It was plain she had attracted attention, for the tall figure, who proved to be a young woman with a baby on her arm, walked slowly to meet her. Maggie looked up in the new face rather tremblingly as it approached, and was reassured by the thought that her aunt Pullet and the rest were right when they called her a gipsy ; for this face, with the bright, dark eyes and the long hair, was really something like what she used to see in the glass before she cut her hair off.

"My little lady, where are you going to ? " the gipsy said, in a tone of coaxing deference.

It was delightful, and just what Maggie expected. The gipsies saw at once that she was a little lady, and were prepared to treat her accordingly.

"Not any farther," said Maggie, feeling as if she were saying what she had rehearsed in a dream. "I'm come to stay with *you*, please."

" That's pretty ; come, then.  Why, what a nice little lady you are, to be sure," said the gipsy taking her by the hand.  Maggie thought her very agreeable, but wished she had not been so dirty.

There was quite a group round the fire when they reached it.  An old gipsy woman was seated on the ground nursing her knees, and occasionally poking a skewer into the round kettle that sent forth an odorous steam ; two small shock-headed children were lying prone and resting on their elbows something like small sphinxes ; and a placid donkey was bending his head over a tall girl, who, lying on her back, was scratching his nose and indulging him with a bite of excellent stolen hay.

The slanting sunlight fell kindly upon them, and the scene was really very pretty and comfortable, Maggie thought, only she hoped they would soon set out the tea cups.  Everything would be quite charming when she had taught the gipsies to use a washing-basin, and to feel an interest in books.  It was a little confusing, though, that the young woman began to speak to the old one in a language which Maggie did not understand, while the tall girl, who was feeding the donkey, sat up and stared at her without offering any salutation.  At last the old woman said :

" What, my pretty lady, are you come to stay with us ?  Sit ye down and tell us where ye come from."

It was just like a story : Maggie liked to be called " pretty lady " and treated in this way.  She sat down and said :

" I'm come from home because I'm unhappy, and I mean to be a gipsy.  I'll live with you if you like, and I can teach you a great many things."

" Such a clever little lady," said the woman with the baby, sitting down by Maggie, and allowing baby to crawl ; " and such a pretty bonnet and frock," she added, taking off Maggie's bonnet and looking at it while she made an observation to the old woman in the unknown language.  The tall girl snatched the bonnet and put it on her own head hind-foremost with a grin ; but Maggie was determined not to show any weakness on this subject, as if she were susceptible about her bonnet.

" I don't want to wear a bonnet," she said ; " I'd rather wear a red handkerchief, like yours " (looking at her friend by her side).  " My hair was quite long till yesterday, when I cut it off ; but I dare say it will grow again very soon," she added apologetically, thinking it probable the gipsies had a strong prejudice in favour of long hair.  And Maggie had forgotten even her hunger at that moment in the desire to conciliate gipsy opinion.

" Oh, what a nice little lady !—and rich, I'm sure," said the old woman.  " Didn't you live in a beautiful house at home ? "

" Yes, my home is pretty, and I'm very fond of the river, where we go fishing ; but I'm often very unhappy.  I should have liked to bring my books with me, but I came away in a hurry, you know.  But I can tell you almost everything there is in my books, I've read them so many times ; and that will amuse you.  And I can tell you something about geography, too—that's about the world we live in—very useful and interesting.  Did you ever hear about Columbus ? "

Maggie's eyes had begun to sparkle and her cheeks to flush ; she was really beginning to instruct the gipsies, and gaining great influence over them.  The gipsies themselves were not without amazement at this talk, though their attention was divided by the contents of Maggie's pocket, which the friend at her right hand had by this time emptied without attracting her notice.

"Is that where you live, my little lady?" said the old woman, at the mention of Columbus.

"Oh, no," said Maggie, with some pity. "Columbus was a very wonderful man, who found out half the world, and they put chains on him and treated him very badly, you know—it's in my Catechism of Geography—but perhaps it's rather too long to tell before tea. . . . *I want my tea so.*"

The last words burst from Maggie, in spite of herself, with a sudden drop from patronising instruction to simple peevishness.

*The tall girl snatched the bonnet and put it on her own head hind-foremost.*

"Why, she's hungry, poor little lady," said the younger woman. "Give her some o' the cold victual. You've been walking a good way, I'll be bound, my dear. Where's your home?"

"It's Dorlcote Mill, a good way off," said Maggie. "My father is Mr. Tulliver, but we mustn't let him know where I am, else he'll fetch me home again. Where does the queen of the gipsies live?"

"What! do you want to go to her, my little lady?" said the younger woman. The tall girl meanwhile was constantly staring at Maggie and grinning. Her manners were certainly not agreeable.

"No," said Maggie, "I'm only thinking that if she isn't a very good queen you might be glad when she died, and you could choose another. If I was a queen, I'd be a very good queen, and kind to everybody."

"Here's a bit o' nice victual, then," said the old woman, handing to Maggie a lump of dried bread, which she had taken from a bag of scraps, "and a piece of cold bacon."

" Thank you," said Maggie, looking at the food without taking it ;
" but will you give me some bread-and-butter and tea instead ?  I don't
like bacon."

" We've got no tea nor butter," said the old woman with something
like a scowl, as if she were getting tired of coaxing.

" Oh, a little bread and treacle would do," said Maggie.

" We han't got no treacle," said the old woman crossly, whereupon
there followed a sharp dialogue between the two women in their unknown
tongue, and one of the small sphinxes snatched at the bread-and-bacon
and began to eat it. . . .

Both the men, who had come up to the tent, now seemed to be inquiring
about Maggie, for they looked at her, and the tone of the conversation
became of that pacific kind which implies curiosity on one side and the
power of satisfying it on the other.  At last the younger woman said in her
previous deferential, coaxing tone :

" This nice little lady's come to live with us.  Aren't you glad ? "

" Ay, very glad," said the younger man, who was looking at Maggie's
silver thimble and other small matters that had been taken from her pocket.
He returned them all except the thimble to the younger woman, with some
observation, and she immediately restored them to Maggie's pocket, while
the men seated themselves and began to attack the contents of the kettle
—a stew of meat and potatoes—which had been taken off the fire and turned
out into a yellow platter.

Maggie began to think that Tom must be right about the gipsies : they
must certainly be thieves, unless the man meant to return her thimble by
and by.  She would willingly have given it to him, for she was not at all
attached to her thimble, but the idea that she was among thieves prevented
her from feeling any comfort in the revival of deference and attention towards
her.  All thieves, except Robin Hood, were wicked people.  The women saw
she was frightened.

" We've got nothing nice for a lady to eat," said the old woman, in her
coaxing tone.  " And she's so hungry, sweet little lady ! "

" Here, my dear, try if you can eat a bit o' this," said the younger woman,
handing some of the stew on a brown dish with an iron spoon to Maggie,
who, remembering that the old woman had seemed angry with her for not
liking the bread-and-bacon, dared not refuse the stew, though fear had
chased away her appetite.  If her father would but come by in the gig and
take her up !  Or even if Jack the Giantkiller, or Mr. Greatheart, or St.
George who slew the dragon, on the halfpennies, would happen to pass that
way !  But Maggie thought with a sinking heart that these heroes were never
seen in the neighbourhood of St. Ogg's—nothing very wonderful ever came
there.

Her ideas about gipsies had undergone a rapid modification in the last
five minutes.  From having considered them very respectful companions,
amenable to instruction, she had begun to think that they meant perhaps
to kill her as soon as it was dark, and cut up her body for gradual cooking :
the suspicion crossed her that the fierce-eyed old man was in fact the devil,
who might drop that transparent disguise at any moment, and turn either
into the grinning blacksmith or else a fiery-eyed monster with dragon's

wings. It was no use trying to eat the stew, and yet the thing she most dreaded was to offend the gipsies by betraying her extremely unfavourable opinion of them, and she wondered, with a keenness of interest that no theologian could have exceeded, whether, if the devil were really present, he would know her thoughts.

" What ! you don't like the smell of it, my dear," said the young woman, observing that Maggie did not even take a spoonful of the stew. " Try a bit—come ! "

" No, thank you," said Maggie, summoning all her force for a desperate effort, and trying to smile in a friendly way. " I haven't time, I think it seems getting darker. I think I must go home now, and come another day, and then I can bring you a basket with some jam-tarts and things."

Maggie rose from her seat as she threw out this illusory prospect, devoutly hoping that Apollyon was gullible ; but her hope sank when the old gipsy woman said : " Stop a bit, stop a bit, little lady ; we'll take you home, all safe, when we've done supper. You shall ride home, like a lady."

Maggie sat down again, with little faith in this promise, though she presently saw the tall girl putting a bridle on the donkey, and throwing a couple of bags on his back.

" Now, then, little missis," said the younger man, rising and leading the donkey forward, " tell us where you live ; what's the name o' the place ? "

" Dorlcote Mill is my home," said Maggie eagerly. " My father is Mr. Tulliver ; he lives there."

" What ! a big mill a little way this side o' St. Ogg's ? "

" Yes," said Maggie. " Is it far off ? I think I should like to walk there, if you please."

" No, no ; it'll be getting dark ; we must make haste. And the donkey'll carry you as nice as can be—you'll see."

He lifted Maggie as he spoke, and set her on the donkey. She felt relieved that it was not the old man who seemed to be going with her, but she had only a trembling hope that she was really going home.

" Here's your pretty bonnet," said the younger woman, putting that recently despised but now welcome article of costume on Maggie's head ; " and you'll say we've been very good to you, won't you ? and what a nice little lady we said you was ? "

" Oh, yes, thank you," said Maggie. " I'm very much obliged to you. But I wish you'd go with me too." She thought anything was better than going with one of the dreadful men alone : it would be more cheerful to be murdered by a larger party.

" Ah, you're fondest of me, aren't you ? " said the woman. " But I can't go—you'll go too fast for me."

It now appeared that the man also was to be seated on the donkey, holding Maggie before him, and she was as incapable of remonstrating against this arrangement as the donkey himself, though no nightmare had ever seemed to her more horrible. When the woman had patted her on the back, and said " Good-bye," the donkey, at a strong hint from the man's stick, set off at a rapid walk along the lane towards the point Maggie had come from an hour ago, while the tall girl and the rough urchin, also

*" What's the meaning o' this ?" he said, while Maggie slipped from the donkey and ran to her father's stirrup*

furnished with sticks, obligingly escorted them for the first hundred yards, with much screaming and thwacking.

At last—oh, sight of joy !—this lane, the longest in the world, was coming to an end, was opening on a broad high road, where there was actually a coach passing ! And there was a finger-post at the corner. She had surely seen that finger-post before—" To St. Ogg's, 2 miles." The gipsy really meant to take her home, then. He was probably a good man after all, and might have been rather hurt at the thought that she didn't like coming with him alone. This idea became stronger as she felt more and more certain that she knew the road quite well, and she was considering how she might open a conversation with the injured gipsy, and not only gratify his feelings but efface the impression of her cowardice, when, as they reached a cross-road, Maggie caught sight of some one coming on a white-faced horse.

" Oh, stop ! stop ! " she cried out. " There's my father ! Oh, father ! father ! "

The sudden joy was almost painful, and before her father reached her she was sobbing. Great was Mr. Tulliver's wonder, for he had made a round from Basset, and had not yet been home.

" Why, what's the meaning o' this ? " he said, checking his horse, while Maggie slipped from the donkey and ran to her father's stirrup.

" The little miss lost herself, I reckon," said the gipsy. " She'd come to our tent at the far end o' Dunlow Lane, and I was bringing her where she said her home was. It's a good way to come arter being on the tramp all day."

" Oh, yes, father, he's been very good to bring me home," said Maggie. " A very kind, good man."

" Here, then, my man," said Mr. Tulliver, taking out five shillings.

" It's the best day's work *you* ever did. I couldn't afford to lose the little wench ; here, lift her up before me."

" Why, Maggie, how's this, how's this ? " he said, as they rode along, while she laid her head against her father, and sobbed. " How came you to be rambling about and lose yourself ? "

" Oh, father," sobbed Maggie, " I ran away because I was so unhappy —Tom was so angry with me. I couldn't bear it."

" Pooh, pooh," said Mr. Tulliver soothingly, " you mustn't think o' running away from father. What 'ud father do without his little wench ? "

" Oh, no, I never will again, father—never."

# A WARNING

## *by* JOHN GAY

THREE children sliding on the ice
Upon a summer's day,
It so fell out they all fell in ;
The rest they ran away.

Now, had these children been at home,
Or sliding on dry ground,
Ten thousand pounds to one penny
They had not all been drowned.

You parents all that children have,
And you that have got none,
If you would have them safe abroad,
Pray keep them safe at home.

# MR. NOBODY

## ANON.

I KNOW a funny little man,
   As quiet as a mouse,
Who does the mischief that is done
   In everybody's house !
There's no one ever sees his face,
   And yet we all agree
That every plate we break was cracked
   By Mr. Nobody.

'Tis he who always tears our books,
   Who leaves the door ajar,
He pulls the buttons from our shirts,
   And scatters pins afar ;
That squeaking door will always squeak
   For, prithee, don't you see,
We leave the oiling to be done
   By Mr. Nobody.

He puts damp wood upon the fire,
   That kettles cannot boil ;
His are the feet that bring in mud,
   And all the carpets soil.
The papers always are mislaid,
   Who had them last but he ?
There's no one tosses them about
   But Mr. Nobody.

The finger marks upon the door
   By none of us are made ;
We never leave the blinds unclosed,
   To let the curtains fade.
The ink we never spill, the boots
   That lying round you see
Are not our boots ; they all belong
   To Mr. Nobody.

# The Dog Crusoe

## by R. M. BALLANTYNE

## CHAPTER I

*The backwoods settlement—Crusoe's parentage and early history—The agonising pains and sorrows of his puppyhood, and other interesting matters.*

THE dog Crusoe was once a pup. Now do not, courteous reader, toss your head contemptuously and exclaim, "Of course he was; I could have told *you* that." You know very well that you have often seen a man above six feet high, broad and powerful as a lion, with a bronzed shaggy visage and the stern glance of an eagle, of whom you have said, or thought, or heard others say, " It is scarcely possible to believe that such a man was once a squalling baby." If you had seen our hero in all the strength and majesty of full-grown doghood, you would have experienced a vague sort of surprise had we told you—as we now repeat—that the dog Crusoe was once a pup,—a soft, round, sprawling, squeaking pup, as fat as a tallow candle, and as blind as a bat.

But we draw particular attention to the fact of Crusoe's having once been a pup, because in connection with the days of his puppyhood there hangs a tale. This peculiar dog may thus be said to have had two tails— one in connection with his body, the other with his career. This tale, though short, is very harrowing, and as it is intimately connected with Crusoe's subsequent history we will relate it here. But before doing so we must beg our reader to accompany us beyond the civilised portions of the United States of America—beyond the frontier settlements of the " far west," into those wild prairies which are watered by the great Missouri River— the Father of Waters—and his numerous tributaries.

Here dwell the Pawnees, the Sioux, the Delawares, the Crows, the Blackfeet, and many other tribes of Red Indians, who are gradually retreating step by step towards the Rocky Mountains, as the advancing white man cuts down their trees and ploughs up their prairies. Here, too, dwell the wild horse and the wild ass, the deer, the buffalo, and the badger ; all, men and brutes alike, wild as the power of untamed and ungovernable passion can make them, and free as the wind that sweeps over their mighty plains.

There is a romantic and exquisitely beautiful spot on the banks of one of the tributaries above referred to—a long stretch of mingled woodland and meadow, with a magnificent lake lying like a gem in its green bosom— which goes by the name of the Mustang Valley. This remote vale, even at the present day, is but thinly peopled by white men, and is still a frontier settlement round which the wolf and the bear prowl curiously, and from which the startled deer bounds terrified away. At the period of which we write, the valley had just been taken possession of by several families of squatters, who, tired of the turmoil and the squabbles of the *then* frontier settlements, had pushed boldly into the far west to seek a new home for themselves, where they could have " elbow room," regardless alike of the dangers they might encounter in unknown lands and of the Redskins who dwelt there.

The squatters were well armed with axes, rifles, and ammunition. Most of the women were used to dangers and alarms, and placed implicit reliance in the power of their fathers, husbands, and brothers to protect them ; and well they might, for a bolder set of stalwart men than these backwoodsmen never trod the wilderness. Each had been trained to the use of the rifle and the axe from infancy, and many of them had spent so much of their lives in the woods that they were more than a match for the Indian in his own peculiar pursuits of hunting and war. When the squatters first issued from the woods bordering the valley, an immense herd of wild horses or mustangs were browsing on the plain. These no sooner beheld the cavalcade of white men than, uttering a wild neigh, they tossed their flowing manes in the breeze and dashed away like a whirlwind. This incident procured the valley its name.

The new-comers gave one satisfied glance at their future home, and then set to work to erect log huts forthwith. Soon the axe was heard ringing through the forests, and tree after tree fell to the ground, while the occasional sharp ring of a rifle told that the hunters were catering successfully for the camp. In course of time the Mustang Valley began to assume the aspect of a thriving settlement, with cottages and waving fields clustered together in the midst of it.

Of course the savages soon found it out and paid it occasional visits. These dark-skinned tenants of the woods brought furs of wild animals with them, which they exchanged with the white men for knives, and beads, and baubles and trinkets of brass and tin. But they hated the " Pale-faces " with bitter hatred, because their encroachments had at this time materially curtailed the extent of their hunting-grounds, and nothing but the numbers and known courage of the squatters prevented these savages from butchering and scalping them all.

The leader of this band of pioneers was a Major Hope, a gentleman whose love for nature in its wildest aspects determined him to exchange barrack life for a life in the woods. The major was a first-rate shot, a bold, fearless man, and an enthusiastic naturalist. He was past the prime of life, and, being a bachelor, was unencumbered with a family. His first act on reaching the site of the new settlement was to commence the erection of a block-house, to which the people might retire in case of a general attack by the Indians.

In this block-house Major Hope took up his abode as the guardian of the settlement. And here the dog Crusoe was born ; here he sprawled in the early morn of life ; here he leaped, and yelped, and wagged his shaggy tail in the excessive glee of puppyhood ; and from the wooden portals of this block-house he bounded forth to the chase in all the fire, and strength, and majesty of full-grown doghood.

Crusoe's father and mother were magnificent Newfoundlanders. There was no doubt as to their being of genuine breed, for Major Hope had received them as a parting gift from a brother officer, who had brought them both from Newfoundland itself. The father's name was Crusoe, the mother's name was Fan. Why the father had been so called no one could tell. The man from whom Major Hope's friend had obtained the pair was a poor, illiterate fisherman, who had never heard of the celebrated " Robinson " in all his life. All he knew was that Fan had been named after his own wife. As for Crusoe, he had got him from a friend, who had got him from another friend, whose cousin had received him as a marriage-gift from a friend of *his* ; and that each had said to the other that the dog's name was " Crusoe," without reasons being asked or given on either side. On arriving at New York, the Major's friend, as we have said, made him a present of the dogs. Not being much of a dog fancier, he soon tired of old Crusoe, and gave him away to a gentleman, who took him down to Florida, and that was the end of him. He was never heard of more.

When Crusoe, junior, was born, he was born, of course, without a name. That was given to him afterwards in honour of his father. He was also born in company with a brother and two sisters, all of whom drowned themselves accidentally in the first month of their existence by falling into the river which flowed past the block-house—a calamity which occurred, doubtless, in consequence of their having gone out without their mother's leave. Little Crusoe was with his brother and sisters at the time, and fell in along with them, but was saved from sharing their fate by his mother, who, seeing what had happened, dashed with an agonised howl into the water, and, seizing him in her mouth, brought him ashore in a half-drowned condition. She afterwards brought the others ashore one by one, but the poor little things were dead.

And now we come to the harrowing part of our tale, for the proper understanding of which the foregoing dissertation was needful.

One beautiful afternoon, in that charming season of the American year called the Indian summer, there came a family of Sioux Indians to the Mustang Valley, and pitched their tent close to the block-house. A young hunter stood leaning against the gate-post of the palisades, watching the movements of the Indians, who, having just finished a long " palaver " or talk with Major Hope, were now in the act of preparing supper. A fire had been kindled on the greensward in front of the tent, and above it stood a tripod, from which depended a large tin camp-kettle. Over this hung an ill-favoured Indian woman, or squaw, who, besides attending to the contents of the pot, bestowed sundry cuffs and kicks upon her little child, which sat near to her playing with several Indian curs that gambolled round the fire. The master of the family and his two sons reclined on buffalo robes, smoking their stone pipes or calumets in silence. There was nothing peculiar in their appearance. Their faces were neither dignified nor coarse in expression, but wore an aspect of stupid apathy, which formed a striking contrast to the countenance of the young hunter, who seemed an amused spectator of their proceedings.

The youth referred to was very unlike, in many respects, to what we are accustomed to suppose a backwoods hunter should be. He did not possess that quiet gravity and staid demeanour which often characterise these men. True, he was tall and strongly made, but no one would have called him stalwart, and his frame indicated grace and agility rather than strength. But the point about him which rendered him different from his companions was his bounding, irrepressible flow of spirits strangely coupled with an intense love of solitary wandering in the woods. None seemed so well fitted for social enjoyment as he ; none laughed so heartily, or expressed such glee in his mischief-loving eye ; yet for days together he went off alone into the forest, and wandered where his fancy led him, as grave and silent as an Indian warrior.

After all, there was nothing mysterious in this. The boy followed implicitly the dictates of nature within him. He was amiable, straightforward, sanguine, and intensely *earnest*. When he laughed he let it out, as sailors have it, " with a will." When there was good cause to be grave, no power on earth could make him smile. We have called him " boy," but in truth he was about that uncertain period of life when a youth is said to be neither a man nor a boy. His face was good-looking (*every* earnest, candid face is) and masculine ; his hair was reddish-brown, and his eye bright blue. He was costumed in the deerskin cap, leggings, moccasins and leathern shirt common to the Western hunter.

" You seem tickled wi' the Injuns, Dick Varley," said a man who at that moment issued from the block-house.

" That's just what I am, Joe Blunt," replied the youth, turning with a broad grin to his companion.

" Have a care, lad ; do not laugh at 'em too much. They soon take offence ; an' them Redskins never forgive."

" But I'm only laughing at the baby," returned the youth, pointing to the child which, with a mixture of boldness and timidity, was playing with a pup, wrinkling up its fat visage into a smile when its playmate rushed away in sport, and opening wide its jet-black eyes in grave anxiety as the pup returned at full gallop.

" It 'ud make an owl laugh," continued young Varley, " to see such a queer pictur' o' itself."

He paused suddenly, and a dark frown covered his face as he saw the Indian woman stoop quickly down, catch the pup by its hind leg with one hand, seize a heavy piece of wood with the other, and strike it several violent blows.

The cruel act drew young Varley's attention more closely to the pup, and it flashed across his mind that this could be no other than young Crusoe, which neither he nor his companion had seen before, although they had often heard others speak of and describe it.

Had the little creature been one of the unfortunate Indian curs, the two hunters would probably have turned away in disgust, feeling that, however much they might dislike such cruelty, it would be of no use attempting to interfere with Indian usages. But the instant the idea that it was Crusoe occurred to Varley he uttered a yell of anger, and sprang towards the woman with a bound, that caused the three Indians to leap to their feet and grasp their tomahawks.

Blunt did not move from the gate, but threw forward his rifle with a careless motion, but an expressive glance, that caused the Indians to resume their seats and pipes with an emphatic " Wah ! " of disgust at having been startled out of their propriety by a trifle ; while Dick Varley snatched poor Crusoe from his painful position, scowled angrily in the woman's face, and, turning on his heel, walked up to the house, holding the pup tenderly in his arms.

Joe Blunt gazed after his friend with a grave, solemn expression of countenance till he disappeared ; then he looked at the ground and shook his head.

Joe was one of the regular out-and-out backwoods hunters, both in appearance and in fact—broad, tall, massive, lion-like ; gifted with the hunting, stalking, running and trail-following powers of the savage, and

*Varley uttered a yell of anger and sprang towards the woman*

with a superabundance of the shooting and fighting powers, the daring and dash of the Anglo-Saxon. He was grave, too—seldom smiled, and rarely laughed. His expression almost at all times was a compound of seriousness and good-humour. With the rifle he was a good, steady shot, but by no means a "crack" one.

After meditating a few seconds, Joe Blunt again shook his head, and muttered to himself: "The boy's bold enough, but he's too reckless for a hunter. There was no need for that yell, now—none at all."

Having uttered this sagacious remark, he threw his rifle into the hollow

*He vented his misery in piteous squeaks as Varley confided him tenderly to the care of his mother*

of his left arm, turned round, and strode off with a long, slow step towards his own cottage.

Blunt was an American by birth, but of Irish extraction, and to an attentive ear there was a faint echo of the *brogue* in his tone, which seemed to have been handed down to him as a threadbare and almost worn-out heirloom.

Poor Crusoe was badly bruised. His wretched tail seemed little better than a piece of wire filed off to a point, and he vented his misery in piteous squeaks as the sympathetic Varley confided him tenderly to the care of his mother. How Fan managed to cure him no one can tell, but cure him she did, for in the course of a few weeks Crusoe was as well and sleek and fat as ever.

## CHAPTER II

*A shooting match and its consequences—New friends introduced to the reader—Crusoe and his mother change masters.*

SHORTLY after the incident narrated in the last chapter, the squatters of the Mustang Valley lost their leader.   Major Hope suddenly announced his intention of quitting the settlement and returning to the civilised world.   Private matters, he said, required his presence there— matters which he did not choose to speak of, but which would prevent his returning again to reside among them.   Go he must, and, being a man of determination, go he did ; but before going he distributed all his goods and chattels among the settlers.  He even gave away his rifle, and Fan and Crusoe. These last, however, he resolved should go together ; and, as they were well worth having, he announced that he would give them to the best shot in the valley. He stipulated that the winner should escort him to the nearest settlement eastward, after which he might return with the rifle on his shoulder.

Accordingly, a long level piece of ground on the river's bank with a perpendicular cliff at the end of it was selected as the shooting-ground, and, on the appointed day, at the appointed hour, the competitors began to assemble.

" Well, lad, first as usual," exclaimed Joe Blunt, as he reached the ground and found Dick Varley there before him.

" I've bin here more than an hour looking for a new kind o' flower that Jack Morgan told me he'd seen.  And I've found it, too.  Look here ;  did you ever see one like it before ? "

Blunt leaned his rifle against a tree, and carefully examined the flower.

" Why, yes, I've seed a-many of them up about the Rocky Mountains, but never one here-away.  It seems to have gone lost itself.  The last I seed, if I remember rightly, wos near the head-waters o' the Yellowstone River, it wos—jest where I shot a grizzly bar."

" Was that the bar that gave you the wipe on the cheek ? " asked Varley, forgetting the flower in his interest about the bear.

" It wos.  An' it nearly ripped the shirt off my back afore I wos done with it."

" I would give my rifle to get a chance at a grizzly ! " exclaimed Varley, with a sudden burst of enthusiasm.

" Whoever got it wouldn't have much to brag of," remarked a burly young backwoodsman, as he joined them.

His remark was true, for poor Dick's weapon was but a sorry affair. It missed fire, and it hung fire ; and even when it did fire, it remained a matter of doubt in its owner's mind whether the slight deviations from the direct line made by his bullets were the result of *his* or *its* bad shooting.

Further comment upon it was checked by the arrival of a dozen or more hunters on the scene of action.  They were a sturdy set of bronzed, bold, fearless men, and one felt, on looking at them, that they would prove more than a match for several hundreds of Indians in open fight.  A few minutes after, the major himself came on the ground with the prize rifle on his shoulder, and Fan and Crusoe at his heels—the latter tumbling, scrambling, and yelping after its mother, fat and clumsy, and happy as possible.

Immediately all eyes were on the rifle, and its merits were discussed with animation.

And well did it deserve discussion, for such a piece had never before been seen on the Western frontier. It was shorter in the barrel and larger in the bore than the weapons chiefly in vogue at that time, and, besides being of beautiful workmanship, was silver-mounted. But the grand peculiarity about it, and that which afterwards rendered it the mystery of mysteries to the savages, was that it had two sets of locks—one percussion, the other flint—so that, when caps failed, by taking off the one set of locks and affixing the others, it was converted into a flint rifle. The major, however, took care never to run short of caps, so that the flint locks were merely held as a reserve in case of need.

" Now, lads," cried Major Hope, stepping up to the point from whence they were to shoot, " remember the terms. He who first drives the nail obtains the rifle, Fan and her pup, and accompanies me to the nearest settlement. Each man shoots with his own gun, and draws lots for the chance."

" Agreed ! " cried the men.

" Well, then, wipe your guns and draw lots. Henri will fix the nail. Here it is."

The individual who stepped, or rather plunged, forward to receive the nail was a rare and remarkable specimen of mankind. Like his comrades, he was half a farmer and half a hunter. Like them, too, he was clad in deer-skin, and was tall and strong—nay, more, he was gigantic. But, unlike them, he was clumsy, awkward, loose-jointed and a bad shot. Nevertheless, Henri was an immense favourite in the settlement, for his good-humour knew no bounds. No one ever saw him frown. Even when fighting with the savages, as he was sometimes compelled to do in self-defence, he went at them with a sort of jovial rage that was almost laughable. Inconsiderate recklessness was one of his chief characteristics, so that his comrades were rather afraid of him on the war-trail or in the hunt, where caution and frequently *soundless* motion were essential to success or safety. But when Henri had a comrade at his side to check him he was safe enough, being humble-minded and obedient. Men used to say he must have been born under a lucky star, for, notwithstanding his natural inaptitude for all sorts of backwoods life, he managed to scramble through everything with safety, often with success, and sometimes with credit.

To see Henri stalk a deer was worth a long day's journey. Joe Blunt used to say he was " all jints together, from the top of his head to the sole of his moccasin." He threw his immense form into the most inconceivable contortions, and slowly wound his way, sometimes on hands and knees, sometimes flat, through bush and brake, as if there was not a bone in his body, and without the slightest noise. This sort of work was so much against his plunging nature that he took long to learn it ; but when, through hard practice and the loss of many a fine deer, he came at length to break himself into it, he gradually progressed to perfection, and ultimately became the best stalker in the valley. This, and this alone, enabled him to procure game, for, being short-sighted, he could hit nothing beyond fifty yards, except a buffalo or a barn-door.

Yet that same lithe body, which seemed as though totally unhinged, could no more be bent, when the muscles were strung, than an iron post.

No one wrestled with Henri unless he wished to have his back broken. Few could equal and none could beat him at running or leaping except Dick Varley. When Henri ran a race even Joe Blunt laughed outright, for arms and legs went like independent flails. When he leaped, he hurled himself into space with a degree of violence that seemed to ensure a somersault ; yet he always came down with a crash on his feet. Plunging was Henri's forte. He generally lounged about the settlement when unoccupied, with his hands behind his back, apparently in a reverie, and when called on to act, he seemed to fancy he must have lost time, and could only make up for it by *plunging*. This habit got him into many awkward scrapes, but his herculean power as often got him out of them. He was a French-Canadian, and a particularly bad speaker of the English language.

We offer no apology for this elaborate introduction of Henri, for he was as good-hearted a fellow as ever lived, and deserves special notice.

But to return. The sort of rifle-practice called " driving the nail," by which this match was to be decided was, and we believe still is, common among the hunters of the Far West. It consisted in this : an ordinary large-headed nail was driven a short way into a plank or a tree, and the hunters, standing at a distance of fifty yards or so, fired at it until they succeeded in driving it home. On the present occasion the major resolved to test their shooting by making the distance seventy yards.

Some of the older men shook their heads.

" It's too far," said one ; " ye might as well try to snuff the nose o' a mosquito."

" Jim Scraggs is the only man as'll hit that," said another.

The man referred to was a long, lank, lantern-jawed fellow, with a cross-grained expression of countenance. He used the long, heavy Kentucky rifle which, from the ball being a little larger than a pea, was called a pea-rifle. Jim was no favourite, and had been named Scraggs by his companions on account of his appearance.

In a few minutes the lots were drawn, and the shooting began. Each hunter wiped out the barrel of his piece with his ramrod as he stepped forward ; then, placing a ball in the palm of his left hand, he drew the stopper of his powder-horn with his teeth, and poured out as much powder as sufficed to cover the bullet. This was the regular *measure* among them. Little time was lost in firing, for these men did not " hang " on their aim. The point of the rifle was slowly raised to the object, and the instant the sight covered it the ball sped to its mark. In a few minutes the nail was encircled by bullet holes, scarcely two of which were more than an inch distant from the mark, and one—fired by Joe Blunt—entered the tree close beside it.

" Ah, Joe ! " said the major. " I thought you would have carried off the prize ! "

" So did not I, sir," returned Blunt, with a shake of his head. " Had it

"*That wins if there's no better,*" *said the major.* "*Who comes next?*"

a-bin a half-dollar at a hundred yards, I'd ha' done better, but I never *could* hit the nail. It's too small to *see*."

"That's 'cos ye've got no eyes," remarked Jim Scraggs, with a sneer, as he stepped forward.

All tongues were now hushed, for the expected champion was about to fire. The sharp crack of the rifle was followed by a shout, for Jim had hit the nail-head on the edge, and part of the bullet stuck to it.

"That wins if there's no better," said the major, scarce able to conceal his disappointment. "Who comes next?"

To this question Henri answered by stepping up to the line, straddling his legs, and executing preliminary movements with his rifle, that seemed to indicate an intention on his part to throw the weapon bodily at the mark. He was received with a shout of mingled laughter and applause. After gazing steadily at the mark for a few seconds, a broad grin overspread his countenance, and looking round at his companions, he said:

"Ha! mes boys, I can-not behold de nail at all!"

"Can ye 'behold' the *tree*?" shouted a voice, when the laugh that followed this announcement had somewhat abated.

"Oh! oui," replied Henri, quite coolly; "I can see *him*, an' a goot small bit of de forest beyond."

"Fire at it, then. If ye hit the tree ye desarve the rifle—leastways ye ought to get the pup."

Henri grinned again, and fired instantly, without taking aim.

The shot was followed by an exclamation of surprise, for the bullet was found close beside the nail.

"It's more be good luck than good shootin'," remarked Jim Scraggs.

"Possiblement," answered Henri modestly, as he retreated to the rear and wiped out his rifle ; "mais I have killed most of my deer by dat same goot luck."

"Bravo, Henri ! " said Major Hope as he passed ; "you *deserve* to win, anyhow. Who's next ? "

"Dick Varley ! " cried several voices ; "where's Varley ? Come on, youngster, an' take yer shot."

The youth came forward with evident reluctance.

"It's of no manner o' use," he whispered to Joe Blunt as he passed ; "I can't depend on my old gun."

"Never give in," whispered Blunt encouragingly.

Poor Varley's want of confidence in his rifle was merited, for, on pulling the trigger, the faithless lock missed fire.

"Lend him another gun," cried several voices.

"'Gainst the rules laid down by Major Hope," said Scraggs.

"Well, so it is ; try again."

Varley did try again, and so successfully, too, that the ball hit the nail on the head, leaving a portion of the lead sticking to its edge.

Of course, this was greeted with a cheer, and a loud dispute began as to which was the better shot of the two.

"There are others to shoot yet," cried the major. "Make way. Look out."

The men fell back, and the few hunters who had not yet fired took their shots, but without coming nearer the mark.

It was now agreed that Jim Scraggs and Dick Varley, being the two best shots, should try over again, and it was also agreed that Dick should have the use of Blunt's rifle. Lots were again drawn for the first shot, and it fell to Dick, who immediately stepped out, aimed somewhat hastily, and fired.

"Hit again ! " shouted those who had run forward to examine the mark. "*Half* the bullet cut off by the nail head ! "

Some of the more enthusiastic of Dick's friends cheered lustily, but the most of the hunters were grave and silent, for they knew Jim's powers, and felt that he would certainly do his best. Jim now stepped up to the line, and, looking earnestly at the mark, threw forward his rifle.

At that moment our friend Crusoe, tired of tormenting his mother, waddled stupidly and innocently into the midst of the crowd of men, and in doing so received Henri's heel and the full weight of his elephantine body on its fore paw. The horrible and electric yell that instantly issued from his agonised throat could only be compared, as Joe Blunt expressed it, "to the last dyin' screech o' a bustin' steam biler ! " We cannot say that the effect was startling, for these backwoodsmen had been born and bred in the midst of alarms, and were so used to them that a "bustin' steam biler" itself, unless it had blown them fairly off their legs, would not have startled them. But the effect, such as it was, was sufficient to disconcert the aim of Jim Scraggs, who fired at the same instant, and missed the nail by a hairbreadth.

Turning round in towering wrath, Scraggs aimed a kick at the poor pup, which, had it taken effect, would certainly have terminated the innocent existence of that remarkable dog on the spot ; but quick as lightning Henri interposed the butt of his rifle, and Jim's shin met it with a violence that caused him to howl with rage and pain.

" Oh, pardon me. broder ! " cried Henri, shrinking back, with the drollest expression of mingled pity and glee.

Jim's discretion, on this occasion, was superior to his valour ; he turned away with a coarse expression of anger and left the ground.

Meanwhile, the major handed the silver rifle to young Varley. " It couldn't have fallen into better hands," he said. " You'll do it credit, lad ; I know that full well ; and let me assure you it will never play you false.

*Turning round in towering wrath, Scraggs aimed a kick at the poor pup*

Only keep it clean, don't overcharge it, aim true, and it will never miss the mark."

While the hunters crowded round Dick to congratulate him and examine the piece, he stood with a mingled feeling of bashfulness and delight at his unexpected good fortune. Recovering himself suddenly, he seized his old rifle, and dropping quietly to the outskirts of the crowd, while the men were still busy handling and discussing the merits of the prize, went up, unobserved, to a boy of about thirteen years of age, and touched him on the shoulder.

" Here, Marston ; you know I often said ye should have the old rifle when I was rich enough to get a new one. Take it *now*, lad, it's come to ye sooner than either o' us expected."

" Dick," said the boy, grasping his friend's hand warmly, " ye're true as heart of oak. It's good of 'ee, that's a fact."

" Not a bit, boy ; it cost me nothing to give away an old gun that I've no use for, an's worth little, but it makes me right glad to have the chance to do it."

Marston had longed for a rifle ever since he could walk ; but his prospects of obtaining one were very poor indeed at that time, and it is a question whether he did not at that moment experience as much joy in handling the old piece as his friend felt in shouldering the prize.

A difficulty now occurred which had not before been thought of : this was no less than the absolute refusal of Dick Varley's canine property to follow him. Fan had no idea of changing masters without her consent being asked or her inclination being consulted.

" You'll have to tie her up for a while, I fear," said the major.

" No fear," answered the youth. " Dog natur's like human natur' ! "

Saying this he seized Crusoe by the neck, stuffed him comfortably into the bosom of his hunting shirt, and walked rapidly away with the prize rifle on his shoulder.

Fan had not bargained for this. She stood irresolute, gazing now to the right and now to the left, as the major retired in one direction and Dick with Crusoe in another. Suddenly Crusoe, who, although comfortable in body, was ill at ease in spirit, gave utterance to a melancholy howl. The mother's love instantly prevailed. For one moment she pricked up her ears at the sound, and then, lowering them, trotted quietly after her new master, and followed him to his cottage on the margin of the lake.

---

# LIGHTING-UP TIME

### by KATHARINE TYNAN

THIS is the time when children go,
And hang their pretty lamps arow,
To toss upon the Summer wind,
When the blue heaven is soft and kind.

The roses in the garden-beds,
And hollyhocks, those sleepy-heads,
Lilies, carnations, wake and cry,
" A score of suns all in the sky."

The funny rabbits run and leap,
The squirrels rub their eyes from sleep ;
What golden fruit is on the trees
Like to huge, splendid oranges ?

When all the nests are well a-drowse,
The children from the Orchard-House
Fling in the air great globes of light.
The garden cannot sleep to-night.

# The Goulden Vanitee

**TRADITIONAL**

THERE was a gallant ship, and a gallant ship was she,
  Ik iddle du, and the Lowlands low ;
And she was called the Goulden Vanitee,
  As she sailed to the Lowlands low.

She had not sailed a league, a league but only three,
  Ik iddle du, and the Lowlands low ;
When she came up with a French gallee,
  As she sailed to the Lowlands low.

Out spoke the little cabin boy, out spoke he,
  Ik iddle du, and the Lowlands low ;
" What will you give if I sink that French gallee,
  As we sail to the Lowlands low ? "

Out spoke the Captain, out spoke he,
  Ik iddle du, and the Lowlands low ;
" We'll give you an estate in the North Countree,
  As ye sail to the Lowlands low."

" Then sew me up in a black bull's skin,
  Ik iddle du, and the Lowlands low ;
And throw me o'er deck-board sink or swim,
  As ye sail to the Lowlands low."

So they sewed him up tight in the black bull's skin,
  Ik iddle du, and the Lowlands low ;
And threw him over deck-board, sink or swim,
  As they sail to the Lowlands low.

About and about and about went he,
  Ik iddle du, and the Lowlands low ;
Until he had swam to the French gallee,
  As she sailed to the Lowlands low.

O some were playing cards, and some were playing dice,
  Ik iddle du, and the Lowlands low ;
When he took out an auger, bored thirty holes at twice,
  And she sailed to the Lowlands low.

And some they ran with cloaks, and some they ran with caps,
  Ik iddle du, and the Lowlands low ;
To try if they could stop the salt water drops,
  As she sailed to the Lowlands low.

About and about and about went he,
  Ik iddle du, and the Lowlands low ;
Until he came back to the Goulden Vanitee,
  As we sailed to the Lowlands low.

" Now heave me o'er a rope, and sway me up aboard,
  Ik iddle du, and the Lowlands low ;
And give me the farm land as good as your word,
  As ye sail to the Lowlands low."

" We'll heave you no rope, nor sway you up aboard,
  Ik iddle du, and the Lowlands low ;
Nor give you an estate, as good as our word,
  As we sail to the Lowlands low."

Outspoke the little cabin-boy, out spoke he,
  Ik iddle du, and the Lowlands low ;
" I'll sink ye as I sunk the French gallee,
  As ye sail to the Lowlands low."

They hove him o'er a rope, and they swayed him up aboard,
  Ik iddle du, and the Lowlands low ;
And they have proved to him much better than their word,
  As they sailed to the Lowlands low.

# Did the Tiger Know?

### by H. M. COSTELLO

"IT'S worth sweltering in Sourabaya all day to be able to appreciate the freshness of this breeze," said the Colonel, and we all grunted assent.

Java is an interesting and intensely hospitable land, but hot—hot with a steaminess peculiarly its own, and when, after a whole day ashore, we were again settled into our deck-chairs, the usually irresistible invitation of the ship's orchestra to " come and join the dance " fell upon indifferent ears.

"Let's tell stories," drawled " The Dynamo," and the suggestion met with general approval.

"What about it, Samson ? " queried the boy. " None of us have a look-in with you, when it comes to experiences worth talking about ! "

Samson reddened and shook his head discouragingly. He was a queer chap—seemed, like so many men who spend their lives in silent places, to have a dream-world of his own, quite apart from the froth and bubble of ours, into which he slipped, at times, with evident relief. Still we all liked him—he was delightful with the youngsters and always willing to join in whatever we wanted to do.

As he did not speak, the girl put a hand on his arm and said, coaxingly, " Please, Mr. Vincent ! I have never heard an adventure told by a person to whom it really happened."

Samson, who had petted and humoured her little ladyship all the voyage, could refuse her nothing, so now said hesitatingly, " I don't know what to tell you. Shall it be of birds, beasts, or fishes ? "

" All three," urged the boy, but the girl—girl-like—said she would sooner hear about some one he loved in that jungle life—some one who shared his dangers, and enjoyed things because he enjoyed them too.

" But there isn't any one just like that in Malaya for me, Princess," he demurred, " and if I tell you of the things which have seemed most wonderful to me, they may, perhaps, not interest you at all. Jungle life is a medley— a medley of beauty and terror. The beautiful things are indescribable without their scented, mysterious, palm-strewn setting, and the terrible ones seem too terrible when told in civilised surroundings. A face, alight with eagerness to forestall one's wishes, stilled by some merciless foe—a perfect tree shattered by a flash of lightning—or a pretty girl dead of the plague—seem natural there, but monstrous—monstrous here," and, pulling hard at his pipe, he stared into the darkness ahead.

An uncomfortable silence fell upon us which Samson quickly realised was the outcome of his words, so shaking his broad shoulders, he laid his hand gently upon that of the girl, and said quietly :

" Well, what is the story to be, Princess ? " Her only answer was to fix her wide eyes expectantly upon his, but the boy—heedless young devil— begged eagerly for " the worst experience you have ever had," and Samson began in a low reminiscent voice :

" The worst experience I ever had was hardly an adventure at all, but will, perhaps, interest you. It is about Grey, my chum out there—a surveyor who spent most of his time off trapping wild animals, which he sold to zoological societies and menagerie proprietors. He was the best shot I have ever seen, and twice saved my life by the quickness of his eye and aim.

" His mother having been a Eurasian, he had a rather thin time socially, but, except for some differences of opinion as to what was—well—' playing the game,' arising probably from his mixed parentage, we got on famously.

" Once, his work being held up by a shipping strike, he proposed we should share a camp in the hills behind Kuala Lumpur, where he might trap some saleable animals, and I find some of the rare butterflies, which were my main objective.

" It was lovely up there, though the growth was much less luxuriant than on the lower levels, and we were both sorry when it was time to return. The day before breaking camp we separated—Grey on the track of a tiger which had been reported prowling in the vicinity—and I on that of what might be a Crœsus butterfly. A Crœsus was what I wanted more than anything just then, and a boy, who had joined us the day before, described some unusual butterflies in a nearby valley, butterflies which sounded so promising that I was longing to investigate. ' The wings,' he said, ' are as the spread of my two palms, the colour of ripe oranges, and of the eyes of night ! '

" We had a long scramble—long because the way absolutely teemed with interest. Streams of sweet-smelling orchids hung like scarves from the trees, and birds and butterflies, brighter than the flowers themselves, flew about them. The boulders, upon which we trod, were decked in moss and coloured lichens, but the most vivid, beautiful thing I'd ever seen was the butterfly hovering over a flowering shrub quite near us. It was about seven inches from tip to tip—seven inches of black and gold velvet! Its own perfection almost made me let it go again, but it is in my cabinet now, and lots of people have enjoyed it with me.

" I'm sorry, Princess," he broke off. " I have digressed badly." But the girl, smiling comprehendingly, said gently, " I like that part, don't stop."

" Well!" went on Samson obediently. " When, late in the morning, we got back to camp, we found a boy impatiently waiting to take me to where Grey was caging a tiger. The boy was very excited and told me, breathlessly, as we hurried along, that ' Master had gone caught the largest " Lord Tiger " in the whole world, this time.' "

" But how, though—however had he caught a tiger ? " interrupted one of the youngsters interestedly.

" They dug a pit, covered it with branches, and baited it with a calf," replied Samson patiently. " One side, at the bottom of the pit, they excavated like a tunnel, tying another calf at the far end. Then they put a bamboo cage, with a trap-door, inside the tunnel, and when the tiger sprang at the second calf, the door fell and imprisoned him."

" Oh! what a thrill—suppose the cage broke ! But do go on quickly, please," said the boy.

Samson continued. " Every one was very excited when we got to the pit, and soon I was as keen as the rest, but we were all thankful when the brute was safely swinging away down the track, his cage, slung from long bamboos, carried on the shoulders of the natives.

" The bearers, their heavy burden swaying, picked their way cautiously from boulder to boulder, with frequent upward glances, and began a weird, droning song. Grey, smiling at me, said quietly, ' The dusk is coming and with it all sorts of hobgoblins, you see ! ' I laughed at the thought of evil spirits who would be frightened by the soothing chant that floated towards us, but as the swift tropical darkness crept like a sentient thing about the track, and fallen trees, clad in their wealth of verdant parasites, became strange monsters as they melted in the gloom, I understood something of the Malayan fear of night in the jungle.

" I don't know why that sunset made such an impression on me, but I shall never forget how the palm fronds grew black against the radiant after-glow which flamed on for ages after the sun had really gone. The sky was extraordinarily transparent, almost as though the colour was shining through a veil of crystal. It was like a bowl of—well ! I was going to say opal—but only in childish dreams of what heaven would look like have I seen anything to compare with that pageant of loveliness.

" The tiger seemed to have vented all his rage whilst being dragged from the pit and, except for a constant nervous twitching of his tail, was perfectly quiet. He was a magnificent animal and his glossy coat was barred as cleanly as if the black had been put on with a ruler.

" After we were settled in camp again, Grey stood gloating over his prize, until I, imagining I saw hatred gleaming in the tiger's eyes, made an excuse to draw him away.

" The fame of our capture soon spread and lots of people came to see it, among them two young Siamese. Grey had a long talk with them, seeming, at first, rather uninterested, but after a while he called me from where I was packing my gorgeous butterflies, and told me that he had agreed to take the tiger to Siam to fight with a young bull which the Siamese wanted to exhibit.

" ' Good Lord, Grey, but you can't entertain such a rotten suggestion, surely,' I said disgustedly, but he, eagerly pointing out the probability of winning a huge sum of money and, at the same time, having a jolly good spree, only laughed and turned to the waiting lads. ' Look here ! ' he said firmly, ' I won't come unless you will have a staging built at one side of the ring for me to photograph the fight from.'

" ' Of course ! ' readily agreed the Siamese, ' that is easily done,' and ignoring my disapproval, they went on arranging the details of the barbarous affair. Seeing it was useless to attempt to influence Grey at the moment, I returned to my job, and presently he came whistling into the tent.

" ' Grey,' I then said firmly, ' please understand that I shall have nothing whatever to do with this show. If you are going on with it, I will make plans to join the Norton crowd, and cut over to Penang with them.'

" Grey looked at me for a minute, in that funny mystified way he so often assumed when our respective points of view wouldn't meet, then said quietly : ' Well ! for the life of me I can't see what there is to object to—you are funny sometimes, Vincent. These fights between wild animals go on in the jungle—it is only a simple, natural thing. What is the difference in letting them have a go where we can watch them at it ? '

" There was logic in what he said, without some inborn understanding of the repugnance all Englishmen feel to the fighting of captive creatures, it probably was impossible for him to appreciate my objections.

" ' See here, Grey,' I finished lamely, after vainly trying to make him see how it struck me, ' it isn't British sport ! '

" ' British sport ! ' he muttered bitterly. ' British sport will put a human being through the tortures of the damned because he has a touch of what they are pleased to call " the tar-brush," but can't stand for two wild animals having a fair fight ! Well ! I don't know much about British sport, but it seems a pretty lop-sided sort of business to me, anyhow.' Then, squaring his shoulders, he added impatiently : ' Anyway, Vincent, it's all arranged, and your clearing off will do nothing to stop the fight and will make it jolly unpleasant for me, because I said you would do all the financial part, so don't be a rotter—see me through. You will ! Won't you ? '

" I suppose I should have stuck to my guns, but he was so genuinely unable to understand, and so evidently hurt by my attitude, that at length —very reluctantly—I agreed to go with him the next week to Siam.

" We were early astir on the morning of the contest and, as a crimson sun rose from behind a mass of black clouds, he said, with an odd seriousness : ' Rather an ominous sunrise, old chap.' ' I don't know about ominous, but it's jolly beautiful,' I replied lightly, and gathering up the camera, we set off.

" When we reached the arena Grey was hailed with welcoming cries, and the applause was tumultuous as he climbed into the staging, and the bull was led in. Evidently scenting battle the animal pawed the earth impatiently, carpeting it with a shower of blossoms from the wreaths about his shoulders. Every one gasped when the tiger stalked in, but he, entirely ignoring them, began to walk quickly round and round. He looked magnificent against the hard-beaten, deep-red earth, as he circled faster—faster—round the ring. His lips were curled back, showing his cruel teeth, and his, eyes narrowed.

" We all grew breathless, waiting, watching, longing for the uncanny circling to cease. Faster, faster he went, and faster—faster—went our pulses too. The bull turned his head perplexedly, then, evidently growing impatient, began to bellow, not loudly, but with blood-curdling intensity, and moved slowly towards the tiger. The tiger stopped just as the bull paused uncertainly below the staging where Grey was feverishly winding off his reel. Down went the bull's head, threateningly, and we were all tense in anticipation of a mighty rush, when, suddenly, there was a tawny flash, and the tiger, hurling himself right across the bull, fastened himself savagely upon Grey's shoulders.

" Paralysed we watched as they rolled heavily to the ground, Grey fighting desperately his apparently hopeless battle. Their movements were so rapid that we scarcely dared to use the pistols we held in readiness, but, as the brute gathered itself for a renewed attack, two bullets reached their mark, and springing forward, as though suddenly aware of new adversaries, he quiveringly stretched his length across Grey's body, reluctant, even in dying, to relinquish his revenge.

" Grey was, by this time, quite unconscious.

" Weeks elapsed before his wounds healed sufficiently for us to return to Kuala Lumpur, and many a time as I sat by his bed he raised himself uncomfortably and looked towards the jungle-clad hills in the blue distance, with a horror that was beastly in a brave man's eyes and said uneasily : ' Nubia is right, Vincent, that brute knew ! '

" I couldn't help remembering the Malayan belief in the malignant power possessed by the soul of a tiger enemy, and that that touch of the tar-brush, of which Grey had spoken so angrily, was definite enough to make the belief very real to him.

" It was a hateful business, and even while I tried to tell him his ideas were all rot, and that the tiger had never intended to spring beyond the bull, the echo of his Malayan boy's trembling, sing-song voice muttering : ' Lord Tiger know who bring him here all right,' passed through my mind, and often, even now, I find myself wondering—wondering——"

.        .        .        .        .        .        .        .        .        .        .        .

Then, raising himself suddenly, Samson passed his hand gently across the bright head beside him and, without another word, walked quickly away to the bow, and we saw no more of him that night.

Again an uncomfortable silence fell upon us. The girl, with her little face cupped in her hands, leant motionless upon the arm of her chair, and I, staring away towards the dim distance in which lay those lovely hills behind Kuala Lumpur, visioned a ghostly tiger stalking—stalking—while a man, whose work forced him to travel those verdant fastnesses, went fearfully upon his way.

## DID THE TIGER KNOW?

There was a tawny flash, and the tiger, hurling himself right across the bull, fastened himself savagely upon Guy's shoulders   (*Page* 128)

THE WHITE KNIGHT'S SONG

" I'll tell thee everything I can ;
There's little to relate " (*Page* 129)

# THE WHITE KNIGHT'S SONG

*by* LEWIS CARROLL

" I 'LL tell thee everything I can ;
　There's little to relate.
I saw an aged, aged man,
　A-sitting on a gate.
' Who are you, aged man ? ' I said.
　' And how is it you live ? '
And his answer trickled through my head
　Like water through a sieve.

" He said ' I look for butterflies
　That sleep among the wheat :
I make them into mutton-pies,
　And sell them in the street.
I sell them unto men,' he said,
　' Who sail on stormy seas ;
And that's the way I get my bread—
　A trifle, if you please.'

" But I was thinking of a plan
　To dye one's whiskers green,
And always use so large a fan
　That they could not be seen.
So, having no reply to give
　To what the old man said,
I cried, ' Come, tell me how you live ! '
　And thumped him on the head.

" His accents mild took up the tale :
　He said ' I go my ways,
And when I find a mountain-rill,
　I set it in a blaze ;
And thence they make a stuff they call
　Rowland's Macassar-Oil—
Yet twopence-halfpenny is all
　They give me for my toil.'

" But I was thinking of a way
　To feed oneself on batter,
And so go on from day to day
　Getting a little fatter.
I shook him well from side to side,
　Until his face was blue :
' Come, tell me how you live,' I cried,
　' And what it is you do ! '

" He said ' I hunt for haddocks' eyes
 Among the heather bright,
And work them into waistcoat-buttons
 In the silent night.
And these I do not sell for gold
 Or coin of silvery shine,
But for a copper halfpenny,
 And that will purchase nine.

" ' I sometimes dig for buttered rolls,
 Or set limed twigs for crabs ;
I sometimes search the grassy knolls
 For wheels of hansom-cabs.
And that's the way ' (he gave a wink)
 ' By which I get my wealth—
And very gladly will I drink
 Your Honour's noble health.'

" I heard him then, for I had just
 Completed my design
To keep the Menai bridge from rust
 By boiling it in wine.
I thanked him much for telling me
 The way he got his wealth,
But chiefly for his wish that he
 Might drink my noble health.

" And now, if e'er by chance I put
 My fingers into glue,
Or madly squeeze a right-hand foot
 Into a left-hand shoe,
Or if I drop upon my toe
 A very heavy weight,
I weep, for it reminds me so
Of that old man I used to know—

" Whose look was mild, whose speech was slow,
Whose hair was whiter than the snow,
Whose face was very like a crow,
With eyes, like cinders, all aglow,
Who seemed distracted with his woe,
Who rocked his body to and fro,
And muttered mumblingly and low,
As if his mouth were full of dough,
Who snorted like a buffalo—
That summer evening long ago
 A-sitting on a gate."

# The Feast of the Moon-Goddess

### by JOHN R. CROSSLAND

THREE men sat round an open fire in front of a tent. It was a hot
night, for the time was early August, and the place Central America.
To the north the twinkling lights in the distance told of civilisation
and life, for Mexico City lay across the plain. To the south the skyline was
blotted out by a huge black shadow, rising like a pyramid from the rocks
that strewed the district.

A hundred feet in the air this monstrous shadow reared its ghostly form,
and darkened the tent and the men who sat by the fire before it. Suddenly from the right of the shadow came a ghostly radiance, that grew ever
stronger and stronger, and as the men unconsciously raised their eyes to
meet the light, the edge of the moon appeared, flooding the camp with its
silver sheen.

It lighted up the faces of the three campers, and showed them to
be men of varying age and build. In the centre, with his back to the
flap of the tent, sat a tall, spare man of middle age, with narrow face
and dark, pointed beard. He was bareheaded, and the moon showed
up the greyness of his hair. He puffed at his pipe and turned to the man
on his right.

" Things look much more cheerful now the moon has come out," he
began, and his companion turned from gazing into the fire and faced the
speaker. He was a well-built, tall and soldierly figure of a man, with close-
cropped hair and a bronzed, clean-shaven face. He took his pipe from
between his strong teeth, knocked out the ashes and yawned.

" Yes, Professor, it was a little too ghostly in the dark. This place seems
to get on one, somehow, at night. When one thinks of the things that used
to happen in the long ago, just here, one almost imagines that savage figures are

moving about as of yore. I almost see the festival processions of the ancient priests and their victims, and hear the weird chanting of the assembled tribe."

The third man sprang from his seat on the Professor's left, and stood there looking up at the moon. He was only a slip of a boy, nineteen or twenty possibly, thin and lanky. His hair shone golden in the moonlight, and the pallor of his face was turned to a silvery whiteness.

"You're right, Captain Standish," he put in, turning to the last speaker. Then he turned to the professor.

"I say, Professor Baker, do you really believe the tales these Indians and half-caste labourers tell of the ghosts round here ? "

The Professor laughed. Then his face became grave as he looked up at the young man before him.

"There are lots of things in this world that sound queer, Geoffrey," he replied, "and there are queer things happening that few men know of. But I shouldn't treat the labourers' tales with too much trust, for they would lie sooner than tell truth, and would, in fairly safe circumstances, murder as soon as befriend."

"Then why do they repeat such stories ? " broke in Captain Standish. "They seem to delight in making each other's flesh creep with their ghastly tales of human sacrifices and bloodthirsty carnivals round the mound. I've heard them at it night after night when I've done the last inspection of their quarters."

"They are only half-castes and natives," replied Professor Baker. "You must remember they cannot read, nor can they write. They have little amusement here, and so, like our own forefathers in Britain, they spend their evening's leisure telling stories of the past."

Geoffrey Bellew was listening to the conversation with wide-open eyes. He was not well, this young man, for the heat had taken its toll on his slight physique.

"Say, Professor," he chimed in, in an awesome voice, "Quixito, the interpreter johnny, was telling me to-day that there will be a special ghost-walk to-morrow night."

Captain Standish laughed loudly in the young lad's face.

"Quixito is a seer, then, as well as a liar ! What a marvellous mixture that man is ! I wouldn't trust him a yard—no, nor an inch ! "

"Yet," broke in Baker, "he's the best interpreter we've had in three expeditions. He can manage the Indian labourers when no other man could. At least grant that in his favour."

Geoffrey Bellew again interrupted. His face was drawn and his eyes staring wildly.

"Do you know how he manages the men, Professor ? " he whispered. "By magic, that's what it is ! Magic ! I've seen him do it."

The Professor rose and crossed to the lad.

"Come now," he said gently, "it's high time we were all under the blankets and mosquito nets. There's much to do to-morrow. We hope to ascend the stairway, now that it's been cleared of lava deposits, and examine the sacrificial temple at the top. Don't you worry about Quixito and his idle tales. . . . And," he added firmly, "a double dose of quinine for you before you turn in, lad. You're shaky, and I can't be nursemaid as well as archæologist. Time is too precious. So get your quinine and have a good night's rest. Come, now, there's a good fellow."

With this he shepherded Bellew to the tent, and it was some moments before he returned to where Standish sat idly kicking the dying embers with his outstretched boot.

" We're going to have some trouble with Bellew if we don't watch him, Standish," he began, as he seated himself again.

" I've seen it coming on for days," returned Standish. " He never ought to have come with us. He can't stand this detestable heat and insect-irritation. He'll have fever as sure as his name's Bellew. Why did you bring him ? "

" Because he *is* Bellew. Family business, you know. Didn't Napoleon once say, ' God save us from our relations,' or something like that ? He's my sister's boy. Did not too badly at Cambridge, but needed a sea voyage and some travel, doctor said. So Elsa, my sister, palmed him on to me, and nothing I could say would satisfy her until I said ' Yes.' She was afraid of his going away alone or in strange company. He's her only son, you see. I really oughtn't to have brought him, but when I took him to the doctor for examination he was pronounced fit for the rough-and-tumble."

" Watch him for a day or two, then, Professor, and don't let him monkey round when it's too hot. And keep Quixito away from him." As he said this, Standish gave a queer look, and the Professor nodded.

" I understand your meaning, Standish. The lad's young and impressionable. He's not well, either, and the rascally interpreter will do him no good at all. I'll warn Quixito to tell no more of his fantastic yarns to our young friend. And now, let's have a word about to-morrow."

The two men talked on for another hour, and by this time the moon, almost at full, shone brightly in a clear sky.

Baker was in charge of exploration work on the " mound." This huge pyramid-like structure was over a hundred feet in height, and was four-sided. Over three hundred feet square, it had been built fully eight thousand years ago, by slave labour, to be a temple of the moon-goddess, in the days before the men of Mexico learned even how to make tools of flint. The temple rose in three sections, each sloping like a pyramid, but with a gallery or platform running round between each two sections. The sides faced north, south, east and west, and on the southern side a broad stairway, with high steps, led to the ruined temple on the summit. The expedition had, during three seasons, cleared away the thick coating of lava cast on the temple through the centuries by volcanic eruptions, and now had come the most interesting task of all—the exploration of the temple itself, the hunt for carvings, picture-writing on the walls, and for rooms or passages inside the huge building.

Native labour had been busy, and even as the two men said good-night and retired to the tent, the noise of chanting and laughter could be heard in the distance, where the native camp lay, on the other side of the mound.

The next day Bellew seemed more normal, but Professor Baker decided that he should not take part in the work on the mound. So the morning was passed for the young man by reading and lying in the shade of the tent.

The afternoon saw him walking around the camp disconsolately, for he had nothing to do. Then he heard footsteps, and looking up, saw a thin dusky figure approaching, clad in cotton short robe, and with broad straw hat throwing his dark face into deeper shadow still. It was Quixito, the interpreter and foreman of the labourers.

Quixito came up with long, athletic strides, and as he approached Bellew he bowed before him.

" Well ? " snapped out Bellew, looking somewhat distastefully at the newcomer.

" Capt'n says you ill, Meester Bellew," began Quixito, " so I come see if you better."

" Much better, Quixito," returned Geoffrey. " But is that all you want ? "

Quixito came nearer and leered into the face of the young man.

" No, Meester Bellew, there is some other thing I will tell. To-night much magic will be at the mound. Would Meester Bellew care to see magic ? "

The temptation was great. Bellew was young, and if not bodily strong, he was adventurous. Should he encourage this strange fellow ? He quickly made up his mind. He would hear more of what was brewing.

" I'd better hear what you're to be up to first, Quixito," he said laughingly. " Some prank or other, I expect."

" No pranks, as you say in your language, Meester Bellew. It is magic that comes to-night. Listen ! " and he came close to his listener's ear.

" To-night is full moon. It is the day when, so much long ago, the savage natives came to the mound. It is the feast of the moon-goddess."

Bellew laughed, though already the spell was on him.

" But that was ages and ages ago, you old fool. What can happen to-night ? The old priests and their wicked ways are dead and done with these eighty centuries or more."

Quixito looked steadily into the eyes of his companion. For a while he did not speak, but those eyes seemed to sear themselves into Bellew's very soul. He felt a strange enthusiasm stirring him, and little by little his thought became confused. Still Quixito did not move or speak.

At last the native raised his right hand and put it high above Bellew's face. Slowly he lowered it, palm stretching upwards, in front of Bellew, until at last it dropped at his side. Then he spoke.

" You will come, Meester Bellew," he whined in a monotonous voice. " You will meet me by the staircase of the mound at moonrise, yes ? "

" I will meet you at the mound at moonrise," almost chanted Bellew, and as he did so the wiry arm was raised again, this time travelling upward before the Englishman's face.

Geoffrey rubbed his eyes, looked around, and tried to remember the events of the past few minutes, but all seemed so hazy. No one was in sight, and still puzzling over what he thought had been a fit of faintness, he slowly returned to his tent and threw himself on his bed, to fall asleep almost instantly.

After the day's work was ended, the Professor and Captain Standish returned to find him still asleep.

" He'll sleep himself better," ventured Standish, as they both bent over the inert form.

Baker gently laid hold of the young man's wrist and took out his watch. " Pulse nearly normal. Yes, I think you're right. Leave him to sleep it out."

They busied themselves with discussions of the day's finds and plans for the morrow's investigations, and were busy at it when they were aware of the presence of their young companion. There he stood, looking into the sky, motionless as a statue.

Baker rose and went across to him.

" Feeling better now, old man ? " he asked kindly, putting an arm round Geoffrey's shoulder.

" *You will meet me by the staircase of the mound at moonrise, yes?* "

The boy started, and then, laughing naturally, replied in the affirmative. " Then have some tea. You must be famished."

Geoffrey assented with alacrity and soon he had demolished quite a respectable supply of food. Then he rose and stretched himself.

" I think I'll have a stroll, now that it's a little cooler. I feel wide awake now, and much better than I've done for days."

" That's good," retorted Baker. " But don't overdo it, and take care. Come back before the damp rises. Cheerio, boy."

So Bellew passed out from the camp and away under the trees toward the mound.

As he neared the structure he began to wonder what to do next. Why he had taken this route was beyond his comprehension. Still he went on, vaguely attempting to gather his wits, which were becoming more and more muddled and hazy.

Soon he reached the foot of the mighty staircase, and there, seated on the lowest stair, was the figure of a man wrapped head and shoulders in a coloured blanket. The figure arose, casting off the blanket, folding it and tossing it across his shoulder. It was Quixito, and as he approached he fixed Bellew with his eye.

"So! You are come, Meester Bellew. It is good! We will see big magic to-night. Come!"

As he spoke he raised his hand and passed it slowly once down the front of Geoffrey's face, and the lad stiffened and lost all expression and interest.

Quixito strode forward to the mound, and Bellew followed like a man asleep. Up the stairs they went, until at last they reached the first platform. Then Quixito turned to the right and rounded one side of the mighty building. At last he stopped, reached forward to the face of the ruin and pulled aside, with difficulty, a huge stone that seemed to swing on a pivot.

Wriggling through the aperture he beckoned for Geoffrey to follow, the lad obeying in silence, and with eyes fixed before him. Once inside, Quixito produced matches and lit a torch that reposed in a recess. Holding this aloft, when at last it flared up properly, he took Bellew's hand and led him on. Turning and twisting they threaded a crooked passage of carved stone, and at last reached a chamber some twenty feet by twelve. Here he fixed his torch in a crack between two of the stones of the wall, and lit another that was already in position.

The chamber was bare, but the walls were a miracle of ancient carving in stone. Around the room, up to the height of a yard, were patterns of key-work, repeating themselves in curious manner. Above were pictures in stone, showing priests and gods of the ancient world.

Bellew stood motionless, like a machine, awaiting the touch of the master to bring it to life and movement. Quixito was not slow in getting to work. First he produced a flask, and after passing his hand upwards before the face of his English companion he offered the drink to the now alive but bewildered lad.

Geoffrey took the flask and drank. How sleepy he felt, somehow. How dark it was! Even the torches were dim. Where was he, where . . . ? Quixito caught him as he fell and laid him on the ground.

.    .    .    .    .    .    .    .    .    .    .    .

There was a sound of chanting, weird and monotonous. Clapping of hands in rhythmic beats, then a high-pitched voice singing in wavering tones what seemed to be a never-ending note.

Bellew stood at the edge of the topmost platform of the temple, looking down on the surging populace below. The moon shone brightly, for it was full, and the sky was cloudless. Bellew felt almost sick as he looked down the broad stone stairway to where, over a hundred feet below, thousands of almost naked, reddish-brown people waved their arms and shouted. The clearing below was like an ant-hill newly disturbed, and every one was in a frenzy of excitement.

Then Geoffrey turned to look behind him.

He was standing at the entrance to the temple of the moon-goddess. The figures of this deity were carved on pillars and on the walls, and in many of the carvings richly apparelled priests were to be seen bending in homage to the queen of the heavens.

The central portion of the temple was filled by a huge circular slab, carved all round its sides, and with a large hole in the centre. Round the slab stood, at attention, three of the chief priests of the goddess, each holding in his hand a long, thin knife of sharpened bone. They stood motionless, waiting. Waiting—for what?

Then a hush in the pandemonium below caused Geoffrey to turn again, and there, down at the base of the temple, he saw the savages part into two sections, leaving an avenue leading to the staircase. The priests above sprang to life, felt the blades of their knives, and turned their eyes to the stairway.

Suddenly Geoffrey was aware of a figure by his side. Turning, he saw a half-clad fellow whose face seemed to resemble that of some one he knew. Yes, it was Quixito, and this worthy began to speak in whispers.

" He's coming now, Meester Bellew. This is the sacrifice to the moon-goddess." The language was flowing English. Geoffrey was so fascinated that he did not think this strange, and he whispered :

" Go on, fellow. Tell me more. Look, there's some one coming to the stairway below."

" That is the victim, Meester Bellew. At this time, the full moon, the most handsome and finest built of our captives is chosen for the sacrifice. He has had a month of freedom and riches. Everything has been his. Now he must come to the sacrifice. Watch ! "

A procession approached the foot of the stairs, and from it came forward a tall, lithe figure of a man, bareheaded and clad only in a white loincloth. Slowly he began to ascend the stair, stopping on each step to tap something on the stone.

" What's he doing ? " whispered Bellew.

" Pretending to break an earthenware flute on each step," came the

*Slowly he began to ascend the stair, stopping on each step*

whispered answer. " It is a sign of the music and joy he is leaving behind him in this life."

The victim had now reached the first platform, where he paused to look back. The crowd yelled in a frenzy and waved him on. Turning again, he looked up at the temple and began the second stage of his ascent. At the second platform he paused again, and Bellew now thought he saw the resolution and grim courage in his handsome face.

Then he commenced the final climb, and as he advanced his fine physique showed to full advantage. The moon lightened the moist darkness of his smooth skin, and Geoffrey noticed the ripples of hard muscle that moved and rolled as he stepped upward.

He now neared the uppermost stair, and the priests struck attitudes of eager anticipation. The chief priest gripped the handle of his bone knife firmly in his right hand and stood gazing at the victim, the fingers of his left hand clutching and opening quickly.

Ignoring Bellew and his companion, the athletic figure of the victim topped the stair and strode resolutely toward the three priests. As he disappeared from the straining eyes of the savages below a loud cry came up from the ground, repeated three times, and then a ghostly silence.

The victim advanced to the chief priest and bowed his head, holding his sinewy arms out before him in supplication. The chief priest stood motionless, looking at this fine specimen of manhood about to be sacrificed to the goddess of the moon.

Quickly Geoffrey whispered to his companion:
" What's to happen to him ? "
Back came the hurried whisper :
" They'll kill him and hurl his body down the stairway to the mob below."
" The devils ! " hissed Bellew. " And what happens to the body ? "
" It will be seized and torn to pieces. Look ! "

The victim still bowed and kept his arms outstretched. The priest approached, knife upraised. He was now within a step of the unfortunate captive, and threw out his left hand to clutch at his throat.

Suddenly the captive straightened himself and shot forth one of his lithe legs. It caught the chief priest in the pit of the stomach and he crumpled up with a long-drawn-out sigh and lay still.

The other priests sprang forward with knives raised, and as one met the clenched fist of the captive the other brought down his blade and pierced the victim's arm. It was his last act, however, for the athlete, with bone knife still fixed in his left arm, took his assailant's throat in his two hands, swung him off his feet and hurled him down the staircase.

Down thumped the body to the populace below. Immediately a cry of triumph arose, and dozens of brown figures began to swarm up the stair to seize what they thought to be their victim.

By this time the chief priest had struggled to his feet and was manœuvring for a good position behind the now retiring captive. He raised his knife to pierce the muscular back of the unprepared fighter, but Bellew sprang forward, hurling his slight weight on the stout priest, pulling down the arm before it completed its deadly design.

Dropping his knife the priest grappled with his new assailant, and

*For a brief moment they hung on the very edge and then, with a sickening movement, they rolled down, locked in each other's arms*

together they rolled on the floor of the temple. The captive turned swiftly, picked up the dead priest as though he were a child and hurled him down upon the now swarming savages on the stairs below.

Again he turned to assist Bellew, but the two wrestlers were on the edge of the top stair. For a brief moment they hung on the very edge and then, with a sickening movement, they rolled down, locked in each other's arms. Down, down, down.

.　　.　　.　　.　　.　　.　　.　　.

" Where's Bellew got to ? "

Baker and Standish had asked each other the question time and time again that night. The whole camp had been roused, and with Quixito in charge a search had been made without success.

All through the night the search had gone on, but no trace of the lad could be found, so when at last dawn broke, Baker and the Captain were wearied and full of despair.

After a breakfast that was more of a habit than a meal the Professor called up all the labourers. Addressing Quixito he said :

" Send them out in parties. Give each party certain boundaries within which they must search every inch of the ground. You come with us, we're going to the mound."

Quixito gabbled and gesticulated for ten minutes, and at last the labourers had all departed on their search.

" Now we'll get forward," snapped out Baker. " Come, Quixito. If you want to regain my respect, do some quick thinking. Where do you think Mr. Bellew went last night ? He wasn't well, you know."

Quixito's face showed no expression. It was a death mask. He thought for a moment, and then spoke : " Meester Professor, I hope I did good. I told the men you would give money for him who find Meester Bellew."

" Well, I don't mind that, if only we find him alive. How much did you promise, rascal ? "

Quixito smiled in a wry manner.

" I said one hundred English pounds, Meester Professor."

Baker gasped. Then he realised the urgency of the search.

" Pretty steep, you old fool. Still, we'll give that if only we can find the lad safe and well. One hundred pounds if we get him alive."

" Let's get over to the ruin, then," put in Standish. " We've wasted enough time already, and this fool won't help us much, I fear."

They followed Quixito, who seemed to desire to lead the party, and came to the foot of the staircase. Here Quixito stopped and waited for the approach of the white men.

" He may have gone up the stairway," he ventured, pointing up the long flight of broad steps.

" That's an idea, anyway," returned Standish. " And the natives wouldn't search here at night, especially as last night was full moon."

" Funny how these superstitions persist through the centuries, isn't it ? " replied Baker, as they began the ascent.

Reaching the first platform they cried a halt, for the Professor was somewhat out of breath.

" Look here, Quixito," ordered Standish. " The Professor is a little tired. You go one way and I'll go the other. We'll meet on the northern side."

Quixito immediately set off to the right, leaving Standish to take the left. Round the platform the Captain walked, examining the broad stone pavement for marks of feet or signs of recent visitors. When he reached the northern side he found a gesticulating Quixito awaiting him.

"Come, Meester Capt'n, I found a hole in the wall. Have you matches? It is much dark in the hole."

Standish sprang forward.

"A hole in the wall? Lead me to it. Hurry!" and he set off at a slow run, with Quixito trotting by his side. Arriving at the hole, Standish scrambled through and struck a match. Then he snuffed the air. "Some one's been here," he snapped. "There's a smell of burning here. Come, let's get on."

They threaded the crooked passage, and at last came out into the chamber where, last night, Quixito had brought the hypnotised Bellew.

The Captain struck another match and held it aloft. Quixito kept behind him, a cunning leer on his swarthy face.

"Good heavens! Geoffrey!" and as Standish uttered the cry the match burned his fingers, and he dropped it. Quickly he struck another, and then saw the burnt-out torches stuck in clefts in the wall.

"There's devil's work here," he snarled, and swung round on Quixito. Then he bent over the inanimate form of Bellew and saw that his knuckles were all bruised and clotted with dried blood.

Quickly he raised him and tore at his shirt. Putting his ear to the lad's breast he listened for the heart beat.

"Thank God he's alive," he gasped. "Quick! We must carry him back to the camp. Come, give a hand."

The box of matches was by this time almost finished, and so he strode over to one of the fragments of a torch.

Prising it from the wall, he lit the fragment that remained, and handed it to Quixito. Suddenly he stopped, and picking up a small object, put it in his pocket.

Motioning for Quixito to lead the way out he picked up the unconscious boy and slung him over his shoulder.

Once in the open air again they found the Professor pacing up and down in despair.

"Hi, Baker. We're here, and here's Geoffrey," bawled Standish, and the look of relief on Baker's face told of his gratitude that the boy had been found.

The journey down the stairway was difficult, but at last they reached the ground, and before long Geoffrey was stretched on his bed, while brandy was being forced between his lips. After half an hour of anxious waiting the two white men were rewarded by a flicker of the lad's eyelids, and soon he was gazing around and murmuring unintelligible words. After a while the words formed themselves. "Did they get him after all? The villains! . . . We fell together. . . . That priest was tough . . ." and then he fell asleep.

Late that afternoon Bellew was sufficiently recovered to take some food and drink, though when questioned as to what had happened the night before his mind was a complete blank.

Standish resolved to return to the chamber and explore. Taking a lamp he ascended the stairway, and when on the first platform whom should he meet but Quixito !

The native started visibly, but recovered his composure and approached.

" How is Meester Bellew, Meester Capt'n ? Is it well with him ? "

" Well enough," retorted Standish. " Why are you here ? "

" Looking round, Meester Capt'n. Just looking round," replied Quixito, staring at the pavement.

Then he lifted his eyes and added :

" I found him after all. I led you to the hole, Meester Capt'n."

" And you want the reward, I suppose ? " Standish's face assumed a curious smile.

" But yes, Meester Capt'n. It is my due." Quixito shuffled his feet. He was undoubtedly uncomfortable.

Standish dived his hand into his pocket and then stretched out his hand.

" I found this in the chamber, under the place where the torch was stuck. Your ear-ring, I believe. Those who hide can find. You took him to the cave. You devil ! "

Quixito turned to flee, but the Captain was there first.

Seizing the wretched interpreter by the shoulders he shook him like a rat until he howled for mercy.

At last he let him go, and stood back to see the effect of the punishment.

But Quixito was sick, dizzy and unbalanced. He swayed and tottered as he tried to pull himself together. Standish sprang forward as the beaten man, winded and half-blinded, staggered backwards. But he was too late.

One foot slipped over the edge of the pavement. The body hung for one brief moment in air, and then hurtled down the smooth slope of the pyramid to crash with a sickening thud on the ground below.

The Moon-goddess had claimed her victim at the time of the full moon.

# LIFE'S BATTLE

*by* Lord Houghton

IF what shone afar so grand,
Turn to nothing in thy hand,
On again ; the virtue lies
In the struggle, not the prize.

# SUMMER

*by* CHRISTINA ROSSETTI

WINTER is cold-hearted,
   Spring is yea and nay,
Autumn is a weather-cock
   Blown every way :
Summer days for me
When every leaf is on its tree ;
When Robin's not a beggar,
   And Jenny Wren's a bride,
And larks hang singing, singing, singing,
   Over the wheat fields wide,
   And anchored lilies ride,
And the pendulum spider
   Swings from side to side.

And blue-black beetles transact business
   And gnats fly in a host,
And furry caterpillars hasten
   That no time be lost,
And moths grow fat and thrive,
And ladybirds arrive.
Before green apples blush,
   Before green nuts embrown,
Why, one day in the country
   Is worth a month in town ;
   Is worth a day and a year
Of the dusty, musty, lag-last fashion
That days drone elsewhere.

# A Surprise for Katy

## by SUSAN COOLIDGE

IT was a pleasant morning in early June. A warm wind was rustling the trees, which were covered thickly with half-opened leaves, and looked like fountains of green spray thrown high into the air. Dr. Carr's front door stood wide open. Through the parlour window came the sound of piano practice, and on the steps, under the budding roses, sat a small figure busily sewing.

This was Clover, and she was now over fourteen. Clover was never intended to be tall. Her eyes were blue and sweet, and her apple-blossom cheeks pink. Her brown pig-tails were pinned into a round knot, and the childish face had gained almost a womanly look. Old Mary declared that Miss Clover was getting quite youngladyfied, and " Miss Clover " was quite aware of the fact, and mightily pleased with it. It delighted her to turn up her hair ; and she was very particular about having her dresses made to come below the tops of her boots. She had also left off ruffles, and wore narrow collars instead, and little cuffs with sleeve-buttons to fasten them. These sleeve-buttons, which were a present from Cousin Helen, Clover liked best of all her things. Papa said that he was sure she took them to bed with her, but of course that was only a joke, though she certainly was never seen without them in the day-time. She glanced frequently at these beloved buttons as she sat sewing, and every now and then laid down her work to twist them into a better position, or give an affectionate pat with her fore-finger.

Very soon the side-gate swung open, and Philly came round the corner of the house. He had grown into a big boy. All his pretty baby curls were cut off, and his frocks had given place to jacket and trousers. In his hand he held something. What, Clover could not see.

" What's that ? " she said, as he reached the steps.

" I'm going upstairs to ask Katy if these are ripe," replied Phil, exhibiting some currants faintly streaked with red.

" Why, of course, they're not ripe ! " said Clover, putting one into her mouth. " Can't you tell by the taste ? They're as green as can be."

" I don't care, if Katy says they're ripe I shall eat 'em," answered Phil defiantly, marching into the house.

" What did Philly want ? " asked Elsie, opening the parlour door as Phil went upstairs.

" Only to know if the currants are ripe enough to eat."

" How particular he always is about asking now ! " said Elsie ; " he's afraid of another dose of salts."

" I should think he would be," replied Clover, laughing. " Johnnie says she never was so scared in her life as when Papa called them, and they looked up, and saw him standing there with the bottle in one hand and a spoon in the other ! "

*Under the budding roses sat a small figure busily sewing*

" Yes," went on Elsie, " and you know Dorry held his in his mouth for ever so long, and then went round the corner of the house and spat it out ! Papa said he had a good mind to make him take another spoonful, but he remembered that after all Dorry had the bad taste a great deal longer than the others, so he didn't. I think it was an *awful* punishment, don't you ? "

" Yes, but it was a good one, for none of them have ever touched the green gooseberries since. Have you got through practising ? It doesn't seem like an hour yet."

" Oh, it isn't ; it's only twenty-five minutes. But Katy told me not to sit more than half an hour at a time without getting up and running round to rest. I'm going to walk twice down to the gate, and twice back. I promised her I would." And Elsie set off, clapping her hands briskly before and behind her as she walked.

" Why—what is Bridget doing in Papa's room ? " she asked, as she came back the second time. " She's flapping things out of the window. Are the girls up there ? I thought they were cleaning the dining-room."

" They're doing both. Katy said it was such a good chance, having Papa away, that she would have both the carpets taken up at once. There isn't going to be any dinner to-day, only just bread and butter, and milk, and cold ham, up in Katy's room because Debby is helping too, so as to get through and save Papa all the fuss. And see," exhibiting her sewing, " Katy's making a new cover for Papa's pincushion, and I'm hemming the ruffle to go round it."

" How nicely you hem ! " said Elsie. " I wish I had something for Papa's room, too. There's my washstand mats—but the one for the soap-dish isn't finished. Do you suppose, if Katy would excuse me from the rest of my practising, I could get it done ? I've a great mind to go and ask her."

" There's her bell ! " said Clover, as a little tinkle sounded upstairs ; " I'll ask her if you like."

" No, let me go. I'll see what she wants." But Clover was already half-way across the hall, and the two girls ran up side by side. There was often a little strife between them as to which should answer Katy's bell. Both liked to wait on her so much.

Katy came to meet them as they entered. Not on her feet ; that alas ! was still only a far-off possibility ; but in a chair with large wheels, with which she was rolling herself across the room. This chair was a great comfort to her. Sitting in it she could get to her closet and her bureau drawers, and help herself to what she wanted without troubling anybody. It was only lately that she had been able to use it. Dr. Carr considered her doing so as a hopeful sign, but he had never told Katy this. She had grown accustomed to her invalid life at last, and was cheerful in it, and he thought it unwise to make her restless by exciting hopes which might after all end in fresh disappointment.

She met the girls with a bright smile as they came in, and said :

" Oh, Clovy, it was you I rang for ! I am troubled for fear Bridget will meddle with the things on Papa's table. You know he likes them to be left just so. Will you please go and remind her that she is not to touch them at all ? After the carpet is put down, I want you to dust the table, so as to be sure that everything is put back in the same place. Will you ? "

" Of course I will," said Clover, who was a born house-wife, and dearly loved to act as Katy's prime minister.

" Shan't I fetch you the pincushion, too, while I'm there ? "

" Oh, yes, please do ! I want to measure."

" Katy," said Elsie, " those mats of mine are almost done, and I would like to finish them and put them on Papa's washstand before he comes back. Mayn't I stop practising now and bring my crochet up here instead ? "

" Will there be plenty of time to learn the new exercise before Miss Phillips comes, if you do ? "

" I think so, plenty. She doesn't come till Friday, you know."

" Well, then, it seems to me that you might just as well as not. And Elsie, dear, run into Papa's room first and bring me the drawer out of his table. I want to put that in order myself."

Elsie went cheerfully. She laid the drawer across Katy's lap, and Katy began to dust and arrange the contents. Pretty soon Clover joined them.

" Here's the cushion," she said. " Now we'll have a nice quiet time all by ourselves, won't we ? I like this sort of day, when nobody comes in to interrupt us."

Somebody tapped at the door as she spoke. Katy called out, " Come in," and in marched a tall, broad-shouldered lad, with a solemn, sensible face, and a little clock carried carefully in both his hands. This was Dorry.

" Here's your clock, Katy," he said. " I've got it fixed so that it strikes all right. Only you must be careful not to hit the striker when you start the pendulum."

" Have you really ? " said Katy. " Why, Dorry, you're a genius ! I'm ever so much obliged."

" It's four minutes to eleven now," went on Dorry. " So it'll strike pretty soon. I guess I'd better stay and hear it, so as to be sure that it is right. That is," he added politely, " unless you're busy and would rather not."

" I'm never too busy to want you, old fellow," said Katy, stroking his arm. " Here, this drawer is arranged now. Don't you want to carry it into Papa's room and put it back into the table ? Your hands are stronger than Elsie's."

Dorry looked gratified. When he came back the clock was just beginning to strike.

" There ! " he exclaimed ; " that's splendid, isn't it ? "

But alas ! the clock did not stop at eleven. It went on—twelve, thirteen, fourteen, fifteen, sixteen !

" Dear me ! " said Clover, " what does all this mean ? It must be the day after to-morrow, at least ! "

Dorry stared with open mouth at the clock, which was still striking as though it would split its sides. Elsie, screaming with laughter, kept count.

" Thirty, thirty-one—Oh, Dorry ! Thirty-two ! thirty-three ! thirty-four ! "

" You've bewitched it, Dorry ! " said Katy, as much entertained as the rest.

Then they all began counting. Dorry seized the clock, shook it, slapped it, turned it upside down. But still the sharp, vibrating sounds continued, as if the clock, having got its own way for once, meant to go on till it was tired out. At last, at the one-hundred-and-thirtieth stroke, it suddenly ceased, and Dorry, with a red, amazed countenance, faced the laughing company.

" It's very queer," he said, " but I'm sure it's not because of anything I did. I can fix it, though, if you'll let me try again. May I, Katy ? I'll promise not to hurt it."

For a moment Katy hesitated. Clover pulled her sleeve, and whispered, " Don't ! " Then, seeing the mortification on Dorry's face, she made up her mind.

" Yes, take it, Dorry. I'm sure you'll be careful. But if I were you, I'd carry it down to Wetherell's first of all, and talk it over with him. Together you could hit on just the right thing. Don't you think so ? "

" Perhaps," said Dorry ; " yes, I think I will." Then he departed with the clock under his arm, while Clover called after him teasingly : " Lunch at 1.32 o'clock ; don't forget."

" No, I won't," said Dorry. Two years before he would not have borne to be laughed at so good-naturedly.

" How could you let him take your clock again ? " said Clover, as soon as the door was shut. " He'll spoil it. And you think so much of it."

" I thought he would feel mortified if I didn't let him try," replied Katy quietly ; " I don't believe he'll hurt it. Wetherell's man likes Dorry, and he'll show him what to do."

" You were real good to do it," responded Clover ; " but if it had been mine, I don't think I could."

Just then the door flew open and Johnnie rushed in.

" Oh, Katy ! " she gasped, " won't you please tell Philly not to wash the chickens in the rain-water tub? He's put in every one of Speckle's, and is just beginning on Dame Durden's. I'm afraid one little yellow one is dead already——"

" Why, he mustn't, of course he mustn't!" said Katy. " What made him think of such a thing? "

" He says they're dirty, because they've just come out of egg-shells! And he insists that the yellow on them is yoke of egg. I told him it wasn't, but he wouldn't listen to me." And Johnnie wrung her hands.

" Clover!" cried Katy, " won't you run down and ask Philly to come up to me? Speak pleasantly, you know."

" I spoke pleasantly—real pleasantly, but it wasn't any use," said Johnnie, on whom the wrongs of the chicks had evidently made a deep impression.

" What a mischief Phil is getting to be!" said Elsie. " Papa says his name ought to be Pickle."

" Pickles turn out very nice sometimes, you know," replied Katy, laughing.

Pretty soon Philly came up, escorted by Clover. He looked a little defiant, but Katy understood how to manage him. She lifted him into her lap, which, big boy as he was, he liked extremely; and talked to him so affectionately about the poor little shivering chicks that his heart was quite melted.

" I didn't mean to hurt 'em, really and truly," he said; " but they were all dirty and yellow—with egg, you know, and I thought you'd like me to clean them up."

" But that wasn't egg, Philly—it was dear little clean feathers, like a canary-bird's wings."

" Was it? "

" Yes, and now the chickies are as cold and forlorn as you would feel if you tumbled into a pond and nobody gave you any dry clothes. Don't you think you ought to go and warm them? "

" How? "

" Well, in your hands, very gently. And then I would let them run round in the sun."

" I will," said Philly, getting down from her lap. " Only kiss me first, because I didn't mean to, you know!"—Philly was very fond of Katy. Miss Pettingill said it was wonderful to see how that child let himself be managed. But I think the secret was that Katy didn't " manage," but tried to be always kind and loving and considerate of Phil's feelings.

Before the echo of Phil's boots had died away on the stairs, old Mary put her head into the door. There was a distressed expression on her face.

" Miss Katy," she said, " I wish *you'd* speak to Alexander about putting the wood-shed in order. I don't think you know how bad it looks."

" I don't suppose I do," said Katy, smiling and then sighing. She had never seen the wood-shed since the day of her fall from the swing which had crippled her. " Never mind, Mary; I'll talk to Alexander about it, and he shall make it nice."

Mary trotted downstairs satisfied. But in the course of a few minutes she was up again.

" There's a man come with a box of soap, Miss Katy, and here's the bill. He says it's resated."

It took Katy a little time to find her purse, and then she wanted her pencil and account-book, and Elsie had to move from her seat at the table.

" Oh dear ! " she said. " I wish people wouldn't keep coming and interrupting us. Who'll be the next, I wonder ? "

She was not left to wonder long. Almost as she spoke there was another knock at the door.

" Come in ! " said Katy, rather wearily. The door opened.

" Shall I ? " said a voice. There was a rustle of skirts, a clatter of boot-

*He looked a little defiant, but Katy knew how to manage him*

heels, and Imogen Clark swept into the room. Katy could not think who it was at first. She had not seen Imogen for almost two years.

" I found the front door open," explained Imogen, in her high-pitched voice, " and as nobody seemed to hear when I rang the bell, I ventured to come right upstairs. I hope I am not interrupting anything private ? "

" Not at all," said Katy politely. " Elsie, dear, move up that low chair, please. Do sit down, Imogen. I'm sorry nobody answered your ring, but the servants are cleaning house to-day, and I suppose they didn't hear."

So Imogen sat down and began to rattle on in her usual manner, while Elsie, from behind Katy's chair, took a wide-awake survey of her dress. It was of cheap material, but very gorgeously made and trimmed with flounces and puffs ; and Imogen wore a jet necklace and long black earrings, which jingled and clicked when she waved her head about. She had little round curls stuck on to her cheeks, and Elsie wondered what kept them in their places.

By and by the object of Imogen's visit came out. She had called to say good-bye. The Clark family were all going back to Jacksonville to live.

" Did you ever see the Brigand again ? " asked Clover, who had never forgotten that eventful tale told in the parlour.

" Yes," replied Imogen, " several times. And I get letters from him quite often. He writes *beau*tiful letters. I wish I had one with me, so that I could read you a little bit. You would enjoy it, I know. Let me see—perhaps I have." And she put her hand into her pocket. Sure enough there *was* a letter.

Clover couldn't help suspecting that Imogen knew it all the time.

The Brigand seemed to write a bold, black hand, and his note-paper and envelope was just like anybody else's. But perhaps his band had surprised a pedlar with a box of stationery.

" Let me see," said Imogen, running her eye down the page. " ' Adored Imogen '—*that* wouldn't interest you—hm, hm, hm—ah, here's something ! ' I took dinner at the Rock House on Christmas. It was lonesome without you. I had roast turkey, roast goose, roast beef, mince pie, plum pudding and nuts and raisins. A pretty good dinner, was it not ? But nothing tastes first-rate when friends are away.' "

Katy and Clover stared, as well they might. Such language from a Brigand !

" ' John Billings has bought a new horse,' " continued Imogen ; " hm, hm, hm—' him.' I don't think there is anything else you'd care about. Oh, yes ! just here, at the end, is some poetry :—

" ' Come, little dove, with azure wing,
And brood upon my breast.'

" That's sweet, ain't it ?"

" Hasn't he reformed ? " said Clover. " He writes as if he had."

" Reformed ! " cried Imogen, with a toss of the jingling earrings. " He was always just as good as he could be ! "

There was nothing to be said in reply to this. Katy felt her lips twitch, and for fear she should be rude, and laugh out, she began to talk as fast as she could about something else. All the time she found herself taking measure of Imogen, and thinking : " Did I ever really like her ? How queer ! Oh, what a wise man Papa is ! "

Imogen stayed half an hour. Then she took her leave.

" She never asked how you were ! " cried Elsie indignantly. " I noticed, and she didn't—not once ! "

" Oh, well—I suppose she forgot. We were talking about her, not about me," replied Katy.

The little group settled down again to their work. This time half an hour went by without any more interruptions. Then the doorbell rang, and Bridget with a disturbed face came upstairs.

" Miss Katy," she said, " it's old Mrs. Worrett, and I reckon she's come to spend the day, for she's brought her bag. Whatever shall I tell her ? "

Katy looked dismayed. " Oh dear ! " she said, " how unlucky. What can we do ? "

Mrs. Worrett was an old friend of Aunt Izzie's, who lived in the country, about six miles from Burnet, and was in the habit of coming to Dr. Carr's for lunch on days when shopping or other business brought her into town. This did not occur often ; and, as it happened, Katy had never had to entertain her before.

" Tell her ye're busy, and can't see her," suggested Bridget. " There's no dinner nor nothing, you know."

The Katy of two years ago would probably have jumped at this idea. But the Katy of to-day was more considerate.

" N—o," she said ; " I don't like to do that. We must just make the best of it, Bridget. Run down, Clover dear, that's a good girl, and tell Mrs. Worrett that the dining-room is all in confusion, but that we're going to have lunch here, and, after she's rested, I should be glad to have her come up. And, oh, Clovy ! give her a fan the first thing. She'll be *so* hot. Bridget, you can bring up the luncheon just the same, only take out some canned peaches, by way of a dessert, and make Mrs. Worrett a cup of tea. She drinks tea always, I believe."

" I can't bear to send the poor old lady away when she has come so far," she explained to Elsie, after the others were gone. " Pull the rocking-chair a little this way, Elsie. And, oh ! push all those little chairs back against the wall. Mrs. Worrett broke down in one the last time she was here—don't you recollect ? "

It took some time to cool Mrs. Worrett off, so nearly twenty minutes passed before a heavy, creaking step on the stairs announced that the guest was on her way up. Elsie began to giggle. Mrs. Worrett always made her giggle. Katy had just time to give her a warning glance before the door opened.

Mrs. Worrett was the most enormously fat person ever seen. Nobody dared to guess how much she weighed, but she *looked* as if it might be a thousand pounds. Her face was extremely red. In the coldest weather she appeared hot, and on a mild day she seemed absolutely ready to melt. Her bonnet-strings were flying loose as she came in, and she fanned herself all the way across the room, which shook as she walked.

" Well, my dear," she said, as she plumped herself into the rocking-chair, " and how do you do ? "

" Very well, thank you," replied Katy, thinking that she never saw Mrs. Worrett look half so fat before, and wondering how she *was* to entertain her.

" And how's your Pa ? " inquired Mrs. Worrett. Katy answered politely, and then asked after Mrs. Worrett's own health.

" Well, I'm so's to be round," was the reply, which had the effect of sending Elsie off into a fit of convulsive laughter behind Katy's chair.

" I had business at the bank," continued the visitor ; " and I thought, while I was about it, I'd step up to Miss Pettingill's and see if I couldn't get her to come and let out my black silk. It was made a long while ago, and I seem to have grown stouter since then, for I can't make the hooks and eyes meet at all. But when I got there she was out, so I'd my walk for nothing. Do you know where she's sewing now ? "

" No," said Katy, feeling her chair shake, and keeping her own countenance with difficulty. " She was here for three days last week to make

Johnnie a school dress. But I haven't heard anything about her since. Elsie, you might run downstairs and ask Bridget to bring a—a—a glass of iced water for Mrs. Worrett. She looks warm after her walk."

Elsie, dreadfully ashamed, made a bolt from the room, and hid herself in the hall closet to have her laugh out. She came back after a while, with a perfectly straight face. Luncheon was brought up. Mrs. Worrett made a good meal, and seemed to enjoy everything. She was so comfortable that she never stirred till four o'clock! Oh, how long that afternoon did seem to the poor girls, sitting there and trying to think of something to say to their vast visitor!

At last Mrs. Worrett got out of her chair and prepared to depart.

"Well," she said, tying her bonnet strings, "I've had a good rest, and feel all the better for it. Aren't some of you young folks coming out to see me one of these days? I'd like to have you first-rate if you will. 'Tain't every girl would know how to take care of a fat old woman, and make her feel at home, as you have me, Katy. I wish your aunt could see you all as you are now. She'd be right pleased; I know that."

Somehow this sentence rang pleasantly in Katy's ears.

"Ah! don't laugh at her," she said later in the evening, when the children, after their tea in the clean, fresh-smelling dining-room, were come up to sit with her, and Cecy, in her pretty pink lawn and white shawl, had dropped in to spend an hour or two; "she's a real kind old woman, and I don't like to have you laugh at her. It isn't her fault that she's fat. And Aunt Izzie was fond of her, you know. It is doing something for her, when we can show a little attention to one of her friends. I was sorry when she came; but now it's over I'm glad."

"It feels so nice when it stops aching," quoted Elsie mischievously, while Cecy whispered to Clover:

"Isn't Katy sweet?"

"Isn't she?" replied Clover. "I wish I was half as good. Sometimes I think I shall really be sorry if she ever gets well. She's such a dear old darling to us all, sitting there in her chair, that it wouldn't seem so nice to have her anywhere else. But, then, I know it's horrid in me. And I don't believe she'd be different, or grow rough and horrid, like some of the girls, even if she were well."

"Of course she wouldn't!" replied Cecy.

It was six weeks after this that, one day, Clover and Elsie were busy downstairs, they were startled by the sound of Katy's bell ringing in a sudden and agitated manner. Both ran up two steps at a time, to see what was wanted.

Katy sat in her chair, looking very much flushed and excited.

"Oh, girls," she exclaimed, "what do you think? I stood up?"

"What?" cried Clover and Elsie.

"I really did! I stood up on my feet! by myself!"

The others were too much astonished to speak, so Katy went on explaining.

"It was all at once, you see. Suddenly, I had the feeling that if I tried I could, and almost before I thought, I *did* try, and there I was, up and out of the chair. Only I kept hold of the arm all the time! I don't know how

I got back, I was so frightened. Oh, girls ! "—and Katy buried her face in her hands.

" Do you think I shall ever be able to do it again ? " she asked, looking up with wet eyes.

" Why, of course you will," said Clover ; while Elsie danced about, crying out anxiously : " Be careful ! Do be careful ! "

Katy tried, but the spring was gone. She could not move out of the chair at all. She began to wonder if she had dreamed the whole thing.

But next day, when Clover happened to be in the room, she heard a sudden exclamation, and, turning, there stood Katy absolutely on her feet.

" Papa ! Papa ! " shrieked Clover, rushing downstairs. " Dorry, John, Elsie—come ! Come and see ! "

Papa was out, but all the rest crowded up at once. This time Katy found no trouble in " doing it again." It seemed as if her will had been asleep ; and now that it had waked up, the limbs recognised its orders and obeyed them. When Papa came in he was as much excited as any of the children. He walked round and round the chair, questioning Katy and making her stand up and sit down.

" Am I really going to get well ? " she asked, almost in a whisper.

" Yes, my love, I think you are," said Dr. Carr, seizing Phil and giving him a toss into the air. None of the children had ever before seen Papa behave so like a boy. But pretty soon, noticing Katy's burning cheeks and excited eyes, he calmed himself, sent the others all away, and sat down to soothe and quiet her with gentle words.

" I think it is coming, my darling," he said, " but it will take time, and you must have a great deal of patience. After being such a good child all these years, I'm sure you won't fail now. Remember, any imprudence will put you back. You must be content to gain a very little at a time. There is no royal road to walking any more than there is to learning. Every baby finds that out."

" Oh, Papa ! " said Katy, " it's no matter if it takes a year—if only I got well at last."

How happy she was that night—too happy to sleep. Papa noticed the dark circles under her eyes in the morning and shook his head.

" You *must* be careful," he told her, " or you'll be laid up again. A course of fever would put you back for years."

Katy knew Papa was right, and she *was* careful, though it was by no means easy to be so with that new life tingling in every limb. Her progress was slow, as Dr. Carr had predicted. At first she only stood on her feet a few seconds, then a minute, then five minutes, holding tightly all the while by the chair. Next she ventured to let go the chair and stand alone. After that she began to walk a step at a time, pushing a chair before her as children do when they are learning the use of their feet. Clover and Elsie hovered about her as she moved, like anxious mammas. It was droll, and a little pitiful, to see tall Katy with her feeble, unsteady progress, and the active figures of the little sisters following her protectingly. But Katy did not consider it either droll or pitiful ; to her it was simply delightful—the most delightful thing possible. No baby of a year old was ever prouder of his first steps than she.

Gradually she grew adventurous, and ventured on a bolder flight. Clover, running upstairs one day to her own room, stood transfixed at the sight of Katy sitting there, flushed, panting, but enjoying the surprise she caused.

" You see," she explained, in an apologising tone, " I was seized with a desire to explore. It is such a time since I saw any room but my own ! But oh dear, how long that hall is ! I had forgotten it could be so long. I shall have to take a good rest before I go back."

Katy did take a good rest, but she was very tired next day. The experiment, however, did no harm. In the course of two or three weeks she was able to walk all over the second story.

This was a great enjoyment. It was like reading an interesting book to see all the new things and the little changes. She was for ever wondering over something.

" Why, Dorry," she would say, " what a pretty book-shelf ! When did you get it ? "

" That old thing ! Why, I've had it two years. Didn't I ever tell you about it ? "

" Perhaps you did," Katy would reply, " but, you see, I never *saw* it before, so it made no impression."

By the end of August she was grown so strong that she began to talk about going downstairs. But Papa said, " Wait."

" It will tire you much more than walking about on a level," he explained, " you had better put it off a little while—till you are quite sure of your feet."

" I think so too," said Clover ; " and besides, I want to have the house all put in order and made nice before your sharp eyes see it, Mrs. Housekeeper. Oh, I'll tell you ! Such a beautiful idea has come into my head ! You shall fix a day to come down, Katy, and we'll be all ready for you, and have a ' celebration ' among ourselves. That would be just lovely ! How soon may she, Papa ? "

" Well, in ten days, I should say, it might be safe."

" Ten days ! that will bring it to the seventh of September, won't it ? " said Katy. " Then, Papa, if I may, I'll come down for the first time on the eighth. It was Mamma's birthday, you know," she added in a lower voice.

So it was settled. " How delicious ! " cried Clover, skipping about and clapping her hands ; " I never, never, never *did* hear anything so perfectly lovely. Papa, when are you coming downstairs ? I want to speak to you *dreadfully.*"

" Right away—rather than have my coat-tails pulled off," answered Dr. Carr, laughing, and they went away together. Katy sat looking out of the window in a peaceful, happy mood.

" Oh ! " she thought, " can it really be ? Is school going to ' let out,' just as Cousin Helen's hymn said ? Am I going to

' Bid a sweet good-bye to Pain ? '

But there was Love in the Pain. I see it now. How good the dear Teacher has been to me ! "

Clover seemed to be very busy all the rest of that week. She was " having windows washed," she said, but this explanation hardly accounted for her long absences, and the mysterious exultation on her face, not to mention certain sounds of hammering and sawing which came from down-stairs. The other children had evidently been warned to say nothing; for once or twice Philly broke out with, "O Katy!" and then hushed himself up, saying, "I most forgot!" Katy grew very curious. But she saw that the secret, whatever it was, gave immense satisfaction to every-body except herself; so, though she longed to know, she concluded not to spoil the fun by asking any questions.

At last it wanted but one day of the important occasion.

"See," said Katy, as Clover came into the room a little before tea-time. "Miss Pettingill has brought home my new dress. I'm going to wear it for the first time to go downstairs in."

*She took a book and tried to read, but she couldn't help listening*

"How pretty!" said Clover, examining the dress, which was a soft, dove-coloured cashmere, trimmed with ribbon of the same shade. "But, Katy, I came up to shut your door. Bridget's going to sweep the hall, and I don't want the dust to fly in, because your room was brushed this morning, you know."

"What a queer time to sweep the hall!" said Katy, wondering. "Why don't you make her wait till morning?"

"Oh, she can't! There are—she has—I mean there will be other things for her to do to-morrow. It's a great deal more convenient that she should do it now. Don't worry, Katy darling, but just keep your door shut. You will, won't you? Promise me!"

"Very well," said Katy, more and more amazed, but yielding to Clover's eagerness, "I'll keep it shut." Her curiosity was excited. She took a book and tried to read, but the letters danced up and down before her eyes, and she couldn't help listening. Bridget was making a most ostentatious noise with her broom, but through it all Katy seemed to hear other sounds—feet on the stairs, doors opening and shutting—once, a stifled giggle. How queer it all was !

"Never mind," she said, resolutely stopping her ears, "I shall know all about it to-morrow."

To-morrow dawned fresh and fair—the very ideal of a September day.

"Katy !" said Clover, as she came in from the garden with her hands full of flowers, "that dress of yours is sweet. You never looked so nice before in your life !" And she stuck a beautiful carnation pink under Katy's breast-pin, and fastened another in her hair.

"There !" she said, "now you're adorned. Papa is coming up in a few minutes to take you down."

Just then Elsie and Johnnie came in. They had on their best frocks. So had Clover. It was evidently a festival-day to all the house. Cecy followed, invited over for the special purpose of seeing Katy walk downstairs. She, too, had on a new frock.

"How fine we are !" said Clover, as she remarked this magnificence. "Turn round, Cecy—a pannier, I do declare—and a sash ! You are getting awfully grown up, Miss Hall."

"None of us will ever be so ' grown up ' as Katy," said Cecy, laughing.

And now Papa appeared. Very slowly they all went downstairs, Katy leaning on Papa, with Dorry on her other side, and the girls behind, while Philly clattered ahead. And there were Debby and Bridget and Alexander peeping out of the kitchen door to watch her, and dear old Mary with her apron at her eyes crying for joy.

"Oh, the front door is open !" said Katy, in a delighted tone. "How nice ! And what a pretty oil-cloth. That's new since I was here."

"Don't stop to look at *that* !" cried Philly, who seemed in a great hurry about something. "It isn't new. It's been there ever and ever so long ! Come into the parlour instead."

"Yes !" said Papa, "dinner isn't quite ready yet, you'll have time to rest a little after your walk downstairs. Are you very tired ? "

"Not a bit !" replied Katy cheerfully. "I could do it alone, I think. Oh ! the bookcase door has been mended ! How nice it looks."

"Don't wait, oh, don't wait !" repeated Phil, in an agony of impatience.

So they moved on. Papa opened the parlour door. Katy took one step into the room—then stopped. What was it that she saw ?

Not merely the room itself, with its fresh muslin curtains and vases of flowers. Not even the wide, beautiful window which had been cut toward the sun, or the inviting little couch and table which stood there evidently for her. No, there was something else ! The sofa was pulled out, and there upon it, her bright eyes turned to the door, lay—Cousin Helen !

Clover and Cecy agreed afterwards that they never were so frightened in their lives as at this moment ; for Katy, forgetting her weakness, let go of Papa's arm, and absolutely *ran* towards the sofa. "Oh, Cousin Helen ! dear, dear Cousin Helen ! " she cried. Then she tumbled down by the sofa somehow, the two pairs of arms and the two faces met, and for a moment or two not a word more was heard from anybody.

" Isn't it a nice 'prise ! " shouted Philly, turning a somersault by way of relieving his feelings, while John and Dorry executed a sort of war-dance.

It appeared that this happy thought of getting Cousin Helen to the " celebration," was Clover's. She it was who had proposed it to Papa, and made all the arrangements. And, artful puss ! she had set Bridget to sweep the hall on purpose that Katy might not hear the noise of the arrival.

" Cousin Helen's going to stay three weeks this time—isn't that nice ? " asked Elsie, while Clover anxiously questioned : " Are you sure that you didn't suspect ? Not one bit ? Not the least tiny, weeny mite ? "

" No, indeed, not the least. How could I suspect anything so perfectly delightful ? " and Katy gave Cousin Helen another rapturous kiss.

Such a short day as that seemed ! There was so much to see, to ask about, to talk over, that the hours flew, and evening dropped upon them all like another great surprise.

Cousin Helen was perhaps the happiest of the party. Besides the pleasure of knowing Katy to be almost well again, she had the additional enjoyment of seeing for herself how many changes for the better had taken place during the four years among the little cousins she loved so much.

It was very interesting to watch them all. Elsie had quite lost her plaintive look and little injured tone, and was as bright and beaming a maiden of twelve as any one could wish to see. Dorry's moody face had grown open and sensible, and his manners were good-humoured and obliging. And to him, as to all the other children, Katy was evidently the centre and the sun.

Cousin Helen looked on as Phil came in crying, after a hard tumble, and was consoled ; as Johnnie whispered an important secret, and Elsie begged for help in her work. She saw Katy meet them all pleasantly and sweetly, without a bit of the dictatorial elder-sister in her manner, and with none of her old impetuous tone. And, best of all, she saw the change in Katy's own face ; the gentle expression of her eyes, the womanly look, the pleasant voice, the politeness, the tact in advising the others without seeming to advise.

" Dear Katy," she said, a day or two after her arrival, " this visit is a great pleasure to me—you can't think how great. It is such a contrast to the last I made, when you were so sick, and everybody so sad. Do you remember ? "

" Indeed I do ! And how good you were, and how you helped me ! I shall never forget that."

" I'm glad ! But what I could do was very little. You have been learning by yourself all this time. And Katy, darling, I want to tell you how pleased I am to see how bravely you have worked your way up. I can perceive it in everything—in Papa, in the children, in yourself. You have won the place which, you recollect, I once told you an invalid should try to gain, of being to everybody ' the heart of the House.' "

" Oh, Cousin Helen, don't ! " said Katy, her eyes filling with sudden tears. " I haven't been brave. You can't think how badly I sometimes have behaved ; how cross and ungrateful I am, how stupid and slow. Every day I see things which ought to be done, and I don't do them. It's too delightful to have you praise me—but you mustn't. I don't deserve it."

But although she said she didn't deserve it, I think that Katy did.

# THE MERMAID

TRADITIONAL

ON Friday morning as we set sail,
It was not far from the land,
O, there I spy'd a fair pretty maid,
With a comb and a glass in her hand.
The stormy winds did blow,
And the raging seas did roar,
While we poor sailors went to the top
And the land-lubbers laid below.

Then up spoke a boy of our gallant ship,
And a well-speaking boy was he,
" I've a father and mother in Portsmouth town,
And this night they weep for me."
The stormy, etc.

Then up spoke a man of our gallant ship,
And a well-speaking man was he,
" I've married a wife in fair London town,
And this night she a widow will be."
The stormy, etc.

Then up spoke the Captain of our gallant ship,
And a valiant man was he,
" For want of a boat we shall be drown'd,
For she sank to the bottom of the sea."
The stormy, etc.

The moon shone bright, and the stars gave light
And my mother was looking for me.
She might look and weep with weary eyes,
She might look to the bottom of the sea.
The stormy, etc.

Three times round went our gallant ship
And three times round went she,
Three times round went our gallant ship,
Then she sank to the bottom of the sea.
The stormy, etc.

## THE FOX AND THE STORK

A FOX one day invited a stork to dinner, and amused himself at the expense of his guest, by providing nothing for the entertainment but some thin soup in a shallow dish.

This the fox lapped up very quickly, while the stork, unable to gain a mouthful with her long, narrow bill, was as hungry at the end of the dinner as when she began.

The fox expressed his regret at seeing her eat so sparingly, and feared that the dish was not seasoned to her liking.

The stork said but little, but begged that the fox would do her the honour of returning the visit next day, which invitation Reynard readily accepted.

The fox kept the appointment, and, having greeted his hostess, turned his attention to the dinner placed before them.

To his dismay Reynard saw that the repast was served in a narrow-necked vessel, and, while the stork was able to thrust in her long bill and take her fill, he was obliged to content himself with licking the outside of the jar.

Unable to satisfy his hunger, he retired with as good grace as he could, knowing that he could hardly find fault with his hostess, for she had only paid him back in his own coin.

MORAL: "Those who love practical jokes must be prepared to laugh when one is made at their expense."

# THE MICE IN COUNCIL

ONCE upon a time a number of mice called a meeting to decide upon the best means of ridding themselves of a cat that had killed so many of their relations.

Various plans were discussed and rejected, until at last a young mouse proposed that a bell should be hung round the tyrant's neck, in future, so that they would have warning of her movements and be able to escape.

The suggestion was received joyfully by nearly all, but an old mouse, who had sat silent for some time, got up and said : " While I consider the plan to be a very clever one, and feel sure that it would prove to be quite successful if carried out, I should like to know who is going to bell the cat ? "

MORAL : " It is easier to make a suggestion than to carry it out."

# THE EAGLE AND THE FOX

AN Eagle and a Fox once struck up a bargain to remain firm friends all their lives and help each other all they could. The Fox made his burrow at the foot of a tree, on the top of which the Eagle had built its nest.

One day when the Fox had gone out to look for food the cunning Eagle swept down to the burrow and carried off the young cubs to its nest to feed its own family. When it was carrying off the last cub, the Fox returned home, and, in great anger, vowed vengeance.

Time went on and one day the Eagle snatched a piece of goat-flesh from the altar where it was being sacrificed and carried it to its nest. A piece of live coal, however, was stuck to the flesh and this set fire to the nest so that the young Eagles all tumbled out. The Fox was waiting below with his mouth wide open. He had his revenge at last.

MORAL : "Punishment always awaits wrong-doers."

THE MICE IN COUNCIL

"I consider the plan to be a very clever one, but who is going to bell the cat?" asked the old mouse

(*Page* 160)

THE ASS AND THE FROGS

The Ass sank into a bog among a host of Frogs. "Woe is me!" he groaned, and sighed as though his heart would break (*Page* 161)

# THE ASS AND THE FROGS

ONE day an Ass, with a burden of wood upon his back, had the ill-luck to sink into a bog among a host of Frogs. " Woe is me ! " he groaned and sighed as though his heart would break.

"Friend," said one of the Frogs to the unhappy Ass, "if you make such a noise about a bog you have just entered, what would you do if you had been here as long as we have ? "

MORAL : " Custom makes things familiar and easy to us."

# THE CAT AND THE FOX

A CAT and a fox were exchanging views upon the difficulties of living in peace and safety from those who were ever ready to take their lives.

" I do not care a jot for any of them," said the fox at last. " Things may be very bad, as you say, but I have a thousand tricks to show my enemies before they can do me harm."

" You are fortunate," replied the cat. " For my part, I have but one way of evading my enemies, and if that fails all is lost."

" I am sorry for you with all my heart," said Reynard. " But that one cannot tell a friend from a foe in these difficult times, I would show you one or two of my tricks."

Hardly had he finished speaking when a pack of hounds burst suddenly upon them.

The cat, resorting to her single trick, ran up a tree, and from the security of the topmost branches witnessed the downfall of the braggart.

Unable to make up his mind which of the thousand tricks he would adopt the fox was torn to pieces before he could put even one of them into operation.

MORAL : " He who considers himself more clever than his neighbour usually fares badly when put to the test."

G.T.B.

F

# THE WISE MEN OF GOTHAM

*by* THOMAS LOVE PEACOCK

IN a bowl to sea went wise men three,
On a brilliant night of June :
They carried a net, and their hearts were set
On fishing up the moon.

The sea was calm, the air was balm,
Not a breath stirred low or high,
And the moon, I trow, lay as bright below,
And as round as in the sky.

The wise men with the current went,
Nor paddle nor oar had they,
And still as the grave they went on the wave
That they might not disturb their prey.

Far, far at sea, were the wise men three,
When their fishing-net they threw ;
And at the throw, the moon below
In a thousand fragments flew.

The sea was bright with a dancing light
Of a million million gleams,
Which the broken moon shot forth as soon
As the net disturbed her beams.

They drew in their net ; it was empty and wet,
And they had lost their pain ;
Soon ceased the play of each dancing ray,
And the image was round again.

Three times they threw, three times they drew,
And all the while were mute ;
And evermore their wonder grew,
Till they could not but dispute.

Their silence they broke, and each one spoke
Full long and loud, and clear ;
A man at sea their voices three
Full three leagues off might hear.

The three wise men got home again
To their children and their wives :
But, touching their trip and their net's vain dip,
They disputed all their lives.

The wise men three could never agree
Why they missed the promised boon ;
They agreed alone that their net they had thrown,
And they had not caught the moon.

# JOYCE of X.Y.2.

## by C. BERNARD RUTLEY

**J**OYCE HILLIARD leaned against the railing of the cross-Channel steamer, and watched the waves as they raced by a few feet below where she stood. A gale was blowing, and, with the exception of Joyce and two men, the passengers had already retired below. The girl glanced at her fellow-survivors. One was a tall, soldierly-looking man, manifestly an Englishman, whilst the other was as evidently a foreigner. He had a thick, black beard, and the girl caught a glimpse of dark eyes gleaming beneath the low brim of his hat. A Russian, Joyce decided, and returned to her own reflections, and soon she had forgotten all about her fellow-passengers in thoughts of the new life which lay ahead.

Joyce was nineteen. She was tall, dark, and very pretty, and she had just left the finishing school in Paris and was returning home for good. Presently the sound of footsteps made the girl look up. The Englishman had disappeared, but the Russian was pacing restlessly along the deck, and as he passed close to where she was standing the girl was conscious of piercing, black eyes boring into her ; then, as though satisfied with what he had seen, the stranger turned away and looked at her no more. Involuntarily Joyce shivered. There was something sinister about the man. She began to wish the Englishman would return, and as though in answer to her thought, the tall, straight figure emerged from the companion-way, and again began to pace the deck.

Joyce watched him out of the corners of her eyes. He was quite young, and had a nice, dependable-looking face. The Russian had stopped his uneasy pacing, and was also watching the Englishman with a look of anxious uncertainty in his eyes. Joyce felt suddenly thrilled. There was some mystery here. The Englishman appeared to be totally unconscious of the Russian's scrutiny—too unconscious, Joyce thought—and did not even turn his head when presently, as though he had just made up his mind about something, the Russian darted across the deck, and in his turn disappeared down the companion-way.

What followed happened so quickly that Joyce had no time to feel surprised. As the Russian disappeared, the Englishman ran to the head of the companion-way and glanced down the stairs ; then in a dozen long strides he had crossed the deck and was thrusting a thin, oilskin packet into the girl's hand.

" You're English, aren't you ? " he asked.   Then, hardly waiting for the girl's reply, he went on, " Take that, and hide it.   It's vitally important, national !  I daren't keep it ;  they'll be after me as soon as Orloff discovers it has gone.   Take it to the Foreign Office as soon as you can.   No, that won't do.   Grant's away, and I may not be there.   Wait till day after tomorrow.   Wednesday.   Understand ?   Ask for department X.Y.2—Captain Travers.   That's me.   If I'm not there, ask to see Major Grant, and give him that packet, and tell him everything.   Don't part with it to any one but Major Grant or me.   Got that ?   Good !   Who are you ? . . . Miss Hilliard, Brent Lodge, Godalming.   I'll remember.   And thank you.   Now go on looking over the side, and don't take any notice of me, and remember that the peace of England may depend upon your getting those papers through in safety."

He slid away from her side, and resumed his pacing up and down the deck.   Joyce hesitated a moment ;  then she turned her back on the man, and when she straightened herself the thin packet was no longer in her hand.   The girl leant on the rail, feeling very pleased with herself.   Bags could be snatched, but if they were going to get that packet from where it lay hidden under the top of her thin, silk stocking they would have to snatch her, and that wasn't so easily done.

To say that Joyce was thrilled is to describe her feelings lamely.   Who was the Englishman ?   A secret service man, surely, else why did he belong to a department with such an alluring title as X.Y.2 ?   And he had called the other man Orloff.   So she was right.   He was a Russian, and an enemy to England, and perhaps . . . The object of the girl's thoughts emerged from the companion-way.   He had another man with him, and they were talking together excitedly, and every now and then darted venomous glances at the pacing Englishman.   What were they going to do ?   Joyce wondered.

For the first time the possible danger of the situation dawned upon the girl.   The foreigners looked like men who would stick at nothing, and the packet she was carrying belonged to them.   The girl shivered, but not from fear.   She glanced at the Englishman.   He appeared wholly unconscious of the other men, and looked quite capable of taking care of himself.   Joyce felt vaguely comforted, but at the same time she realised a little of how important the papers must be.   That there might be danger to herself, if the Russians discovered that the Englishman had not got the packet, she did not doubt, for they would immediately become suspicious of her.   Yet the Englishman had not hesitated to expose her to the peril, and he did not look the sort of man to expose a girl to danger unless the occasion was of such supreme importance as to overshadow all personal feelings.   Joyce squared her shoulders.  Well, if the packet was as important as all that, she would get it through to its destination, no matter what the danger might be.

It soon became apparent that the enemy intended to take no immediate action.  Once or twice Joyce caught the Russians looking in her direction, but they made no efforts to speak to her, and presently she turned away to look after her luggage.  They were already entering Dover harbour, and soon she would be passing through the customs.  After all, the adventure promised to end tamely.  Once the Englishman had led the foreigners away from her, all risk of being followed would have ended, and there would be nothing to prevent her delivering the packet at X.Y.2 on the day after the morrow.

*" Take that, and hide it.  It's vitally important, national ! "*

But the voyage was not to end so tamely as Joyce feared.  There was a crush at the gangway, and as she waited her turn she was suddenly pushed violently from behind.  With a cry, the girl stumbled forward, colliding with a man in front, and at the same time she felt her bag jerked from beneath her arm.

" Hallo ! anything wrong ? " asked the man with whom she had collided.

" No.  I'm so sorry.  I stumbled," apologised the girl hastily as she turned round to look for her assailant.

But there was no one whom she could accuse.  Just behind her was a tall woman dressed in expensive clothes, and who returned her look with a frosty stare.  Joyce glanced beyond.  A lady and gentleman were next in the queue, but neither of them looked in the least like people who would snatch bags.  But one of them must have snatched it.  Somebody had pushed her, and had——

" Will you please move on. I am in a hurry, and you are holding every one back from the gangway."

The voice of a lady immediately behind her interrupted Joyce's thoughts, and after a moment's hesitation the girl obeyed. What was the good of making a fuss ? The bag was an old one, there was very little money in it, and nothing else of value. At that moment too she caught sight of her father waiting on the quay, and forgetting everything else she hurried across the gangway and flung herself into his arms, and it was not until they were speeding homeward in the car that Joyce remembered her lost bag. At the same moment she remembered the Englishman, and the Russians, and the papers she carried, and with remembrance came knowledge. The bag had not been stolen by an ordinary snatch-thief. Somehow the Russians had stolen it because they suspected her, and because they guessed that even if the papers weren't inside they would find her address in it, and so would be able to find her if the need arose. Suddenly Joyce felt afraid. There were two letters from home in her bag. How long, she wondered, before the Russians discovered that the young Englishman had not got the packet, and by the process of elimination decided that she and she alone could have taken their precious papers from him.

Mr. Hilliard found his daughter very quiet during the rest of the journey, but she brightened up when they reached home, and after she had had tea, and had heard all the news, Joyce went for a stroll round the garden. She visited the greenhouses, the potting shed, she talked with old Angus, the gardener, and so at last came to another shed hidden away in a corner of the grounds.

It was a shed which had always been the especial domain of Joyce and her brother Bob. There were odds and ends of furniture, a gramophone, and at one end, resting against the wall, stood Joyce's bicycle. The girl looked at the machine. It had a dilapidated appearance, but her brother had kept it oiled, and the tyres were still good. Joyce smiled. She would take up cycling again. It was awfully old-fashioned, of course, but why not ? For ten minutes longer she remained in the shed ; then she went out, locking the door carefully behind her, and returned to the house. It was fine being home again. Her thoughts went to the young Englishman. Had he eluded his enemies ? She hoped so. Joyce looked about her. It was too early yet for the enemy to appear, but if they caught the Englishman she might expect them before many hours were out.

Somewhat to Joyce's surprise, and to her great relief, the night passed uneventfully. For the first time in her life she had slept with closed windows, and as she flung them open to let in the morning sunshine she called herself all sorts of a coward. After all, she might be imagining the danger. The Russians might not have stolen her bag, in which case they did not know her address, and she would deliver the papers the next morning without interference. The girl decided to forget all about the precious packet for the day. She was playing golf in the morning ; in the afternoon some friends were coming to tennis ; and the next morning she would go up to town and deliver the packet. In spite of the thrill attached to its possession, she would be glad to get rid of it. Ever since she had spoken to the young Englishman she had felt as though she were living on the top of a volcano, where nothing ever did happen, but where something might happen with startling suddenness at any moment.

Joyce enjoyed her golf ; the tennis party was a great success ; and it was not until she was running upstairs to change, after saying good-bye to her guests, that she remembered the packet. With her fingers gripping the handle of the door, she paused. The enemy had made no sign, and surely that must mean that either the Englishman had escaped, or that they had been unable to trace her. Joyce was conscious of relief as she opened the door ; the next moment all her sense of security was shattered, and she stood gazing into her room with eyes wide with dismay and apprehension.

The room presented a scene of turmoil and devastation. The coverings had been torn from the bed, and the mattress slit open. All her drawers had been pulled out, and her clothes lay in a tumbled pile in the middle of the room, as though every garment she possessed had been examined before it had been tossed aside. The door of her wardrobe was open, and her dresses and coats had been flung out. Even the pictures on the walls hung awry, whilst the shelves of her bookcase stood empty, and all her cherished books lay torn and bent in a heap upon the floor.

Joyce's first impulse was to rush downstairs and proclaim her discovery, and she had reached the top of the stairs before she stopped herself. Ought she to tell her people what had happened ? Her father would immediately demand the packet, and she had promised not to part with it to any one but the young Englishman or the man he had named. Besides, would the papers be any safer with her father than with her ? Joyce decided to say nothing of her discovery, and having locked herself in her room, she started to tidy up the turmoil her enemies had made. As she did so her dismay

*The room presented a scene of turmoil and devastation*

turned to anger. She would beat the brutes yet! They had searched her room when every one was in the garden, but they hadn't found the papers, and they wouldn't find them, and if she were careful they would never know who had had them, or how they reached their destination in department X.Y.2.

Joyce lay awake a long time that night making her plans for the morrow. She did not imagine that the Russians would be satisfied with searching her room. They would guess that she had hidden the packet in some other place, and would have set a watch upon her, and the real danger would begin when she started for town the next morning. Somehow she had got to outwit them, and persuade them that she had not got the papers. But how? Joyce had plenty of pluck, but when at last she thought of a plan it took her a long time to summon up enough courage to carry it through. The enemy might let her pass unsuspecting, but if they didn't she would be putting her head right in the lion's mouth. Yet what a glorious way of outwitting the foreigners. Besides, she could think of no other plan which, in spite of the risks, held such promise of success. The Russians would never imagine . . . Joyce fell asleep, and dreamed that all foreign spies and trouble-makers were fleeing the country in terror lest she should discover them and hand them over to justice.

.   .   .   .   .   .   .   .   .   .   .   .   .   .

"I'm going for a bicycle ride this morning, mother."

The Hilliard family were seated at breakfast, and despite Joyce's effort to speak naturally her announcement created a small sensation.

"A bicycle ride, my dear," repeated Mrs. Hilliard; "but surely——"

"A bicycle ride!" Bob Hilliard, folding his napkin preparatory to starting for town, guffawed loudly. "My dear old girl, what's wrong with you? Miss Hilliard, fresh from Paris——"

"I'm going for a bicycle ride!" Joyce interrupted doggedly. "And for the life of me I can't see why everybody should jeer."

"I am not jeering, my dear," her father assured her with a twinkle in his eyes. "Cycling is a very healthy exercise, and I should much prefer to see you adopt it in preference to motoring. Where are you going?"

The girl looked at her father suspiciously.

"Oh, just round about," she answered vaguely. "And I'm not sure I shall take it up definitely. I'm just going to—just going to—oh, dash it all, why must you all laugh just because I want to take the old bike out this morning?"

Half an hour later Joyce set out. She turned her back on Godalming and the London Road, and started along a lane leading into the country. As she rode she kept a sharp look out. A farm hand passed her, and bade her a cheerful "good-morning"; a motor cyclist whizzed by; a motor van from Godalming overtook her, and disappeared round a bend ahead; but she saw no one in the least like a foreigner, and gradually, as she cycled along, she began to think that her plan had succeeded, and that if anyone had been on the watch he had concluded she was merely going for a country spin, and had let her pass. A feeling of elation took possession of the girl, and as she covered mile after mile and nothing happened, her sense of security increased, and she gave herself up to the enjoyment of the ride.

Joyce had ridden five miles. She had passed a few houses, but most of the way lay between fields and woodland, and she was riding along a particularly lonely stretch of road when, on rounding a corner, she saw before her a steep hill, with the van, which had passed her some way back, drawn up by the roadside half-way up the rise. Joyce rode up the hill until the slope became too steep ; then she jumped off and started to walk. It was warm work pushing the bicycle up the hill, and as she neared the van the thought came to Joyce that she might beg a lift for the rest of the way, and so save valuable time. But where was the driver ? The girl stopped and looked about her, but the driver of the van was nowhere in sight, and she was about to start forward again when a rustling amongst the undergrowth by the side of the road caused her to look round in alarm. Who was hiding amongst the bushes ? Suddenly Joyce felt very much afraid, and she was turning her bicycle round when two masked men rose out of the bushes and rushed at her across the road.

Joyce had just time to utter a cry of fear ; then her assailants were upon her, a sack had been thrown over her head, and rough hands were tying her wrists together. In vain she struggled. She was helpless against her adversaries, and a moment later she was lifted bodily from the ground, and thrown down inside the van. From in front came the roar of the engine starting up ; she heard her bicycle being put in beside her ; then came the sound of doors being shut, and the next moment the van was speeding up the hill away from the scene of the brief struggle by the roadside.

Where were they taking her ? Joyce was feeling very frightened. She had been so sure that she had outwitted the Russians, and here she was a helpless prisoner, and being carried she knew not whither. Desperately she strove to conquer her fears. What would her captors do when they discovered that she had not got the papers ? Would they let her go, or would they resort to threats or worse to make her tell them where they were ? The girl tried to comfort herself with the thought that her enemies would not have masked themselves had they intended to keep her indefinitely a prisoner. But it was poor comfort. She began bitterly to regret her determination to carry the adventure through alone. No one knew where she had been going, or what she had intended to do. No one. . . . A sudden bumping interrupted the girl's thoughts, and she guessed that the van had turned off the road, and was proceeding along a rough track. For perhaps five minutes the bumping continued before the van stopped, and Joyce felt herself lifted out and carried some distance. She heard the creak of a door and the thud of heavy boots on bare boards, voices reached her speaking in some foreign language ; then she was set upon her feet, and some one began to untie the rope which bound her arms together.

Joyce struggled free from the suffocating sack, and drew a deep breath of relief. She was in an empty room. The rotting boards were covered with grime, and the colour wash had long ago flaked off the crumbling walls. Sunshine streamed through a broken window, showing great cobwebs festooning the dirty ceiling, whilst beyond the window lay a thick wall of green foliage. Joyce decided that she was in a forsaken cottage buried deep in the heart of a wood ; then she turned to confront the other occupants of the room.

The girl saw a tall woman. A black mask covered the top half of the woman's face; yet, despite the disguise, there was something vaguely familiar to Joyce in the firm chin and tall, commanding figure of her gaoler. Where had she seen the woman before? The next instant the answer came to her. She remembered her snatched bag, and the woman who had been standing behind her, and had coldly requested her to move on. This was the same woman, and she was about to put her accusation into words, when something checked her. She mustn't let the woman know she had recognised her. If she——

"Take off your clothes."

The words, uttered in the cool, precise voice of her gaoler, brought Joyce's reflections to an abrupt end.

"Take my clothes off," the girl repeated slowly. Then, with rising anger, "Whatever do you mean? How dare you bring me here, and make such a ridiculous demand? Of course I shall do nothing of the kind."

"Don't be a fool, child," answered the other impatiently. "Oh! I know you are young and strong, but I am strong also, stronger than you. So obey. We mean you no harm, but I am here to search you, and search you I will if I have to tear every garment off your body."

"You beast," cried Joyce in helpless rage, "you utter, utter beast! What is it you want? I have got nothing."

The woman shrugged her shoulders.

"I will forgive your hard words," she said, "and as for the rest, we shall see. If——"

She broke off with a cry of anger. Joyce had suddenly made a spring for the door, and the girl had her hand upon the latch before the woman reached her and dragged her back.

"So," snapped the woman, "you would try tricks and, little one, it is not wise to try tricks with me."

Her grip on Joyce tightened, and suddenly the girl felt a numbing pain shoot through her limbs, and all strength seemed to flow out of her body so that she could hardly stand.

"You see," continued the woman, releasing her hold, "I am your master. Now do you obey, or do I find that little nerve again, and press on it harder than before? Come, child, in five minutes it will be done, and you will be free, so why all this fuss?"

It was perhaps the thought of freedom and all that freedom meant, more than the fear of physical pain, which made Joyce submit to the in-dignity of being searched. One by one she handed her garments to the woman, but when ten minutes later she stood facing her gaoler, again fully dressed, nothing incriminating had been found upon her.

"It would seem that we have been mistaken," the woman admitted grudgingly. "But who has them?" she went on, evidently speaking to herself. "Curses on the Englishman, he was cleverer than we thought." She turned again to the girl. "Now listen, child," she warned. "I am leaving here, but if you value your life you will remain in this room for ten minutes before you leave the cottage. At the end of that time you are free. You will find your bicycle outside, and if you are wise you will say nothing to anybody of what has happened this morning."

Next moment Joyce was alone.

Joyce ran to the window. From the front of the cottage came the sound of a motor, and as she listened the sound gradually receded in the distance until it died away altogether. The girl looked at her watch. She had no intention of disobeying the woman by leaving the cottage before the ten minutes were up—something in the other's voice had warned Joyce that it was no idle threat her enemy was uttering—and now the girl eagerly watched the hands of her watch tick out the stipulated time. It was eleven o'clock. In eight minutes she would be free to go. There was a train at eleven forty-five from Cranleigh to London. She might just do it. Five minutes more. She had been right in making for Cranleigh instead of going up to town from Godalming. There was no knowing what those foreigners

*Joyce had her hand upon the latch before the woman reached her*

might have done if they had been driven to desperation, but now she had put her head right into the lion's mouth and had come out unharmed, and they would no longer be suspicious of her. Slowly a smile of triumph overspread the girl's face. She had won. She looked at her watch. It was eight minutes past eleven. Time to go.

It is not a very usual sight to see a pretty girl, dressed in expensive clothes, riding a battered old bicycle down Whitehall, and many people turned to watch Joyce's progress down the historic thoroughfare. Still more unusual is it for such a person to stop at the main entrance to the Foreign Office, and to demand an instant interview with the head of a very important branch of the secret service.

"Captain Travers, he ain't here, miss, and I don't know that Major Grant'll be able to see you," replied the commissionaire, gazing dubiously at Joyce's battered machine.

"Oh! Yes, he will," retorted Joyce stoutly. "Tell Major Grant that I come from Captain Travers, and have an important message for him. And please take my bicycle with you. I don't want to leave it outside."

"The bicycle, miss, but surely——"

Joyce stamped her foot.

"Man," she cried impatiently, "don't stand there dithering. I tell you it's important, desperately important." She picked up the bicycle and walked past the commissionaire. " If you won't carry it, I will, but I'm going to see Major Grant, and the bicycle goes with me ! "

It may have been Joyce's manner, or it may have been that she always looked her prettiest when flushed with excitement, but all at once the commissionaire ceased to dither, and having called a messenger he bade him carry the bicycle for the young lady, and led her to the office of the head of X.Y.2.  So it happened that some minutes later Joyce found herself facing a short, grey-haired, little man whose steely blue eyes seemed to go right through her, and to read the secrets of her inmost soul.

" Miss Joyce Hilliard," said the little man, looking at the card he held in his hand.  " I don't know you, Miss Hilliard, but still sit down.  And why the bicycle ? "

" I'll tell you about that later," said Joyce quickly.  " But first tell me where Captain Travers is."

" I am afraid that is impossible," replied the little man.

" Impossible !  Why ? " snapped Joyce.  " Because you won't, or because you can't ! "

For some seconds Major Grant sat regarding the girl before him ; then he answered :

" Because I can't."

" So they have him."

The little man leant suddenly forward.

" Who have him ?  Answer me.  Quick !  What do you know about Captain Travers ? "

" Why, Orloff and his Russians have him, of course," replied the girl.  " The Russians who were in the steamer with us, and who kidnapped me and searched me two hours ago."

" Kidnapped you and searched you ! "  The little man leaned back in his chair, and for the first time the frosty eyes softened.  " We are putting the cart before the horse, Miss Hilliard," he said.  " I see you have a tale to tell.  Suppose you tell it from the beginning, and then I will tell you all I know, and perhaps between us we may be able to do something to help Captain Travers.  He is a very valued assistant of mine, and I should regret to lose him."

Joyce smiled.  Suddenly the little man with the cold, blue eyes had become human, and settling herself comfortably in her chair she told her story from beginning to end.  Major Grant listened without interrupting and it was not until Joyce ceased speaking that he asked the question which must have been hammering in his brain for many minutes past.

" And the packet ? "

Joyce smiled.

" Why, I——"

The door of the room was suddenly flung open, and a tall, young man appeared on the threshold.  For a moment he stood poised in the doorway ; the next his eyes alighted on Joyce, and a look of relief overspread his good-looking face.

" Thank Heaven, you're safe ! " he cried.  " Those swine nabbed me, and when they found I hadn't got the papers they told me they knew who had, and that they were going down to Godalming to get them.  I was in a terrible stew. All yesterday they watched me as a cat watches a mouse, but this morning I managed to escape, and went straight down to Godalming, only to discover that you had gone for a bicycle ride. Heavens, but I had the wind up! Though I couldn't understand the bicycle. Why go——"

His eyes fell upon the bicycle leaning against the wall, and opened with wide surprise.

" You don't mean to say you rode all the way up here with——"

" Sit down, Travers." Major Grant's voice interrupted the younger man's excited question. " I am very glad to see you, for, from what Miss Hilliard has been telling me, I confess I was beginning to feel rather anxious about you. Now sit down, my good fellow. Miss Hilliard is quite all right despite various adventures, and if I guess rightly she was going to tell me something about that bicycle when you came dashing into the room. Was it not so, Miss Hilliard ? " Joyce turned her eyes to the older man, and nodded.

" Yes," she began. " You see, when I arrived home with the papers I naturally wondered what I should do with them. I had to hide the packet where no one would find it, and also to think of some way of getting it here without having it stolen on the way."

" So you thought of your bicycle, and killed two birds with one stone," put in the little man calmly. Again Joyce nodded.

" Will you please turn my bicycle upside down ? " she said, turning to Captain Travers.

The young man obeyed, and would have helped her further, but she waved him back. With breathless interest the two men watched the girl. She let the air out of the front tyre ; then, with the aid of two levers which she took from her bag, she prised the outer cover away from the steel rim, and thrust her slim fingers into the space between the inner tube and the tyre. For some seconds she spun the wheel slowly round ; then she stopped it, and the next moment Joyce had turned to face the men, a smile of triumph on her lips.

" The papers," she said, holding out a thin, oilskin packet to Captain Travers.

.    .    .    .    .    .    .    .    .    .    .    .    .    .

Two hours later Joyce and Captain Travers returned to department X.Y.2 after having partaken of the most perfect lunch Joyce had ever eaten. They found Major Grant sitting at his desk, gazing straight in front of him, but as they entered he rose to his feet, and took the girl by the hand.

" My dear," he said, " I hope you are not expecting a speech, for I am a man of few words. The papers in that packet contain the plans for a great revolutionary upheaval in this country, together with a list of all the foreign agents and communists who are doing their best to create unrest." He paused a moment, and then went on: " There are many brave and clever men and women belonging to my department, but I do not think that any one of them has ever performed a greater service to this country, or has displayed more wit and courage in carrying through the allotted task, than you have done in bringing those papers safely through to me. What do you say, Travers ? I think Miss Hilliard is a credit to X.Y.2."

" I am with you there all the way, sir," replied the young man heartily, gazing admiringly at the blushing girl.

# THE PEDLAR'S CARAVAN

### by WILLIAM BRIGHTY RANDS

I WISH I lived in a caravan,
With a horse to drive, like the pedlar-man !
Where he comes from nobody knows,
Or where he goes to, but on he goes !

His caravan has windows two,
And a chimney of tin, that the smoke comes through ;
He has a wife, with a baby brown,
And they go riding from town to town.

Chairs to mend, and delf to sell !
He clashes the basins like a bell ;
Tea-trays, baskets ranged in order,
Plates, with alphabets round the border !

The roads are brown, and the sea is green,
But his house is like a bathing-machine ;
The world is round, and he can ride,
Rumble and slash, to the other side !

With the pedlar-man I should like to roam,
And write a book when I came home ;
All the people would read my book,
Just like the Travels of Captain Cook !

# Macbeth

### by CHARLES AND MARY LAMB

WHEN Duncan the Meek reigned king of Scotland, there lived a great thane, or lord, called Macbeth. This Macbeth was a near kinsman to the king, and in great esteem at court for his valour and conduct in the wars ; an example of which he had lately given, in defeating a rebel army assisted by the troops of Norway in terrible numbers.

The two Scottish generals, Macbeth and Banquo, returning victorious from this great battle, their way lay over a blasted heath, where they were stopped by the strange appearance of three figures like women, except that they had beards, and their withered skins and wild attire made them look not like any earthly creatures. Macbeth first addressed them, when they, seemingly offended, laid each one her choppy finger upon her skinny lips, in token of silence ; and the first of them saluted Macbeth with the title of Thane of Glamis.

The general was not a little startled to find himself known by such creatures ; but how much more, when the second of them followed up that salute by giving him the title of Thane of Cawdor, to which honour he had no pretensions ; and again the third bid him : " All hail ! king that shalt be hereafter ! " Such a prophetic greeting might well amaze him, who knew that while the king's sons lived he could not hope to succeed to the throne.

Then turning to Banquo, they pronounced him, in a sort of riddling terms, to be *lesser than Macbeth and greater ! not so happy, but much happier !*

and prophesied that though he should never reign, yet his sons after him should be kings in Scotland. They then turned into air, and vanished ; by which the generals knew them to be the weird sisters, or witches.

While they stood pondering on the strangeness of this adventure, there arrived certain messengers from the king, who were empowered by him to confer upon Macbeth the dignity of Thane of Cawdor ; an event so miraculously corresponding with the prediction of the witches as to astonish Macbeth, and he stood wrapt in amazement, unable to make reply to the messengers ; and in that point of time swelling hopes arose in his mind that the prediction of the third witch might in like manner have its accomplishment, and that he should one day reign king in Scotland.

Turning to Banquo, he said : " Do you not hope that your children shall be kings, when what the witches promised to me has so wonderfully come to pass ? "

" That hope," answered the general, " might enkindle you to aim at the throne ; but oftentimes these ministers of darkness tell us truths in little things, to betray us into deeds of greatest consequence."

But the wicked suggestions of the witches had sunk too deep into the mind of Macbeth to allow him to attend to the warnings of the good Banquo. From that time he bent all his thoughts how to compass the throne of Scotland.

Macbeth had a wife, to whom he communicated the strange prediction of the weird sisters, and its partial accomplishment. She was a bad, ambitious woman, and so as her husband and herself could arrive at greatness, she cared not much by what means. She spurred on the reluctant purpose of Macbeth, who felt compunction at the thoughts of blood, and did not cease to represent the murder of the king as a step absolutely necessary to the fulfilment of the flattering prophecy.

It happened at this time that the king, who out of his royal condescension would oftentimes visit his principal nobility upon gracious terms, came to Macbeth's house, attended by his two sons, Malcolm and Donalbain, and a numerous train of thanes and attendants, the more to honour Macbeth for the triumphal success of his wars.

The castle of Macbeth was pleasantly situated, and the air about it was sweet and wholesome, which appeared by the nests which the martlet, or swallow, had built under all the jutting friezes and buttresses of the building, wherever it found a place of advantage ; for where those birds most breed and haunt, the air is observed to be delicate. The king entered, well pleased with the place, and not less so with the attentions and respect of his honoured hostess, Lady Macbeth, who had the art of covering treacherous purposes with smiles ; and could look like the innocent flower, while she was indeed the serpent under it.

The king being tired with his journey, went early to bed, and in his state-room two grooms of his chamber (as was the custom) slept beside him. He had been unusually pleased with his reception, and had made presents to his principal officers before he retired ; and among the rest, had sent a rich diamond to Lady Macbeth, greeting her by the name of his most kind hostess.

Now was the middle of night, when over half the world nature seems dead, and wicked dreams abuse men's minds asleep, and none but the wolf and the murderer is abroad. This was the time when Lady Macbeth waked to plot the murder of the king. She would not have undertaken so horrible a deed, but that she feared her husband's nature was too kind. She knew him to be ambitious, but withal to be scrupulous, and not yet prepared for such a monstrous crime. She had won him to consent to the murder, but she doubted his resolution ; and she feared that the natural tenderness of his disposition (more humane than her own) would come between and defeat the purpose.

So she herself approached the king's bed ; having taken care to ply the grooms of his chamber so with wine that they slept intoxicated, and careless of their charge. But she had not the courage to proceed, and returned to

*She had won him to consent to the murder, but she doubted his resolution*

confer with her husband ; his resolution had begun to stagger. He considered that there were strong reasons against the deed. In the first place, he was not only a subject, but a near kinsman to the king ; and he had been his host and entertainer that day, whose duty, by the laws of hospitality, it was to shut the door against his murderers.

Then he considered how just and merciful a king this Duncan had been, how clear of offence to his subjects, how loving to his nobility, and in particular to him ; that such kings are the peculiar care of Heaven, and their subjects doubly bound to revenge their deaths. Besides, by the favours of the king, Macbeth stood high in the opinion of all sorts of men, and how would those honours be stained by the reputation of so foul a murder !

In these conflicts of the mind Lady Macbeth found her husband inclining to the better part and resolved to proceed no further. But she being a woman not easily shaken from her evil purpose, began to pour in at his ears words which infused a portion of her own spirit into his mind, assigning reason upon reason why he should not shrink from what he had undertaken ; how easy the deed was ; how soon it would be over ; and how the action of one short night would give to all their nights and days to come sovereign sway and royalty !

Then she threw contempt on his change of purpose, and accused him of fickleness and cowardice. Then she added how practicable it was to lay the guilt of the deed upon the drunken, sleepy grooms. And with the valour of her tongue she so chastised his sluggish resolutions that he once more summoned up courage.

So, taking the dagger in his hand, he softly stole in the dark to the room where Duncan lay. Getting rid of his fear, he entered the king's room, whom he despatched with one stroke of his dagger. Just as he had done the murder, one of the grooms, who slept in the chamber, laughed in his sleep, and the other cried " Murder ! " which woke them both ; but they said a short prayer ; one of them said : " God bless us ! " and the other answered " Amen " and addressed themselves to sleep again. Macbeth, who stood listening to them, tried to say " Amen " when the fellow said " God bless us ! " but, though he had most need of a blessing, the word stuck in his throat, and he could not pronounce it.

Again he thought he heard a voice which cried : " Sleep no more : Macbeth doth murder sleep, the innocent sleep, that nourishes life." Still it cried, " Sleep no more," to all the house. " Glamis hath murdered sleep, and therefore Cawdor shall sleep no more, Macbeth shall sleep no more."

With such horrible imaginations Macbeth returned to his listening wife, who began to think he had failed of his purpose, and that the deed was somehow frustrated.

Morning came, and with it the discovery of the murder, which could not be concealed ; and though Macbeth and his lady made great show of grief, and the proofs against the grooms were sufficiently strong, yet the entire suspicion fell upon Macbeth, whose inducements to such a deed were so much more forcible than such poor silly grooms could be supposed to have ; and Duncan's two sons fled. Malcolm, the eldest, sought for refuge in the English court ; and the youngest, Donalbain, made his escape to Ireland.

The king's sons, who should have succeeded him, having thus vacated the throne, Macbeth as next heir was crowned king, and thus the prediction of the weird sisters was literally accomplished.

Though placed so high, Macbeth and his queen could not forget the prophecy of the weird sisters, that, though Macbeth should be king, yet not his children, but the children of Banquo, should be kings after him. The thought of this, and that they had done so great crimes, only to place the posterity of Banquo upon the throne, so rankled within them that they determined to put to death both Banquo and his son, to make void the prediction of the weird sisters, which in their own case had been so remarkably brought to pass.

For this purpose they made a great supper, to which they invited all the chief thanes ; and, among the rest, with marks of particular respect, Banquo and his son Fleance were invited. The way by which Banquo was to pass to the palace at night was beset by murderers appointed by Macbeth, who stabbed Banquo ; but in the scuffle Fleance escaped. From that Fleance descended a race of monarchs who afterwards filled the Scottish throne, ending with James the Sixth of Scotland and the First of England, under whom the two crowns of England and Scotland were united.

At supper, the queen, whose manners were in the highest degree affable and royal, played the hostess with the gracefulness and attention which conciliated every one present, and Macbeth discoursed freely with his thanes and nobles, saying that all that was honourable in the country was under his roof, if he had but his good friend Banquo present, whom yet he hoped he should rather have to chide for neglect than to lament for any mischance.

Just at these words the ghost of Banquo entered the room and placed himself on the chair which Macbeth was about to occupy. Though Macbeth was a bold man, at this horrible sight his cheeks turned white with fear, and he stood quite unmanned with his eyes fixed upon the ghost. His queen and all the nobles, who saw nothing, but perceived him gazing (as they thought) upon an empty chair, took it for a fit of distraction, and they reproached him.

But Macbeth continued to see the ghost, and gave no heed to all they could say, while he addressed it with distracted words, yet so significant, that his queen, fearing the dreadful secret would be disclosed, in great haste dismissed the guests, excusing the infirmity of Macbeth as a disorder he was often troubled with.

To such dreadful fancies Macbeth was subject. His queen and he had their sleep afflicted with terrible dreams, and the death of Banquo troubled them not more than the escape of Fleance, whom now they looked upon as father to a line of kings who should keep their posterity out of the throne. With these miserable thoughts they found no peace, and Macbeth determined once more to seek out the weird sisters, and know from them the worst.

He sought them in a cave upon the heath, where they, who knew by foresight of his coming, were engaged in preparing their dreadful charms, by which they conjured up spirits to reveal to them futurity. Their horrid ingredients were such things as toads, bats, and serpents, the eye of a newt, the leg of a lizard, and the wing of the night-owl, the scale of a dragon, the tooth of a wolf, and the root of the poisonous hemlock (this to have effect must be digged in the dark). All these were set on to boil in a great kettle, or cauldron, and by their charms they bound the spirits to answer their questions.

It was demanded of Macbeth whether he would have his doubts re-solved by them, or by their masters, the spirits. He, nothing daunted by the dreadful ceremonies which he saw, boldly answered : " Where are they ? let me see them." And they called the spirits, which were three. And the first arose in the likeness of an armed head ; and he called Macbeth by name, and bid him beware of the Thane of Fife ; for which caution Macbeth thanked him ; for Macbeth had entertained a jealousy of Macduff, the Thane of Fife.

And the second spirit arose in the likeness of a child, and he called Macbeth by name, and bid him have no fear, but laugh to scorn the power of man, for none of woman born should have power to hurt him ; and he advised him to be bold and resolute. " Then live, Macduff ! " cried the king. " What need I fear of thee ? but yet I will make assurance doubly sure. Thou shalt not live ; that I may tell pale-hearted Fear it lies, and sleep in spite of thunder."

That spirit being dismissed, a third arose in the form of a child crowned, with a tree in his hand. He called Macbeth by name, and comforted him against conspiracies, saying that he should never be vanquished until the wood of Birnam to Dunsinane Hill should come against him. " Sweet bodements ! good ! " cried Macbeth ; " who can unfix the forest, and move it from its earth-bound roots ? I see I shall live the usual period of man's life, and not be cut off by a violent death. But my heart throws to know one thing. Tell me, if your art can tell so much, if Banquo's issue shall ever reign in this kingdom ? "

Here the cauldron sank into the ground, and a noise of music was heard, and eight shadows, like kings, passed by Macbeth, and Banquo last, who bore a glass which showed the figures of many more, and Banquo smiled upon Macbeth, and pointed to them ; by which Macbeth knew that these were the posterity of Banquo, who should reign after him in Scotland ; and the witches, with a sound of soft music, and with dancing, making a show of duty and welcome to Macbeth, vanished. And from this time the thoughts of Macbeth were all dreadful.

The first thing he heard when he got out of the witches' cave was that Macduff, Thane of Fife, had fled to England, to join the army which was forming against him under Malcolm, the eldest son of the late King, with intent to displace Macbeth and set Malcolm, the right heir, upon the throne. Macbeth, stung with rage, attacked the castle of Macduff, and set upon all who claimed the least relationship to Macduff.

These and such-like deeds alienated the minds of all his chief nobility from him. Such as could, fled to join with Malcolm and Macduff, who were now approaching with a powerful army which they had raised in England ; and the rest secretly wished success to their arms, though for fear of Macbeth they could take no active part. His recruits went on slowly. Everybody hated the tyrant ; nobody loved or honoured him ; but all suspected him, and he began to envy the condition of Duncan, whom he had murdered, who slept soundly in his grave, against whom treason had done its worst : steel nor poison, domestic malice nor foreign levies, could hurt him any longer.

While these things were acting, the queen, who had been the sole partner in his wickedness, in whose bosom he could sometimes seek a momentary repose from those terrible dreams which afflicted them both nightly, died, unable to bear the remorse of guilt and public hate ; by which event he was left alone, without a soul to love or care for him, or a friend to whom he could confide his wicked purposes.

He grew careless of life, and wished for death ; but the near approach of Malcolm's army roused in him what remained of his ancient courage, and he determined to die (as he expressed it), " with armour on his back." Besides this, the hollow promises of the witches had filled him with a false confidence, and he remembered the saying of the spirits, that none of woman born was to hurt him, and that he was never to be vanquished till Birnam wood should come to Dunsinane, which he thought could never be.

So he shut himself up in his castle, whose impregnable strength was such as defied a siege : here he sullenly waited the approach of Malcolm. When, upon a day, there came a messenger to him, pale and shaking with fear, almost unable to report that which he had seen ; for he averred that as he stood upon his watch on the hill he looked towards Birnam, and to his thinking the wood began to move ! Macbeth now began to faint in resolution, and to doubt the equivocal speeches of the spirits.

He was not to fear till Birnam wood should come to Dunsinane ; and now a wood did move ! "However," said he, "if this which he avouches be true, let us arm and out. There is no flying hence, nor staying here. I begin to be weary of the sun, and wish my life at an end." With these desperate speeches he sallied forth upon the besiegers, who had now come up to the castle.

The strange appearance, which had given the messenger an idea of a wood moving, is easily solved. When the besieging army marched through the wood of Birnam, Malcolm, like a skilful general, instructed his soldiers to hew down every one a bough and bear it before him, by way of concealing the true number of his host. This marching of the soldiers with boughs had at a distance the appearance which had frightened the messenger. Thus were the words of the spirit brought to pass, in a sense different from that in which Macbeth had understood them, and one great hold of his confidence was gone.

And now a severe skirmishing took place, in which Macbeth, though feebly supported by those who called themselves his friends, but in reality hated the tyrant and inclined to the party of Malcolm and Macduff, yet fought with the extreme of rage and valour till he came to where Macduff was fighting.

Seeing Macduff, and remembering the caution of the spirit who had counselled him to avoid Macduff above all men, he would have turned, but Macduff, who had been seeking him through the whole fight, opposed his turning, and a fierce contest ensued. Macbeth, whose soul was charged enough with blood of that family already, would still have declined the combat ; but Macduff still urged him to it, calling him tyrant, murderer, and villain.

Then Macbeth remembered the words of the spirit, how none of woman born should hurt him ; and smiling confidently he said to Macduff, " Thou losest thy labour, Macduff. As easily thou mayest impress the air with thy sword as make me vulnerable. I bear a charmed life, which must not yield to one of woman born."

" Despair thy charm," said Macduff, " and let that lying spirit whom thou hast served tell thee that Macduff was never born of woman, never as the ordinary manner of men is to be born."

" Accursed be the tongue which tells me so," said the trembling Macbeth, who felt his last hold of confidence give way ; " and let never man in future believe the lying equivocations of witches and juggling spirits, who deceive us in words which have double senses, and while they keep their promise literally, disappoint our hopes with a different meaning. I will not fight with thee."

" Then live ! " said the scornful Macduff ; " we will have a show of

*He threw himself upon Macduff, who in the end overcame him*

thee, as men show monsters, and a painted board, on which shall be written, ' Here men may see the tyrant ! ' "

"Never," said Macbeth, whose courage returned with despair ; " I will not live to kiss the ground before young Malcolm's feet, and to be baited with the curses of the rabble. Though Birnam wood be come to Dunsinane, and though opposed to me who wast never born of woman, yet will I try the last."

With these frantic words he threw himself upon Macduff, who, after a severe struggle, in the end overcame him. Malcolm took upon him the government which, by the machinations of the usurper, he had so long been deprived of, and ascended the throne of Duncan the Meek, amid the acclamations of the nobles and the people.

---

# GRACE FOR A CHILD

*by* ROBERT HERRICK

HERE a little child I stand,
Heaving up my either hand ;
Cold as Paddocks though they be,
Here I lift them up to thee,
For a Benison to fall
On our meat, and on us all.

# THE FAIRIES

*by* WILLIAM ALLINGHAM

UP the airy mountain,
  Down the rushy glen,
We daren't go a-hunting
  For fear of little men—
Wee folk, good folk,
  Trooping all together;
Green jacket, red cap,
  And white owl's feather.

Down along the rocky shore
  Some make their home;
They live on crispy pancakes
  Of yellow tide-foam;
Some in the reeds
  Of the black mountain lake,
With frogs for their watch-dogs,
  All night awake.

High on the hill-top
  The old king sits;
He is now so old and grey
  He's nigh lost his wits.
With a bridge of white mist
  Columbkill he crosses,
On his stately journeys
  From Slieveleague to Rosses;
Or going up with music,
  On cold starry nights,
To sup with the queen
  Of the gay Northern Lights.

They stole little Bridget
   For seven years long ;
When she came down again
   Her friends were all gone.
They took her lightly back
   Between the night and morrow ;
They thought that she was fast asleep,
   But she was dead with sorrow.
They have kept her ever since
   Deep within the lake,
On a bed of flag leaves,
   Watching till she wake.

By the craggy hillside,
   Through the mosses bare,
They have planted thorn-trees
   For pleasure here and there.
Is the man so daring
   As dig them up in spite ?
He shall find their sharpest thorns
   In his bed at night.

Up the airy mountain,
   Down the rushy glen,
We daren't go a-hunting
   For fear of little men—
Wee folk, good folk,
   Trooping all together ;
Green jacket, red cap,
   And white owl's feather.

MILDRED
R. LAMB.

# The Wood Maiden

### by PARKER FILLMORE

BETUSHKA was a little girl. Her mother was a poor widow, with nothing but a tumble-down cottage and two little nanny-goats. But, poor as they were, Betushka was always cheerful. From spring till autumn, she pastured the goats in the birch wood. Every morning, when she left home, her mother gave her a little basket with a slice of bread and a spindle.

"See that you bring home a full spindle," her mother always said.

Betushka had no distaff, so she wound the flax around her head. Then she took the little basket and went romping and singing behind the goats to the birch wood. When they got there, she sat down under a tree and pulled the fibres of the flax from her head with her left hand, and with her right hand let down the spindle, so that it went humming along the ground. All the while she sang until the woods echoed, and the little goats nibbled away at the leaves and grass.

When the sun showed midday, she put the spindle aside, called the goats, and gave them a mouthful of bread, so that they wouldn't stray, and ran off into the woods to hunt berries or any other wild fruit that was in season. Then, when she had finished her bread and fruit, she jumped up, folded her arms, and danced and sang.

The sun smiled at her through the green of the trees, and the little goats, resting on the grass, thought: "What a merry little shepherdess we have!"

After her dance she went back to her spinning and worked industriously. In the evening, when she got home, her mother never had to scold her because the spindle was empty.

One day at noon, just after she had eaten and, as usual, was going to dance, there suddenly stood before her a most beautiful maiden. She was

185

dressed in white gauze that was fine as a spider's web. Long golden hair fell down to her waist, and on her head she wore a wreath of woodland flowers.

Betushka was speechless with surprise and alarm.

The maiden smiled at her, and said in a sweet voice :

" Betushka, do you like to dance ? "

Her manner was so gracious that Betushka no longer felt afraid, and answered :

" Oh, I could dance all day long ! "

" Come, then, let us dance together," said the maiden. " I'll teach you."

With that she tucked up her skirt, put her arm about Betushka's waist, and they began to dance. At once such enchanting music sounded over their heads that Betushka's heart went one-two with the dancing. The musicians sat on the branches of the birch trees. They were clad in little frock coats, black and gray, and many-coloured. It was a carefully chosen orchestra that had gathered at the bidding of the beautiful maiden : larks, nightingales, finches, linnets, thrushes, blackbirds, and showy mocking-birds.

Betushka's cheeks burned, her eyes shone. She forgot her spinning, she forgot her goats. All she could do was gaze at her partner, who was moving with such grace and lightness that the grass didn't seem to bend under her slender feet.

They danced from noon till sundown and yet Betushka wasn't the least bit tired. Then they stopped dancing, the music ceased, and the maiden disappeared as suddenly as she had come.

Betushka looked around. The sun was sinking behind the wood. She put her hands to the unspun flax on her head and remembered the spindle that was lying unfilled on the grass. She took down the flax and laid it with the spindle in the little basket. Then she called the goats and started for home.

She reproached herself bitterly that she had allowed the beautiful maiden to beguile her, and she told herself that another time she would not listen to her. She was so quiet that the little goats, missing her merry song, looked around to see whether it was really their own little shepherdess who was following them. Her mother, too, wondered why she didn't sing, and questioned her.

" Are you sick, Betushka ? "

" No, dear mother, I'm not sick, but I've been singing too much and my throat is dry."

She knew that her mother did not reel the yarn at once, so she hid the spindle and the unspun flax, hoping to make up to-morrow what she had not done to-day. She did not tell her mother one word about the beautiful maiden.

The next day she felt cheerful again, and as she drove the goats to pasture she sang merrily. At the birch wood she sat down to her spinning, singing all the while, for with a song on the lips work falls from the hands more easily.

Noonday came. Betushka gave a bit of bread to each of the goats and ran off to the woods for her berries. Then she ate her luncheon.

"Ah, my little goats," she sighed, as she brushed up the crumbs for the birds. "I mustn't dance to-day."

"Why mustn't you dance to-day?" a sweet voice asked, and there stood the beautiful maiden, as though she had fallen from the clouds.

Betushka was worse frightened than before and she closed her eyes tight. When the maiden repeated her question, Betushka answered timidly:

"Forgive me, beautiful lady, for not dancing with you. If I dance with you, I cannot spin my stint, and then my mother will scold me. To-day, before the sun sets, I must make up for what I lost yesterday."

"Come child, and dance," the maiden said. "Before the sun sets, we'll find some way of getting that spinning done!"

*The little goats looked around to see whether it was really their own little shepherdess*

She tucked up her skirt, put her arm about Betushka, the musicians in the tree-tops struck up, and off they whirled. The maiden danced more beautifully than ever. Betushka couldn't take her eyes from her. She forgot her goats, she forgot her spinning. All she wanted to do was to dance on for ever.

At sundown the maiden paused and the music stopped. Then Betushka clasping her hands to her head, where the unspun flax was twined, burst into tears. The beautiful maiden took the flax from her head, wound it round the stem of a slender birch, grasped the spindle, and began to spin. The spindle hummed along the ground and filled in no time. Before the sun sank behind the woods, all the flax was spun, even that which was left over from the day before. The maiden handed Betushka the full spindle, and said:

" Remember my words :

Reel and grumble not !
Reel and grumble not ! ' "

When she said this, she vanished as if the earth had swallowed her.

Betushka was very happy now, and she thought to herself on her way home : " Since she is so good and kind, I'll dance with her again if she asks me. Oh, how I hope she does ! "

She sang her merry little song as usual, and the goats trotted cheerfully along.

She found her mother vexed with her, for she had wanted to reel yesterday's yarn, and had discovered that the spindle was not full.

" What were you doing yesterday," she scolded, " that you didn't spin your stint ? "

Betushka hung her head. " Forgive me, mother. I danced too long." Then she showed her mother to-day's spindle, and said : " See, to-day I more than made up for yesterday."

Her mother said no more but went to milk the goats, and Betushka put away the spindle. She wanted to tell her mother her adventure, but she thought to herself : " No, I'll wait. If the beautiful lady comes again, I'll ask her who she is, and then I'll tell mother." So she said nothing.

On the third morning she drove the goats as usual to the birch wood. The goats went to pasture, and Betushka, sitting down under a tree, began to spin and sing. When the sun pointed to noon, she laid her spindle on the grass, gave the goats a mouthful of bread, gathered some strawberries, ate her luncheon, and then, giving the crumbs to the birds, she said cheerily :

" To-day, my little goats, I will dance for you ! "

She jumped up, folded her arms, and was about to see whether she could move as gracefully as the beautiful maiden, when the maiden herself stood before her.

" Let us dance together," she said. She smiled at Betushka, put her arm about her, and, as the music above their heads began to play, they whirled round and round with flying feet. Again Betushka forgot the spindle and the goats. Again she saw nothing but the beautiful maiden whose body was lithe as a willow shoot. Again she heard nothing but the enchanting music to which her feet danced of themselves.

They danced from noon till sundown. Then the maiden paused and the music ceased. Betushka looked around. The sun was already set behind the woods. She clasped her hands to her head, and, looking down at the unfilled spindle, she burst into tears.

" Oh, what will my mother say ? " she cried.

" Give me your little basket," the maiden said, " and I will put something in it that will more than make up for to-day's stint."

Betushka handed her the basket, and the maiden took it and vanished. In a moment she was back. She returned the basket and said:

" Look not inside until you're home !
Look not inside until you're home ! "

As she said those words she was gone, as if a wind had blown her away. Betushka wanted awfully to peep inside, but she was afraid to. The basket was so light that she wondered whether there was anything at all in it. Was the lovely lady only fooling her? Half-way home she peeped in to see.

Imagine her feelings when she found that the basket was full of birch leaves! Then indeed did Betushka burst into tears and reproach herself for being so simple. In her vexation she threw out a handful of leaves, and was going to empty the basket, when she thought to herself:

"No, I'll keep what's left as litter for the goats."

She was almost afraid to go home. She was so quiet that again the little goats wondered what ailed their shepherdess.

Her mother was waiting for her in great excitement.

"For heaven's sake, Betushka, what kind of a spool did you bring home yesterday?"

"Why?" Betushka faltered.

"When you went away this morning I started to reel that yarn. I reeled and reeled and the spool remained full. One skein, two skeins, three skeins, and still the spool was full. 'What evil spirit has spun that?' I cried out impatiently, and instantly the yarns disappeared from the spindle, as if blown away. Tell me, what does it mean?"

So Betushka confessed and told her mother all she knew about the beautiful maiden.

"Oh," cried her mother in amazement, "that was a wood maiden! At noon and midnight the wood maidens dance. It is well you are not a little boy or she might have danced you to death! But they are often kind to little girls, and sometimes make them rich presents. Why didn't you tell me? If I hadn't grumbled, I could have had yarn enough to fill the house!"

Betushka thought of the little basket and wondered if there might be something under the leaves. She took out the spindle and unspun flax and looked in once more.

"Mother!" she cried. "Come here and see!"

Her mother looked and clapped her hands. The birch leaves were all turned to gold!

Betushka reproached herself bitterly: "She told me not to look inside until I got home, but I didn't obey."

"It's luck you didn't empty the whole basket," her mother said.

The next morning she herself went to look for the handful of leaves that Betushka had thrown away. She found them still lying in the road, but they were only birch leaves.

But the riches which Betushka brought home were enough. Her mother bought a farm, with fields and cattle. Betushka had pretty clothes, and no longer had to pasture goats.

But no matter what she did, no matter how cheerful and happy she was, still nothing ever again gave her quite so much pleasure as the dance with the wood maiden. She often went to the birch wood in the hope of seeing the maiden again. But she never did.

# THE CAROL SINGERS

*by* MARGARET G. RHODES

LAST night the carol singers came
When I had gone to bed,
Upon the crisp white path outside
    I heard them softly tread.

I sat upright to listen, for
    I knew they came to tell
Of all the things that happened on
    The very first Noel.

Upon my ceiling flickering
    I saw their lantern glow,
And then they sang their carols sweet
    Of Christmas long ago.

And when at last they went away,
    Their carol-singing done,
There was a little boy who wished
    They'd only just begun.

# The Skating Match

### *by* MARY M. DODGE

## I

TWENTY boys and twenty girls. The latter by this time are standing in front, braced for the start, for they are to have the first run. Hilda, Rychie, and Katrinka are among them—two or three bend hastily to give a last pull at their skate-straps. It is pretty to see them stamp to be sure that all is firm. Hilda is speaking pleasantly to a graceful little creature in a red jacket and a new brown petticoat. Why, it is Gretel! What a difference those pretty shoes make, and the skirt, and the new cap.

Annie Bouman is there too. Even Janzoon Kolp's sister has been admitted—but Janzoon himself has been voted out by the directors, because he killed the stork, and only last summer was caught in the act of robbing a bird's nest, a legal offence in Holland.

This Janzoon Kolp, you see, was—— There, I cannot tell the story just now. The race is about to commence.

Twenty girls are formed in a line. The music has ceased.

A man, whom we shall call the Crier, stands between the columns and the first judges' stand. He reads the rules in a loud voice :—

" The girls and boys are to race in turn, until one girl and one boy has beaten twice. They are to start in a line from the united columns—skate to the flag-staff line, turn, and then come back to the starting point ; thus making a mile at each run."

A flag is waved from the judges' stand. Madame van Gleck rises in her pavilion. She leans forward with a white handkerchief in her hand. When she drops it, a bugler is to give the signal for them to start.

The handkerchief is fluttering to the ground. Hark! They are off! No. Back again. Their line was not true in passing the judges' stand. The signal is repeated. Off again. No mistake this time. Whew! how fast they go!

The multitude is quiet for an instant, absorbed in eager, breathless watching.

Cheers spring up along the line of spectators. Huzza! five girls are ahead. Who comes flying back from the boundary mark? We cannot tell. Something red, that is all. There is a blue spot flitting near it, and a dash of yellow nearer still. Spectators at this end of the line strain their eyes and wish they had taken their post nearer the flag-staff. The wave of cheers is coming back again. Now we can see. Katrinka is ahead!

She passes the Van Holp pavilion. The next is Madame van Gleck's. That leaning figure gazing from it is a magnet. Hilda shoots past Katrinka, waving her hand to her mother as she passes. Two others are close now, whizzing on like arrows. What is that flash of red and gray? Hurrah, it is Gretel! She too waves her hand, but towards no gay pavilion.

The crowd is cheering, but she hears only her father's voice, " Well, done, little Gretel!" Soon Katrinka, with a quick merry laugh, shoots past Hilda. The girl in yellow is gaining now. She passes them all, all except Gretel. The judges lean forward without seeming to lift their eyes from their watches. Cheer after cheer fills the air ; the very columns seem rocking. Gretel has passed them. She has won.

" Gretel Brinker—one mile!" shouts the crier.

The judges nod. They write something upon a tablet which each holds in his hand.

While the girls are resting—some crowding eagerly around our frightened little Gretel, some standing aside in high disdain—the boys form in a line. Mynheer van Gleck drops the handkerchief this time. The buglers give a vigorous blast!

The boys have started.

Half-way already! Did you ever see the like!

Three hundred legs flashing by in an instant. But there are only twenty boys. No matter, there were hundreds of legs I am sure! Where are they now? There is such a noise one gets bewildered. What are the people laughing at? Oh, at that fat boy in the rear. See him go! See him! He'll be down in an instant—no, he won't. I wonder if he knows he is all alone ; the other boys are nearly at the boundary line. Yes, he knows it. He stops! He wipes his hot face. He takes off his cap and looks about him. Better to give up with a good grace. He had made a hundred friends by that hearty, astonished laugh. Good Jacob Poot!

The fine fellow is already among the spectators, gazing as eagerly as the rest.

A cloud of feathery ice flies from the heels of the skaters as they " bring to " and turn at the flag-staffs.

Something black is coming now, one of the boys — it is all we know. He has touched the *vox humana* stop of the crowd; it fairly roars. Now they come nearer—we can see the red cap. There's Ben—there's Peter— there's Hans !

Hans is ahead ! Young Madame van Gend almost crushes the flowers in her hand; she had been quite sure that Peter would be first. Carl Schummel is next, then Ben, and the youth with the red cap. The others are pressing close. A tall figure darts from among them. He passes the red cap, he passes Ben, then Carl. Now it is an even race between him and Hans. Madame van Gend catches her breath.

It is Peter ! He is ahead ! Hans shoots past him. Hilda's eyes fill with

*Now they come nearer—we can see the red cap*

tears, Peter *must* beat. Annie's eyes flash proudly. Gretel gazes with clasped hands—four strokes more will take her brother to the columns.

He is there ! Yes, but so was young Schummel just a second before. At the last instant, Carl, gathering his powers, had whizzed between them and passed the goal.

" Carl Schummel ! One mile ! " shouts the crier.

Soon Madame van Gleck rises again. The falling handkerchief starts the bugle ; and the bugle, using its voice as a bow-string, shoots off twenty girls like so many arrows.

It is a beautiful sight, but one has not long to look ; before we can fairly distinguish them they are far in the distance. This time they are close upon one another ; it is hard to say as they come speeding back from the flag-staff which will reach the columns first. There are new faces among the foremost—eager, glowing faces, unnoticed before. Katrinka is there, and Hilda, but Gretel and Rychie are in the rear.

Gretel is waving, but when Rychie passes her, she starts forward afresh. Now they are nearly beside Katrinka. Hilda is still in advance, she is almost home. She has not faltered since that bugle note sent her flying ; like an arrow still she is speeding toward the goal. Cheer after cheer rises in the air. Peter is silent but his eyes shine like stars. " Huzza ! Huzza ! "

The crier's voice is heard again.

" Hilda van Gleck, one mile ! "

A loud murmur of approval runs through the crowd, catching the music in its course, till all seems one sound, with a glad rhythmic throbbing in its depths. When the flag waves all is still.

Once more the bugle blows a terrific blast. It sends off the boys like chaff before the wind—dark chaff I admit, and in big pieces.

It is whisked around at the flag-staff, driven faster yet by the cheers and shouts along the line. We begin to see what is coming. There are three boys in advance this time, and all abreast. Hans, Peter, and Lambert. Carl soon breaks the ranks, rushing through with a whiff ! Fly Hans, fly Peter, don't let Carl beat again : Carl the bitter, Carl the insolent. Van Moumen is flagging, but you are strong as ever. Hans and Peter, Peter and Hans ; which is foremost ? We love them both. We scarcely care which is the fleeter.

Hilda, Annie, and Gretel, seated upon the long crimson bench, can remain quiet no longer. They spring to their feet—so different, and yet one in eagerness. Hilda instantly reseats herself ; none shall know how interested she is, none shall know how anxious, how filled with one hope. Shut your eyes then, Hilda—hide your face rippling with joy, Peter has beaten.

" Peter van Holt, one mile ! " calls the crier.

The same buzz of excitement as before, while the judges take notes, the same throbbing of music through the din — but something is different. A little crowd presses close about some object near the column. Carl has fallen. He is not hurt, though somewhat stunned. If he were less sullen he would find more sympathy in these warm young hearts. As it is they forget him as soon as he is fairly on his feet again.

## II

THE girls are to skate their third mile.

How resolute the little maidens look as they stand in a line ! Some are solemn with a sense of responsibility, some wear a smile half bashful, half provoked, but one air of determination pervades them all.

This third mile may decide the race. Still, if neither Gretel nor Hilda win, there is yet a chance among the rest for the Silver Skates.

Each girl feels sure that this time she will accomplish the distance in one half the time. How they stamp to try their runners, how nervously they examine each strap—how erect they stand at last, every eye upon Madame van Gleck !

The bugle thrills through them again. With quivering eagerness they spring forward, bending, but in perfect balance. Each flashing stroke seems longer than the last.

Now they are skimming off in the distance.

Again the eager straining of eyes—again the shouts and cheering, again the thrill of excitement as, after a few moments, four or five, in advance of the rest, come speeding back, nearer, nearer to the white columns.

Who is first ? Not Rychie, Katrinka, Annie, nor Hilda, nor the girl in yellow—but Gretel—Gretel, the fleetest sprite of a girl that ever skated. She was but playing in the earlier race, now she is in earnest, or rather something within her has determined to win. That lithe little form makes no effort ; but it cannot stop—not until the goal is passed !

In vain the crier lifts his voice—he cannot be heard. He has no news to tell—it is already ringing through the crowd. *Gretel has won the Silver Skates !*

Like a bird she has flown over the ice, like a bird she looks about her in a timid, startled way. She longs to dart to the sheltered nook where her father and mother stand. But Hans is beside her—the girls are crowding round her. Hilda's kind, joyous voice breathes in her ear. From that hour, none will despise her. Goose-girl or not, Gretel stands acknowledged Queen of the Skaters !

With natural pride Hans turns to see if Peter van Holp is witnessing his sister's triumph. Peter is not looking toward them at all. He is kneeling, bending his troubled face low, and working hastily at his skate-strap. Hans is beside him at once.

" Are you in trouble, mynheer ? "

" Ah, Hans ! that you ? Yes, my fun is over. I tried to tighten my strap —to make a new hole—and this botheration of a knife has cut it nearly in two."

" Mynheer," said Hans, at the same time pulling off a skate—" you must use my strap ! "

" Not I, indeed, Hans Brinker," cried Peter, looking up, " though I thank you warmly. Go to your post, my friend, the bugle will sound in a minute."

" Mynheer," pleaded Hans in a husky voice. " You have called me your friend. Take this strap—quick ! There is not an instant to lose. I shall not skate this time—indeed I am out of practice. Mynheer, you must take it,"—and Hans, blind and deaf to any remonstrance, slipped his strap into Peter's skate and implored him to put it on.

" Come, Peter ! " cried Lambert, from the line, " we are waiting for you."

" For madame's sake," pleaded Hans, " be quick. She is motioning to you to join the racers. There, the skate is almost on ; quick, mynheer, fasten it. I could not possibly win. The race lies between Master Schummel and yourself."

" You are a noble fellow, Hans ! " cried Peter, yielding at last. He sprang to his post just as the white handkerchief fell to the ground. The bugle sends forth its blast, loud, clear, and ringing.

Off go the boys !

" See them ! " cries a tough old fellow from Delft. " They beat everything, these Amsterdam youngsters."

See them, indeed ! They are winged Mercuries every one of them. What mad errand are they on ? Ah, I know ; they are hunting Peter van

Holp. He is some fleet-footed runaway from Olympus. Mercury and his troop of winged cousins are in full chase. They will catch him! Now Carl is the runaway—the pursuit grows furious—Ben is foremost!

The chase turns in a cloud of mist. It is coming this way. Who is hunted now? Mercury himself. It is Peter, Peter van Holp; fly, Peter—Hans is watching you. He is sending all his fleetness, all his strength into your feet. Your mother and sister are pale with eagerness. Hilda is trembling and dare not look up. Fly, Peter! the crowd has not gone deranged, it is only cheering. The pursuers are close upon you! Touch the white column! It beckons—it is reeling before you—it——

Huzza! Huzza! Peter has won the Silver Skates!

"Peter van Holp!" shouted the crier. But who heard him? "Peter van Holp!" shouted a hundred voices, for he was the favourite boy of the place. Huzza! Huzza!

Now the music was resolved to be heard. It struck up a lively air, then a tremendous march. The spectators, thinking something new was about to happen, deigned to listen and to look.

The racers formed in single file. Peter, being tallest, stood first. Gretel, the smallest of all, took her place at the end. Hans, who had borrowed a strap from the cake-boy, was near the head.

Three gaily twined arches were placed at intervals up the river facing the Van Gleck pavilion.

Skating slowly, and in perfect time to the music, the boys and girls moved forward, led on by Peter. It was beautiful to see the bright procession glide along like a living creature. It curved and doubled, and drew its graceful length in and out among the arches—whichever way Peter

*Suddenly something dazzling is placed in her hand*

the head went, the body was sure to follow. Sometimes it steered direct for the centre arch, then, as if seized with a new impulse, turned away and curled itself about the first one ; then unwound slowly and, bending low, with quick, snakelike curvings, crossed the river, passing at length through the farthest arch.

When the music was slow the procession seemed to crawl like a thing afraid ; it grew livelier, and the creature darted forward with a spring, gliding rapidly among the arches, in and out, curling, twisting, turning, never losing form until, at the shrill call of the bugle rising above the music, it suddenly resolved itself into boys and girls standing in double semicircle before Madame van Gleck's pavilion.

Peter and Gretel stand in the centre in advance of the others. Madame van Gleck rises majestically. Gretel trembles, but feels that she must look at the beautiful lady. She cannot hear what is said, there is such a buzzing all around her. She is thinking that she ought to try and make a curtsey, such as her mother makes to the *meester*, when suddenly something so dazzling is placed in her hand that she gives a cry of joy.

Then she ventures to look above her. Peter, too, has something in his hands—" Oh ! oh ! how splendid ? " she cries, and " Oh ! how splendid ! " is echoed as far as people can see.

Meantime the silver skates flash in the sunshine, throwing dashes of light upon those two happy faces.

Mevrouw van Gend sends a little messenger with her bouquets. One for Hilda, one for Carl, and others for Peter and Gretel.

At sight of the flowers the Queen of the Skaters becomes uncontrollable. With a bright stare of gratitude she gathers skates and bouquet in her apron —hugs them to her bosom, and darts off to search for her father and mother in the scattering crowd.

----

# THE EVENING SUN

### *by* EMILY BRONTË

THE evening sun was sinking down
    On low green hills and clustered trees ;
It was a scene as fair and lone
    As ever felt the soothing breeze.

That cools the grass when day is gone,
    And gives the waves a brighter blue,
And makes the soft white clouds sail on—
    Like spirits of ethereal dew.

Which all the morn had hovered o'er
    The azure flowers, where they were nursed,
And now return to Heaven once more,
    Where their bright glories shone at first.

# CHOOSING THEIR NAMES

### by TOM HOOD

OUR old cat has kittens three—
What do you think their names should be?

One is a tabby, with emerald eyes,
    And a tail that's long and slender,
And into a temper she quickly flies
    If you ever by chance offend her.
    I think we shall call her this—
    I think we shall call her that ;—
Now, don't you think that Pepperpot
    Is a nice name for a cat ?

One is black, with a frill of white,
    And her feet are all white fur, too ;
If you stroke her she carries her tail upright
    And quickly begins to purr, too !
    I think we shall call her this—
    I think we shall call her that ;—
Now, don't you think that Sootikin
    Is a nice name for a cat ?

One is a tortoiseshell, yellow and black,
    With plenty of white about him ;
If you tease him, at once he sets up his back:
    He's a quarrelsome one, ne'er doubt him.
    I think we shall call him this—
    I think we shall call him that ;—
Now, don't you think that Scratchaway
    Is a nice name for a cat ?

Our old cat has kittens three
And I fancy these their names will be ;
Pepperpot, Sootikin, Scratchaway—there !
Were ever kittens with these to compare ?
And we call the old mother—
        Now, what do you think ?
Tabitha Longclaws Tiddley Wink

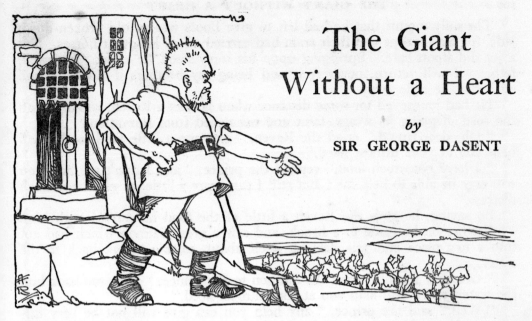

# The Giant
# Without a Heart

*by*

**SIR GEORGE DASENT**

IN days long past, a king had seven sons whom he loved so passionately that he could never endure being parted from them all at the same time. If six went out together, the seventh had always to remain with his father.

When they were grown up, the princes desired to get married. The king gave the six eldest permission to seek for wives, but kept with him the youngest, whose name was Boots, telling his brothers that they might bring back a princess for him.

His elder sons, the king dressed in clothing so sumptuous that they glittered from afar. Each rode a magnificent horse, and thus they set forth in state.

After visiting many palaces and seeing numerous princesses, at last the brothers came to a king who had six daughters, so lovely that the princes had never seen their like. In hot haste they set about wooing them, and when they had won the princesses, they departed homeward with their brides, too much in love to remember that they had promised to bring back a wife for their youngest brother, Boots.

After travelling some distance, they passed by a hillside, steep and upright as a wall, where a giant had his dwelling. The giant appeared and fixed his eyes upon them, and forthwith they were changed into stone, both princes and princesses.

For many months the king waited for his sons, and as they did not return, he fell into great trouble and distress of mind, declaring that he would never know happiness again.

" If I had not you still," he said to Boots, " I could no longer live, so full of sorrow am I for the loss of your brothers."

"Well," replied Boots, "I desire your permission to go in search of them."

" Nay," cried his father, " my permission you shall not have ; for if you go away, you will never come back again."

But Boots was resolute, and he entreated his father so earnestly that the king was obliged to consent.

The only mount that he had left to give Boots was an old broken-down jade, for his six sons and their train had carried off all his other horses. Not a jot did Boots care. Springing upon his sorry steed, he cried, " Farewell, father ; I will return, never fear, and bring my brothers if I can ; " and with that he rode away.

He had journeyed for some distance when he met a Raven, which lay on the road, flapping its wings, faint and exhausted from starvation.

" Oh, dear friend," cried the Raven, " give me a little food, and I will help you at your utmost need."

" I have not much food," replied the prince, " and I don't see how you will ever be able to help me ; but still I can spare a little, as you are in such distress."

So saying, he gave the Raven a little of the food he carried with him.

Farther on he came to a brook, and saw a great Salmon which had got into a dry place and was dashing itself about, unable to get back to the water.

" Oh, dear friend," cried the Salmon to the prince, " push me back into the water, and I will help you at your utmost need."

" Well," said the prince, " any help you can give will not be very important, but it is a pity you should lie there and be suffocated ; " and he pushed the fish back into the stream.

After he had travelled some distance, he met a Wolf, so famished that it could hardly crawl.

" Dear friend," the Wolf implored him, " do let me have your horse ; I am so hungry that the wind whistles through my ribs. I have had nothing to eat these two years."

" Nay," cried Boots, " this will never do ; first I meet a Raven, and am forced to give him my food ; next a Salmon persuades me to throw him back into the water ; and now you request my horse. It can't be done, for I should have nothing to ride upon."

" Nay, dear friend," begged Greylegs, " you can help me if you will. Give me your horse, and you can ride upon my back, and I will help you at your utmost need."

" Any help I get from you will not be great," laughed the prince, " but you may take my horse, since you are in such need."

When the Wolf had finished his meal, the prince put the bit between his jaws, and laid the saddle on his back. After his feast Greylegs had become so strong that he set off like the wind, faster than the prince had ever ridden before.

" When we have gone a little farther," said Greylegs, " I will show you the giant's house."

Presently the Wolf cried, " See, there it is ; and there are your six brothers, whom the giant has turned into stone, and these are their brides beside them. Yonder is the door by which you must enter."

" Nay," exclaimed the prince, " I dare not. He would take my life."

" No," replied the Wolf ; " in the house is a princess who will explain what you must do to make an end of the Giant. See that you carry out her instructions in every particular."

Boots entered the house, but, truth to tell, he was sorely afraid. The

Giant was absent, but in one of the rooms, just as the wolf had asserted, there sat the loveliest princess that Boots had ever beheld.

" Heaven help you," she exclaimed, as soon as she observed him. " Whence come you ? This will surely be your death. No one can slay the Giant who lives here, for he has no heart in his body."

" Well, well," said Boots, " now that I am here, I must do my utmost to set free my brothers who are standing out there turned into stone ; and you too I will try to save, you may be assured of that."

" Well," replied the princess, " if you are determined, let us see if we cannot invent some plan. But here comes the Giant ; just creep under the sofa and listen to what he says. Pray lie as still as a mouse while he is present."

Boots crept under the sofa, and was scarcely underneath before the Giant came.

" Ha ! " roared he, " my eyes and limbs, what horrible smell of Christian blood ! "

" Yes," the princess replied, " a magpie flew by with a man's bone in its bill and let it fall down the chimney. I made all the haste possible to get it out, but the odour still remains."

The Giant appeared satisfied, and after a little conversation, the princess continued, " There is something I should like to ask you, if only I dared."

" Well," said the Giant, " what is it ? "

" I should so like to know where you keep your heart, since you do not carry it about with you."

" That you have no right to ask," replied the Giant, " but since you are so inquisitive, it is under the door-step."

" Oh, ho ! " quoth Boots to himself in his hiding-place, " then we shall see if we can't find it."

Next morning the Giant rose early and strode off to the woods. He was scarcely out of the house before Boots and the princess looked under the door-step for his heart, but dig and search as they might, no heart could they discover.

" He has baulked us this time," declared the princess mournfully ; " but never mind, we will try him once more."

They replaced the door-step in its proper position, and the princess, picking all the prettiest flowers she could find, strewed them over it.

That evening, when it was time for the Giant to return, Boots crept under the sofa again. Scarcely had he concealed himself, before the Giant returned, complaining of the smell of Christian blood. The princess made excuses which quieted his suspicions, and, after a while, he asked who had strewn flowers over the door-step.

" Why, I, of course," said the princess.

" And pray, what is the meaning of this ? "

" Ah," cried the princess, " I am so fond of you that I had to strew them about, when I knew that your heart lay beneath."

" You are very kind," laughed the Giant ; " but as it happens, you are mistaken, for it does not lie there."

Thereupon the princess asked him once more where he kept his heart, saying she was most anxious to know.

" Well," growled the Giant, " if I must tell you, it lies in the cupboard yonder." Getting up, he went off to bed, and Boots crept softly to the chamber in which he had slept the previous night.

Next morning the Giant strode off betimes to the wood, and no sooner was he gone than the princess and Boots were at the cupboard, hunting for his heart ; but search as they might, not the slightest trace of a heart could they discover.

" Well," exclaimed the princess, " we must try him once more."

She decked the cupboard out with flowers and garlands, and when it was time for the Giant to return, Boots crept under the sofa again.

The Giant declared that he smelt Christian blood, but the princess continued to distract his attention. A little while afterwards, seeing the cupboard decked with flowers and garlands, he asked who had done it.

Who could it be but the princess ?

" And pray, what is the meaning of this nonsense ? " he asked.

" Why, how could I help doing it, when I knew your heart lay there ? " said the princess.

" How can you be so silly as to believe any such thing ? "

" Naturally I believe it, when you say it," she answered.

" Then you are a goose, for where my heart is, you will never come."

" All the same," said the Princess, " it would give me great pleasure if you would reveal where you really do keep it."

The poor Giant could resist her pleading no longer. " Far away, on a lake," he said, " there is an island ; on that island stands a church ; in the church is a well ; on the well swims a duck ; in the duck's nest lies an egg, and in that egg my heart is enclosed."

In the morning early, while it was yet gray dawn, the Giant strode off to the woods.

" Now I must set off too," said Boots, " if only I could find out the way."

He took a long farewell of the princess, and was scarcely outside the door when he beheld the Wolf, standing waiting for him. Boots related what had befallen, declaring that he was resolved to go to the well in the church, if only he could find out the way.

The Wolf bade the prince jump on his back, saying he would carry him thither ; and away they went with the wind whistling after them, over hedge and field, hill and dale.

For many days they travelled, and finally reached a lake. Boots felt at a loss how to cross it, but the Wolf bade him have no fear, and, plunging in with the prince on his back, swam over to the island.

They came to the church, but the keys hung high on the tower, and the prince was unable to get them down.

" You must call for the Raven," said the Wolf.

The prince called, and immediately the Raven flew up and fetched the keys, so that the prince could get into the church. He went to the well, and there was the Duck swimming about in front of its nest, just as the Giant had described. The prince wheedled and coaxed the creature until it came to him, when he grasped it in his hand ; but just as he was about to lift it from the water, it contrived to throw its egg down the well.

Boots was beside himself with disappointment, but the Wolf bade him summon the Salmon. The prince called, and the Salmon, immediately appearing, fetched up the egg from the bottom of the well.

The Wolf advised him to squeeze the egg; and directly he did so the Giant cried out with pain.

"Squeeze it again," said the Wolf, upon which the Giant screamed yet more piteously and begged to be spared, promising to fulfil all the prince desired if he would not squeeze his heart in two.

"Tell him to restore to life your six brothers and their brides, whom he has turned to stone," suggested the Wolf.

The Giant was willing to do this; he changed the six brothers into king's sons again, and their brides into king's daughters.

*" The loveliest of all is the bride of Boots," he declared*

"Now, squeeze the egg in two," advised the Wolf.

Boots squeezed the egg in two, and the consequence was that the Giant flew into splinters.

Having made an end of the Giant, Boots mounted the Wolf and hastened to the dwelling in the hill, where he found his six brothers alive and merry, each with his bride. Having fetched his own princess from the hillside, he and the whole party started on their homeward journey.

You may imagine the joy of the old king when he received all his seven sons back again, each with his betrothed.

"The loveliest of all is the bride of Boots," he declared; "he shall sit uppermost at the table, with her by his side."

He summoned a numerous company of guests from every district to the wedding. The merry-making was both loud and long, and if the party have not done feasting, the probability is that they are at it still.

# TRAVEL

*by* R. L. STEVENSON

I SHOULD like to rise and go
Where the golden apples grow ;—
Where below another sky
Parrot islands anchored lie,
And, watched by cockatoos and goats,
Lonely Crusoes building boats ;—
Where in sunshine reaching out
Eastern cities, miles about,
Are with mosque and minaret
Among sandy gardens set,
And the rich goods from near and far
Hang for sale in the bazaar ;—
Where the great Wall round China goes,
And on one side the desert blows,
And with bell and voice and drum,
Cities on the other hum ;—
Where are forests, hot as fire,
Wide as England, tall as a spire ;
Full of apes and cocoa-nuts
And the negro hunters' huts ;—
Where the knotty crocodile
Lies and blinks in the Nile,
And the red flamingo flies
Hunting fish before his eyes:—
Where in jungles, near and far,
Man-devouring tigers are,

Lying close and giving ear
Lest the hunt be drawing near,
Or a comer-by be seen
Swinging in a palanquin ;—
Where among the desert sands
Some deserted city stands,
All its children, sweep and prince,
Grown to manhood ages since,
Not a foot in street or house,
Not a stir of child or mouse,
And when kindly falls the night,
In all the town no spark of light.
There I'll come when I'm a man
With a camel caravan ;
Light a fire in the gloom
Of some dusty dining-room ;
See the pictures on the walls,
Heroes, fights, and festivals ;
And in a corner find the toys
Of the old Egyptian boys.

# WINDS

### by CHARLOTTE DRUITT COLE

THE little winds are all at play,
   And when I join their merry race,
I feel their fingers in my hair,
   I feel their kisses on my face.

I hear them sing their wild, sad songs,
   Which echo through the swaying trees ;
And oh ! their faces must be sweet—
   Those faces which one never sees.

Yet as we swiftly race along,
   I sometimes fancy I can see
Their thin and misty forms, sad eyes,
   And slender hands which beckon me.

And once I climbed a little hill,
   And spread my skirt in childish play,
Hoping the winds would carry me
   Above the clouds and far away.

# A Question of Equality

## by CAPTAIN MARRYAT

*(Mr. Midshipman Easy has been taught by his father that all men are equal and have equal rights. This extract shows how the idea worked out in actual practice on board ship.)*

WHEN Jack Easy had gained the deck, he found the sun shining gaily, a soft air blowing from the shore, and the whole of the rigging and every part of the ship loaded with the shirts, trousers, and jackets of the seamen, which had been wetted during the heavy gale, and were now hanging up to dry ; all the wet sails were also spread on the booms or triced up in the rigging, and the ship was slowly forging through the blue water.

The captain and first lieutenant were standing on the gangway in converse, and the majority of the officers were with their quadrants and sextants ascertaining the latitude at noon. The decks were white and clean, the sweepers had just laid by their brooms, and the men were busy coiling down the ropes. It was a scene of cheerfulness, activity, and order, which lightened his heart after the four days of suffering, close air, and confinement from which he had just emerged.

The captain, who perceived him, beckoned to him, asked him kindly how he felt : the first lieutenant also smiled upon him, and many of the officers, as well as his messmates, congratulated him upon his recovery.

The captain's steward came up to him, touched his hat, and requested the pleasure of his company to dinner in the cabin. Jack was the essence of politeness, took off his hat, and accepted the invitation. Jack was standing on a rope which a seaman was coiling down ; the man touched his hat and requested he would be so kind as to take his foot off. Jack took his hat off his head in return, and his foot off the rope. The master touched his hat, and reported twelve o'clock to the first lieutenant,—the first lieutenant touched his hat, and reported twelve o'clock to the captain,—the captain touched his hat, and told the first lieutenant to make it so. The officer of the watch touched his hat, and asked the captain whether they should pipe to dinner,—the captain touched his hat, and said,—" If you please."

The midshipman received his orders, touched his hat, and gave them to the head boatswain's mate, who touched his hat, and then the calls whistled cheerily.

" Well," thought Jack, " politeness seems to be the order of the day, and every one has an equal respect for the other." Jack stayed on deck ; he peeped through the ports, which were open, and looked down into the deep blue wave ; he cast his eyes aloft, and watched the tall spars sweeping and tracing with their points, as it were, a small portion of the clear sky, as they acted in obedience to the motion of the vessel ; he looked forward at the range of carronades which lined the sides of the deck, and then he proceeded to climb one of the carronades, and lean over the hammocks to gaze on the distant land.

" Young gentleman, get off those hammocks," cried the master, who was officer of the watch, in a surly tone.

Jack looked round.

" Do you hear me, sir ? I'm speaking to you," said the master again.

Jack felt very indignant, and he thought that politeness was not quite so general as he supposed.

It happened that Captain Wilson was upon deck.

" Come here, Mr. Easy," said the captain ; " it is a rule in the service, that no one get on the hammocks, unless in case of emergency—I never do—nor the first lieutenant—nor any of the officers or men,—therefore, upon the principle of equality, you must not do it either."

" Certainly not, sir," replied Jack, " but still I do not see why that officer in the shining hat should be so angry, and not speak to me as if I were a gentleman as well as himself."

" I have already explained that to you, Mr. Easy."

" Oh, yes, I recollect now, it's zeal : but this zeal appears to me to be the only unpleasant thing in the service. It's a pity, as you said, that the service cannot do without it."

It will be observed that this day may be considered as the first in which Jack really made his appearance on board, and it also was on this first day that Jack made known, at the captain's table, his very peculiar notions. If the company at the captain's table, which consisted of the second lieutenant, purser, Mr. Jolliffe, and one of the midshipmen, were astonished at such heterodox opinions being stated in the presence of the captain, they were equally astonished at the cool, good-humoured ridicule with which they were received by Captain Wilson.

The report of Jack's boldness, and every word and opinion that he had uttered (of course much magnified) was circulated that evening through the whole ship ; it was canvassed in the gunroom by the officers ; it was decanted upon by the midshipmen as they walked the deck ; the captain's steward held a levee abreast of the ship's funnel, in which he narrated this new doctrine. The sergeant of marines gave his opinion in his berth that it was detestable. The boatswain talked over the matter with the other warrant officers till the grog was all gone, and then dismissed it as too dry a subject ; and it was the general opinion of the ship's company that, as soon as they arrived at Gibraltar Bay, our hero would bid adieu to the service, either by being sentenced to death by a court-martial, or by being dismissed, and towed ashore on a grating.

In all societies, however small they may be, provided that they do but amount to half-a-dozen, you may invariably meet with a bully. And it is also generally the case that you will find one of that society who is more or less the butt. You will discover this even in occasional meetings, such as a dinner-party, the major part of which have never met before.

Previous to the removal of the cloth, the bully will have shown himself by his dictatorial manner, and will also have selected the one upon whom he imagines that he can best practise. In a midshipman's berth, this fact has become almost proverbial, although now perhaps it is not attended with that disagreeable despotism which was permitted at the time that our hero entered the service.

The bully of the midshipmen's berth of H.M. sloop *Harpy* was a young man about seventeen, with light, curly hair, and florid countenance, the son of the clerk in the dockyard at Plymouth, and his name was Vigors.

The butt was a pudding-faced boy of fifteen, whose intellect, with fostering, if not great might at least have been respectable had he not lost all confidence in his own powers from the constant jeers and mockeries of those who had a greater fluency of speech without perhaps so much real power of mind. Although slow, what he learnt he invariably retained. This lad's name was Gossett. His father was a wealthy yeoman of Lynn, in Norfolk. There were at the time but three other midshipmen in the ship, of whom it can only be said that they were like midshipmen in general, with little appetite for learning but good appetites for dinner, hating everything like work, fond of everything like fun, fighting " *à l'outrance* " one minute, and sworn friends the next—with general principles of honour and justice, but which were occasionally warped according to circumstances ; with all the virtues and vices so heterogeneously jumbled and heaped together that it was almost impossible to ascribe any action to its true motive, and to ascertain to what point their vice was softened down into almost a virtue, and their virtues from mere excess degenerated into vice. Their names were O'Connor, Mills, and Gascoigne.

After Jack had dined in the cabin, he followed his messmates Jolliffe and Gascoigne down into the midshipmen's berth.

" I say, Easy," observed Gascoigne, " you are a free and easy sort of a fellow to tell the captain that you considered yourself as great a man as he was."

" I beg your pardon," replied Jack, " I did not argue individually, but generally, upon the principles of the rights of man."

" Well," replied Gascoigne, " it's the first time I ever heard a middy do such a bold thing ; take care your rights of man don't get you in the wrong box—there's no arguing on board a man-of-war. The captain took it amazingly easy, but you'd better not broach that subject too often."

" Gascoigne gives you very good advice, Mr. Easy," observed Jolliffe ; " allowing that your ideas are correct, which it appears to me they are not, or at least impossible to be acted upon, there is such a thing as prudence, and however much this question may be canvassed on shore, in His Majesty's service it is not only dangerous in itself, but will be very prejudicial to you."

" Man is a free agent," replied Easy.

" I'll be shot if a midshipman is," replied Gascoigne, laughing, " and that you'll soon find."

" And yet it was in the expectation of finding that equality that I was induced to come to sea."

" On the first of April, I presume," replied Gascoigne. " But are you really serious ? "

Hereupon Jack entered into a long argument, to which Jolliffe and Gascoigne listened without interruption. At the end of it, Gascoigne laughed heartily, and Jolliffe sighed.

" From whence did you learn all this ? " inquired Jolliffe.

" From my father, who is a great philosopher, and has constantly upheld these opinions."

" And did your father wish you to go to sea ?"

" No, he was opposed to it," replied Jack, " but of course he could not combat my right and free-will."

" Mr. Easy, as a friend," replied Jolliffe, " I request that you would as much as possible keep your opinions to yourself. I shall have an opportunity of talking to you on the subject, and will then explain to you my reasons."

As soon as Jolliffe had ceased, down came Vigors and O'Connor, who had heard the news of Jack's heresy.

" You do not know Mr. Vigors and Mr. O'Connor," said Jolliffe to Easy.

Jack, who was the essence of politeness, rose and bowed, at which the others took their seats, without returning the salutation. Vigors had, from what he had heard and now seen of Easy, thought he had somebody else to play upon, and without ceremony he commenced.

" So, my chap, you are come on board to raise a mutiny here with your equality—you came off scot free at the captain's table ; but it won't do, I can tell you, even in the midshipman's berth : some must knock under, and you are one of them."

" If, sir," replied Easy, " you mean by knock under that I must submit, I can assure you that you are mistaken. Upon the same principle that I would never play the tyrant to those weaker than myself, so will I resent oppression if attempted."

" He's a regular sea lawyer already : however, my boy, we'll soon put your mettle to the proof."

" Am I then to infer that I am not on an equality with my messmates ? " replied Jack, looking at Jolliffe. The latter was about to answer him, but Vigors interrupted.

"Yes, you are on an equality as far as this,—that you have an equal right to the berth, if you are not knocked out of it for insolence to your masters : that you have an equal share to pay for the things purchased for the mess, and an equal right to have your share, provided you can get it ; you have an equal right to talk, provided you are not told to hold your tongue. The fact is, you have an equal right with every one else to do as you can, get what you can, and say what you can, always provided that you can do it ; for here the weakest goes to the wall, and that is midshipman's berth equality. Now, do you understand all that ; or will you wait for a practical illustration ? "

" I am then to infer that the equality here is as much destroyed as among savages, where the strong oppress the weak, and the only law is club law— in fact, much the same as it is at a public or large school on shore ? "

" I suspect you are right for once. You were at a public school : how did they treat you there ? "

" As you propose treating people here,—' the weakest went to the wall.' "

" Well, then, a nod's as good as a wink to a blind horse ; that's all, my hearty," said Vigors.

But the hands being turned up, " Shorten sail " put an end to the altercation for the present. As our hero had not yet received orders to go to his duty, he remained below.

As soon as the watch was called, Vigors, O'Connor, Gossett, and Gascoigne came down into the berth. Vigors, who was the strongest in the berth, except Jolliffe, had successively had his superiority acknowledged, and, when on deck, he had talked of Easy's impertinence, and his intention

*Jack very coolly divested himself of his upper garments*

of bringing him to his senses.  The others, therefore, came down to see the fun.

"Well, Mr. Easy," observed Vigors, as he came into the berth, "you take after your name, at all events;  I suppose you intend to eat the king's provision, and do nothing."

Jack's mettle was already up.

"You will oblige me, sir, by minding your own business," replied Jack.

"You impudent blackguard, if you say another word, I'll give you a good thrashing and knock some of your equality out of you."

"Indeed," replied Jack, who almost fancied himself back at Mr. Bonny-castle's;  "we'll try that."

Whereupon Jack very coolly divested himself of his upper garments, neckerchief, and shirt, much to the surprise of Mr. Vigors, who little contemplated such a proof of decision and confidence, and still more to the delight of the other midshipmen, who would have forfeited a week's allowance to see Vigors well thrashed.  Vigors, however, knew that he had gone too far to retreat;  he therefore prepared for action;  and, when ready, the whole party went out into the steerage to settle the business.

Vigors had gained his assumed authority more by bullying than fighting;  others had submitted to him without a sufficient trial;  Jack, on the contrary, had won his way up in school by hard and scientific combat;  the result, therefore, may easily be imagined.  In less than a quarter of an hour Vigors, beaten dead, with his eyes closed, and three teeth out, gave in:  while Jack, after a basin of water, looked as fresh as ever, with the exception of a few trifling scratches.

The news of this victory was soon through the ship;  and before Jack had resumed his clothes it had been told confidently by Sawbridge to the captain.

"So soon !" said Captain Wilson, laughing;  "I expected that a midshipman's berth would do wonders;  but I did not expect this yet awhile.  This victory is the first severe blow to Mr. Easy's equality, and will be more valuable than twenty defeats.  Let him go to his duty, he will soon find his level."

# Georgie

## by JACOB ABBOTT

A SHORT distance from where Rollo lives, there is a small but very pleasant house, just under the hill, where you go down to the stone bridge leading over the brook. There is a small white gate that leads to the house, from the road; and there is a pleasant path leading right out from the front door, through the garden, down to the water. This is the house that Georgie lives in.

One evening, just before sunset, Rollo was coming along over the stone bridge towards home. He stopped a moment to look over the railing, down into the water. Presently he heard a very sweet-toned voice calling out to him.

" Rol-lo ! "

Rollo looked along in the direction from which the sound came. It was from the bank of the stream, a little way from the road, at the place where the path from Georgie's house came down to the water. It was a place where Rollo had often been to sail boats with Georgie. There was a little smooth sandy place on the shore, at the foot of the path, and they used to call it Georgie's Landing; and there was a seat close by, under the bushes.

Rollo thought it was Georgie's voice that called him, and in a minute he saw him sitting on his little seat, with his crutches by his side. Georgie was a sick boy. He could not walk, but had to sit almost all day at home, in a large easy-chair, which his father had bought for him. In the winter his chair was established in a particular corner, by the side of the fire, and he had a little case of shelves and drawers, painted green, by the side of him. In these shelves and drawers he had his books and playthings—his pen and ink—his paint-box, brushes and pencils—his knife, and a little saw—and a great many things which he used to make for his amusement. Then, in the summer, his chair and his shelves and drawers were moved to the end window, which looked out upon the garden and brook. Sometimes, when he was better than usual, he could move about a little upon crutches ; and, at such times, when it was pleasant, he used to go out into the garden, and down, through it, to his landing at the brook.

Georgie had been sick a great many years, and when Rollo and Jonas first knew him, he used to be very sad and unhappy. It was because the poor little fellow had nothing to do. His father had to work pretty hard to get food and clothing for his family ; he loved little Georgie very much, but he could not buy him many things. Sometimes people who visited him used to give him playthings ; and they would amuse him for a little while, but he soon grew tired of them, and had them put away. It is very hard for anybody to be happy who has not anything to do.

It was Jonas that taught Georgie what to do. He lent him his knife, and brought him some smooth, soft pine wood, and taught him to make windmills and little boxes. Georgie liked this very much, and used to sit by his window in the summer mornings and make playthings, hours at a time. After he had made several things, Jonas told the boys that lived about there that they had better buy them from him, when they had a few cents to spend for toys ; and they did. In fact, they liked the little windmills and wagons and small framed houses that Georgie made better than sugar-plums and candy. Besides, they liked to go and see Georgie, for, whenever they went to buy anything of him, he looked so contented and happy, sitting in his easy-chair, with his small and slender feet drawn up under him, and his work on the table by his side.

Georgie at length earned in this way quite a little sum of money. It was nearly all in cents ; but there was one quarter which a lady gave him for a four-wheeled wagon that he made. He kept this money in a corner of his drawer, and, at last, there was quite a handful of it.

One summer evening, when Georgie's father came home from his work, he hung up his hat, and came and sat down in Georgie's corner by the side of his little boy. Georgie looked up to him with a smile.

" Well, father," said he, " are you tired to-night ? "

" You are the one to be tired, Georgie," said he, " sitting here alone all day."

" Hold up your hand, father," said Georgie, reaching out his own at the same time, which was shut up and appeared to have something in it.

" Why, what have you got for me ? " said his father.

" Hold fast all I give you," replied he ; and he dropped the money all into his father's hand, and shut up his father's fingers over it.

" What is all this ? " said his father.

" It is my money," said he, " for you. It is 'most all cents, but there is *one* quarter."

" I am sure I am much obliged to you, Georgie, for this."

" Oh, no," said Georgie ; " it is only a *little* of what you have to spend for me."

Georgie's father took the money, and put it in his pocket, and the next day he went to ask Jonas to spend it in buying things he thought would be useful to Georgie, either playthings or tools or materials to work with.

Jonas said he should be very glad to do it, for he thought he could buy him some things that would help him very much in his work. Jonas carried the money into the city the next time he went, and bought him a small hone to sharpen his knife, a fine-toothed saw, and a bottle of black varnish, with a little brush to put it on with. He brought these things home, and gave them to Georgie's father; and he carried them into the house, and put them in a drawer.

That evening, when Georgie was at supper, his father slyly put the things that Jonas had bought on his table, so that when he went back after supper he found them there. He was very much surprised and pleased. He examined them all very particularly, and was especially glad to have the black varnish, for now he could varnish his work, and made it look much more handsome. The little boxes that he made, after this, of a bright black outside, and lined neatly with paper within, were thought by the boys to be elegant.

He could now earn money faster, and, as his father insisted on having all his earnings expended for Georgie's own use, and Jonas used to help him about expending it, he got at last quite a variety of implements and articles.

So Georgie was a great friend of both Rollo and Jonas, and they often used to come and see him and play with him; and that was the reason that Rollo knew his voice so well when he called to him from the landing when Rollo was standing on the bridge.

Rollo ran along to the end of the bridge, clambered down to the water's edge, went along the shore among the trees and shrubbery, until he came to the seat where Georgie was sitting. Georgie asked him to sit down and stay with him; but Rollo said he must go directly home, and so Georgie took his crutches, and they began to walk slowly together up the garden walk.

" Where have you been, Rollo ? " said Georgie.

" I've been to see my cousin James, to ask him to go to the city with us to-morrow."

" Are you going to the city ? "

" Yes. Uncle George gave James and me half a dollar a piece the other day; and mother is going to carry us into the city to-morrow to buy something with it."

" Is Jonas going with you ? "

" Yes," said Rollo. " He is going to drive. We are going in our carry-all."

" I wish you would take some money for me then, and get Jonas to buy me something with it."

" Well, I will," said Rollo. " What shall he buy for you ? "

" Oh, he may buy anything he chooses."

" Yes, but if you do not tell him what to buy, he may buy something you have got already."

" Oh, Jonas knows everything I have got as well as I do."

Just then they came up near the house, and Georgie asked Rollo to look up at the golden pippin tree and see how full it was.

" That is my branch," said he.

He pointed to a large branch which came out on one side, and which hung down loaded with fruit. It would have broken down, perhaps, if there had not been a crotched pole put under it to prop it up.

" Come here," said he, " Rollo, and let me lean on you, while I knock some down for us to eat."

So Rollo came and stood near him, while Georgie leaned on him, and with his crutch gave a gentle tap to the apples, and they fell down upon the soft grass, safe and sound.

They then went into the house, and Georgie gave Rollo his money, wrapped up in a small piece of paper ; and then Rollo, bidding him good-bye, went out of the little white gate and walked along home.

The next morning, soon after breakfast, Jonas drove the carry-all up to the front door, and Rollo and his mother walked out of it. Rollo's mother took the back seat, and Rollo and Jonas sat in front, and they drove along.

They called at the house where James lived, and found him waiting for them on the front steps, with his half-dollar in his hand.

They came after a while to the foot of a long hill, and Jonas said he

*With his crutch he gave the apples a gentle tap*

believed that he would get out and walk up, and he said James might drive the horse. So he put the reins into James's hand, and jumped out. Rollo climbed over the seat, and sat by his side. Presently James saw a large stone in the road, and he asked Rollo to see how well he could drive round it ; for, as the horse was going, he would have carried one wheel directly over it. So he pulled one of the reins, and turned the horse away ; but he contrived to turn him out just far enough to make the *other* wheel go over the stone. Rollo laughed, and asked him to let him try the next time ; and James gave him the reins ; but there was no other stone till they got up to the top of the hill.

Then James said that Rollo might ride on the front seat now, and when Jonas got in, he climbed back to the back seat and took his place by the side of Rollo's mother.

"Come, mother," then said Rollo, "please tell us a story."

"Very well, if you are all ready."

So she began as follows :—

### The Story of the Shallow, Selfish and Wise

Once there were three boys going into town to buy some playthings; their names were Shallow, Selfish and Wise. Each had half a dollar. Shallow carried his in his hand, tossing it up in the air and catching it as he went along. Selfish kept teasing his mother to give him some more money: half a dollar, he said, was not enough. Wise walked along quietly, with his cash safe in his pocket.

Presently Shallow missed catching his half-dollar, and—chink!—it went on the sidewalk, and it rolled along down into a crack under a building. Then he began to cry. Selfish stood by, holding his own money tight in his hand, and said he did not pity Shallow at all; it was good enough for him. He had no business to be tossing it up. Wise came up, and tried to get the money out with a stick, but he could not. He told Shallow not to cry; said he was sorry he had lost his money, and that he would give him half of his as soon as they could get it changed at the shop.

So they walked along to the toy-shop.

Their mother said that each one might choose his own plaything; so they began to look around on the counter and shelves.

After a while Shallow began to laugh very loudly and heartily at something he found. It was an image of a grinning monkey. It looked very droll indeed. Shallow asked Wise to come and see. Wise laughed at it, too, but said he should not want to buy it, as he thought he should soon get tired of laughing at anything, if it was ever so droll.

Shallow was sure that he should never get tired of laughing at so very droll a thing as the grinning monkey; and he decided to buy it, if Wise would give him half of his money, and so Wise did.

*So Shallow, Selfish and Wise walked along home*

Selfish found a rattle, a large, noisy rattle, and went on springing it until they were all tired of hearing the noise.

"I think I shall buy this," said he. "I can make believe that there is a fire, and can run about springing my rattle, and crying 'Fire! Fire!' or I can play that a thief is breaking into a store, and can rattle my rattle at him, and call out 'Stop thief!'"

"But that will disturb all the people in the house," said Wise.

"What care I for that?" said Selfish.

Selfish found that the price of his rattle was not so much as the half-dollar; so he laid out the rest of it in cake, and sat down on a box and began to eat it.

Wise passed by all the images and gaudy toys, only good to look at a few times, and chose a soft ball, and finding that it did not take all of his half of the money, he purchased a little morocco box with an inkstand, some wafers, and one or two short pens in it. Shallow told him that it was not a plaything; it was only fit for a school; and as to his ball, he did not think much of that.

Wise said he thought they could all play with the ball a great many times, and he thought, too, that he should like his little inkstand on rainy days and winter evenings.

So the boys walked along home. Shallow stopped every moment to laugh at his monkey, and Selfish to spring his rattle, and they looked with contempt on Wise's ball, which he carried quietly in one hand, and his box done up in brown paper in the other.

When they got home, Shallow ran in to show his monkey. The people smiled a little, but did not take much notice of it, and, in fact, it did not look half so funny, even to himself, as it did in the shop. In a short time it did not make him laugh at all, and then he was vexed and angry with it. He said he meant to go and throw the ugly old baboon away; he was tired of seeing that same old grin on his face all the time. So he went and threw it over the wall.

Selfish ate his cake up, on his way home. He could not give his brothers any, for he said they had had their money as well as he. When he got home, he went about the house, up and down, through parlour and chamber, kitchen and shed, springing his rattle, and calling out, "Stop thief! Stop thief!" or "Fire! Fire!" Everybody got tired, and asked him to be still; but he did not mind, until at last his father took his rattle away from him and put it up on a high shelf.

Then Selfish and Shallow went out and found Wise playing beautifully with his ball in the yard; and he invited them to play with him. They would toss it up against the wall, and learn to catch it when it came down; and then they made some bat-sticks, and knocked it back and forth to one another about the yard. The more they played with the ball, the more they liked it, and as Wise was always very careful not to play near any holes, and to put it away safe when he had done with it, he kept it a long time, and gave them pleasure a great many times all summer long.

And then his inkstand box was a great treasure. He would get it out in the long winter evenings, and lend Selfish and Shallow each one of his pens; and they would all sit at the table and make pictures and write little letters and seal them with small bits of the wafers. In fact Wise kept his inkstand box safe till he grew up to be a man. That is the end of the story.

"I wish I could get an inkstand box," said Rollo when the story was finished.

"I think he was very foolish to throw away his grinning monkey," said James. "I wish I could see a grinning monkey."

They continued talking about this story for some time, and at length they drew nigh to the city. They drove to a stable where Jonas had the horse put up, and then they all walked in search of a toy-shop.

They passed along through one or two streets, walking very slowly, so that the boys might look at the pictures and curious things in the shop windows. At length they came to a toy-shop and all went in.

*"Don't you think you could let me have it for ten cents?"*

They saw at once a great number and variety of playthings exhibited to view. All around the floor were arranged horses on wheels, little carts, wagons, and baskets. The counter had a great variety of images and figures —birds that would peep, and dogs that would bark, and drummers that would drum—all by just turning a little handle. Then the shelves and the window were filled with all sorts of boxes, and whips, and puzzles, and tea-sets, and dolls (dressed and not dressed). There were bows and arrows, and darts, and jumping-ropes, and glass dogs, and little rocking-horses, and a thousand other things.

When the boys first came in there was a little girl standing by the counter with a small slate in her hand. She looked like a poor girl, though she was neat and tidy. She was talking with the shopman about the slate.

"Don't you think," said she, "you could let me have it for ten cents?"

"No," said he, "I could not afford it for less than fifteen. It cost me more than ten."

The little girl laid the slate down and looked disappointed and sad. Rollo's mother came up to her, took up the slate, and said :

" I should think you had better give him fifteen cents. It is a very good slate. It is worth as much as that, certainly."

" Yes, madam, so I tell her," said the shopman.

" But I have not got but ten cents," said the little girl.

" Have you not ? " said Rollo's mother. She stood still thinking a moment, and then she asked the little girl what her name was.

She said it was Maria.

She asked her what she wanted the slate for ; and Maria said it was to do sums on, at school. She wanted to study arithmetic and could not do so without a slate.

Jonas then came forward, and said that he should like to give her five cents of Georgie's money, and that, with the ten she had, would be enough. He said that Georgie had given him authority to do what he thought best with his money, and he knew if Georgie was here he would wish to help the little girl.

Rollo and James were both sorry they had not thought of it themselves ; and, as soon as Jonas mentioned it they wanted to give some of their money to the girl ; but Jonas said he knew that Georgie would prefer to do it. At last, however, it was agreed that Rollo and James should furnish one cent each and Georgie the rest. This was all agreed upon after a low conversation by themselves in a corner of the store; and then Jonas came forward and told the shopman that they were going to pay the additional five cents, and that he might let the girl have the slate. So Rollo paid the money, and it was agreed that Rollo and James should pay him back their share when they got their money changed. The boys were very much pleased to see the little girl go away so happy with her slate in her hand. It was neatly done up in paper with two pencils which the shopman gave her done up inside.

After Maria was gone, the boys looked around the shop, but could not find anything which exactly pleased them ; or at least they could not find anything which pleased them so much more than anything else that they could decide in favour of it. So they concluded to walk along and look at another shop.

They succeeded at last in finding some playthings that they liked, and Jonas bought a variety of useful things for Georgie. On their way home the carry-all stopped at the house where Lucy lived, and Rollo's mother left him and James there, to show Lucy their playthings.

One of the things they bought was a little boat with two sails, and they went down behind the house to sail it. The other playthings and books they carried down too, and had a fine time playing with them, with Lucy and another little girl who was visiting her that afternoon.

# SPRING, THE SWEET SPRING

*by* THOMAS NASH

SPRING, the sweet Spring, is the year's pleasant
    king ;
Then blooms each thing, then maids dance in a ring,
Cold doth not sting, the pretty birds do sing :
    *Cuckoo, jug, jug, pu we, to witta woo !*

The Palm and May make country houses gay,
Lambs frisk and play, the shepherds pipe all day,
And we hear aye birds tune this merry lay :
    *Cuckoo, jug, jug, pu we, to witta woo !*

The fields breathe sweet, the daisies kiss our feet,
Young lovers meet, old wives a-sunning sit,
In every street these tunes our ears do greet :
    *Cuckoo, jug, jug, pu we, to witta woo !*
        *Spring, the sweet Spring !*

# Wimbry Keep

## by CATHERINE B. MacLEAN

" WHY——?" began Molly.

"How? . . . When?" cried Alan and Fred at the same time.

"Stop," cried Uncle Dick, putting his hands over his ears, "I can only repeat what I have said : I do not know why the house was built like this."

"But, Uncle Dick," said Molly, "it is terribly exciting to have a moat, to cross a bridge to the front door, and to enter upstairs."

"And to go downstairs to bed!" went on Alan. "Wimbry Keep is a jolly queer name, too."

"I quite agree, but if the old owners knew the reason why, the secret must have been buried with them. What was that puff of wind——?"

"A question, Uncle Dick—a question!" cried the trio joyfully, and at that moment the clock gave a curious whirr, as it prepared to strike four.

Granny laughed. "That's good," she said ; "even Uncle Dick can't help asking questions about this new, old house of his. But those odd puffs of wind are strange ; I have noticed them before."

"Oh, Granny, do you think the house is haunted?" asked Fred.

"Another question," sighed Uncle Dick. "Look here, I'll give each of you half a crown if you ask no questions about the house between now and tea-time to-morrow ; and another half-crown to the one who finds out, or invents, the best story of how the house is built below the ground."

"Done," cried the trio, and soon they went off to explore once more.

Supper-time found them no nearer a solution of the mystery, and they all went *down* to bed, determined to rise early to explore further.

Molly had not been long in bed, when she sat up with a start. There was the queerest hollow noise just at her head.

"Whirr, whirr," it went ; then, "boom, boom, boom——"

"It's only the clock," she said, lying down again. "I'd forgotten that my bed was just beneath it ; still, the walls must be hollow to make it sound like that."

She was soon dozing, but could not get very fast asleep, for the noise of the clock always aroused her. At last she determined to move the bed, and as she turned to do so, she noticed a panel in the wall behind it. She pressed her hands all over it ; suddenly it sprang back, a little gust of wind blew on her, and at that moment the clock whirred again. The whirring caught her and carried her up, till she found herself standing on a roof, with towers and battlements. All round, the wind kept repeating, with a long, whispering sigh:

"Windy-brae, windy-brae, windy-brae heath," then in shorter, sharper gusts, "Wimbry, Wimbry, Wimbry Keep."

Molly looked over the battlements at her uncle's house lying low, squat, and sheltered, with its wide moat all round. Between her and it was a great space, where the winds blew gently, holding up by their breath the roof on which she stood, as you would hold a soap bubble in the air. A puff of wind laughed in her face, then " One-two-three-four," struck the clock, and, with a thud, Molly found herself standing by her bed. She crept in again among the blankets, and lay listening to the clock, telling her a thrilling tale of Wimbry Keep.

She woke in the morning with a lovely, exciting feeling, and thought of Uncle Dick's promise. Vaguely she remembered that something had happened in the night, and all day she wandered about, trying to remember what, but in vain. It was a very sad and almost tearful Molly who entered the drawing-room about tea-time.

" Now, Uncle Dick," cried the boys, as she entered.

" Well done," said Uncle Dick, as he gave a half-crown to each of them. " Now for the stories. Alan had better begin, as he is youngest."

At that moment the clock whirred ; a tiny puff of wind stirred Molly's hair and laughed in her face. As the clock struck four, she remembered all that had happened and the tale the clock had told.

But Alan was speaking.

" Long ago," he began, " a man called Sir Boris Wimbry built a castle, full of dungeons, which he called ' Wimbry Keep.' He caught all his enemies and shut them up in the dungeons, and one day he did the same with the king's son. The king came with an army and destroyed the castle and rescued his son. Instead of putting Sir Boris to death, he commanded that he and his family should live always in the dungeons, which were all that remained of the castle. But Sir Boris was clever, and dug a wide moat all round, to let in the light, and changed the dungeons into rooms. That is why you enter Wimbry Keep from upstairs."

" I say, old man," said Uncle Dick, " that is good. Molly, can you beat it ? "

" Very long ago," said Molly, " there was a place called Windy-brae Heath, that the Four Winds loved so much they kept repeating its name, till once, when they had carried off a beautiful lady, they changed their cry to ' Windy-brae (or Wimbry) Keep.'

" A knight, who heard them, rode straight for Windy-brae Heath to see what the new cry meant. He found the beautiful lady and rescued her, but the wind was so strong they could not get right away till he dug a deep shelter in the ground. The Four Winds now knew that they were beaten and fled, but the ' other little wind,' that blows when everything is still, laughed in their faces. The knight took the lady back to her father's house, promising to return and marry her as soon as he had a home where she would be safe from the winds.

" He gathered workmen and, right on Windy-brae Heath, began to dig deep foundations for his house. He dared not build Wimbry Keep high, for fear of the winds, but he hoped that some day the house could have a roof, with high towers and battlements, and he left a secret stair to lead up to it. The roof was never made, for the winds stole the plan and held it over the house in threat ; they still hold it there, but only the ' other little wind ' knows of the secret passage, for he discovered it one day, at four o'clock."

"Your story is good, too. Fred, what about yours?"

Fred shrugged his shoulders. "I think the chaps who built the house did it this way because it was easier to roll stones down than to lift them up."

Uncle Dick laughed. "You are out of the running, anyhow. Granny, can you decide between Alan and Molly?"

"Alan's tale is more convincing, but Molly's accounts for the puffs of wind we have noticed."

"But, Granny, dear," said Molly, "mine is true. I went through the secret passage last night and saw the winds holding up the roof, with its towers and battlements."

"Prove it," cried the boys.

"Come, then," said Molly, leading the way down to her bedroom. She drew back the bed, and began to press the panel behind it. It sprang back and showed a narrow staircase. They climbed up, and found another entrance behind the old clock. Up and up they all went, till the stair ended abruptly, where the present roof had been built over it.

All agreed then that Molly had won the half-crown.

---

# THE WORLD

### by W. B. RANDS

GREAT, wide, beautiful, wonderful world,
With the wonderful water round you curled,
And the wonderful grass upon your breast—
World, you are beautifully drest.

The wonderful air is over me,
And the wonderful wind is shaking the tree,
It walks on the water, and whirls the mills,
And talks to itself on the tops of the hills.

You friendly Earth! how far do you go,
With the wheat-fields that nod, and the rivers that flow,
With cities and gardens, and cliffs and isles,
And people upon you for thousands of miles?

Ah! you are so great, and I am so small,
I tremble to think of you, World, at all;
And yet, when I said my prayers to-day,
A whisper inside me seemed to say,
"You are more than the Earth, though you are such a dot:
You can love and think, and the Earth can not!"

WIMBRY KEEP

All round, the wind, kept repeating, with a long, whispering sigh—" Windy-brae, windy-brae, windy-brae heath " (*Page* 222)

H

HOW MAID MARIAN CAME TO THE GREENWOOD

Maid Marian made her home in the Greenwood and lived very happily with Robin Hood and his Merry
Men   (*Page* 229)

# How Maid Marian came to the Greenwood

*by* LAVINIA DERWENT

ROBIN HOOD, the bold outlaw, who, with his Merry Men, ruled over Sherwood Forest, was wandering about under the trees one day, feeling unusually sad. It was many months since he had seen Marian, the fair lady who had won his heart. In bygone days, her father, Baron Fitzwater, had welcomed him to Trenton Castle, for then he was known as the noble Earl of Huntingdon, but now he was an outcast whom many sought to trap.

His change of fortune, however, had not affected Marian's feelings. She loved the outlawed Robin Hood as much as she had loved the Earl of Huntingdon, but her father stormed and raged whenever his name was mentioned.

"Never shall you wed an outlaw," he cried angrily to his daughter. "If Robin Hood shows face near here, it will be the worse both for him and for you!"

When Robin Hood heard this decree, he was forced, for Marian's sake, to keep away from Trenton Castle and bide his time. Often he hungered for a sight of her lovely face, and to-day he could no longer curb his impatience. Mounting his favourite horse, he rode hastily till he was within sight of his lady's home, then, dismounting and making his horse secure, he moved silently nearer the grim castle.

To his delight, a figure that he knew and loved well appeared in the garden and wandered slowly in the direction of a little stream that ran by the foot. Quietly, with beating heart, Robin Hood followed her, then, "Marian!" he said, softly.

The girl started. Could that voice be the one she had been thinking of ever since the young Earl of Huntingdon had been sent away by her stern father? "Robin Hood," she whispered, and swung round to find her lover close behind her. The next moment she was in his arms and all the loneliness and despair of the last few weeks vanished.

Presently, however, Marian recollected where they were. "We must part, Robin," she said, in a trembling voice. "If my father finds you here, his anger will be terrible."

"How can I part from you like this?" Robin Hood cried, earnestly. "It is so long since I saw you last. I must——"

"*Must?*" roared a terrific voice behind them. With a startled cry, Marian looked round to find the angry Baron striding towards them like a raging lion.

"Robin," she screamed, "save yourself! Flee before it is too late!"

"I prefer to stay," said he, in a calm voice, and turning to Baron Fitzwater addressed him, "I await your pleasure, sir."

"My pleasure!" spluttered the Baron. Then, beckoning some of his retainers, cried, "Throw him in the dungeon and keep him there till I have sent for the Sheriff from Nottingham."

"Oh, no, father!" protested Marian in alarm, but her father caught her roughly by the arm.

"To your room, girl!" he thundered. "You shall stay there under lock and key till you come to your senses."

Thus was the lovers' brief moment of happiness rudely shattered. Marian, her lovely face stained with tears, paced restlessly about her room, wondering what she could do to save Robin Hood from her angry father's clutches. Suddenly, she called for Cedric, the little page, and whispered urgently to him: "Find out Robin Hood's men in the Greenwood and bring them to his aid at once."

"That I will, mistress," said the page, gallantly, though he knew that before him lay a hard task indeed.

As he was crossing the hall to start on his quest, the Baron met him with an order.

"Take this letter without delay to the Sheriff at Nottingham. Long has he tried to catch Robin Hood, and now here he is, holed like a rat."

Cedric accepted the message and went off, but not to deliver it. His young mistress's orders were more to him than those of his master. First, he must find out where Robin Hood's men were hidden. But how?

Suddenly his troubled face lit up. There was Robin Hood's horse, tethered to a bush in a meadow that ran at the foot of the garden. "She'll know her way home," cried Cedric, in glee, and hurrying towards the horse, jumped on its back and allowed it to take its own course.

Sure enough, the horse scampered off into the forest, and at last they came, through devious pathways, to the haunt of the Merry Men.

When Robin Hood's followers saw their master's horse returning without him, they were filled with alarm, and when Cedric gasped out his story, their alarm deepened. Hurriedly, they held a conclave, and it was decided that Friar Tuck should be sent off at once to the castle to try his skill in freeing Robin Hood.

By the time he arrived there, the Baron was feeling somewhat uneasy and sorry for himself. He was missing his daughter's company and feeling that perhaps he had acted too hastily in throwing Robin Hood in the dungeon.

When Friar Tuck arrived he was feeling very miserable, but a sight of that good man's cheery face raised his spirits.

"You have come in good time, Friar, to sup with me. I am in need of company to-night."

"Indeed!" said the Friar, innocently. "Where is the Lady Marian to-night?"

The Baron's brow clouded. "Marian keeps her room to-night," he said. Then, changing the subject, he invited the Friar to sample his hospitality.

Soon they were seated at the groaning board, and Friar Tuck cunningly kept plying his host with the strong wine which he had provided. So convivial became the feast that the Baron was quite overcome and sank back in his chair and soon fell into a deep slumber. Now was Friar Tuck's chance! Stealthily he retrieved a bunch of keys from its place at the Baron's waist.

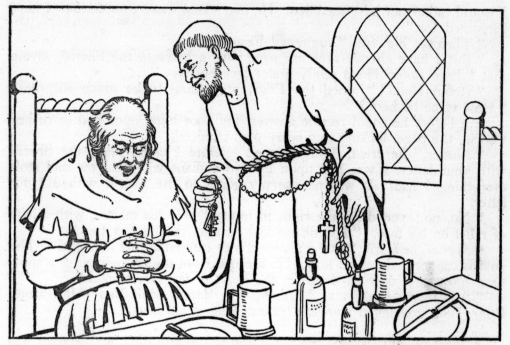

*The Baron sank back in his chair and soon fell into a deep slumber*

Off he went to the dungeon, telling the men who were guarding the door
that he had come to shrive the prisoner.

The guards stepped back and allowed him to enter.  " And now, my
brave master," he cried to Robin Hood, who, sunk in gloom, was seated
in a corner of the dungeon, " haste back to the Greenwood. You can easily
crack a few skulls and make your way out safely."

Robin Hood was on his feet in an instant.  " Thanks, good Friar," he
cried, clasping his rescuer by the hand.  " But Marian ? "

" I will attend to her.  Off with you ! "

Robin Hood needed no second bidding, and made his way safely to the
Greenwood, while Friar Tuck hastened back to his host.

The Baron was awakening from his sleep, which had been an uneasy
one, filled with visions of his daughter and of Robin Hood.  He awoke,
remorseful and sad, and, looking round at the remains of the feast, said to
the Friar, " Poor Marian must be hungry.  There is still enough food left
for her."

" Why not ask her down ? "

The Baron looked relieved.  " I will," he decided, and gave orders to
a servant to see that his daughter was freed and brought down immediately.

Marian arrived, looking pale and worn, but when Friar Tuck contrived
to whisper to her that Robin Hood was now safe, her eyes brightened and
she found appetite enough to eat the food with which her father plied her.

" You look worried," said the wily Friar, as the Baron sat back with
a frown on his brow.

" I am !  As a matter of fact, there is a fellow in my dungeon with whom

I would rather not have meddled. He may cause more trouble than I have bargained for."

"Then set him free," suggested Friar Tuck.

"But I have already sent my page with a letter to the Sheriff, saying that I have Robin Hood safely under lock and key."

"Robin Hood!" cried the Friar, pretending to be much surprised. "How came he here?"

But before he could receive answer, the door burst open and in rushed Cedric, the page, looking in a sorry plight indeed.

"Master," he cried, "forgive me! Before I could reach the Sheriff with your letter, I was laid upon by two ruffians who beat me and stole everything I had. It was no use my going to the Sheriff without your letter."

"No, no; you did quite right to return," said his master, with a look of relief on his face. "I think we had best set that outlaw free."

"Master, he *is* free," said a retainer, who entered at that moment. "The guards cannot understand how. He escaped from under their noses a short time ago and is now no doubt in the heart of the Greenwood."

"And there let him stay," breathed the Baron, while Lady Marian and Friar Tuck exchanged knowing glances behind his back.

.    .    .    .    .    .    .    .    .    .    .

A short time afterwards the old Baron fell ill and died, and Marian was left fatherless. Her first thought was to find Robin Hood in his Greenwood haunt, for now that her father was dead there was no barrier between them. How to manage the journey in safety puzzled the girl, till at last she hit on the plan of arranging herself as a young knight. There would be less danger,

*"Marian! Have I been fighting you whom I love so much?"*

she imagined, journeying through the forest in this guise than if she travelled alone as Lady Marian.

Accordingly, garbed as a knight and carrying a sword which, in earlier days, Robin Hood had taught her how to use, Marian boldly made her way into the forest and wandered for many miles in search of the haunt of Robin and his Merry Men.

That day Robin Hood, very cleverly disguised as a beggar, had gone to Nottingham on an errand, and was returning when he spied, coming towards him, a youth, who seemed to have a lost air about him.

" How now, young fellow," cried Robin, " what are you doing here ? You cannot pass this way," and brandished his sword in a threatening manner. He had no notion to fight with one so small and weak, but he thought it best to frighten the youth in case he should stumble on the forest home of the outlaws.

" Back ! " he cried. But the youth came calmly towards him, and with bared sword showed that he meant to put up a fight. Amused, Robin Hood made a few passes with him, and, though the youth fought gallantly, soon laid him low with a slight wound on the arm. In the fall, the young knight's hat had tumbled to the ground and a mass of beautiful curls was let loose. In amazement, Robin Hood stared at the slight figure at his feet.

" Marian ! " he cried, and kneeling down, gathered her in his arms, " is it really you ? Have I been fighting *you* whom I love so much ? "

" Robin ! " Equally amazed, Marian stared up at the beggar who was speaking to her in Robin Hood's voice. " Have I been fighting *you* ? "

Tender explanations followed and the re-union ended happily. Marian's hurt was slight and soon healed under her lover's fond care.

Proudly, Robin Hood carried his lady to the Greenwood, and, sounding a blast on his horn, called his loyal men together.

" Here is your Queen, my men," he told them, drawing forward the blushing Lady Marian.

" This is Maid Marian, whom I am going to marry and who is going to share with us our forest home."

The cheers that greeted this speech told Marian that her welcome was indeed sincere, and as she and Robin Hood wandered hand in hand over the greensward, the very birds seemed to be crooning a blessing over their heads.

# JOG ON !

### *by* WILLIAM SHAKESPEARE

JOG on, jog on, the foot-path way,
   And merrily hent the stile-a :
A merry heart goes all the day,
   Your sad tires in a mile-a.

# - - THE - -
# ENCHANTED SHIRT

*by* JOHN HAY

THE King was sick.  His cheek was red
  And his eye was clear and bright :
He ate and drank with kingly zest,
  And peacefully snored at night.

But he said he was sick, and a king should
    know,
  And doctors came by the score,
They did not cure him.  He cut off their
    heads
  And sent to the schools for more.

At last two famous doctors came,
  And one was poor as a rat ;
He had passed his life in studious toil,
  And never found time to grow fat.

The other had never looked into a book ;
  His patients gave him no trouble ;
If they recovered they paid him well,
  If they died their heirs paid double.

Together they looked at the royal tongue,
  As the King on his couch reclined ;
In succession they thumped his august
    chest,
  But no trace of disease could find.

The old sage said : " You're as sound
    as a nut,"
  " Hang him up ! " roared the King in
    a gale,
In a ten-knot gale of royal rage ;
  The other leech grew a shade pale ;

But he pensively rubbed his sagacious
    nose,
  And thus his prescription ran :
*The King will be well if he sleeps one
    night*
*In the shirt of a Happy Man.*

Wide o'er the realm the couriers rode,
  And fast their horses ran :
And many they saw, and to many they
    spoke,
  But they found no Happy Man.

They saw two men by the roadside sit,
  And both bemoaned their lot ;
For one had buried his wife, he said,
  And the other one had not.

At last they came to a village gate,
  A beggar lay whistling there ;
He whistled and sang and laughed and
    rolled
  On the grass in the soft June air.

The weary couriers paused and
    looked
  At the scamp so blithe and gay ;
And one of them said : " Heaven
    save you, friend,
  You seem to be happy to-day."

" O yes, fair sirs," the rascal laughed,
  And his voice laughed free and glad,
" An idle man has so much to do,
  That he never has time to be sad."

"This is our man," the courier said;
  "Our luck has led us right.
I will give you a hundred ducats, friend,
  For the loan of your shirt to-night."

The merry blackguard lay back on the
      grass,
  And laughed till his face was black;
"I would do it, indeed," and he roared
      with the fun,
  "But I haven't a shirt to my back."

Each day to the King the reports came in
  Of his unsuccessful spies,
And the sad panorama of human woes
  Passed daily under his eyes.

And he grew ashamed of his useless life,
  And his maladies hatched in gloom;
He opened his windows and let the air
  Of the free heaven into his room.

And out he went in the world and toiled
  In his own appointed way;
And the people blessed him, the land was glad,
  And the King was well and gay.

# A COMEDY OF TERRORS

## by ROBERT MOSS

OUTSIDE a certain study door in the Sixth Form passage at Saintbury School, four little fags stood in breathless silence, listening. From within floated strange, sad sounds.

*Thwack!*—" Bend over farther, Potts "—*Thwack!*—" This may teach you not to play tricks on a prefect ! "—*Thwack!*—" Next time you offer to get my bath ready "—*Thwack!*—" see that it hasn't been newly enamelled."—*Thwack!*—" Being stuck to the bottom of a bath for several minutes "—*Thwack!*—" is not only very unpleasant "—*Thwack!*—" but exceedingly "—*Thwack!*—" painful ! "

" He's given him a cool eight ! " breathed Caudle Minor, with awe.

" Poor old Potts ! " whispered Pulteney-Dix. " He *will* be sore ! "

" Charley's a beast ! " piped up little Blackmore eagerly. " You know he's trying to grow a moustache ?  Well, I chalked on his door the other day, ' Cat's whiskers fourpence a set '—just for fun, you know. He found out who did it and gave me three stingers—one, he said, because I spelt ' fourpence ' with an ' s ' instead of a ' c.' You'd hardly believe a fellow could be so mean over a joke, would you ? "

" Charley," declared Smith Secundus firmly, " *is* mean ! "

At that moment the door opened, and Potts, curiously stiff and erect, walked out. In silence the subdued group wended its way to the third-form common-room.

" Something will have to be done about Charley," declared Pulteney-Dix impressively, seating himself on the table.

Potts didn't sit.

" Being a prefect has gone to his head," said Caudle Minor.

" To his *arm*, you mean," muttered Potts, feeling himself tenderly.

" I simply can't bear the fellow," cried little Blackmore.

" It's his cane *I* can't bear ! " said Smith Secundus sadly.

There was no doubt that something would have to be done about C. B. Charlemagne, otherwise " Charley." To the small boys in the Third Form, Charley had become a daily terror. Being a prefect, he had authority to use the cane on unruly fags. Being in charge of a dormitory of unruly fags, he used the cane often. Being five feet ten inches high and broad of shoulder, he used the cane with alarming effect.

" Revenge is sweet ! " said Pulteney-Dix with a bloodthirsty hiss. " We'll make Charley pay ! I have an idea. From now on we'll *haunt* him ! "

" What d'you mean, dress up in white sheets and pounce out on him at night and—and things like that ? " cried little Blackmore excitedly. " I —I say, Pult, there are an awful lot of holes in my pyjamas ; I should get beastly cold ! "

" I wouldn't have you seen outside in those sky-blue pyjamas of yours for a term's tuck," cried Pulteney-Dix hastily. " The dormitory would never live them down if they became known. No, my idea of haunting is different. Listen . . ."

Five little heads drew close together, five little voices sank to low whispers, and presently from five little collars came five dark little chuckles.

. . . . . . . . . . .

That night, an uneasy quietude brooded over the Third Form dormitory. From little Blackmore's bed came a curious sound, like a row of exclamation marks set to music. *Pip* !—haha—*pip* !—hah *pip* !—hah. It was little Blackmore's idea of snoring. Charley, the prefect, in the bed nearest the door, reached fiercely for a slipper.

" I used to wonder why the nose was called a nasal *organ*," he snorted. " After sleeping near young Blackmore for a term I know ! "

He lifted the slipper and took aim. But at that instant he became suddenly stiff. Through the stillness of the dormitory floated a shrill mocking voice that chanted these words :

" Cluck — cluck — Charley cluck — Charley, Charley — cluck — *cluck* — CLUCK ! "

C. B. Charlemagne could hardly believe his reddening ears. He sat up in bed, startled and incredulous. Again the small insulting voice began :

" Cluck—cluck—Charley cluck—Charley, Charley—cluck— ! "

With an exclamation so fierce that five little fags snuggled deeper into five little beds, Charley leapt out of bed. He rushed to the electric-light switch. In the dark his big toe struck violently against somebody's boot. He yelped. Then he *yelled*, for the electric-light switch refused to produce light.

" Who has removed the electric-light bulb ? " demanded he in a terrible voice.

From five little beds came five little innocent snores. Snore ! SnORe ! SNOre ! SnoRe ! SNoRe !

Charley strode towards the five little beds. " WHO REMOVED THE ELECTRIC-LIGHT BULB ? " he repeated, very slowly, and very, *very* distinctly.

From five little beds came—No. Unluckily, at that moment Smith Secundus had an accident. He sat on the electric-light bulb, which he had thoughtfully taken to bed with him.

BANG !

Smith Secundus jumped. So did Charley. Then Charley jumped again —at Smith Secundus.

Thwack !—" Ow ! "—" Next time you hide an electric-light bulb "— " OW ! "—*Thwack* !—" Smith Secundus—take care you don't "—*Thwack* ! —" give yourself away "—*Thwack* !—" Ow ! "—" by sitting on it ! "— " Ow ! "

" A cool four," murmured Caudle Minor sadly to his pillow.

" Now what I want to know," said Charley hotly, " is, which of you horrible little grubs had the impudence to sing out those insulting—— ? "

Pulteney-Dix, with a polite wave of his hand, interrupted him.

" Excuse me, Charlemagne," he murmured in his most innocent tones, " I think Mr. Senior is waiting to speak to you."

Charley spun round. Then he sagged. Framed in the doorway, in all the glory of a spotted night-gown, bare spindle legs, and a candle, stood Mr. Senior, the housemaster.

" I—I—— " stuttered Charley, taken aback.

" May I point out, Charlemagne," said the housemaster coldly, " that this is the middle of the night ? "

" I—I was only just —that is—these little demons—er—boys—— " began Charley, floundering hopelessly.

" Just so," agreed Mr. Senior. " But may I suggest that it would be better in future to postpone punishment for misdeeds until a more reasonable hour ? Perhaps you will consider the idea. Good-night."

" G—g—g—good-night, sir," stammered Charley, nearly bursting with emotion.

From five little beds came five little voices, each of which sang softly : " G—g—g—good-night, sir ! "

*Bang ! Smith Secundus jumped. So did Charley*

Most of the next day, from dawn onwards, was spent by five little fags in trying to avoid the wrath of Charley. But the wrath of Charley would not be avoided. By evening five little fags had met, had *felt*, the wrath of Charley.

" Never mind," said Pulteney-Dix woefully. " My idea of haunting him with a voice *was* jolly good. We'll keep on till in sheer desperation he stops caning us."

" Oh, will we ! " exclaimed Smith Secundus. " It was *my* voice that was the first to haunt him, and I've been haunted with pain ever since."

" I know," piped up little Blackmore, very anxious to be heard. " Let's play a trick on him every time he whops one of us. Then he'll know why it is and stop—— ! "

" Oh, sit on him, somebody ! " growled Potts gloomily.

"Yes, that's a good idea," agreed little Blackmore eagerly, thinking Potts was speaking of Charley. "But who—oh!—you meant to sit on—oo—*me*!"

Having sat on little Blackmore, and so relieved their feelings, the little group decided to adopt his plan. During the next two weeks Charley found:

Soot in his boots;

A hen in his bed;

No buttons where there had been trouser-buttons before;

Pins where there had been no pins before;

Nothing but trouble.

But Charley did not flinch. His rule grew stricter. His cane smote harder. Fags fled merely at the sound of his approach.

"If this goes on," declared Pulteney-Dix feelingly, after a specially long visit to Charley's study, "I shall have to buy another Latin Grammar. I'm wearing my only one."

"The thing to do," spoke up Potts, "is to teach Charley a severe lesson —one that he won't forget. And I've thought out how to do it. Listen! Every morning, for the past week, Charley has been for a bathe before breakfast. He goes to the river, over a mile away. Now there isn't a public bathing place in the river, so *he must leave his clothes on the bank*! Do you see the idea?"

Four little fags looked thoughtfully at Potts. Four little fags looked thoughtfully at each other. Then four little fags, breaking into four little smiles, said, slowly and very meaningly, "Ah!"

.    .    .    .    .    .    .    .    .    .    .    .

Very early next morning the great Charley rose from his bed, dressed and silently left the dormitory. Two minutes later, Pulteney-Dix began the task of getting his fellow-conspirators to leave *their* beds.

"I'm not fond of early-morning bathing, if Charley is," grumbled Smith Secundus, as he picked fragments of chilly wet sponge from between his neck and his pyjamas.

"Hurry!" hissed Pulteney-Dix, "Charley will have bathed, curled his silly moustache and had breakfast by the time we reach the river if you don't look sharp."

At last five little fags, shivering in the sharp morning air, were on their way to the river.

"Now, all we need to do," said Pulteney-Dix, "is to find Charley's clothes and then run for it. Ah! I have it! The disused boathouse. That's just the place where he'd be likely to leave them."

Keeping in the shelter of a coppice, Pulteney-Dix led the way at a run towards the old boathouse.

"I saw Charley then," announced little Blackmore suddenly, breathless with excitement. "He's a long way downstream, but I think he is swimming."

The boathouse reached, five joyous chuckles floated out on the still morning air.

Within was a pile of clothes. Pulteney-Dix made one quick grab at the pile. Potts secured a pair of braces. Little Blackmore managed to capture a sock from the heap. Smith Secundus found himself without a prize, so he thoughtfully rescued a pair of shoes from the greedy hands of Caudle Minor.

" We'll leave these here," he chortled. " If he ran all the way back to school, Charley might get corns on his bare feet. Besides, he'll look funnier with only a pair of shoes on."

In frantic haste, almost bursting with mirth, the five dashed off, bearing the clothes in triumph with them.

" I say, I'd give anything to see Charley's face when he finds his clothes gone ! " bubbled little Blackmore.

" He'll be awfully cold ! " grinned Caudle Minor.

" His shoes will keep his tootsies warm," said Smith Secundus cheerfully.

But at that moment a wild cry of rage broke from the direction of the river.

Like scuttling rabbits, the five dived hurriedly into a clump of bushes. Presently Pulteney-Dix cautiously raised his head and peeped towards the boathouse. Then he sank back, quivering with laughter.

" He—he's jumping about like a dancing bear ! " he gasped out weakly. " He's tied some old sacking or something about his waist, and he's waving his arms about as if he'd been stung by a horde of wasps ! "

" Perhaps he's trying to attract somebody's attention," suggested Smith Secundus. " Now, if he were one of the babes in the wood, the birds might come to the rescue with some leaves."

" Ha ! Ha ! Ha ! " roared Caudle Minor.

" He ! He ! He ! " gurgled little Blackmore.

" That's a very bright joke you are all enjoying," spoke a deep, grim voice suddenly behind them. " I should like to hear it. Hullo, what is that you have there—somebody's clothes ? "

Five little fags became suddenly stiff and still. Fearfully their eyes turned to behold the intruder.

*Before them, a bicycle by his side, stood a big familiar figure—Charley !*

Then they shrank.

Before them, a bicycle by his side, stood a big familiar figure—Charley!

" Ch—ch—ch—ch—Charley ! " breathed Pulteney-Dix stupidly.

" Ch—ch—ch—— " began Potts, and then his whisper trailed away into horrified silence.

In two minutes Charley had penetrated the plot. " So my habit of taking an early morning dip inspired another of your bright ideas, eh ? " he said. " As it happened, I chose a cycle ride this morning instead of a bathe. But you have evidently succeeded in taking *somebody's* clothes. Whose, I wonder ? "

He stared down at the pile of clothes, and then his gaze became fixed.

" Great Scott ! " he exclaimed, and his voice trembled with a great awe. " Do you know whose clothes you have purloined ? There's only one person at Saintbury besides myself who sometimes has a swim before breakfast, and there's only one person in all the school who wears a collar of that pattern—and that one is your own housemaster—Mr. Senior."

Five little faces became five shades paler. From their limp bodies the earth seemed to be slipping away.

" Mr. S—s—s—s—Senior ! " gasped Pulteney-Dix.

Charley nodded. Then he braced himself. " There he is now, by the boathouse ; he's signalling to me. I'll say only one word to you. That is : GO!"

Five little fags, crushed, mute, went.

.  .  .  .  .  .  .  .  .  .  .

In Charley's study, five little fags stood in a subdued row.

" Mr. Senior is not a suspicious man," said Charley. " He thought it was a tramp who stole his clothes. I didn't enlighten him. If I had, I daren't guess what would happen to you. As it is, I *know* what is going to happen to you. You first, Pulteney-Dix."

Ten minutes later, five little fags filed stiffly out into the passage.

" Charley's a splendid brick ! " cried little Blackmore enthusiastically.

Pulteney-Dix nodded. " After not giving us away to Mr. Senior, we'll never rag him again," he said.

Four little hands rubbed four little tender spots, and four little voices echoed heartily, with rare feeling : " Never again ! "

---

# THE YEAR'S AT THE SPRING

*by* ROBERT BROWNING

THE year's at the spring,
  And day's at the morn ;
Morning's at seven ;
The hill-side's dew-pearled ;
The lark's on the wing ;
The snail's on the thorn ;
God's in His Heaven—
All's right with the world !

# THE CHILDREN IN THE MOON

*by* ROBERT BUCHANAN

HEARKEN, child, unto a story !
For the moon is in the sky,
And across her shield of silver,
See ! two tiny cloudlets fly.

Watch them closely, mark them sharply,
As across the light they pass,—
Seem they not to have the figures
Of a little lad and lass ?

See, my child, across their shoulders
Lies a little pole ; and lo !
Yonder speck is just the bucket,
Swinging softly to and fro.

It is said, these little children,
Many and many a summer night,
To a little well far northward
Wandered in the still moonlight.

To the wayside well they trotted,
Filled their little buckets there,
And the Moon-man, looking downward,
Saw how beautiful they were.

Quoth the man, " How vexed and sulky
Looks the little rosy boy !
But the little handsome maiden
Trips behind him full of joy.

" To the well behind the hedgerow
  Trot the little lad and maiden ;
From the well behind the hedgerow
  Now the little pail is laden.

" How they please me ! how they tempt me !
  Shall I snap them up to-night ?
Snatch them, set them here for ever
  In the middle of my light ?

" Children, ay, and children's children,
  Should behold my babes on high,
And my babes should smile for ever,
  Calling others to the sky ! "

Thus the calm and thoughtful Moon-man
  Muttered many years ago,
Set the babes with pole and bucket,
  To delight the folks below.

Never is the bucket empty,
  Never are the children old ;
Ever when the moon is shining
  We the children may behold.

Ever young and ever little,
  Ever sweet and ever fair !
When thou art a man, my darling,
  Still the children will be there !

Ever young and ever little,
  They will smile when thou art old ;
When thy locks are thin and silver,
  Theirs will be still shining gold.

They will haunt thee from their heaven,
  Softly beckoning down the gloom—
Smiling in eternal sweetness
  On thy cradle, on thy tomb !

# The Glass Brain

## by WILLIAM GILBERT (*Adapted*)

### I

AT the latter end of the fifteenth century, there lived in Bishopsgate Street, London, a merchant of the name of Walter Courcy. He was between forty-five and fifty years of age, tall, well-built, and handsome. He was honourable and generous, but at the same time proud and full of ambition. He was a widower, with one daughter, Bertha, about nineteen years of age.

His ships sailed chiefly to Italy, and his business with Venice was greater than that of any other merchant in England. Vast quantities of valuable goods, jewels, and rich stuffs were sent to him by his agent, who had orders to forward anything new and uncommon.

One novelty, of which the merchant had heard but had not seen, was a glass mirror. These articles had lately been invented, and a manufactory had been established near Venice; but, as it was in the hands of the Government, who generally presented the mirrors to crowned heads, as gifts of great price, it was difficult for the English merchant to obtain one.

He had several of the largest metal mirrors, both of silver and of bronze, but, according to all accounts, they were not to be compared in beauty with those made of glass.

At last, however, by a lucky or perhaps unlucky chance, Master Walter became the owner of a glass mirror. It was of oval shape, and of one entire piece of crystal. On the top of the glass, just beneath the carved frame, were some letters, in ruby-coloured glass, so brilliant that it almost dazzled the eye to look on them. Of what language these letters were no one knew, so that it was impossible to tell their meaning.

" If my brain were made of crystal as pure as this," said the merchant, " I believe I should succeed in everything I undertook."

" But, my dear father, how would that benefit you ? " his daughter asked. " At present you are one of the richest men in England, and what can you wish for more ? "

" To be the richest, my dear. Yes, I sincerely wish my brain were made of glass as clear as that, and I would make you, my child, the wealthiest heiress in the world."

That same evening, when the merchant returned from business, he looked so pale that his daughter asked if he were unwell.

" Never better," he replied ; " with the exception of a slight headache there is nothing the matter."

" Then something has happened to annoy you."

" On the contrary," he answered, smiling faintly, " everything to-day has gone on in the most satisfactory manner."

They now sat down to their meal, for which, however, the merchant seemed to have little appetite. He ate scarcely anything, and soon rose from his chair.

" I feel somewhat tired, my dear," he said in his usual kind tone, " and will go to bed."

Next morning, having business with the Lord Mayor, he went to the Guildhall, where the train-bands were assembled in the courtyard. He watched them for some time, and noticed that their dress was much faded and in bad condition ; but he said nothing to any one on the subject.

Then he proceeded to the Exchange, where he seemed to be looking for some person who was not there. Presently, when two Flemings made their appearance, he walked towards them.

" Good-morning, gentlemen," he said, " I am glad to see you have not yet left England."

" Not yet," replied the elder of the two ; " but we leave to-morrow."

" May I ask what takes you away ? "

" Simply that we can do no business here, and are only wasting our time."

" Is not that your own fault ? " asked Master Walter. " I am afraid it is rather from the high price you ask for your cloth, than from any want of will on the part of our merchants to purchase."

" Not so," said they. " The sum we asked was so small that it scarcely covered the cost of our venture."

" I wish I had known this before," observed Master Walter, " but it is too late now."

" Perhaps not. It is true we have re-shipped the cloth, but if you think of buying we can go to examine it."

When they arrived on board the ship, the Flemings ordered some of the bales of cloth to be brought upon deck, and they were opened one after the other. After some talk the merchant bought the whole of the cloth, and had it removed at once to his warehouse.

He now returned to the Guildhall, where the Lord Mayor and aldermen were in council. The king had promised to dine with them in a fortnight's time, and they wished to provide new uniforms for the train-bands.

" But," said the Lord Mayor sadly, " we do not know where to buy the cloth, no one that we can hear of having sufficient for the purpose. Perhaps Master Walter can advise us on the subject."

" My lord," said the merchant, " I can ; but if I do, you may think me somewhat selfish."

" How so ? "

" Because, at this moment, I happen to be the largest holder of cloth in London, and I should not feel disposed, even to do honour to His Majesty, to sell it under its full value."

" At such a time," said the Lord Mayor, " we cannot haggle about price. Tell us how much cloth you have, and what you ask for it, and we will give you an answer."

The merchant thereupon asked just twice the amount he had paid, and the aldermen, finding they could do no better, at length agreed to buy the material on his own terms.

## II

MASTER WALTER now rose rapidly, until he reached the height of his good fortune. He was a member of the Privy Council ; he was the richest man in London, and everything happened exactly as he wished. His daughter was presented at Court, and was received most graciously. Yet, in spite of all his success, the merchant did not appear to be a happy man.

The evening for the feast in the Guildhall arrived. The king was on a raised throne at one end. Nearest to his right hand sat the Lord Mayor, and to his left Master Walter. Several ladies, with Bertha amongst them, were seated in a gallery. At the sight of her father sitting so near the king, her heart beat with pride ; yet she was not altogether free from anxiety, so weak and ill did he appear.

Master Ambrose, the king's leech, saw this also, and asked the merchant if he were unwell.

" I have not been in good health lately," he replied, " and I have been thinking on calling on you for advice."

" Do so," said the doctor ; " I will remain at home for you to-morrow morning."

The next day, according to promise, the merchant called on Master Ambrose.

" Now tell me what is the matter with you," the doctor began ; " or, rather, I think I can tell you."

" What ? " asked Master Walter.

" You have lately had something to annoy you, and it has preyed on your spirits."

" You were never farther from the truth in your life. For some time past everything has prospered with me."

" You must be a very happy man."

" Again you are in error. A more miserable person does not exist ; my life is hateful to me. I receive every blessing, and yet am not grateful. The king honours me, and I care not at all. My daughter loves me dearly, yet I have no affection for her in return."

" But you did not always feel like this ? "

" Certainly not ; it has only been for the last few weeks."

" What do you think is the cause ? "

" I am almost afraid to say, lest you should laugh at me ; but, for what reason I know not, I have felt recently as if my brain were made of glass."

" What causes you to think that ? " asked the doctor.

" In the first place, my head is so heavy that I can hardly hold it up. In the second, it is like ice. Thirdly, I see everything so clearly that no one can get the better of me. Nothing either pleases or distresses me. I am no more able to feel than a mass of rock crystal."

The doctor looked at him carefully for some time. " Master Walter," said he at last, " as soon as the State ball is over you must leave London, and think no more of business for some time."

The merchant's health did not improve, and on the night of the ball he was too unwell to leave his room. Bertha wished to stay at home, but this he would not permit, and it was arranged that she should go with the wife of the Lord Mayor. She looked very beautiful, and it was with a proud smile that, before joining her friends, she took a last glance at herself in the mirror. When they had gone, the merchant, feeling ill and weary, retired to bed.

It was late when Bertha returned from the ball, and the house was in darkness. Her maid, carrying a heavy lamp, lighted her upstairs. At the door of the chamber Bertha, finding she had dropped her fan, asked the maid to look for it. Meanwhile she herself, entering the room in the darkness, stumbled against the wonderful mirror and broke it. Here was a misfortune ! What would her father say when he learned what had occurred ?

*She took a last glance at herself in the mirror*

But a very curious thing was to happen ! When she had left her father, he had risen with difficulty from his seat to bid her farewell. Next morning he walked into the breakfast-room with light step and smiling face.

" Well, my little Bertha," he laughed, " you did not expect to see me down to breakfast, did you ? "

" In truth, father, I did not ; but it makes me happy to see you look so much better."

" It is wonderful," said he, beginning breakfast. " When I went to bed last night the pain in my head was terrible. Suddenly it vanished, and I never felt better in my life."

" I am most happy, dear father, to hear it ; but when did you say the pain ceased ? "

" Some few minutes after your return from the ball. I thought I heard a noise of some glass falling, and the pain left me immediately."

Bertha glanced at her father for a moment and then said, " Father, you did hear the noise of falling glass ; I have broken the mirror."

To her surprise her father showed not the faintest sign of either anger or sorrow. He seemed to be thinking deeply, and presently said, " Bertha, I have several times thought the mirror had something to do with my illness, and now I am sure of it. Had we been able to understand the writing on the frame, we might have learned the secret. However, let us be thankful that the danger is over, and dismiss the subject from our minds."

It is certainly curious that, after the breaking of the mirror, the merchant's strange illness never returned. He lived to a good old age, honoured and respected by every one for his good faith in all his dealings. As for Bertha, she married a young merchant, made an excellent wife and mother, and lived to see her eldest son elected Lord Mayor of London.

# SLEEP

*by* CHARLOTTE DRUITT COLE

IN the dark and lonely night,
When the stars are all alight,
Sleep comes creeping up the street,
With her naked, silent feet,
Carrying upon her back,
Dreams of all kinds in a sack ;
Though the doors are bolted, still
She can enter where she will ;
And she lingers, it is said,
Longest by the children's bed—
Smooths their pillows, strokes their curls,
Happy little boys and girls !
But her prettiest dreams she keeps
For the Baby, where he sleeps.

# THE PINK VEST

### by LOUEY CHISHOLM

JANE thought she was not clever, and she knew she was not pretty, and she ought to have been quite sure she was not good. But the worst of it was, she did not care whether she was good or not.

Of all Jane's faults the worst was grumbling. There were so many things she did not like. For instance, she could not bear her own name. Why should people not choose what they should be called ? Jane was such a plain name, and she would rather have had no grandmother than have been forced to be her namesake. And the provoking thing was it would have been quite as easy to have called her after Aunt Beatrice. Jane was so short and plain and snappy—such a " bare " name, Jane said ; and Beatrice you could linger over, and it made you think of pretty clothes. Such a name as Jane should be given to no one except as a punishment, and she had been an unoffending baby when it became hers for life.

Jane grumbled too about the colour of her hair. It was neither golden fair nor raven-black, and all the little girls in Jane's story-books had either one or the other. Hers was just a brown-red colour, and she hated it. She would look in the glass and say to herself : " It's my carroty hair that makes me so ugly," but really that wasn't it at all, for it was her pouting lips and scowling forehead that spoilt what should have been a sweet little face.

Jane grumbled too over her lessons, and she grumbled when she had to go to bed, and she grumbled when she had to get up in the morning.

But of all Jane's grumblings the worst were to be heard at meal-times. There was hardly a day passed but Jane didn't like or didn't want what was on the table.

Mrs. Brown, Jane's mother, corrected her little girl over and over again, but as things remained as bad as ever, she determined to punish the naughty child next time she grumbled during a meal.

Jane had also a bad habit of fidgeting at table, and she would fiddle with the salt-spoon or anything within reach, and she was a child that did not hesitate to interrupt her father or mother.

Such a state of things could not continue, so one day at breakfast, when Jane began to hum, while her parents were talking, Mrs. Brown corrected her.

Jane stopped humming, but in a moment was tilting back her chair. " Sit properly, Jane," said her mother.

" I want another lump of sugar," said Jane, slowly bringing forward her chair, and at the same time thrusting out the hand that held her cup and saucer. Over went the cup, and its contents were spilt into the marmalade jar and over the table-cloth.

Now Mr. Brown was a dear daddy, but he had some peculiarities. One was that he could not eat a chop without ketchup. Indeed his wife said that he would rather have the ketchup without the chop. Nor could he eat mutton

246

without red-currant jelly, nor pork without apple sauce. It also happened that he could not eat breakfast without marmalade, and so he was extremely annoyed when Mrs. Brown told him she had not another jar in the house.

Jane's mother was annoyed for another reason. As it was Monday, the clean table-cloth had reached only the second day of its life and it was now unfit to use.

Mr. Brown muttered something, but Jane could not be sure whether he was saying how tiresome children were or how good marmalade was. But there was no doubt about what her mother said.

"Jane, if you misbehave again, you shall be punished. Eat your bacon."

Jane gave her plate a push. "I did eat part of it," she said. "The rest is fat. I don't like it. I don't want it. I won't eat it."

Mrs. Brown took the plate in her hand. "Come upstairs, Jane." The little girl followed her mother to the box-room in the attic. "I shall lock you in till my work is done," said her mother. "Then I shall come to see if you have finished your breakfast. If you have you shall come downstairs. If not, you shall remain where you are until you have eaten every morsel."

Then Jane's mother left her. Jane heard the key turn in the lock. The box-room was nothing but boxes, and every one of them was empty.

From the window, Jane could see nothing but the sky; and what a blue sky it was!

*The little girl followed her mother to the box-room in the attic*

MILDRED·R·LAMB·

It was too bad to be locked up on such a day ! She would make her mother very sorry for treating her so. She would scream at the top of her voice so that all the neighbours could hear, and then they would tell Mrs. Brown what an unkind mother she was.

So Jane screamed and screamed with all her might. Then when she paused for breath, she thought she heard voices beneath the window. She could see no one, but she distinctly overheard these words : " I'm sorry for that girl's mother. The child needs a good beating, that's what she does, disturbing the whole neighbourhood like that. Poor Mrs. Brown, to have such a daughter ! "

" So it's Mother they're sorry for, is it ? " thought Jane. " Nobody cares about me, but I'll make Mother sorry for me. If I'm very quiet, she'll think I've cried till I've fainted and when she comes up she'll find I have, and then she'll get a nice fright." And Jane lay down on her back on the uncarpeted floor, stretched out her legs very stiff and straight, closed her eyes, lips and fists tight. " I wonder if that is right," she thought. " No ; I believe my mouth should be open." And Jane opened her mouth wide. Then in a few minutes, although to Jane it seemed hours, she thought : " I hope Mother will be quick or I'll have to come out of this faint. The floor is so hard and there's a fly keeps tickling my tongue."

But her mother did not come and Jane could bear it no longer. She got up. She must do something. But what ? Her daddy often said that " Satan finds some mischief still for idle hands to do," but that was not true to-day. She was deserted by every one, and she felt very miserable and utterly lonely. Time dragged slowly on. Would her mother ever come?

At last Jane smiled a watery smile. She had an idea.

Slowly she began to undress. One by one she took off her things. No sooner had she done this than she began to put them on again—all but her little pink vest.

Jane could knit and she had made that vest last winter. With it in her hand she now sat down on one of the empty boxes and she nibbled at the edge of the vest until she could get hold of an end of the wool. At last there was something to do. Mischief had been found for those idle hands.

She gave the wool one pull after another, and she went on pull, pull, pulling. Then she began to roll the wool into a neat ball. And the neat little ball began to grow, and Jane went on roll, rolling until at last she had a big ball of wool in her hand and not a suspicion of the little pink vest remained.

Jane now had something to play with, and for some time she was happy tossing and catching the ball. But before long she grew tired and wondered what she should do next. She was beginning to feel hungry, and her eye fell, not for the first time, on the cold fat bacon.

" If I shut my eyes and hold my nose, I believe I can eat it," she said. And she did, for when her mother came in five minutes later, Jane's plate was as bare as old Mother Hubbard's cupboard. " Come along, Jane," she said. " Bring your plate and wash it."

Jane followed her mother downstairs and all that day she was very subdued. She watered the flowers in the garden plot, and she went to buy

*The neat little ball began to grow*

marmalade for her father's tea, and altogether it seemed as if she had made up her mind to turn over a new leaf. But when night came and Jane undressed, her mother noticed that she had on no vest.

"You naughty girl, how dare you leave off your warm underclothing without my leave! Bring me your vest at once and see that you put it on to-morrow morning."

Jane tried to speak, but not a word would come.

"Where is your vest?"

Before Jane could reply, her mother, who was hanging up her little girl's dress, muttered to herself: "What can this be in the child's pocket?"

Jane made a queer sound. It was half a laugh and half a cry, for Mrs. Brown now held in her hand the ball of pink wool.

"Good-night, Jane," said her mother in a cold voice.

"Good-night, Mother," whispered her wondering little daughter as she crept into bed.

If Mrs. Brown had been angry, Jane could have understood that, but what could her silence mean? Was it possible that she did not connect the pink ball with the missing vest?

Whether that was so or not, the next morning a clean one lay with Jane's clothes. As soon as she was dressed and had had breakfast, her mother sent her on various errands. As the day went on, Jane breathed freely, and by dinner time had forgotten all about the ball of pink wool.

I must tell you that while Jane was a child that grumbled when she did not get her own way, no one enjoyed a treat more than she did. So it was with great excitement that she said to her mother after dinner, "I am so glad it is such a fine day. What a treat it will be to go to the seaside for the afternoon ! "

" The seaside did you say, my dear Jane ? "

" Yes, Mother. You remember, Mrs. White said a week ago that she would take me to-day if it was fine. Shall I wear my straw hat, and where are my spade and pail, and will you let——"

" Before you go to the seaside," interrupted Mrs. Brown, " you must find the vest you wore yesterday. You had better look for it at once."

Jane tried to get off her chair, but she could not. Her knees were knocking against each other. She could not move, but sat with her eyes cast upon the ground.

" You will find nothing as long as you sit there, Jane. If you bring your vest to me before two o'clock, you shall go to the seaside with Mrs. White. If not, you must knit another. In that case this ball of pink wool may be useful. Strange to say I found it in your pocket." So saying, Mrs. Brown left the room.

But her mother's words were too much for Jane. She burst into tears and cried as if her heart would break, and she was still sobbing when the door opened suddenly. There stood Aunt Beatrice, looking so sweet and wearing the pretty clothes that, according to Jane, her name gave her the right to possess.

" Why, Pigeon, what is the matter ? " and the young aunt bent down and kissed the angry little face.

" I hate everything in the world," said Jane. " I hate my bare name, and I hate my carroty hair, and I hate fat bacon and I hate, hate, hate knitting pink vests."

" Something has happened," said Aunt Beatrice. " Tell me all about it."

And Aunt Beatrice's voice was so gentle and her face was so kind that Jane told her everything. She even told her how she had fainted in the attic and how the fly had tickled her tongue. And Aunt Beatrice did not even smile, but listened quite solemnly, for she knew how very unhappy and miserable her little niece had been.

At last Jane finished her truthful story, which, of course, included how she had ruined both a clean table-cloth and her father's appetite. " For," she explained, " daddy really likes marmalade as much as I hate fat."

Then Aunt Beatrice took Jane on her lap. " You see, Pigeon," she said (and how Jane loved to be called Pigeon instead of bare Jane !), " you see, you think too much about a little girl called Jane Brown, and about the things she likes and the things she doesn't like. If you could forget her and think a little more about other people and the things they like, and the things they don't like, you wouldn't grumble any more, and you would be a much happier child. Will you try, Pigeon ? "

Jane flung her arms round Aunt Beatrice's neck. " Indeed, I will, Aunty, I will, I will ; but I'll always hate fat bacon and pink vests."

THE GREY CHAMPION
BY NATHANIEL HAWTHORNE

THERE was once a time when New England groaned under the actual pressure of heavier wrongs than those threatened ones which brought on the Revolution. James II., the bigoted successor of Charles the Voluptuous, had annulled the charters of all the colonies, and sent a harsh and unprincipled soldier to take away our liberties and endanger our religion. The administration of Sir Edmund Andros lacked scarcely a single characteristic of tyranny; a Governor and Council, holding office from the King, and wholly independent of the country; laws made and taxes levied without concurrence of the people, immediate or by their representatives; the right of private citizens violated, and the titles of all landed property declared void; the voice of complaint stifled by restrictions on the press; and finally, disaffection overawed by the first band of mercenary troops that ever marched on our free soil. For two years our ancestors were kept in sullen submission, by that filial love which had invariably secured their allegiance to the Mother Country, whether its head chanced to be a Parliament, Protector, or Popish Monarch. Till these evil times, however, such allegiance had been merely nominal, and the colonists had ruled themselves, enjoying far more freedom than is even yet the privilege of the native subjects of Great Britain.

At length, a rumour reached our shores that the Prince of Orange had ventured on an enterprise, the success of which would be the triumph of civil and religious rights and the salvation of New England. It was but a doubtful whisper; it might be false, or the attempt might fail; and, in either case, the man that stirred against King James would lose his head. Still the intelligence produced a marked effect. The people smiled mysteriously in the streets, and threw bold glances at their oppressors; while, far and wide, there was a subdued and silent agitation, as if the slightest signal would rouse the whole land from its sluggish despondency. Aware of this danger, the rulers resolved to avert it by an imposing display of strength, and perhaps to confirm their despotism by yet harsher measures.

One afternoon in April, 1689, Sir Edmund Andros and his favourite councillors, being warm with wine, assembled the red-coats of the Governor's Guard, and made their appearance in the streets of Boston. The sun was near setting when the march commenced.

The roll of the drums, at that unquiet crisis, seemed to go through the streets, less as the martial music of the soldiers than as a muster call to the inhabitants themselves. A multitude, by various avenues, assembled in King Street, which was destined to be the scene, nearly a century afterwards, of another encounter between the troops of Britain and a people struggling against her tyranny. Though more than sixty years had elapsed since the Pilgrims came, this crowd of their descendants still showed the strong and sombre features of their character, perhaps more striking in such a stern emergency than on happier occasions. There were the sober garb, the general severity of mien, the gloomy but undismayed expression, the scriptural forms of speech, and the confidence in Heaven's blessing on a righteous cause, which would have marked a band of the original Puritans when threatened by some peril of the wilderness. Indeed, it was not yet time for the old spirit to be extinct ; since there were men in the street that day who had worshipped there beneath the trees, before a house was reared to the God for whom they had become exiles. Old soldiers of the Parliament were here, too, smiling grimly at the thought that their aged arms might strike another blow against the house of Stuart. Here, also, were the veterans of King Philip's war, who had burned villages and slaughtered young and old, with pious fierceness, while the godly souls throughout the land were helping them with prayer. Several ministers were scattered among the crowd, which, unlike all other mobs, regarded them with such reverence as if there were sanctity in their very garments. These holy men exerted their influence to quiet the people, but not to disperse them. Meantime, the purpose of the Governor, in disturbing the peace of the town at a period when the slightest commotion might throw the country into a ferment, was almost the universal subject of inquiry, and variously explained.

" Satan will strike his master-stroke presently," cried some, " because he knoweth that his time is short. All our godly pastors are to be dragged to prison ! We shall see them at a Smithfield fire in King Street ! "

" The Pope of Rome has given orders for a new St. Bartholomew ! " cried others. " We are to be massacred, man and male child ! "

Neither was this rumour wholly discredited, although the wiser class believed the Governor's object somewhat less atrocious. His predecessor under the old charter, Bradstreet, a venerable companion of the first settlers, was known to be in town. There were grounds for conjecturing that Sir Edmund Andros intended at once to strike terror by a parade of military force, and to confound the opposite faction, by possessing himself of their chief.

" Stand firm for the old charter, Governor ! " shouted the crowd, seizing upon the idea. " The good old Governor Bradstreet ! "

While this cry was at the loudest, the people were surprised by the well-known figure of Governor Bradstreet himself, a patriarch of nearly ninety, who appeared on the elevated steps of a door, and, with characteristic mildness, besought them to submit to the constituted authorities.

" My children," concluded this venerable person, " do nothing rashly.

Cry not aloud, but pray for the welfare of New England, and expect patiently what the Lord will do in the matter ! "

The event was soon to be decided. All this time, the roll of the drum had been approaching through Cornhill, louder and deeper, till with reverberations from house to house, and the regular tramp of martial footsteps, it burst into the street. A double rank of soldiers made their appearance, occupying the whole breadth of the passage, with shouldered matchlocks, and matches burning, so as to present a row of fires in the dusk. Their steady march was like the progress of a machine that would roll irresistibly over everything in its way. Next, moving slowly, with a confused clatter of hoofs on the pavement, rode a party of mounted gentlemen, the central figure being Sir Edmund Andros, elderly, but erect and soldier-like. Those around were his favourite councillors and the bitterest foes of New England. At his right hand rode Edward Randolph, our arch-enemy, that " blasted wretch," as Cotton Mather calls him, who achieved the downfall of our ancient government, and was followed with a sensible curse through life and to his grave. On the other side was Bullivant, scattering jests and mockery as he rode along. Dudley came behind, with a downcast look, dreading, as well he might, to meet the indignant gaze of the people, who beheld him, their only countryman by birth, among the oppressors of his native land. The captain of a frigate in the harbour, and two or three civil officers under the Crown, were also there. But the figure which most attracted the public eye, and stirred up the deepest feeling, was the Episcopal clergyman of King's Chapel, riding haughtily among the magistrates in his priestly vestments, the fitting representative of prelacy and persecution, the union of church and state, and all those abominations which had driven the Puritans to the wilderness. Another guard of soldiers brought up the rear.

The whole scene was a picture of the condition of New England, and its moral, the deformity of any government that does not grow out of the nature of things and the character of the people. On one side the religious multitude, with their sad visages and dark attire, and on the other, the group of despotic rulers, with the High Churchman in the midst, all magnificently clad, flushed with wine, proud of unjust authority, and scoffing at the universal groan. And the mercenary soldiers, waiting but the word to deluge the street with blood, showed the only means by which obedience could be secured.

" O Lord of Hosts," cried a voice among the crowd, " provide a Champion for Thy people ! "

This ejaculation was loudly uttered, and served as a herald's cry, to introduce a remarkable personage. The crowd had rolled back, and were now huddled together nearly at the extremity of the street, while the soldiers had advanced to more than a third of its length. The intervening space was empty—a paved solitude between lofty edifices, which threw almost a twilight shadow over it. Suddenly, there was seen the figure of an ancient man, who seemed to have emerged from the people, and was walking by himself along the centre of the street, to confront the armed band. He wore the old Puritan dress, a dark cloak and a steeple-crowned hat, in the fashion of at least fifty years before, with a heavy sword upon his thigh, but a staff in his hand to assist the tremulous gait of age.

When at some distance from the multitude, the old man turned slowly round, displaying a face of antique majesty, rendered doubly venerable by the hoary beard that descended on his breast. He made a gesture at once of encouragement and warning, then turned again, and resumed his way.

" Who is this grey patriarch ? " asked the young men of their sires.

" Who is this venerable brother ? " asked the old men among themselves.

But none could make reply. The fathers of the people, those of fourscore years and upwards, were disturbed, deeming it strange that they should forget one of such evident authority, whom they must have known in their early days, the associates of Winthrop, and all the old councillors, giving laws, and making prayers, and leading them against the savage. The elderly men ought to have remembered him, too, with locks as grey in their youth as their own were now. And the young ! How could he have passed so utterly from their memories—that hoary sire, the relic of long-departed times, whose awful benediction had surely been bestowed on their uncovered heads in childhood ?

" Whence did he come ? What is his purpose ? Who can this old man be ? " whispered the wondering crowd.

Meanwhile, the venerable stranger, staff in hand, was pursuing his solitary walk along the centre of the street. As he drew near the advancing soldiers, and as the roll of the drum came full upon his ear, the old man raised himself to a loftier mien, while the decrepitude of age seemed to fall from his shoulders, leaving him in grey but unbroken dignity. Now, he marched onward with a warrior's step, keeping time to the military music. Thus the aged form advanced on one side, and the whole parade of soldiers and magistrates on the other, till, when scarcely twenty yards remained between, the old man grasped his staff by the middle, and held it before him like a leader's truncheon.

" Stand ! " cried he.

The eye, the face, and attitude of command ; the solemn, yet warlike peal of that voice, fit either to rule a host in the battlefield or to be raised to God in prayer, were irresistible. At the old man's word and outstretched arm, the roll of the drum was hushed at once, and the advancing line stood still. A tremulous enthusiasm seized upon the multitude. That stately form, combining the leader and the saint, so grey, so dimly seen, in such an ancient garb, could only belong to some old champion of the righteous cause whom the oppressor's drum had summoned from his grave. They raised a shout of exultation, and looked for the deliverance of New England.

The Governor, and the gentlemen of his party, perceiving themselves brought to an unexpected stand, rode hastily forward, as if they would have pressed their snorting and affrighted horses right against the hoary apparition. He, however, blenched not a step, but glancing his severe eye round the group, which half encompassed him, at last bent it sternly on Sir Edmund Andros. One would have thought that the dark old man was chief ruler there, and that the Governor and Council, with soldiers at their back, representing the whole power and authority of the Crown, had no alternative but obedience.

" What does this old fellow here ? " cried Edward Randolph fiercely. " On, Sir Edmund ! Bid the soldiers forward, and give the dotard the same choice that you give all his countrymen—to stand aside or be trampled on ! "

" Nay, nay, let us show respect to the good grandsire," said Bullivant, laughing. " See you not, he is some old round-headed dignitary who hath lain asleep these thirty years and knows nothing of the change of times ? Doubtless, he thinks to put us down with a proclamation in Old Noll's name ! "

" Are you mad, old man ? " demanded Sir Edmund Andros, in loud and harsh tones. " How dare you stay the march of King James's Governor ? "

" I have stayed the march of a King himself ere now," replied the grey figure, with stern composure. " I am here, Sir Governor, because the cry of an oppressed people hath disturbed me in my secret place ; and beseeching

" *Stand !* " *cried he.   The eye, the face, and attitude of command were irresistible*

this favour earnestly of the Lord, it was vouchsafed me to appear once again on earth, in the good old cause of His saints.  And what speak ye of James ? There is no longer a Popish tyrant on the throne of England, and by to-morrow noon his name shall be a byword in this very street, where ye would make it a word of terror.  Back, thou that wast a Governor, back !  With this night thy power is ended—to-morrow the prison !—back lest I foretell the scaffold ! "

The people had been drawing nearer and nearer, and drinking in the words of their champion, who spoke in accents long disused, like one unaccustomed to converse except with the dead of many years ago.  But his voice stirred their souls.  They confronted the soldiers, not wholly without arms, and ready to convert the very stones of the street into deadly weapons.  Sir Edmund Andros looked at the old man ; then he cast his hard and cruel eye over the multitude, and beheld them burning with that lurid wrath so difficult to kindle or to quench ; and again he fixed his gaze on the aged form, which stood obscurely in an open space, where neither friend nor foe had thrust himself. What were his thoughts, he uttered no word which might discover. But whether the oppressor was overawed by the Grey Champion's look, or perceived his peril in the threatening attitude of the people, it is certain that he gave back, and ordered his soldiers to commence a slow and guarded retreat. Before another sunset, the Governor, and all that rode so proudly with him, were prisoners, and long ere it was known that James had abdicated, King William was proclaimed throughout New England.

But where was the Grey Champion? Some reported that when the troops had gone from King Street, and the people were thronging tumultuously in their rear, Bradstreet, the aged Governor, was seen to embrace a form more aged than his own. Others soberly affirmed that while they marvelled at the venerable grandeur of his aspect, the old man had faded from their eyes, melting slowly into the hues of twilight, till, where he stood, there was an empty space. But all agreed that the hoary shape was gone.

And who was the Grey Champion? I have heard that whenever the descendants of the Puritans are to show the spirit of their sires, the old man appears again. When eighty years had passed, he walked once more in King Street. Five years later, in the twilight of an April morning, he stood on the green, beside the meeting-house, at Lexington, where now the obelisk of granite, with a slab of slate inlaid, commemorates the first fallen of the Revolution. And when our fathers were toiling at the breast-work on Bunker's Hill, all through that night the old warrior walked his rounds. Long, long may it be ere he comes again! His hour is one of darkness, and adversity, and peril. But should domestic tyranny oppress us, or the invader's step pollute our soil, still may the Grey Champion come; for he is the type of New England's hereditary spirit: and his shadowy march, on the eve of danger, must ever be the pledge that New England's sons will vindicate their ancestry.

*His hour is one of darkness, and adversity, and peril*

THE GREY CHAMPION

The old man grasped his staff by the middle and held it before him like a leader's truncheon. " Stand ! "
cried he  (*Page* 254)

THE GIRLHOOD OF BEATRICE AND HERO

But Lady Giustina drew back. " Save her ! Save Beatrice ! " exclaimed the aged countess, pointing to her niece (*Page* 271)

# The Girlhood of Beatrice and Hero

### by MARY COWDEN CLARKE

## I

### THE MEETING OF THE COUSINS

A SOUND cuff.

"What do you hit me for?"

Another. "Give it up! Will you give it up?"

"No!"

Another cuff. And a box on the ear. "Give it up, I say!"

Another "No" was about to be bawled, and a look in the lout's eye gave token that it would probably be accompanied by a return of the blows he had received; but suddenly he seemed to think better of it. Muttering something about being "too near Master Constable's house, or he'd ha' kept it as sure as he was alive," the boy flung down the demanded toy, turned on his heel, and made off.

The little girl who was thus left victress of the field, picked up the doll, brushed the dust off its smart skirts, arranged its rumpled headdress, then triumphantly walked up to another little girl who had stood aloof during the affray, and restored the plundered favourite to her arms.

"Oh, I'm so glad to have her back! My beautiful new doll that my father gave me only yesterday!" exclaimed the child, hugging it to her, and smiling through the tears that still glittered on her cheeks.

"Why did you let him snatch it from you?" said the other little girl. "Why didn't you run after him and force him to give it up?"

"He was such a great fierce lad—I couldn't—I didn't dare," replied she.

"Why didn't your sister run after him then, for you, and thump him till he gave it up?" persisted the first little girl, looking towards a young boy who stood by rubbing his knees, his back, and his elbows alternately, looking very scared and very disconsolate, with a few big tears rolling down his face.

" I'm not a girl, miss ! " he blurted out, with a half-shamefaced, half-indignant glance at the beautiful, spirited face that was eyeing him. " What made you take me for a girl ? Don't you see my dress ? " And he cast a look of sheepish pride at his legs, which certainly were cased in masculine fashion.

" Don't I see your tears ? What's crying but the trick of a girl ? " said she, with a motion of her lips that made him wince. " Why didn't you fly after the fellow, instead of standing blubbering there ? "

" He knocked me down ! " said the boy. " He took good care to make sure of me before he snatched at Hero's doll. How could I fly, miss, when he knocked me down ? It's not so easy to fly, let me tell you, when a fellow sends you sprawling."

" But I suppose you could have scrambled up again, couldn't you ? Unless you thought it more prudent to lie still. But, for the sake of your sister's doll, you might have——"

" She isn't my sister—she's my cousin ! " interrupted the boy, glad to seize upon any point of defence.

" Never mind, Gaetano, I have my doll again," said its owner, and then, with her kind, sweet tone, she turned to the little girl who had so bravely rescued it for her, and thanked her in a manner so pretty and earnest as to prove her the young lady born and bred.

The children fell into talk, and began to question each other how they happened to be out alone, how they had met, who they were, and so forth.

It appeared that the little girl, Hero, was the daughter of the governor of Messina, his sole child and heiress, that the young boy, Gaetano, was the son of her uncle, Antonio ; that they had left the palace in the morning for a walk, attended by a servant, but that some show or public procession had suddenly attracted a crowd, in which they had been separated from their attendant.

The other little girl, when she learned their names, uttered an exclamation of surprise. She told them that she was their cousin, that her name was Beatrice, that she was bound for their house at the very time she met them, and that, singularly enough, the crowd had also separated her from the person who was bringing her from her native place to Messina.

Beatrice was an orphan. Her mother had married a poor lieutenant, contrary to the will of a rich maiden aunt, and, in consequence, had been cast off, disavowed, denounced. On her death-bed she bequeathed her little girl to the guardianship of Leonato, beseeching him to be a father to her orphan child.

It was on her way to her future home that Beatrice happened to witness the incident which made her so unexpectedly acquainted with her young relations. She saw the ruffianly lad snatch the child's doll, she saw neither the little girl nor her companion make any attempt at resistance, and her own immediate impulse was to force him to yield his prey. How she succeeded has been seen.

" But what shall we do ? We none of us know our way ? I don't—you don't, Hero ; and, of course, you don't, miss ?—Beatrice, I mean. My father and my uncle will both be rarely angry with Matteo when they hear how he lost us staring about him."

"But how are they to hear?" returned she. "You are no tale-bearer, sure, to bring a poor serving-man into disgrace?"

"Why, when a servant neglects his duty, what are we to do, miss?" said Gaetano.

"Not tell tales, miss; certainly not tell tales," replied she.

"Why do you call me ' miss,' Cousin Beatrice? I've told you already I'm no girl."

She laughed. "And you should recollect that it isn't so easy to treat you as a boy when I see you behave like a girl. Meantime, cheer up, put on a bold face, and inquire our way for us at some house," she said.

"I don't know—I never did—I'm not accustomed to speak to strangers," hesitated he.

"Shall we try if this way will lead us right?" said Hero, pointing down a street that looked invitingly cool; there was a fountain in the centre, shaded by a broad-spreading chestnut-tree, round which stood a group of women, washing and filling pitchers; some men watering their mules, the animals whisking away the flies with their tails, shaking their long ears, and drawing refreshing draughts from the marble basin, through their bright and tasselled headgear.

"Stay, suppose I just ask that lad who is lounging in yonder doorway, whether this turning will do," said Beatrice, stepping forward as she spoke to a sturdy hobbledehoy, who was idly chipping splinters off the door-post with the end of a bill he poised in his hand.

"Thou know'st not whom thou'rt questioning, little girl," he said, looking over his shoulder at her in a lordly manner; " 'twere a pity of thy life, an thou wert to question me too closely, seeing that I am the constable's eldest son, and seeing, moreover, that thou art, or I'm much mista'en, no better than thou shouldst be. 'Tis my father's calling to apprehend all aspicious people, and vagroms."

"We are neither beggars nor thieves," she replied; "we but seek to know our way—we only ask——"

"You only ' ask !' What is asking but begging, I should like to know? What is wandering but going astray, what is going astray but erring, what is erring but wickedness, and what is wickedness but the highroad to thieving? Trust me, I think you're no more virtuous than you should be."

"Who is? Let us all try to be as good as we may, we can scarce hope to be more good than we should and ought to be."

Beatrice turned away with Hero and Gaetano, who had been for the last few minutes plucking at her skirts to prevent her from getting them into trouble with this foolish lad.

They instinctively turned down the inviting-looking street, and when they reached the spot where the fountain stood, Hero said she should like to sit down and rest under the shady tree. A wooden bench ran round its trunk, and here the three children seated themselves, watching the good-humoured women as they laughed and talked over their splashing task with the muleteers and the rest of the men grouped around.

"I'm so thirsty !" said Gaetano in his lackadaisical tone of lament.

"Why don't you drink, then?" said Beatrice. "But you are tired, Hero, and would be glad of a draught from the fountain. I'll try what can be done."

Beatrice advanced among the men and women, and said in a frank, raised voice : " Is there any one here who will lend a horn or a cup of any kind to a little girl who is thirsty ? "

For a moment there was a look of wonder at the beautiful child who stood thus amidst them, with her clear eyes and fearless voice : the next, several pocket drinking-cups of horn, leather, or wood, with which most of them were provided, were heartily proffered.

After they had all three partaken of the welcome refreshment, Beatrice

*Several drinking-cups were heartily proffered*

said, in her firm, ringing tone : " If any one of you will show us the way to the governor's palace, Signor Leonato will join his thanks to ours, for the kindness his daughter has received at your hands, good friends."

A murmur of surprise ran through the crowd, and then there was a loud shout : " Evviva Signor Leonato ! Long live our noble governor ! "

Beatrice was warmly welcomed to her new home by all its inmates. Her Uncle Leonato grew to love her no less proudly and fondly than his own child ; her Uncle Antonio was entertained with her sprightliness and confirmed bearing, so different from his own boy's ill-assured ways ; Hero felt as if she had found a sister, and Gaetano was perplexed, pleased, vexed, and interested with her all at once.

He had been a sickly infant, was still a delicate child, and was, therefore, petted, humoured, and indulged in all his whims and whinings, his fears and his fancies, until he was a spoiled boy—the half-girl—that so amazed and amused Beatrice when she first saw him.

" Hark ! There's that unhappy boy ! Howling again, I declare ! " said

Beatrice to Hero, as sounds of lamentation reached them in an alley of the garden, where the two little girls were walking together.

" You ought to have been a boy yourself, Cousin Beatrice, you are so fearless and so firm, and know so well what a boy ought to be," said Hero.

" I like courage, in boy or girl," said Beatrice. " A girl needn't be unseemly bold, or forward, for having a strong heart any more than a boy need be an unfeeling brute for knowing how to face danger. But here comes unhappy Gaetano."

He was making his way hastily towards them when a large hornet happening to fly close by his ear, made him start aside, his foot tripped, he stumbled and fell headlong, his face flat upon the gravel-path. He cried lustily. The girls both ran to pick him up.

" His nose bleeds ! " exclaimed Hero.

" Oh, the blood ! " he said, turning pale ; " and my hands are grazed ! See here ! Oh dear ! oh dear ! " and he burst out a-crying afresh.

" Dear little cherub ! " said Beatrice. " Here, let me wipe away the marks, and when you don't see them perhaps you'll forget the wounds ; they're not very deep, only a scratch or two."

" But they smart so, you can't think. And my nose, oh, my nose ! See how it keeps bleeding ! "

" Stay, I'll run into the house for something to stop it," said Beatrice, " and when the blood has done flowing, you can dry up your tears, you know, at the same time."

" Are you angry with her, Gaetano ? " said his Cousin Hero, peeping into his face, as Beatrice flew away to bring sponge and water and to get help.

" Oh, no ! I'm never angry with Cousin Beatrice, tease me as much as she will," said he, his tears subsiding into sobs ; " she never seems to do it from malice—but as if she couldn't help the fun of it. I suppose it's funny to her, though it's not so to me."

" If it's not pleasant to you, what if we beg her not to tease you any more ? " said Hero.

" No, no ; I don't wish her to give up teasing me. I don't know how it is, but somehow, though I'm provoked with her, I rather like it."

" I'm glad of it, for that shows you have a good temper of your own, dear Gaetano," said Hero, " and so, I know, you have. But so has Beatrice, too, for all she loves to plague and torment you a little. See how good naturedly she helped you up, and now runs off to fetch something that'll cure you. Let us go and meet her."

## II

### THE VISIT TO MONTASPRO

SOME few years had gone by without incident, after Beatrice had made her home at her Uncle Leonato's house, when, unexpectedly, he received a message from the Countess Giustina, his aunt, to say that now his young daughter was beyond babyhood, she wished to see her, and make acquaintance with her, as the individual in whose person would eventually centre the honours of their house.

This Countess Giustina was the aunt whom the mother of Beatrice had mortally offended by her marriage. In the pang of finding that she was not all-in-all to this beloved niece, as her niece was to her, she resolved never more to communicate with or behold her. She remained shut up in her castle, with a few faithful retainers, and held little intercourse with the world, save an occasional interchange of messengers bearing greetings between her two nephews and herself.

She never lost the habit of authority with them, which she had acquired during the years when they were boys left to her care ; and now, when she wrote to her nephew Leonato, bidding him give her the pleasure of seeing his daughter, she dictated entirely the conditions of the visit. She told him neither his brother Antonio nor himself were to come this time. She forbade the attendance of any hand-maidens, saying that her own woman should wait upon the young ladies. She begged that Hero might be accompanied by her female cousin only.

Leonato was glad that the young girls should have the pleasant change of a country holiday. The old lady's castle lay up among the mountains, a long day's journey from Messina, in a wild solitude, and the fresh breezes of the high ground would be healthful after the heat of the plains.

" Will it not be charming ? " said Beatrice to her cousin.

" Well, I suppose so—most charming," repeated Hero, but in a tone anything but the echo of her cousin's eager delight.

" Why, thou say'st ' charming ' in a most lugubrious voice, worthy to be that of Gaetano himself ! " said the laughing Beatrice.

" I could tell you such things I have heard of the strictness of our great-aunt, Lady Giustina. She never forgives the smallest fault, or over-looks the slightest misbehaviour. Think what it will be to live all day long, and for many weeks and months together, beneath her severe eye. I fancy I feel it upon me now," said Hero, shivering, " even your courage would quail beneath that severe eye, I think, Beatrice. By day Lady Giustina's terrible eye ; and by night——"

Hero broke off. Beatrice could see her actually tremble.

" But if you dread it, why not ask my uncle to allow you to give it up ? " said Beatrice.

" Oh, I would not on any account object to going," said Hero. " My father respects our aunt. I have heard him say he owes her a large debt of gratitude ; she was a friend to him in his boyhood, she was like a mother to him and his brother and sister—Uncle Antonio and Aunt Beatrice—when they were all three left orphans. She is very, very good, although so strict, I know."

" If she be good and just we have nothing to fear," said Beatrice. " I was too young when my mother died," she went on gravely, " to understand much of what she felt and thought ; but I think I can make out, from what I remember of words she dropped at the time, that she reproached herself with ingratitude towards one who, with all her severity, had been bountiful in goodness and care.

" One comfort : we shall go together," said Hero, " and you will help me to bear difficulties cheerfully, and teach me to meet them bravely. With you, Beatrice, I shall be ashamed to be a coward, and with you time must always pass happily."

There was a handsome retinue appointed to conduct the two young ladies to their destination, for Leonato knew that his aunt would be displeased were her grand-nieces not to travel in a style befitting their rank. Their journey was to be performed in a kind of coach, or litter, drawn by mules, well suited to the rugged mountain-paths they would have to traverse.

Their way lay through scenery of the most picturesque beauty. It almost immediately arose from the plains, and wound among the uplands, commanding a grand view of sea and land. Beneath them lay the city, with its amphitheatre of palaces, beyond it stretched its sickle-shaped harbour, bearing stately vessels within its bosom, at safe anchorage. Still farther might be seen the sparkling waters of the Faro di Messina, bounded by the opposite Calabrian coast, with the cliffs of Scylla.

The early morning sun shone brilliantly, and as yet temperately, upon all, for they had commenced their journey with the dawn, and were to halt at noon-tide in order to avoid the greatest heat of the day, and that they might reach Montaspro before nightfall.

Hero enjoyed the journey to the full as much as her cousin, and it was not until the sun was sinking towards the west that she began to show signs of fear. The path became wilder and wilder, as they penetrated farther up among the mountain solitudes ; the purple glow of evening threw a less brilliant light upon all around ; the shadows deepened and lengthened among the rocks ; there were fewer trees and barer and more rugged crags on every side. Her tone fell, her admiring exclamations became fewer and fewer, and at length sank into silence.

" What's that ? " she cried suddenly.—" Hark ! don't you hear a noise ? If it should be banditti ! "

" It sounds to me like the rush of waters," said Beatrice. She paused to listen. Then she pointed through the curtains on her side. " Look ! is not that a grand sight ? " she said.

Through an opening in the rocks appeared the castle of Montaspro. It stood perched, as it were, in mid-air, on the summit of a precipitous crag that jutted out from amid the surrounding heights. Its walls, rough and solid, looked part of the rock from which it reared its frowning crest. No shrubs or trees feathered the sides of the yawning chasm beneath, no draping ivy, or vine, hung its festoons amid the rifts to grace and conceal the stony bareness ; but instead abrupt and jagged points, shelving ledges, and sheer depths, among which leaped, and tore, and boiled a fierce mountain torrent.

" And that is Montaspro ? " whispered Hero. " It looks a fit residence for our stern grand-aunt. How shall we ever venture to encounter her ? I have not a spark of bravery in me, when I think of being so near."

" We are yet some distance—the road winds," answered Beatrice. " Come, call thy courage to thee. Remember, she's no ogress, she will neither eat thee nor murder thee. Let her looks be never so terrible, she will not harm thee, believe it."

As the litter proceeded across the drawbridge and beneath the massive gateway, and they entered a spacious courtyard, where a body of retainers received them by torchlight, the scene was so strange, so impressive, that it might well have struck more experienced travellers than the two young cousins with awe.

They were assisted to alight with much ceremonial deference. They found stationed in the great hall a gray-headed old man, very stately and upright—the countess's steward, and a gray-headed old dame, also very stately and upright and very angular—the countess's own woman, or duenna. By these two personages they were accosted in a grave manner, and begged to state which of their two young ladyships was his lordship the governor's daughter.

Hero got out a word or two announcing herself, and then the two stately personages, giving her the preference, led the cousins in a silent and stately manner into a spacious apartment where sat the lady of Montaspro. She occupied an easy-chair by the hearth, but she sat perfectly erect. She was surrounded by all the tokens of wealth and of a magnificent taste, but her own person was simply attired. She was entirely in black—her gown of a homely stuff, her headgear a plain coif, but there was that in herself which denoted her, unmistakably, the gentlewoman. She sat there, a noblewoman in her whole aspect, in her very look, in the slightest turn of her head, in the least motion of her hand.

She had marked features, but her complexion retained its delicacy—that, and the silver-white of her hair, made her face and hands show in almost snowy contrast with her swart garments. There were two points of colour in her countenance. Her eyes were jet-black, of piercing brilliancy, and her lips were of a vivid red, no less remarkable at her age.

"And you are Hero?" she said, taking a hand of her young grand-niece in hers.

"Yes, madam," replied Hero, "and here is Beatrice," she added, looking towards her cousin, who had followed her up to the countess's chair.

But the lady Giustina kept her eyes fixed upon Hero's face, saying: "I see your father in your look, maiden. How is he? How doth my good nephew Leonato?"

"My father is well, madam, and bade me present his dutiful greetings to your ladyship. My cousin is charged with them, no less than myself." And again she turned to where Beatrice stood waiting to pay her respects.

But the countess went on: "And how doth my worthy nephew Antonio? He hath a son, I hear. Doth he give promise of being as hasty as his sire could be, when a boy?"

"My cousin, Gaetano, is the most gentle creature living, madam, and Beatrice will tell you that——"

Again Hero moved towards Beatrice, and again Lady Giustina took no notice.

"Too gentle is scarce commendable in a boy, whatever it may be in a girl," she said, "and when thou talk'st of the most gentle of living creatures, what can a young thing like you know of degrees of gentleness in so large a range of beings? Speak ever within bounds, little maiden, lest thou chance to outstate fact, and so prove thyself either ignorant or false."

Abashed at having already incurred her aunt's rebuke, Hero had no voice for a reply. There was a pause. And then the countess put her two hands upon the arms of her chair, and turning her face in the direction of Beatrice, said in a suppressed voice: "Come hither, child."

Beatrice advanced a step and stood immediately before her. The old lady's eyes were fixed upon her own lap for another instant, then raised as if by an effort of will and directed full upon the face of the young girl.

The keen black eyes never wavered, their lids never stirred, the muscles of the mouth never altered, but the red lips waned in colour until they blanched to the whiteness of the pale face itself.

Beatrice, while the countess thus continued to gaze upon her, had it in her heart to say that she had no greetings to bring from a living parent, but that her mother's parting hour had been embittered by the thought of dying unforgiven by her aunt, but something arose within her to check the reproachful speech.

The Lady Giustina raised her hand as if to screen her eyes from the

*The old lady's eyes were directed full upon the face of the young girl*

glare of light. " Remove that lamp farther back," she said to one of the attendants, then, turning again to Beatrice, she said : " Welcome to Mont-aspro, child ; I am well pleased that you should have accompanied Hero, well pleased to have both my young cousins to spend some time with me, and trust they are well pleased to come."

" I have rejoiced ever since I learned we were to visit the castle, madam," replied Beatrice.

" And now, Prisca," said the Lady Giustina, addressing her stately gentlewoman, " these young ladies will doubtless be glad to see their rooms. Lead them thither, and assist them with what change of apparel they think fit and refreshing, ere they return to take some refection with me. They must need some, after their long day's journey."

The ancient handmaiden performed her mistress's bidding, by beckon-ing an attendant to precede them with lights. She led the way up a flight of stairs, of wood so dark with age as to look like ebony, and so bright with polishing as to reflect the lights the attendant carried like a mirror. They passed on into a corridor so lofty and so long that it looked like the aisle of a cathedral, it opened by side doors, into different chambers. One of these doors the stately gentlewoman threw open, while she looked at Hero, and said : " Yours, young lady ! "

As Hero peeped into its depths she thought it looked like a chill cavern, but the stately gentlewoman did not tarry for her to examine it, or to enter, but led the way straight on to the end of the corridor, till she came to another flight of stairs, as wide, as dark, as polished as the other. At the top they found themselves in a narrow gallery, which seemed to lead somewhere out upon the ramparts of the castle, certainly into the open air, for there was a strong draught which threatened to extinguish the lights. After traversing this gallery they came to another long and lofty corridor, at one of the doors in which the ancient duenna stopped, and throwing it open in like manner as before, she looked at Beatrice and said : " Yours, young lady ! "

The two girls exchanged a dismayed glance : they had always, since their living together, been accustomed to occupy the same sleeping-room, and Beatrice knew her cousin would not like this solitary arrangement— especially as they were so far distant from each other.

Hero stood aghast, and said nothing. But Beatrice said : " We are in the habit of having but one room between us, Mistress Prisca ; either of these we have seen will serve for us both."

" If you wish alteration you must ask my lady," said the duenna.

" No, no ; pray, Beatrice, no, no," eagerly whispered Hero ; then she added aloud : " Let it be as it is, since it is my aunt's wish, we are satisfied."

During supper Lady Giustina was very gracious to her young cousins, and afterwards dismissed them to their night's rest with words of hospitable courtesy.

At the door of Hero's room the cousins parted for the night. Mistress Prisca being present, they only exchanged a good-night kiss and a silent squeeze of the hand ; but Beatrice, as she took her way on to her own chill cavern, thought of Hero's white cheeks, and could not get to sleep for some time, from sympathy with the discomfort she knew her cousin was suffering.

Next morning, the first glimpse she had of them showed how accurately she had guessed ; they were still more wan, and poor Hero had evidently had little or no rest.

There was no time for question or sympathy, however, for Mistress Prisca told them her lady was already in the breakfast-room expecting them. Beatrice, who had hastened to Hero's room, now helped her cousin to get ready, and, after as speedy dressing as might be, the two girls hurried down.

The Lady Giustina was seated at the breakfast-table, when Beatrice and Hero approached to pay her their morning respects.

" Your journey somewhat excuses your late-rising, maidens," said the countess, " but remember, for the future, my breakfast-hour is earlier, and it is but fitting respect that youth should not keep age waiting."

There was no want of colour in Hero's cheeks now, but as she took her seat at the breakfast-table she found courage to say : " Beatrice would have been ready, madam, but that she waited for me."

This pleased the old lady, and she said : " Perhaps you slept badly, and that made you late. How did you rest ? "

Unfortunately, Hero, anxious to please her aunt, answered : " Thank you, madam, quite well."

The countess had noticed the pale young cheeks, and guessing their cause, had half resolved to indulge Hero—who she at once saw was a gentle, timid child—with companionship at night, but this denial of having rested ill she deemed untruthful, and resolved to punish it by taking no further notice of her tremors.

" In future, then, let me find you with your cousin, here, in the breakfast-room when I come down. As I said before, better youth should wait for age, than age for youth."

" I am in higher than tiptopmost spirits this morning," said Beatrice, " at the thought of the delightful mountain ramble you are going to allow us to take, madam."

" Am I, child ? No, not a mountain ramble ; these wild passes might not be so safe for you. Montaspro hath not a neighbour roof within many miles of it, and the rocks and caverns harbour gentry, they say, who are not pleasant to meet with. What makes you tremble, Hero ? " said Lady Giustina, interrupting herself and fixing her jet eyes upon the young girl's face. " There is no fear of these lawless people, while you are within the walls of Montaspro. I hope you do not give way to idle fears. I despise a dastardly spirit ! Your father's child should be no coward."

" My cousin belies neither her father's name nor her own, madam," said Beatrice. " Hero is no coward."

" She seems no great heroine," said Lady Giustina. " How wouldst thou be able to meet a real danger, maiden, if thou quak'st now at the mere mention of one ? Keep thy heart brave, and thy spirit strong, and then they will serve thee in time of need."

" Hero hath a tender heart and a gentle spirit, madam, but they neither of them want for courage when occasion calls for it," said Beatrice. " But shall we not, indeed, be allowed to enjoy a ramble among this fine scenery ? "

" Beyond the demesnes you must not go," said the countess. " But the castle grounds are extensive, and command several fine points of view. You shall walk abroad, attended by my gentlewoman, after breakfast."

The grounds belonging to Castle Montaspro were indeed, as their mistress had described them, both fine and extensive. They were magnificent in their wild luxuriance, grand in their uncultivated beauty.

" Come, Hero ! Let you and me have a good race together, as far as yonder pine-clump! " exclaimed Beatrice, with a glance at her cousin, and in another moment the two girls had set off at a rate of speed that quickly left Mistress Prisca far in the rear. By dint of appointing fresh goals, as often as the duenna gained upon them, Beatrice and Hero contrived to get some snatches of talk together.

" Dear Hero, you are unhappy, I fear ; tell me what grieves you."

" Not unhappy, Beatrice, but I wish we were at home. This wild place —this gloomy old castle—my terrible aunt——"

" Nay, she is not so terrible, surely, as we had pictured to ourselves. Though she can look seriously enough when she chooses, yet she can also look pleasantly. Did you see ?—She all but smiled this morning."

" I wish I had your courage, Beatrice," sighed Hero. " It was very kind of you to say what you did for me this morning, of my being no coward, but I fear sometimes that I am a bit of one."

" Then don't let yourself grow into a whole one," said Beatrice.

" But when night returns we shall be sundered again, dear coz ! " said Hero. " They will make us sleep in separate rooms, and I don't like to be away from thee. I confess, I dread to be alone in the dark—darkness fills me with I know not what alarms. Especially after what I have heard of Montaspro," and she visibly shuddered.

" What hast thou heard, dear ? " said Beatrice gently.

" A tall figure, dressed in white, and veiled with black, they say, has been seen to wander through the corridors and chambers of the castle ; it wrings its hands and moans sadly—that it is fearful to see and hear," whispered Hero.

" Most likely the moonbeams gliding in phantom shapes upon the old walls, and the wind sobbing and sighing as it bears them company," said Beatrice. " How came you to say you slept well, when Lady Giustina asked this morning how you rested ? You must not let your fancies make you a coward in speech, dearest coz ; that is worse than any other cowardice— it leads you to be afraid of the truth."

" I meant not to tell a falsehood," said Hero ; " but I hardly know what I answer my aunt—I stand so in awe of her."

" If you do not like to ask her leave that we have one room, I will," said Beatrice.

" No, no, Beatrice ; if you love me, don't do that. I should rather any- thing than that ! She will think me a coward ! She will reproach me with my dastardly spirit. Promise me that you won't speak of it to my aunt. Anything better than that. The very thought of the veiled spirit itself is less terrible to me than Lady Giustina's displeasure."

Beatrice had but just time to calm Hero by giving her promise before the angular Mistress Prisca overtook them.

She made no remark, but her looks censured them severely. Of these, however, the cousins took no notice, and they returned in silence to the castle.

## III

### THE FIRE

DAY followed day, and week succeeded to week, and yet Hero's awe of the countess lessened no jot. Her night terrors were as powerful as ever ; then came the late waking, the hurried dressing, and the hurrying downstairs.

Hero grew daily more hollow-eyed, more wan, more languid. Beatrice noticed that her meals were scarcely touched and that she started at the most trifling noise. Beatrice watched for an opportunity of speaking in private with her, but none could she obtain.

At last she determined to take a bold measure, which should secure to them an uninterrupted interview, besides affording the means of remaining with Hero long enough to comfort and reassure her.

That very night she stole through the darkness—for she would not take

*" Dear, dear Beatrice ! Is that you ? " exclaimed Hero*

the lamp with her—along the corridor, and into the narrow gallery. She hastened onward, glided down the dark staircase, and found her way into the corridor below. She crept along, carefully counting the doors as she passed, that she might be sure of the one belonging to Hero's chamber ; and when she reached it, she opened it softly and spoke, that her cousin might at once recognise her voice.

" Is it possible ! Dear, dear Beatrice ! Is that you ? " exclaimed Hero, starting up at the welcome sound and clinging to her cousin with delight.

" To be sure ! to be sure ! It is I ! Who should it be, you foolish trembler ? I'll wager now, you have been watching the door, fancying the veiled spectre would steal in, and make you pop your head under the bed-clothes like a goose as you are. But you see it's no ghost, only your own sauce-box cousin, come to rate you for scaring yourself out of your wits, and the roses out of your cheeks, with such idle fancies. Come, confess : you have never seen such a thing as the shadow of a shade, the ghost of a spectre, have you ? "

" But I've had such terrible dreams, Beatrice," whispered Hero. " If you only knew ! Here, get into bed : you'll take cold. How good you are to come to me ! And through those long dark passages, too ! Oh, how brave of you to venture—and how kind, for my sake ! Dear, dear Beatrice ! " As Hero hugged her cousin and nestled close to her, she again whispered of the fearful dreams she had had.

" Oh, such nights as I have spent in this dreadful castle," she cried.

" You shall spend no more such ! At least, if my lying by your side can prevent your imagination from running wild, and playing you such painful tricks as these, my poor Hero ! " said her cousin. " I will steal down from my room each night, as soon as Dragoness Prisca leaves me, so do you keep a brave heart for that short time, and then we'll sleep cosily together, holding the ghosts at bay till cock-crow."

" Dear coz ! And then you will be sure to call me early, and make me get up ; and then I shall escape the disgrace of being too late, as I so often am," said Hero.

As she spoke, Beatrice started up in bed, and remained motionless.

" Do you not perceive a strong smell of burning, Hero ? "

" Certainly—yes—I surely do ! " returned Hero.

" Now there is real danger—true cause for alarm—show yourself a brave girl, dear coz," said Beatrice. " You who have owned to being a coward about ghosts, and that you are afraid of the dark—will yet prove yourself of good courage in the hour most needful. I fear the castle is on fire. Get up, dress yourself quickly, make the best of your way downstairs, across the hall, into the offices, and rouse the household. I will join you as soon as possible."

" Are you not going with me ? " said Hero, who had sprung out of bed.

" No, but I shall be below scarcely a moment after you."

Volumes of smoke rolled through the spacious hall, and curled up towards its lofty roof. Beatrice could hear the crackling of the flames—and the splitting of timbers as she made her way straight across the hall towards the door which she knew opened into the gallery communicating with the turret where Lady Giustina slept alone.

She had just attained the entrance to the turret when a portion of the inner wall of the gallery gave way and a volume of flame and smoke came bursting through into the space she had passed, as if pursuing her. She instinctively closed the door behind her, as if to put a barrier between herself and the approaching fire, and then sped up the winding stair. She reached the door at the top—her aunt's chamber door ; opened it softly, lifted the tapestry, and entered. The room was in perfect stillness. Its mistress lay in a deep sleep.

Beatrice leaned over Lady Giustina whispering : " Awake, dear aunt, awake ! "

The countess opened her eyes, fixed them on the beautiful young face hanging over her, and said : " Already morning, darling ? And so my Beatrice is come, as usual, to help me arise. Methought I dreamed a long and ugly dream, that you were gone from me, my Beatrice ! "

The tenderness in the tone—the name—such as never before had the young girl heard from those lips, the fond look, such as never before had she seen in that rigidly-calm face, all told Beatrice that the old countess's thoughts had gone back to that period of her life when her other Beatrice, her own child-niece, used daily to awaken her, hanging lovingly over her.

" Dear aunt ! it is not morning. It is night. But there is danger. The castle is on fire. You must get up."

Another moment or two and the door at the foot of the turret, which Beatrice had closed behind her as she came up, crashed in, and the flames came pouring through the breach, caught to the first steps of the staircase, and sent their spiral tongues, darting and threatening, up the interior of the turret.

Beatrice uttered no sound. She fixed her eyes upon her aunt's face, mutely took her hand between both hers, and grasped it very tight.

" Brave wench ! " exclaimed the old countess, now fully awake and self-possessed ; her eye dilating and her lip regaining its ruddy colour in the proud delight of noting a fearless spirit, worthy of the noble race from which they sprang. She ejaculated with an emotion which the thought of her own danger had never once called forth : " And must she perish ? Is there no way to save her ? So young ! So brave ! So beautiful ! " Her voice sank to a whisper as she added : " *Her* child ! "

At that moment there was a sound at one of the windows—the window that looked across the castle grounds. Backed by the red glare outside, Beatrice could perceive the dark figure of a man attempting to effect an entrance through the casement. It was Pietro, one of the countess's faithful retainers, who had reared a scaling-ladder against the wall of the turret and had climbed up, to attempt the rescue of his aged mistress.

" See, aunt ! There is help at hand ! They are coming to save us ! " Beatrice sprang to the casement to unfasten it.

" The countess ! My lady !—where is she ? " shouted the man, as he put the young girl aside and leaped into the chamber.

But Lady Giustina drew back. " Her child ! Save her ! Save Beatrice ! " exclaimed the aged countess, pointing to her niece.

But Beatrice in her turn refused to be rescued first.

" My child—my Beatrice—obey my wish " said Lady Giustina in her impressive tone.

Pietro, merely saying, " My lady must not be gainsaid," lifted Beatrice in one of his stalwart arms, bidding her lean her weight as much across his shoulder as might be, climbed the window-sill, firmly planted his foot upon the first rung of the ladder, and commenced his descent.

As the man appeared from the window with his human burden there arose a shout from those anxiously assembled below, but the next instant it was hushed : a solemn silence took its place, as breathlessly his progress was watched. Pietro bore her carefully, steadily. They were still some feet from the ground, when Beatrice threw herself out of his arms, exclaiming : " Return ! return ! Go up again ! Hasten ! hasten ! "

The man needed no urging ; he had scarcely felt himself freed from his load ere he was remounting towards the turret window. But by this time the flames had made their way into the chamber. Their dread light could be seen through the casement, flickering and glaring, now obscured and dull, anon in a sudden blaze, fitfully revealing the interior of the room to the night-sky.

Intensely the watching eyes beneath followed Pietro's every movement, as he neared the burning window. They saw him gain it—boldly step in —into the very midst of the smoke and flames.

A pause ensued, of unspeakable suspense. Nothing could be discerned of what passed within the room, but the next moment a tremendous rushing sound—a crumbling and mighty yielding—and then the floor sank in burning ruins, the roof collapsed and fell in, leaving the outer walls of the turret a hollow tower—a mere shell, from which spouted forth a volume of fire, waving and flaming upward in fatal splendour.

A cry of horror burst from the crowd of faithful retainers, while the two cousins clung to each other, weeping and awe-stricken.

## IV

### THE RETURN JOURNEY

THE morning dawned upon the ruins of Montaspro. The old steward asked the young ladies if they would not have a messenger despatched to Messina that the Lord Governor might be informed of the calamity which had befallen, and that he might come and fetch away his daughter and niece from so melancholy a scene.

"Dear Beatrice," said Hero, "let us leave at once. We shall arrive at home as soon as the messenger."

"The litter and mules are safe, young lady," said Domenico. "The outhouses where they were bestowed have escaped the fire. There is naught need detain you in this scene of desolation. I will undertake that all diligent search be made for the remains of mine honoured mistress, and see that all care be taken to give them reverent burial."

"Be it so, good Domenico," said Hero. "Bid them harness ; in less than half an hour my cousin and I will be ready to set forth."

The sun had scarcely arisen when the little train wound along the mountain path leading from Montaspro. The still-smoking walls lay a disfigured heap, where late they had stood erect in strength and seeming security.

Both girls presently fell asleep and some hours must have elapsed, for when Beatrice awoke, she saw that the sun was high in the heavens. Hero still slept, and her cousin, unwilling to disturb her, watched in silence.

The mules were slowly toiling up a long rise, the attendants were strolling on leisurely ahead, when Beatrice, attracted by the leafy coolness of a grove of trees that skirted the road, felt inclined to walk a while. She softly unfastened the door of the litter without awakening her cousin, and sprang lightly to the ground. The beauty, the stillness, won upon her. She wandered on among the trees.

A moment she lingered to gather for Hero a branch of ripe oranges that hung temptingly near, ere she should bound onward to overtake the litter. She had secured the golden fruit when her attention was caught by a purple cluster of grapes, that nestled amid some vine-leaves, drooping just above her head. As she scrambled up the tangled bank where they grew, and reached among the leaves and tendrils for her prize, she became suddenly aware of two strange faces that peered at her from above. They shone like burnished metal—their deep olive complexion, bronzed by constant exposure to the sun ; they were hung about with black elf-locks of matted hair, and had eyes that sparkled with mingled keenness and ferocity.

Beatrice's heart beat as the thought of Hero's tales of banditti crossed her mind, but hastily resolving that her best chance of safety was to behave as if they were harmless peasants, until she found them hostile, said, as she nodded up in their direction : "Good-day, friends ! I suppose this ground is no enclosed vineyard, and that it is hardly a theft for a thirsty traveller to help herself to a handful of fruit ? "

"And so you're a traveller, are you, signorina ? " said one of them.

" As sure as my name's Filippino, it's my opinion that you have only just stepped out of yonder litter trotting down hill there, and that it's in that you've been travelling."

" Well guessed," said Beatrice, and she suddenly gave a loud ringing call ; but it failed to reach those to whom it was addressed.  She could see the litter and the attendant horsemen still plodding on.

One of the men started, half drew his knife, and muttered a curse, but the other laughed and said : " Don't be in a hurry to leave us, signorina ; we can't part with you yet.  It isn't every day we have the honour of seeing the Governor of Messina's daughter in our mountain solitudes."

" And now we'll make him not only thank us, but pay us, for returning her to him safely," said the other.  " But come, signorina, you must go see our captain."

The two men walked on either side of her, leading the way through the grove of trees, along the skirts of which she had so lately passed.  It thickened into a close wood, but the men threaded their way unhesitatingly, until at length they came to a comparatively open space, though surrounded on all sides by rock and wood.  In the midst, on the margin of a small lake, there stood an old dismantled watch-tower or stronghold.  Its roof was open to the sky, its walls were rent and ruined, and it was covered with ivy. Filippino struck three smart blows against a rock near which they stood. A portal, so well constructed that it seemed, when closed, like a portion of the solid crag itself, receded at the signal, and gave entrance to a cavern, part natural, part hewn out.

Beatrice, on being led in, found herself in an arched space that seemed like a vast hall supported by irregular pillars.  At the farther end several men were employed spreading a board with food and wine, while near to them paced a man with folded arms and lowering brow, as if lost in moody thought. Beatrice's conductors went toward their chief, and exchanged a few hasty words with him.  The short colloquy ended by his saying, in a harsh voice, as he flung himself on a kind of settle, spread with the skins of wild animals, " Bring her hither."

The two men returned to where Beatrice stood and said : " Our captain desires to speak with you, young lady."

" Your people lack discipline, Signor Capitano," said Beatrice, advancing ; " you should teach them better manners than to keep a young lady waiting in the entrance while they parley with their master ; and they would doubt-less learn to doff their hats in her presence were they to see you set them an example," added she, glancing at the broad beaver which shaded his brow, already darkened by a heavy frown.

Involuntarily—in his surprise at her coolness—the man's hand stole to his hat, and lifted it from his head, but he was yet more surprised to see the young girl quietly seat herself beside him upon the settle, saying : " Well, they told me you wanted to speak to me.  What have you to say ? "

" I am in the habit of putting questions, not of answering them, young lady," said the man sternly.  " Those who are brought before me, stand there and reply, in lieu of sitting here questioning me."

" I sit here from no wish to come so close, believe me," answered she ; " but I saw no other seat at hand, and I am tired with my ramble.  If you have not the courtesy to offer me a chair, I must help myself and take one. That is the mode here, I fancy."

" We have learned to help ourselves, since none will help us," said the robber-chief, in his harsh voice. " I see you guess our calling. We live upon what we can seize, or extort, from the fears of those who have made us out-casts. Trusty Filippino and Matteo saw the litter approaching this morning, and decided that it was not probable that two girls travelling alone would carry much worth taking. But on recognising one of them for the Governor of Messina's daughter, they knew that by detaining her they could secure heavy ransom."

" My only concern is that you should get it," said Beatrice.

" We shall surely do that," he replied. " Meantime, signorina, you must be content to remain here."

" Remain I must ; contentedly is more than you can compel me to, or I can answer for," interrupted she.

" To remain here our prisoner," he resumed, " though you shall have all courteous treatment."

" That is glad hearing, if it be only as a welcome change from what I have already had," said she. " Suppose you begin your courtesy by offering me something to eat and drink, for I am half-famished. I have had but scant breakfast this morning, and travelling sharpens the appetite."

" We were about to sit down to our noontide meal, when you entered. Will you share it with us ? " said the brigand.

" Corpo di Bellona ! " exclaimed one of the men. " I would thou wert a few years older, little one, and thou shouldst stay here, and be our queen ! 'Tis a million pities thou'rt not old enough to marry our captain, and share his sway ! I'll drink your health, young lady ! "

" Fill me a cup, and I'll pledge you all, good gentlemen," said Beatrice. " But I have no ambition to be your queen. I should soon be an unpopular monarch among you, for I should begin my rule by reforming your ways. No molestation of peaceful travellers—no waylaying of unoffending pas-sengers—no detaining people against their will and extorting unjust ransoms from their anxious friends. Liberty, not licence, on the road, should then be your maxim, and I would make you observe what now I only give you as a toast—' Freedom for *all* upon the highway ! ' "

She nodded gracefully round to them as she put her lips to the wine-cup, and the robbers shouted a loud " Evviva ! " to her honour.

" And now, as I am a prisoner, a dungeon is to be my withdrawing-room, I presume," she said. " Let me begone to it at once."

" If you will pass your word not to attempt escape, young lady," said the grim captain, " you shall have free range throughout our fastness ; I think I can trust you."

" If I were so simple as to promise, you might be so simple as to trust me. No, no, best be free altogether, where neither promise nor trust are like to be preserved."

" The strong-room in the tower must be your portion then, wilful one," said the robber-chief, nodding to Filippino, who led the way with Beatrice out of the cavern hall.

The young girl, the moment she was alone, eagerly inspected her prison.

It was a middle-sized room bare of furniture, with the exception of a pallet-bed, a rough table, a stool, and an iron lamp. There was but one window—if that might be called a window which was a mere grated outlet. But it was not very high up in the wall, and the embrasure was so deep that Beatrice could lean upon it and look out upon the magnificent view that spread in front of the tower.

She remained here for some time, feasting her eyes upon the beauties of rock, lake, and wood, while her thoughts flew to Hero—to her uncles, to what would be the consternation of the former on waking, and discovering her cousin no longer by her side in the litter, to what would be the anxiety of the latter on learning that she had not returned home. As she leaned, musing, her eyes closed, her head dropped upon her arms, and she slept.

*" Fill me a cup, and I'll pledge you all, good gentlemen "*

It was late in the afternoon when she was awakened by the unfastening of her prison-door and the entrance of Filippino.

" I have brought you some supper, young lady," he said, " and I am but a rough chambermaid, but I'll try to make your bed a bit tidy for you, against you go to rest. I shall never cease to regret that you were born a lady, when you might have been a brigand. Cospetto! Che vergogna! Che peccato! But it can't be helped! Buona notte, signorina. Felice notte ! "

" Good-night, good Filippino. May thy dreams be undisturbed by regrets for me."

" Good-night ! " repeated Filippino, as he withdrew muttering.

When she was again left to herself, Beatrice for the first time felt a little downhearted. Night was coming on ; here, in this wild place, among these wild and lawless men, with no friend at hand to cheer or aid her, a sense of loneliness crept over her, and she sat for a space lost in saddened thought.

Then she took some of the bread and fruit from the supper Filippino had brought, and took them to her old leaning-place, the deep window-ledge, and ate them there, that her eyes might imbibe comfort and hope from the view of Nature in her serene aspect. The moon had risen, and the lovely sequestered spot lay steeped in her soft beams. The lake was like a mirror, save where the night breeze from the mountain gently stirred its surface.

As she gazed, the thought of her friends, and above all Hero's misery, at her prolonged absence, made her writhe with impatience at her captivity, and, in an impulse of longing to get to them, she clutched at one of the bars of the iron grating before her.

To her surprise and delight it moved beneath her grasp. She felt it sensibly give way. She applied all her strength in pulling at it, and to give still greater purchase she climbed up into the deep embrasure. It yielded more and more, and at length she succeeded in wrenching it out of its rusty socket entirely, leaving sufficient space for her to pass her body through the opening thus made. The bedclothes torn into lengths and fastened together might form a means of letting her down outside, but she remembered that the watch-tower stood immediately on the brink of the lake, and she was uncertain whether the walls might not go sheer down into the water. She determined to try, however. She set to work and at length succeeded in forming her knotted ladder. She fastened one end securely to the loose iron bar that it might form a steadying weight, and the other end to the grating. She then lowered it out, and by the tightened strain found that it could not have reached to the ground.

Notwithstanding, she crept through the opening of the grating, and trusted herself to the strength of the new-made rope. Luckily she had been accustomed to active sports, and constant out-of-door exercise, which gave her strength of limb as well as good command of them. Firmly she clung to her bed-clothes ladder, carefully letting herself down from knot to knot, until at length she had the joy of feeling that she had arrived at the friendly iron bar. She planted her feet steadily upon it as it hung crosswise, and then ventured to look down, which she had refrained from doing till now.

She found that she was within a few feet of the bottom of the tower, so she quitted her hold, slid down, and fell safely to the ground. Before endeavouring to regain her feet, she lay still for a moment that she might recover from the giddiness that she felt, and then she leaned over the grassy edge and dipped her hands in the cold water, and laved some on her face, and then the giddiness passed quite off.

She had nothing to guide her in the choice of a path, but any direction seemed well, so that it led away from the tower walls. She struck at once across a grassy plain, dotted with trees that lay stretched before her, the lake abruptly diverging to her right, leaving a way open and unimpeded. She kept as much as possible within the shadow of the trees, that her progress might be unnoted should there be any stragglers of the troop abroad.

After a time the way became steeper : it arose from the plain she had passed, among the rocks and higher ground. Gradually it had less and less of tree and vegetation, and she began to fear that she might be getting back again among the mountain range from which on the previous day she had journeyed. She had no means of judging her course, but she kept forward that she might, at any rate, leave the robber-hold in the rear.

*Firmly she clung to her bed-clothes ladder, carefully letting herself down*

She wandered on for some hours, when, just as day broke, she discovered, to her great mortification, that she was not far from the spot where she had yesterday morning first encountered the two robbers. She could not be mistaken, there was the road, winding down the declivity where she had last seen the litter, trotting away in the distance, hopelessly unhearing of her cry to stop ; there was the tangled bank up which she had scrambled to pluck the fruit for Hero ; there the very spot whence she had beheld the brigands' faces glaring down upon her.

Notwithstanding that she was by this time much tired with her long night ramble, she walked, or rather ran, with her best speed down the hill, avoiding the open road, lest she should be seen, but skirting it to keep it in view, that she might be sure of her way.

She had nearly reached the more level ground at the foot of the descent when she saw a man with a sickle in his hand ; there was a mule beside him fastened to a tree, grazing, and into the large baskets that were slung on either side of the animal the man was loading the green fodder as he reaped. He was shouting a rustic song at the full stretch of his lungs. His garb was coarse, and his look was unmistakably countrified. " He looks safely a peasant—a peasant—a rude peasant—I may surely trust him," thought Beatrice, as she eyed the man, who looked up at her approaching step.

" Hallo, little one ! Where did you start from ? From the earth, or from the bole of a tree ? Or did you drop from the clouds ? Out of breath, panting, dusty ! Are you pursued ? "

" No, no ; I have been seized by the bandits—have made my escape from them, and fear lest they should discover it and recover me. Hide me, good man ; give me rest and shelter for a while, and then be my guide to Messina—to my home—where you shall have both thanks and reward."

" Softly, softly, little one ! how glibly your tongue runs on," said the peasant. " Let me understand this matter. You have been taken by the bandits. Good. You call them no friends, but enemies. Good again ; so far as you are concerned ; but it's different in my case. They are no enemies of mine—but very good friends and neighbours—as friends and neighbours go."

" That's to say, they neither rob nor murder you," said Beatrice.

" Exactly," assented the peasant. " And it would be a poor return on my part if I were to rob them of their hope of gain. They'd think I joined to defraud them, if they knew I helped you out of their clutches. They expect ransom for you, and if their hostage slips away, how are they to get it, I should like to know ? Be just, and tell me that. Be reasonable."

" Well, then, I need your kindness ; how do you propose to aid me, and yet keep all smooth with your worthy friends ? "

" Thus. You want to get away from them, very natural. They want to keep you, very fair. I want to please both parties, very right. If I manage your escape, unknown to them, well and good in all ways ; you are saved, and they remain unoffended—that's the main thing."

" And how is this to be done ? Quick, quick, good man ! They may even now be upon us."

" 'Tis for that very reason I must contrive a way to take you to my hut unseen, little one," said the peasant ; " it is at some distance, and on your way there we might, as likely as not, stumble upon one or other of the brigands. Here, step into this basket ; you will ride softly and easily upon this couch of new-cut grass, and I will cover you lightly over with more, so that no matter whom we meet I shall be seen in no awkward company, and my mule will seem to carry a no less innocent load than green fodder."

" Put some stones in the opposite basket," said Beatrice, " that it may weight down the grave charge you consent to carry in this one, otherwise you'll be betrayed by a lop-sided appearance."

The peasant, after putting the final touch to his arrangements, led the animal by the rein, with an easy air, resuming his rustic song, as he went his way. It was not long ere he had occasion to rejoice at his forethought.

A voice called lustily after him : " Girolamo ! Ohe ! Girolamo ! "

" Ah, messer Matteo ! " said the peasant, turning to salute the bandit with every appearance of hearty greeting ; " you are early abroad this morning. Ah, well, you can't be too early at work."

" Let's to business, then," said the robber. " Our people got hold of a young girl yesterday, whom we've reason to know is none other than the Governor of Messina's daughter. It stands to reason that we ought to get a good ransom for such as she, and we took care of her, according. But see the heartlessness of the world ! So far from feeling grateful this young hussy must needs take advantage of our all being peacefully asleep, to steal away in the night and leave us without so much as good-bye t'ye, or thanks for the food and the shelter she had."

" And you are out this morning to look after her, and see if you can reclaim her ? " said Girolamo.

" Even so," answered he. " When Filippino went to look in upon her at daybreak, just to see that she was all safe and comfortable, he found the bird flown, and I was despatched to try to bring her back to cage. You haven't happened to see her pass by, have you ? " continued Matteo, twitching out one or two of the blades of grass that overhung the basket in which Beatrice lay hidden. " A little gay-eyed red-lipped thing, that looks too bright and fearless to mind anything."

" Just such a child as you describe I saw this very morning, not half an hour ago," said the peasant. " She was wandering about. I questioned her, as in duty bound. She told me she had made her escape from your hands. I washed mine of the concern, as became me. I said you would not approve of my helping her away if it should come to your ears that I had done so, and that I liked to live in peace with my neighbours."

" Well said, good Girolamo," said Matteo ; " our captain shall know of the good turn you have done him. And so you left the little one to do as well as she could. Quite right. And whereabouts was this ? "

" Close by ; just up there, yonder," said the peasant, pointing to the spot where the colloquy had taken place between himself and Beatrice.

" And you think I shall find here there still ? " said Matteo.

" She can't have got far," replied Girolamo. " I shouldn't wonder but she's crouching among the long grass, hiding somewhere quite near."

" Thanks, good friend, I'll not forget to report you to our captain, and, in return for your neighbourliness, it shall go hard, but we'll spare you a token of our goodwill out of the chit's ransom, when it is ours," said the robber, as he strode off in the direction pointed out.

" I'm much bounden to you, messer Matteo," said the peasant ; " lest I seem selfish, I'll not say I wish you may get it."

And taking up his song again at the very note and turn of the tune where he had been interrupted, Girolamo jogged on by the side of his mule as before. At length the mule, of its own accord, turned out of the main path ; the glare of the sun was exchanged for the cool green light of trees overhead ; the dust of the road no longer arose in clouds about them ; there was the loose rich earth of cultivated ground beneath their feet ; and the panniers brushed their way past lines of maize, vines, canes, and waving broom plants. She could discern that they were entering a small *campagna* of humble pretensions, but well tilled, and kept in order. There were apple, walnut, and peach trees ; and near the house she noted the usual broad trays made of canes, on which lay figs spread to dry for winter provision.

The house was a mere cottage, built in the rudest form, but of stone, with thick walls as a protection against the heat ; while the side trellis, overrun with vine-leaves and drooping clusters, the bunches of bright orange-coloured ears of Indian corn that hung round the windows to ripen and dry, with here and there a long-necked bottle-gourd, and a huge tawny pumpkin, gave a picturesque effect to the spot, which a place of greater elegance and exactness might have lacked.

Peasant Girolamo did the honours of his *campagna* with much courtesy, after his own phlegmatic fashion, bidding Beatrice abide beneath the vine-trellis. When he had concluded his arrangements, he went to the door and beckoned Beatrice in.

He glanced with a sort of meek triumph, a kind of composed pride, upon the repast he had set forth ; as though he knew its super-excellence, but that he was capable of the heroism of bestowing it upon his new acquaintance, since he had already done so much for her.

It looked certainly very tempting, a crusty loaf of barley-bread upon an olive-wood trencher ; cheese made of ewes' milk, embedded in cool green leaves ; honey, looking like liquid topaz ; and heaps of fruit, golden oranges, burnished pomegranates, rough walnuts, purple grapes, rosy apples, and bloomy peaches, piled into a pyramid that looked as though Amalthea's horn had tumbled its contents upon the board.

The young girl's many-hours' fast, and long wanderings in the open air, had given her an appetite which lent the crowning zest to this pleasant meal ; and the relish with which she evidently enjoyed, and did justice to his entertainment, was not lost upon her host. He looked on approvingly from time to time, in the intervals of his own eating ; cut for her huge corner hunks of bread, and selected for her the choicest fruit. He pledged her in some of the rough new wine which formed his own beverage ; but seeing that she merely put her lips to it from courtesy, he went and filled a gourd with water cold and fresh from the well, for her especial drinking.

" To some palates, water comes more welcome than wine," he said ; " a young lady's mouth hath mostly this delicacy of taste ; to please it, I grudge not the trouble of fetching."

" Mine host is as gallant as he is hospitable," said Beatrice. " In this delicious draught, refreshing and grateful, I drink his health. You lead a very quiet life here, I conjecture ? "

" I live quite alone ; but he who hath virtuous thoughts to keep him company cannot complain of solitude, young lady," said Girolamo ; " they are better than visitors ; they never come inopportunely, they never tire, their very sweets never cloy. Let me give you some of this honey, by the bye ; it is very fine—my swarms originally came from thymy Hybla."

" I have already had abundance of good things—good things to repletion," said Beatrice. " But you will not think me wanting in acknowledgment if I seem eager to quit them the moment I have had enough. Pity my impatience to reach home, to see my friends, to relieve their anxiety, to embrace them all once more."

" Far be it from me to thwart so natural, so worthy a desire," said the peasant. " Orecchiutone, my good mule, will have rested and dined by this time. Let us away then, in the same order we came."

Through the afternoon they went jogging on again, until at length, towards evening, they arrived within view of the gates of Messina.

. . . . . . . . . . . .

Leonato was pacing up and down one of his saloons, anxiously hoping for news of his lost niece from some one of the several parties he had sent forth in search of her, when an attendant hastily entered the saloon to say that there was a strange man, a peasant mountaineer, who was in the courtyard insisting upon seeing his lordship the Lord Governor of Messina himself.

" Perchance he brings news of my niece ; bring him hither ; why did you not admit him at once ? "

" My lord, he will neither be brought hither, nor admitted, nor anything else," said the attendant. "He will not wait upon your lordship, but says forsooth your lordship must come down to him, as he can't leave his mule. We offered to take charge of the beast; he wouldn't hear of it. Had we not feared that he might bring news of my young lady Beatrice, he should soon have seen the outside of the palace gates."

Half of the attendant's ireful speech at this insult to his master's dignity was lost to Leonato, who had hurried out of the saloon as soon as he had gathered that the peasant would only tell what he had to say to himself.

At sight of the Lord Governor entering the courtyard, the crowd of lackeys, and guards, and attendants that had gathered round the stranger,

*Beatrice sprang up, throwing off the heap of green fodder*

gave way, and Leonato advanced to the spot where stood Girolamo holding his mule by the bridle, with an air perfectly grave and cool.

"I am come to offer you a bargain, my Lord Governor; will you buy this load of green hay? Will you give me a fair price for it?" he said.

"I will give thee thine own price for it, good fellow, if, as I hope, thou bring'st me news of my dear child, my lost niece, my Beatrice. Tell me what thou know'st of her. Speak, man!" said Leonato eagerly.

"Every one for his own pet interest, my lord, as is natural; your thoughts run all upon your niece, mine all upon the contents of my panniers, quite natural," said Girolamo. "But you bid fairly, you offer mine own price. If I name a high one—as I shall—don't wonder. You'll think it cheap."

"What thou wilt. But Beatrice—you say you have brought her—where does she tarry—why is not she home? She was ever all impatience to fly to me."

"She has had much ado to restrain it," said Beatrice, springing up, throwing off the heap of green fodder, and leaping from the midst of it into her uncle's embrace.

"And now, good friend, tell me what I can do for thee in return for the happiness thou hast bestowed," said Leonato, turning to peasant Girolamo, after the first transports of finding Beatrice restored, "this purse of gold shall acquit my promise of purchasing the load of hay, but I would have thee tell me if there be anything in which I can further pleasure thee, as a recompense for the care thou hast taken of my wanderer. Speak frankly."

"Since you bid me, my Lord Governor, I will honestly tell you there are three things in which you can mainly oblige me. Firstly, let your treasurer exchange me this purse of gold for the like value in copper coins ; secondly, allow it not to get wind how my young lady, your niece, made her way home ; and thirdly, give me your lordship's promise that you will not visit their late misdemeanour upon my neighbours."

"Grant him his petition for my sake, dear uncle, and I will explain all," said Beatrice, observing some surprise and hesitation in her uncle's look. "Friend Girolamo is of a cautious turn of mind, and would fain not attract the attention of his neighbours by any ostentatious display of an unwonted kind of metal, when next he hath occasion to disburse coin, which would be the case had he gold pieces to change ; therefore he modestly and wisely preferreth copper.

"Friend Girolamo is of a peaceable turn of mind, and would fain not run the chance of giving offence by having it known that he aided me to find my way back to Messina unransomed. And lastly, friend Girolamo is of a generous turn of mind, and therefore speaks a good word on behalf of those who have it in their power to give him a helping hand now and then, as his very good friends and neighbours."

Peasant Girolamo, who had checked off on his fingers each clause of her speech in succession as they were uttered by Beatrice, at its conclusion, nodded gravely : "Well set forth, little one ; I could hardly have better delivered it, mine own self."

"It shall all be as thou wishest, good fellow," said Leonato, "but the copper coins will be a heavy burthen for thee to carry."

"Friend Girolamo hath the prudence to let his mule bear all troublesome charges for him," said Beatrice. The young girl patted the good animal's neck, and then extended her hand in a kindly farewell to its master ; upon which Girolamo made his parting obeisance, and took his departure towards his mountain home.

"And now for Uncle Antonio and my dear Hero, and Cousin Gaetano ! " exclaimed Beatrice. "Where are they all ? "

"Here come my brother and Hero ! " said her uncle. "As for poor Gaetano, he's in bed."

"In bed ! "

"Ay ; he was so distressed when he found you were missing that he was obliged to lie down, and he has not been up since. Poor lad ! I believe he was really ill : he worked himself into such a fever of inquietude, it was quite pitiable."

"Pitiable, indeed ! " exclaimed Beatrice. "To take it to heart, he must take to his bed ! Alack, most infelicitous of Gaetanos ! "

# RAIN IN SUMMER

### *by* H. W. Longfellow

HOW beautiful is the rain !
After the dust and the heat,
In the broad and fiery street,
In the narrow lane,
How beautiful is the rain !

How it clatters along the roofs,
Like the tramp of hoofs !
How it gushes and struggles out
From the throat of the overflowing spout !
Across the window-pane
It pours and pours ;
And swift and wide,
With a muddy tide,
Like a river down the gutter roars
The rain, the welcome rain !

The sick man from his chamber looks
At the twisted brooks ;
He can feel the cool
Breath of each little pool ;
His fevered brain
Grows calm again,
And he breathes a blessing on the rain.

From the neighbouring school
Come the boys,
With more than their wonted noise
And commotion ;
And down the wet streets
Sail their mimic fleets,
Till the treacherous pool
Engulfs them in its whirling
And turbulent ocean.
In the country on every side,
Where far and wide,
Like a leopard's tawny and spotted hide,
Stretches the plain,
To the dry grass and the drier grain
How welcome is the rain !

In the furrowed land
The toilsome and patient oxen stand ;
Lifting the yoke-encumbered head,
With their dilated nostrils spread,
They silently inhale
The clover-scented gale,
And the vapours that arise
From the well-watered and smoking soil.
For this rest in the furrow after toil
Their large and lustrous eyes
Seem to thank the Lord,
More than man's spoken word.

Near at hand,
From under the sheltering trees,
The farmer sees
His pastures and his fields of grain,
As they bend their tops
To the numberless beating drops
Of the incessant rain.
He counts it as no sin
That he sees therein
Only his own thrift and gain.

# THE SHADOWLESS MAN

## by ADELBERT VON CHAMISSO

### CHAPTER I

AT last, after a fortunate, but to me most tedious, passage, we reached our destined haven. As soon as the boat had landed me on the shore, I loaded myself with my little possessions, and, forcing my way through the swarming crowd, entered the first and meanest house distinguished by a signboard. I ordered a chamber; the waiter measured me with a glance, and sent me up to the garret.

I ordered fresh water, and inquired for the abode of Mr. Thomas Jones. "Near the North Gate, the first country house on the right-hand side; a large new house of red and white marble, supported by many pillars." Well, it was yet early. I opened my bundle, laid out my newly-turned black coat, clad myself in my sprucest garments, put my letter of introduction into my pocket, and bent my way to the man who, I modestly hoped, was destined to befriend me.

After I had gone through the long North Street, and reached the gate, I saw the columns glimmering through the green trees. "It is here, then," I thought. I wiped the dust from my feet with my pocket-handkerchief, arranged my cravat, and rang the bell. The door flew open; the servants narrowly examined me, in the hall, but the porter at last announced me, and I had the honour of being summoned into the park, where Mr. Jones was walking with a small company. I knew him instantly by his portly self-complacency.

He received me tolerably well—as a rich man is wont to receive a poor dependent ; looked towards me, but without turning from the rest of the company, and took from me the letter I held in my hand. " Ay, ay ! from my brother ; I have not heard from him for a long time. Is he well ? There," he continued, addressing the company without waiting for an answer, and pointed with the letter to a hill,—" There I have ordered a new building to be erected." He broke the seal, but not the conversation, of which wealth became the subject. " He who is not the master of at least a million," he interposed, " forgive the expression, is a ragamuffin."

" That is true, indeed," exclaimed I, with full overflowing feeling.

He smiled on me and said, " Remain here, young friend : I shall perhaps have time to tell you by-and-by, what I think of it." He pointed to the letter, put it into his pocket, and turned again to the company.

He then offered his arm to a young lady ; other gentlemen were busied with other fair ones ; every one found some one to whom he attached himself, and they walked towards the rose-encircled hill.

We reached the rose-grove. The lovely Fanny—the queen, as it seemed, of the day—was capricious enough to wish to gather for herself a blooming branch ; a thorn pricked her, and a stream, as bright as if from damask roses, flowed over her delicate hand. This accident put the whole company in motion. English court-plaster was instantly inquired after.

A silent, meagre, pale, tall, elderly man, who stood next to me, and whom I had not before observed, instantly put his hand into a close-fitting breast-pocket of his old-fashioned grey taffeta coat, took out a small pocket-book, opened it, and with a lowly bow gave the lady what she had wished for ; she took it without any attention to the giver, and without a word of thanks. The wound was bound up, and they ascended the hill, from whose brow they admired the wide prospect over the park's green labyrinth, extending even to the immeasurable ocean.

Refreshments were produced ; the rarest fruits of every climate, served in the richest dishes. They would willingly have remained longer on the sod of the sloping hill, and have stretched themselves over the outspread turf, had they not feared its dampness.

" Now it would be enchanting," said somebody of the company, " if we had Turkey carpets to spread here."

The wish was hardly expressed ere the man in the grey coat had put his hand into his pocket, and began to draw out a richly embroidered Turkey carpet. It was received by the attendants as a matter of course, and laid down on the appointed spot. Without further ceremony the company took their stand upon it.

I looked with new surprise on the man, the pocket, and the carpet, which was about twenty paces long and ten broad. I rubbed my eyes, not knowing what to think, and especially as nobody else seemed moved by what had passed.

The sun now began to shine more intensely, and to annoy the ladies. The lovely Fanny carelessly addressed the grey man—whom, as far as I know, nobody had addressed before—with the frivolous question, " Had he a marquee ? " His hand was already in his pocket, from which I perceived canvas, bars, ropes, iron-work—everything, in a word, belonging to the most sumptuous tent—issuing forth. The young men helped to erect it ; it covered the whole extent of the carpet and no one appeared to consider all this as at all extraordinary.

If my mind was confused—nay, terrified—with these proceedings, how was I overpowered when the next-breathed wish brought from his pocket three riding-horses ! I tell you, three great and noble steeds, with saddles and appurtenances !

I determined to steal away from the company ; and this was easy for one who had acted a part so little conspicuous. I wished to hasten back to the city, and to return in pursuit of my fortune the following morning to Mr. Jones, and, if I could muster up courage enough, inquire something about the extraordinary grey man. Oh, had I been thus privileged to escape !

I had hastily glided through the rose-grove, descended the hill, and found myself on a wide grass-plot, when I saw the old man in the grey coat behind, and advancing towards me ! He immediately took off his hat, and bowed to me more profoundly than any one had ever done before. It was clear he wished to address me, and without extreme rudeness I could not avoid him.

" Will the gentleman forgive the intrusion of one who has stopped him in this unusual way ? I have a request to make, but pray pardon——"

" In the name of heaven, sir ! " I cried out, " what can I do for one who——" We both started back, and methought both blushed deeply.

After a momentary silence he again began:—

" During the short time when I enjoyed the happiness of being near you, I observed with admiration the beautiful shadow in the sun which, with a certain noble contempt, and perhaps without being aware of it, you threw off from your feet ; would you be inclined to transfer it to me ? "

He was silent, and my head turned round like a water-wheel. " He is crazy ! " thought I ; and, with an altered tone, I replied :—

" How is this, good friend ? Is not your own shadow enough for you ? This seems to me a whimsical sort of bargain indeed."

He began again : " I have in my pocket many matters which might not be quite unacceptable to the gentleman ; for this invaluable shadow I deem any price too little."

A chill came over me : I remembered what I had seen, and knew not how to address him whom I had just ventured to call my good friend. I spoke again, and assumed an extraordinary courtesy, that I might set matters in order.

" Pardon, sir, pardon your most humble servant ; I do not quite understand your meaning. How can my shadow——"

He interrupted me : " I only beg your permission to be allowed to lift up your noble shadow, and put it in my pocket : how to do it is my own affair. As a proof of my gratitude to the gentleman, I leave him the choice of all the treasures that my pocket affords ; but better that you should have Fortunatus's wishing-cap, restored spick and span new ; and also a fortune-bag which belongs to him."

" Fortunatus's fortune-bag ! " I exclaimed ; and, great as had been my terror, all my senses were now enraptured by the sound.

*I instantly drew from it ten pieces of gold*

"Condescend, sir, to inspect and make a trial of this bag." He put his hand into his pocket, and drew from it a moderate-sized, firmly-stitched purse of thick cordovan, with two convenient leather cords hanging to it, which he presented to me.

I instantly dipped into it, drew from it ten pieces of gold, and ten more, and ten more, and yet ten more. I stretched out my hand. "Done! the bargain is made; I give you my shadow for that purse."

He grasped my hand, and knelt down behind me, and I perceived him with wonderful dexterity loosening my shadow from the ground from head to foot; he lifted it up; he rolled it together and folded it, and at last put it into his pocket. He then stood erect, bowed to me again, and returned to the rose-grove.

I thought I heard him laughing softly to himself. I held, however, the purse tight by its strings—the earth was sunbright all around me,—and my senses were still wholly confused.

## CHAPTER II

AT last I came to myself, and hastened from a place where apparently I had nothing more to do. I first filled my pockets with gold, then firmly secured the strings of the purse round my neck, taking care to conceal the purse in my bosom. I left the park unnoticed, reached the high road, and bent my way to the town. I was walking thoughtfully towards the gate, when I heard a voice behind me :—

THE SHADOWLESS MAN

With a swift movement he made a slight wound in my hand. " Sign ! " he cried, and thrust the parchment
and pen into my hand  (*Page* 299)

FINETTE

The prince, who was handsome and charming, came to kiss her hand. Shouts arose of " Long live the princess, who will be our queen " (*Page* 317)

"Hallo! young Squire! hallo! don't you hear?" I looked round—an old woman was calling after me: "Take care, sir, take care: you have lost your shadow!"

"Thanks, good woman." I threw her a piece of gold for her well-meant counsel, and walked away under the trees.

At the gate I was again condemned to hear from the sentinel, "Where has the gentleman left his shadow?" and immediately afterwards a couple of women exclaimed, "Good heavens! the poor fellow has no shadow!"

I continued sadly discomposed, when the coach stopped before the old tavern. I was shocked at the thought of again entering that vile garret. I sent for my baggage, took up the miserable bundle with contempt, threw the servants some pieces of gold, and ordered myself to be driven to the principal hotel. The house faced the north, so I had nothing to fear from the sun. I dismissed the driver with gold, selected the best front room, and locked myself in as soon as possible.

And how do you imagine I employed myself?—oh! my beloved Chamisso, I blush to confess it even to you—I drew forth the luckless purse from my bosom, and, impelled by a sort of madness, I shook out the gold, and gold, and gold, and still more gold; strewed it over the floor, trampled on it, and made it tinkle, and feasting my weak senses on the glitter and the sound, I added pile to pile, till I sank exhausted on the golden bed. I rolled about and wallowed in delicious delirium. And so the day passed by, and so the evening. My door remained unopened, and night found me still reposing on the gold when sleep at length overcame me.

I awoke: it seemed to be yet early—my watch had stopped—I felt as if I had been bastinadoed—yet I was both hungry and thirsty, for since the previous morning I had eaten nothing.

With weariness and disgust I pushed away from me the gold; in my perplexity, I knew not how to dispose of it. But it could not remain there. I tried to put it again into the purse—no; none of my windows opened upon the sea. I was obliged to content myself by dragging it with immense labour and difficulty to a large cupboard which stood in a recess, where I packed it up. I left only a few handfuls lying about. When I had finished my labour, I sat down in an arm-chair, and waited till the people of the house began to stir. I ordered breakfast, and begged the landlord to be with me as soon as practicable.

With this man I arranged the future management of my household. He recommended to me for my personal servant a certain Bendel, whose honest and intelligent countenance instantly interested me. I passed the whole day in my apartments with servants out of place, shoemaker, tailors and shopkeepers; I provided myself with all necessaries, and bought large quantities of jewels and precious stones, merely to get rid of some of my piles of gold; but it seemed scarcely possible to diminish the heap.

Meanwhile, I contemplated my situation with most anxious doubts. I dared not venture one step from my door, and at evening ordered forty wax-lights to be kindled in my saloon, before I left the dark chamber. I thought with horror of the dreadful scene with the schoolboys, and determined, whatever it might cost, once more to sound public opinion. The moon, at this season, illumined the night. Late in the evening I threw a

G.T.B. K

wide cloak around me, pulled down my hat over my eyes, and glided out of the house, trembling like a criminal. I walked first along the shadows of the houses to a remote open place : I then abandoned their protection, stepped out into the moonshine, resolving to learn my destiny from the lips of the passers-by.

But spare me, my friend, the painful repetition of what I was condemned to undergo ! I could bear it no longer. With a broken heart I tremblingly hurried back into darkness. I was obliged to grope along by the houses, in order to feel my steps secure, and slowly and late I reached my dwelling.

That night was a sleepless one. My first care at daybreak was to order the man in the gray coat to be everywhere sought for. I sent for Bendel ; he seemed both apt and active. I described to him minutely the man who held in his possession that treasure without which life was but a torment to me. I told him the time and the place where I had seen him ; particularised to him all the persons who could assist his inquiries ; and added, that he should especially ask after a gold embroidered Turkish carpet, a superb tent, and also the black riding-horses ; whose history—I did not state how—was closely connected with that of the unintelligible man whom nobody seemed to notice, and whose appearance had destroyed the peace and happiness of my life.

When I had done, I brought out as much gold as I was able to carry. I laid jewels and precious stones to a still greater amount upon the pile. " Bendel," I said, " this levels many a path, and makes many a difficult thing easy ; be not sparing—you know I am not ; but go and rejoice your master with the information on which his only hopes are built."

He went—he returned—and returned late and sorrowful. None of the merchant's servants, none of his guests—he had spoken to all—knew anything about the man in the gray coat. I beckoned gloomily to him that he should leave me alone.

But he resumed : " I have informed you, sir, of everything connected with the affair which most interests you. I have also a message to deliver, which was given to me this morning, early, by a person whom I met at the door, while I was going out on the business in which I have been so unfortunate. His own words were, ' Say to Mr. Peter Schlemihl, he will see me here no more, as I am going to cross the sea, and a favourable wind beckons me to the haven. But after a year and a day I shall have the honour to seek him out, and perhaps to propose to him another arrangement which may then be to his liking. Remember me to him, and assure him of my thanks.' I asked him who he was : and he replied, that you know."

" What was the man's appearance ? " I cried, full of forebodings. And Bendel described the man in the gray coat, feature by feature, word for word, precisely as I had depicted him.

" Miserable mortal ! " exclaimed I, wringing my hands, " it was he ! it was he himself ! "

He looked as if scales had fallen from his eyes. " Yes, it was he, it was indeed he ! " he cried in agony ; " and I, silly deluded one, did not know him."

" Bendel ! " I called to him ; " Bendel ! you who alone see and respect my sufferings, not curiously prying into them, but secretly and devoutly sharing them with me—come to me, Bendel, be the nearest to my heart. The store of my gold I have not concealed from you ; from you I will not hide the store of my anguish. Bendel, forsake me not. You know I am wealthy, kind, and generous, and perhaps you think the world should honour me for that ; but you see I shun the world ; I hide myself from its observation. Bendel, the world has judged me and condemned me—and Bendel, too, perhaps will turn from me when he possesses my dreadful secret. Bendel, I am indeed rich, liberal, and independent, but—heavens ! I have no shadow ! ''

He was silent, and I hid my face in my hands. At last I tremblingly said, '' Bendel, you have now my confidence—betray it if you will—away ! and bear witness against me.''

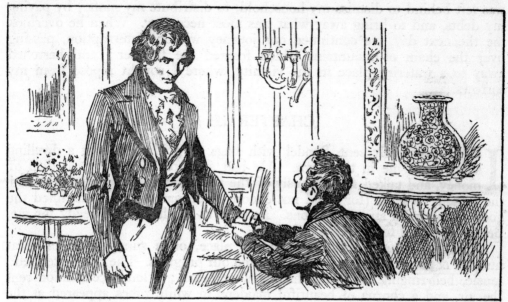

'' I will not leave my good master for the sake of a shadow ''

He seemed struggling with internal emotion ; he threw himself at my feet, and seized my hand. '' No,'' he said, '' let the world say what it may, I will not leave my good master for the sake of a shadow ; I will do what is right and not what is prudent. I will remain with you ; I will lend you my shadow ; I will help you where I can.''

From that moment my fate and my mode of life changed. It is indescribable how carefully Bendel sought to cover my defects. He was ever before me and with me, foreseeing everything, arranging everything, and, where unexpected danger threatened, covering me with his shadow, for he was fortunately taller and stouter than I. Again I mingled with mankind, and acted my part in the scenes of the world.

According to my custom, one lovely evening I had assembled a large company in an illuminated garden. I was wandering about with the beautiful Fanny arm-in-arm, separated from the rest of the guests, and endeavouring to amuse her with well-timed conversation.

At this moment the moon unexpectedly burst through the clouds : her shadow alone was there,—she started, looked alarmed at me, then at the earth, as if her eyes were asking for my shadow. All her emotions were painted so faithfully on her countenance, that I should have burst into a loud laugh, had I not felt an icy chilliness creeping over me.

She sank down from my arms in a swoon. I flew like an arrow through the alarmed company, reached the door, threw myself into the first coach I found waiting there, and hurried back to the city, where to my misfortune, I had left the worthy Bendel. He was startled at seeing me—but a word told all. Post-horses were instantly ordered. I took only one of my servants with me, an interested villain called Rascal, who had learned to make himself useful by his dexterity, and who could suspect nothing of what had occurred. We travelled a hundred miles before night. Bendel was left behind to dismiss my household, to distribute my money by paying my debts, and to bring away what was most necessary. When he overtook me the next day, we continued our journey without interruption, passing over the chain of mountains which formed the frontier ; and hastened away to a watering-place in the vicinity, where I sought repose from my sorrows.

## CHAPTER III

I HAD previously sent Bendel with bags of gold to fit out a dwelling suitable for me in the town. He had scattered about a great deal of money, and talked mysteriously of the illustrious stranger whom he had the honour to serve (for I did not choose to be named), and this filled the good people with strange notions. As soon as the house was ready for me, Bendel returned to convey me thither.

About an hour's distance from the place, on a sunny plain, a great number of persons in gala dresses arrested our progress. The coach stopped : music, bell-ringing, and cannonading were heard ; a loud acclamation rent the air, and a chorus of beautiful maidens in white robes appeared at the door of the carriage, one of whom, surpassing the rest as the sun surpasses in brightness the stars of evening, stepped forward, and with graceful and modest blushes kneeling before me, presented to me on a silken cushion a wreath of laurel, olive, and rose branches, garlanded together. The chorus began, and sang the praise of a good monarch, and the happiness of his people.

And this happened, my friend, in the bright sunshine : she continued to kneel some two steps before me, and I, shadowless, dared not move. What would I not have given at that moment for a shadow ! I was obliged to conceal my despair, by sinking back into the carriage. Bendel relieved me from my embarrassment : he leaped out from the other side—I called him back, and gave him out of my casket, which lay close at hand, a rich diamond crown which had been intended to adorn the lovely Fanny.

He moved forward, and spoke in his master's name, " who neither could," he said, " nor would accept such flattering marks of honour ; there must have been some error ; though he could not but thank the worthy townspeople for their expressions of kindness."

He then took the garland of flowers from its place, and put there instead of it the crown of diamonds. His hand assisted the beautiful maiden to rise and with a look of dignity he dismissed the clergy, magistrates, and deputies.

I knew not yet what all this meant, nor who I was imagined to be. I sent out Rascal to get information. He discovered that the people believed they had certain information that the good king of Prussia was travelling through the country, under the title of count ;—that my adjutant had been recognised, and had discovered both himself and me. I was not a little flattered by even the illusion of being mistaken for the head of the kingdom.

I ordered a feast to be provided on the following evening, under the trees which overshadowed the expanse in front of my house, and caused the whole town to be invited.

Evening darkness came on ; the guests appeared, and were introduced to me. The word " majesty " was no more whispered ; but I often heard, uttered in deep awe and humility, " the count." What could I do ? The word Count satisfied me, and from that moment I was Count Peter.

But in the midst of the festival crowd I sought but one ; at last she appeared ; she *was* the crown, and she wore it. The forest-master, his wife, and daughter were introduced. I said much that was agreeable and obliging to the old people ; but I stood before their daughter like a timid boy, and could not utter a single word. At last I stammered a request that she would honour the festival by undertaking that office whose badge she bore.

On the following morning, Bendel communicated to me, in confidence, that the suspicions he had formed in regard to Rascal's integrity were fully confirmed ; he had yesterday purloined several bags of gold.

" Let us not envy," I replied, " the poor fellow this trifling booty ; I scatter my money about profusely ; why not to him ? Yesterday, he and everybody else served me nobly, and arranged a delightful festivity."

It appeared very soon in the newspapers, that the reported journey of the king was wholly without foundation. But I had been a king, and a king I was unfortunately compelled to remain ; and certainly I was one of the richest who had ever appeared.

I told Mina I was not that which I was supposed to be ; I was only a wealthy but an infinitely wretched man. There was, I said, a curse upon me, which should be the only secret between her and me ; for I had not yet lost the hope of being delivered from it.

I announced to the approaching forest-master my determination to ask the hand of his daughter for the first day of the coming month. I fixed that period because in the meanwhile many an event might occur which would have great influence on my fortunes.

The day so big with fate rolled onwards, heavy and dark, like a thunder-cloud. Its eve had arrived ; I could scarcely breathe. I had been foresighted enough to fill some chests with gold. I waited for midnight—it tolled.

And there I sat, my eyes directed to the hand of the clock ; the seconds, the minutes, as they tinkled, entered me like a dagger. I rose up at every sound I heard. The day began to dawn ; the leaden hours crowded one on another ; it was morning—evening—night. The hands of the time-piece moved slowly on, and hope was departing. It struck eleven, and nothing appeared. The last minutes of the last hour vanished—still nothing appeared ; the first stroke—the last stroke of *twelve* sounded. I sank hopeless on my couch, in ceaseless tears. To-morrow—shadowless for ever !—to-morrow I should solicit the hand of my beloved.

Towards morning, a heavy sleep closed my eyes.

## CHAPTER IV

IT was yet early, when I was awakened by the sound of voices violently disputing in my ante-chamber. I listened : Bendel was forbidding access to my door. Rascal swore loudly and deeply that he would take no orders from his fellow-servant, and insisted on rushing into my apartment. The good Bendel warned him that if such language reached my ears, he might perchance lose a profitable place ; but Rascal threatened to lay violent hands upon him if he impeded his entrance any longer.

I had half dressed myself. I angrily flung the door open, and called out to Rascal, " What dost want, thou scoundrel ? " He retreated two paces, and answered with perfect coldness, " Humbly to request that it may please your lordship for once to show me your shadow ; the sun is shining so beautifully in the court."

Bendel, pale and trembling, made me a sign to seek a resource in the silence-imposing gold. It had, however, lost its power ; Rascal flung it at my feet. " I will take nothing from a shadowless being."

He turned his back upon me, put his hat on his head, and, whistling a tune, went slowly out of the apartment. I stood there like a petrifaction —looking after him, vacant and motionless.

Heavy and melancholy, I prepared to redeem my promise, and to show myself in the forester's garden. I ascended to the dark arbour which had been called by my name, where an appointment had been made to meet me. Mina's mother came forward to meet me, gay and free from care. Mina was seated there, pale and lovely as the earliest snow when it kisses the last autumnal flower.

With irregular steps the forest-master paced the arbour backwards and forwards ; he stood for a moment before me, looked into a paper which he held, and said with a most penetrating glance : " Count! and do you indeed know one Peter Schlemihl ? "—I was silent—" a man of reputable character, and of great accomplishments ? " He waited for my answer.

" And what if I were he ? "

" He," added he vehemently, " who has in some way got rid of his shadow ! "

" Oh, my forebodings ! my forebodings ! " exclaimed Mina. " Alas ! I knew long ago that he had no shadow ! "

" And so," cried the forest-master furiously, " your matchless impudence has sought to betray that poor girl and me ! "

He spoke angrily : " Explain to me, sir, explain how you got rid of your shadow."

I was compelled again to lie : " A vulgar fellow trod so clumsily upon my shadow that he tore a great hole in it ; I sent it to be mended—gold can do everything ; I ought to have received it back yesterday."

" Very well, sir, very well," he replied. " You sue for my daughter—

" *Show me your shadow !* "

others do the same ; as her father, I must take care of her. I give you three days' respite, which you may employ in procuring a shadow. Come to me after this, and if you have one that suits you, you will be welcome : but if not, on the fourth day my daughter shall be the wife of another."

I attempted to address a word to Mina ; but she clung, violently agitated, closer to her mother, who silently motioned to me that I should retire. I slunk away as if the world's gates had closed behind me.

Escaped from Bendel's affectionate guidance, I wandered with erring footsteps through fields and woods. I know not how long it had lasted, when on a sunny heath I found myself held by the sleeve—I stood still and looked around me. It was the gray-coated stranger ; he seemed to have followed me till he was out of breath.

He instantly began : " I had announced myself for to-day ; you have hardly been able to wait so long ; but all is well—you will take good counsel. Exchange your shadow again—it only awaits your commands—and then turn back. You will be welcome in the forester's garden. It was but a jest. Rascal, who has betrayed you, and who is a suitor to your betrothed, I will dispose of—the fellow is ripe."

I stood still there, as if I were asleep. " Announced for to-day ? "—I reckoned the time over again. It was so. I had erred in my calculations. I put my right hand on the bag in my bosom ; he discovered my meaning and drew back two paces.

" No, Sir Count, that is in good hands ; that you may retain." I looked on him with staring and inquiring eyes. He spoke : " May I ask for a trifling memento ? Be so good as to sign this note."

The following words were on the parchment he held : " I hereby promise to deliver over my soul to the bearer after its natural separation from my body."

I shook my head. " Forgive me, sir, for I will not sign."

" Not ! " replied he, with seeming surprise. " Why not ? "

" 'Tis an affair that requires some consideration to add my soul to my shadow in the bargain."

" Oh ! Oh ! " he exclaimed ; " Consideration ! " and burst into a laugh. " I am sorry, Mr. Schlemihl, that you push away the favours which are presented to you ; but I may be more fortunate another time. Farewell —till our speedy meeting ! By the way, you will allow me to mention that I do not by any means permit my purchases to get mouldy ; I hold them in special regard, and take the best possible care of them."

With this he took my shadow out of his pocket, and with a dexterous

*Lifting up his blackthorn cudgel, he required the man to give up the shadow*

fling it was unrolled and spread out on the heath on the sunny side of his feet, so that he stood between the two attendant shadows, mine and his, and walked away.

Bendel, who had followed my steps to the present spot, approached me full of sadness at this instant. The kind-hearted fellow observed my shadow, which he could not mistake, attached to the figure of the extraordinary gray unknown one, and he endeavoured by force to put me in possession of my property ; but not being able to lay firm hold on this subtle thing, he ordered the old man, in a peremptory tone, to abandon what did not belong to him. He, for reply, turned his back upon my well-meaning servant and marched away. Bendel followed him closely, and lifting up the stout blackthorn cudgel which he carried, required the man to give up the shadow, enforcing the command with the strength of his nervous arm ; but the man, accustomed perhaps to such encounters, bowed his head, raised his shoulders, and walked calmly over the heath, accompanied by my shadow and my faithful man.

## CHAPTER V

THUS left behind on the dreary heath, I gave vent to countless tears which seemed to lighten my bosom of its intolerable weight.

The day rolled by. I calmed my hunger with wild fruits, my thirst from the nearest mountain stream. Night approached ; I stretched myself under a tree. The damp dawn awoke me from a heavy sleep. Bendel had surely lost my traces, and I rejoiced to think so. I determined to return no more among men, from whom I fled like the shy beasts of the mountain. Thus I existed through three weary days.

On the morning of the fourth day I found myself on a shady plain, where the sun was shining brightly. I sat down there on the fragment of rock in its beam, for I enjoyed basking again in its long-forbidden glance.

I was alarmed by a gentle rustling. I looked around me, preparing to fly—I saw no one; but there passed by on the sunny sand a man's shadow not unlike my own, wandering about alone ; it appeared to be straying from its owner.

A mighty impulse was roused within me. " Shadow," thought I, " art thou seeking thy master ? I will be he ; " and I sprang forward to possess myself of it. I imagined that, if I were lucky enough to get into its track, I could so arrange that its feet should just meet mine ; it would then attach and accommodate itself to me.

The shadow on my moving fled before me, and I was compelled to begin an active chase after it. I gained, approached it nearer and nearer—I was within reach of it. It stopped suddenly and turned round towards me ; like the lion pouncing on its prey, I sprang forward upon it with a mighty effort to take possession. I felt most unexpectedly that I had dashed against some thing which made a bodily resistance—I received from an unseen power the most violent thrust which a human being ever felt. The working of terror was acting dreadfully within me ; its effect was to close my arms as in a spasm, to seize on what stood unseen before me. I staggered onwards, and fell prostrate on the ground. Beneath me, on his back was a man whom I held fast, and who now was visible.

The whole affair was thus naturally explained. The man must have possessed the viewless charm which makes the possessor, but not his shadow, invisible. He first held it, and afterwards had thrown it away. I looked round, and immediately discovered the shadow of the invisible charm. I leaped up and sprang towards it, and did not miss at last the valuable spoil ; unseen and shadowless, I held the charm in my hand which gave me the means and the disposition to mingle again among my fellow-men.

I longed to go to the forest-garden, in order to inform myself of the truth of what the hated one had announced to me. But I knew not where I was ; and in order to inform myself as to the neighbourhood, I mounted the nearest hill, and saw from its brow the tower of the forest-garden lying at my feet.

I walked into the garden, my bosom trembling with the alarm of expectation. A laugh approached me. I shook, looked eagerly around me, but could perceive nobody. I moved farther forward, and a noise as of the pacing of human feet seemed near me. Still I could see nothing. I thought my ears were deceived ; but it was early and nobody was in Count Peter's arbour—the garden was empty. I rambled over the familiar paths, until I came near to the mansion. I heard the same sound more distinctly. I sat down with a sorrowful heart upon a bank immediately opposite the front door, in a sunny spot. It appeared to me as if I heard the invisible imp laughing insultingly. The key was turned in the door, which opened, and the forest-master walked out with papers in his hand. I felt something like a mist around my eyes—I looked round—and, oh, horrible ! the man in the gray coat was sitting close to me. He had drawn his wishing-cap over my head. At his feet my shadow and his own lay peacefully one against the other ; he was playing carelessly with the well-known parchment, which he held in his hand ; and while the forest-master was walking backwards and forwards in the shade of the arbour, he bent himself to my ear, and whispered these words :—

"Now, then, you have at last accepted my offer, and so we set two heads under one cap. Very good ! very good ! But pray give me my charm again —you do not want it any more, and are too honourable a man to keep what does not belong to you : no thanks—I assure you I lent it to you from my heart." He took it gently from my hand, put it into his pocket, laughed insultingly at me, and so loudly that the forest-master looked round, attracted by the noise. I sat there as if I had been petrified.

"You must agree," he continued, "that such a cap is much more convenient. It does not cover its possessor alone, but his shadow also, and as many people besides as he likes to have with him. Look, now, to-day I get two of you." He laughed again. "You must know, Schlemihl, that what is not done by fair means at first may be enforced at last. I still thought you would have bought the trifle. Take back your bride (there is yet time), and send Rascal to swing on the gallows ; that is an easy matter while we have a rope at hand. I give you the cap into the bargain. Hearken ! "

The man in the gray coat laughed and looked full in my face. The door opened, and Mina came out ; she was supporting herself on her maid's arm ; silent tears were flowing over her pale and lovely cheeks. She sat down in a chair placed for her under the lime-trees, and her father seated himself beside her.

"Thou art my dearest child ; " he said, "thou wilt be prudent, too ; thou wilt not grieve thy old father, who thinks only of making thee happy. I well understand, my sweet girl, that this has sadly shaken thee. Thou hast wonderfully escaped from misery. Listen, my Mina : a lover addresses thee who does not dread the sun ; an honourable man, who is no Count indeed, but who possesses ten times more than thou hast ever possessed ; a man who will make my beloved child happy. Do not oppose me ; make no reply ; be my good, obedient daughter. Let they affectionate father care for thee, and dry thy tears. Promise me to give thy hand to Mr. Rascal ; say, wilt thou promise me ? "

She answered in a low voice, "I have no further will nor wish on earth ; let my father's will be accomplished ! "

On this Mr. Rascal was announced, and daringly joined the circle. Mina lay in a swoon. My hated evil genius fixed his eyes angrily on me, and whispered in these rapid words, " Can you bear *that* too ? What runs in your veins instead of blood ? " With a swift motion he made a slight wound in my hand—blood gushed forth : he cried, " Red blood, truly ! sign !

The parchment and the pen were in my hand.

## CHAPTER VI

WHILE preparing to sign, I fell into a deep swoon, and lay a long time as in the arms of death.

On coming to my recollection, the first tones that reached my ears were the stamping of feet and cursing. I opened my eyes ; it was dark ; my hated companion was there holding me, but scolding thus : " Now, is not that behaving like a silly old woman ? Let the gentleman rise up—conclude the business—as he intended—or perhaps he has other thoughts— would like still to weep."

With difficulty I raised myself from the ground and looked around me. The evening was advanced ; festive music broke from the brightly-lighted forest-house, and groups of company were scattered over the garden walks. Some drew near who were engaged in conversation, and seated themselves on the benches. They spoke of the nuptials of the daughter of the house with the rich Mr. Rascal—they had taken place in the morning. All—all was over !

With my hand I struck away from my head the wishing-cap of the instantly-vanishing unknown one, and fled in silence to conceal myself in the deepest darkness of the wood, hurrying to the garden gate before Count Peter's arbour.

*He was always behind me, ever present*

But my evil genius accompanied me unseen, pursuing me with bitter words : "This, then, is the reward one is to get for the trouble of taking care, through the live-long day, of the nervous gentleman ! And I am then to be fooled at last ? Very well, very well, Mr. Wronghead : fly from me. But we are inseparable. You have my gold, and I your shadow ; they leave no rest to either. Did anybody ever hear of a shadow abandoning its master ? Yours draws me after you, till you condescend to take it again, and I get rid of it."

He continued to talk in the same tone, and I fled from him in vain— he was always behind me, ever present, and speaking sneeringly of gold and shadow.

Through untrodden, vacant streets I hastened to my abode. I rang and a light appeared. Bendel asked from within, "Who is there ?" When he heard my voice, the poor fellow could scarcely contain his joy. He was greatly changed—weak and ill. His hair had become wholly gray.

He led me through the vacant chambers to an inner apartment, which remained furnished. He fetched meat and drink—we sat down—he again began to weep. He then told me that he had lately beaten the gray-clad meagre man, whom he had met with my shadow, so lustily and so long that he had lost all trace of me, and had sunk exhausted to the earth ; that after- wards, not being able to discover me, he had returned home, and that the mob, excited by Rascal, had raised a tumult, broken the windows of the house, and given full reins to their love of destruction.

"Bendel," said I, "you know my fate. Not without certain guilt does the heavy penalty fall on me. You, innocent being as you are, shall no longer bind your destiny to mine ; I will no longer let it be so. To-night I will hasten away. Saddle me my horse—I ride alone. You must remain— I require it. Some chests of gold must yet be here. They are now yours. I shall wander restlessly through the world ; but if a happier day should dawn, and bliss should again smile upon me, I will faithfully think of you."

The honest fellow obeyed with a broken heart this last command of his master. He brought the horse to me, I sprang into the saddle, and pursued my way indifferent as to the direction my horse might take. On the earth I had no goal—no wish—no hope.

## CHAPTER VII

A FOOT-PASSENGER soon joined me, and, after walking some time by my horse's side, begged me, as we were bound the same way, to be allowed to throw the cloak which he carried on the crupper ; I quietly allowed him to do so.

In the meanwhile time passed on, and morning dawn had imperceptibly stolen over the heaven. I trembled as I looked around, and saw the mag- nificent colours blending in the east and heralding the ascending sun; and at that hour, when the shadows stretched themselves out in all their extension, no shelter, no protection was to be discovered—and I was not alone ! I looked upon my companion, and again I trembled : it was even the man in the gray coat.

He smiled at my alarm, and, without allowing me to utter a word, began :
" Let us, as is the custom of the world, unite our different advantages
for a while ; we have always time to separate. The road alongside the
mountain is the only one which you can prudently take. You dare not
descend into the valley ; and over the hill you will hardly think of returning ;
and the road in which you are is just mine. I see the uprising sun makes
you look pale ; I will lend you your shadow while we remain together, and
this may induce you to bear my being near to you."

The sun had arisen ; travellers were approaching us on the road, and
I accepted his offer. He smiled, and let my shadow fall on the ground ; it
took its station upon that of my horse, and cheerfully moved forward.

*One day we were sitting before a cave*

He came on carelessly by my side, and whistled a tune—he on foot, I
on horseback. A dizziness seized me—the temptation was too great ; I
hastily turned the reins, drove both spurs into the horse, and thus went
off at full speed through a cross road. I could not elope with the shadow ;
it slipped away when the horse started, and waited on the road for its lawful
owner. I was obliged to turn round, ashamed ; the man in the gray coat
began to laugh at me, and, fixing the shadow again in its place, informed
me it would only stick to me, and remain with me, when I had properly
and lawfully become possessed of it.

I continued my journey on the same road as before. I possessed all the
comforts of life, and all its luxuries. I could move about freely and easily ;
and I possessed a shadow, too, though but a borrowed one ; and I imposed
everywhere that reverence which wealth commands. My marvellous conductor never separated himself from my side, and incessantly plagued me,
exhibiting the greatest assurance in order that I might conclude the bargain
with him respecting the shadow, if it were only to get rid of him.

One day we were sitting before a cave, which the travellers who had to cross the mountain were accustomed to visit. He depicted to me, as he had often done, careful and detailed pictures of the brilliant figure I might make in the world by means of my purse, if I had only my shadow again in my possession.

I held out the purse to him.

" At the price ? "

" No ! "—I sighed deeply, and began again : " Well, then, I insist upon it, we must part. Do not stop up my way any longer in the world which is wide enough for both of us."

He smiled, and replied : " I go, sir ; but I will first instruct you how to summon me, when you wish for the presence of your most humble slave. You need only shake your purse, that its exhaustless pieces may tinkle, and the sound will draw me instantly to you."

There was something in his speech that pierced my soul. I dashed the clinking purse hastily into the abyss, and uttered these last words : " I conjure thee in the name of God, monster, begone, and never again appear before these eyes."

He rose up with a gloomy frown, and vanished instantaneously behind the dark masses of rock which surrounded that wild and savage place.

## CHAPTER VIII

I OPENED my eyes at last—the sun was in the heavens, but in the east ; I had slept through the night. I took this for a sign that I ought not to return to the inn. I willingly abandoned that which I had so lately left there, and determined to take on foot a by-road which led through the forest-girdled base of the hill, leaving it to fate to determine what might be my lot. I looked not back ; I thought not even of applying to Bendel, whom I had left in wealth behind me, though I might easily have done so.

A couple of rainy days helped me far on my way, but at the cost of my boots, whose soles were made to suit Count Peter, and not a running foot-man. I soon walked on my naked feet, and was obliged to procure another pair of boots. The next morning I attended earnestiy to this affair in a village where a fair was held, and where old and new boots were exposed for sale in a shop. I selected and bargained for a long time, but I was obliged to abandon a new pair which I wished to possess—I was frightened by the extravagant price—and satisfied myself, therefore, with old ones, which were yet firm and strong, and which the fair and light-haired shop-boy handed to me for my ready cash with a smile, while he wished me a prosperous journey. I put them on immediately, and went away through a door which lay to the north.

I was lost in my own thoughts, and hardly observed where I put my foot—for I was planning about a certain mine, where I hoped to find work underground, though I hardly knew how I should manage to introduce myself there. I had not advanced two hundred paces ere I discovered that I had lost my way. I looked round, and found myself in an ancient and desert wood of firs, to the roots of which it appeared the axe had never been laid. I still hastened onwards a few steps, and perceived I was among

*The cold was intolerable. Another bewildered step and I was on to the ice-borders of the ocean*

dreary rocks, surrounded only by moss and stones, between which lay piles of snow and ice. I moved forward for a few minutes—it was burning hot: around me were richly-cultivated rice-fields under mulberry trees, in whose shadow I sat down, and, looking at my watch, I found it was only a quarter of an hour since I left the village.

I fancied I was dreaming ; I bit my tongue to awake myself, and I was aroused most thoroughly. I went towards a tree—and all was again changed. I walked forward like a drilled recruit, with slow paces. Wonderful varieties of countries—fields, meadows, mountains, wastes, and sandy deserts— rolled along before my astounded sight. Doubtless, I had seven-leagued boots on my feet.

## CHAPTER IX

I FELL down on my knees in speechless devotion, and shed tears of gratitude—my future destiny seemed bright in my soul. Shut out from human society by my early guilt, nature, which I had ever loved, was given me for my enjoyment, spread out like a rich garden before me, an object of study for the guidance and strength of my life, of which science was to be the end. It was no decision of my own.

I rose up hastily, in order that by a rapid survey I might take possession of the field in which I wished to make my harvest. I stood upon the mountains of Tibet, and the sun, which had risen a few hours before, was now sinking in the evening sky. I journeyed from the east towards the west of Asia, overtaking the sun in his progress, and passed the boundaries of Africa. I looked round with great curiosity, and crossed the country in all directions. As I glanced over the old pyramids and temples of Egypt,

I observed in the deserts, near the hundred-gated Thebes, the caverns once occupied by Christian anchorites : instantly it occurred impressively and distinctly to me—There is thy abode. I chose for my future dwelling one of the most secret chambers, which was at the same time roomy and convenient, and moved forward with my staff.

As soon as I had taken some repose, and the day had dawned upon Europe, my first care was to provide for my necessities. First, stop-shoes ; for I had discovered that, however inconvenient it might be, there was no way of shortening my pace in order to move conveniently in my immediate neighbourhood, except by drawing off my boots. A pair of slippers, however, produced the wished-for effect. My watch was an admirable chronometer ; but I required a sextant, philosophical instruments, and books.

In order to obtain all these things, I made some tedious journeys to London and Paris, which were both overshadowed by friendly fogs. As I had exhausted the remainder of my magic gold, I brought with me, for the purposes of payment, some African elephants' teeth.

I had a love of a little dog, that watched my Theban cave ; and when I returned to it laden with new treasures, it sprang forward to meet me, making me feel the spirit of humanity within me, and that I was not quite alone on the earth. But, notwithstanding this, calamity was yet to drive me back to the haunts of men !

## CHAPTER X

ONCE, on the northern coast, having drawn on my boots while I was gathering together my straggling plants and seaweeds, a bear approached unawares the verge of the rock on which I stood. I wished to throw off my slippers and move off to an adjacent island, which I expected to reach over a rock whose head towered above the waves. With one foot I reached the rock ; I stretched out the other, and fell into the sea : I had not observed that my foot was only half-released from the slipper.

Overpowered by the tremendous cold, I had the greatest difficulty in rescuing my life from this peril ; but as soon as I reached the land, I hurried off to the wastes of Libya to dry myself there in the sun. I had, however, scarcely set out ere the burning heat so oppressed my head, that I reeled back again to the north, very ill. I sought relief in rapid movements ; and with uncertain and hurried steps I hastened on.

I know not how long I thus wandered over the earth. A burning fever glowed through my veins, and with dreadful agony I felt that my intellect was abandoning me. Misfortune would have it that I should carelessly tread on a traveller's heel : I must have hurt him, for I received a violent blow ; I staggered, and fell.

When I recovered my senses, I was comfortably stretched on an excellent bed, which stood among many others in a roomy and handsome apartment. Somebody was sitting near my pillow ; many persons passed through the hall, going from one bed to another. They stood before mine, and I was the subject of their conversation. They called me *Number Twelve*, and on the wall at the foot of my bed that number certainly stood—it was no illusion, for I could read it most distinctly. There was a black marble slab, on which was inscribed in large golden letters my name,

## PETER SCHLEMIHL,

quite correctly written. Under my name were two lines of letters, but I was too weak to connect them, and closed my eyes again.

I heard something of which Peter Schlemihl was the subject loudly and distinctly uttered, but I could not collect the meaning. I saw a friendly man and a beautiful woman in black apparel standing before my bed. Their forms were not strangers to me, though I could not recognise them.

My boots were, as I was assured, to be found, with everything else that had been discovered with me, in good and safe keeping, and ready to be delivered to me on my recovery. The place in which I lay ill was called the *Schlemihlium*; and there was a daily exhortation to pray for Peter Schlemihl, as the founder and benefactor of the hospital. The friendly man whom I had seen at my bedside was Bendel; the lovely woman was Mina.

I lived peaceably in the *Schlemihlium*, quite unknown; but I discovered that I was in Bendel's native place, and that he had built this hospital with the remainder of my once unhallowed gold. The unfortunate blessed me daily, for he had built it in my name, and conducted it wholly under his own inspection.

Mina was a widow: an unlucky criminal process had cost Mr. Rascal his life, and taken from her the greatest part of her property. Her parents were no more. She dwelt here like a pious widow, and dedicated herself to works of charity.

I doubted whether I should discover myself, or set out unknown from the place. I decided, however; I ordered paper and pencil to be brought to me, and wrote these words,—

" Your old friend is better provided for than formerly, and if he do penance, it is the penance of reconciliation."

On this, finding myself better, I desired to dress myself. The keys were deposited on the little trunk which stood close to my bed. I found in it everything that belonged to me. I put on my clothes, and hung over my black coat my botanical case, in which I found again, with joy, my northern plants. I drew on my boots, laid the note which I had written on my bed, and when the door opened was far on my way towards Thebes.

I found everything there in order, and returned again, as my strength came back, to my former engagements and habits of life. And now for a whole twelvemonth I have refrained from exposing myself to the unbearable winter's cold.

And thus, my beloved Chamisso—thus do I yet live. My boots have not lost their virtues; their power is unbroken. But my strength is failing; though I have confidence I have applied the boots to their proper end, and not fruitlessly. And you, my beloved Chamisso—you have I chosen to be the keeper of my marvellous history, which, when I shall have vanished from the earth, may tend to the improvement of many of its inhabitants. But, my friend, while you live among mankind, learn above all things first to reverence your shadow, and next to that your money. If you will only live for Chamisso and his better self, you need no counsel of mine.

# O'ER THE VALLEY

*by* GEORGE DARLEY

O'ER the valley, o'er the mountain !
　By the pathway of the foam
Leading down from yonder fountain,—
　Like a honey-bird, I roam !

Thro' the wild and the bower,
　Like the golden-coated fly
Kissing ev'ry lady-flower,
　As I pass her beauty by ;

Tripping round and round the blossoms
　That bespeck the grassy steep,
Into all their rosy bosoms
　As I run away, I peep !

O'er the meadows gaily winging
　Like an idle elf I rove,
My unheeded song a-singing
　To the melody I love !

# FINETTE

### by COUNTESS D'AULNOY

LONG ago a king and a queen, who had managed their affairs very badly, were driven out of their kingdom. They sold their crowns to support themselves, then their wardrobes, their linen, their lace, and all their furniture piece by piece. The shopkeepers grew tired of buying, for every day something or other fresh was sent for sale.

When nearly everything had been sold, the king said, " We are out of our own country and have no longer any property ; we must do something to obtain a living for ourselves and our poor children. Consider a little what we can do ; for up to this time I have known no trade but a king's, which is a very agreeable one."

The queen, who had much good sense, asked for eight days to think over the matter, and at the end of that time she said, " Sire, we must not make ourselves unhappy. You have only to make nets, with which you may catch both fowl and fish. As the lines wear out, I will spin to make new ones. With respect to our three daughters, they are downright idle girls, who still think themselves fine ladies, and would fain live in that style without work. We must take them to such a distance that they can never find their way back again, since it is impossible for us to keep them as fine as they would like to be."

The king began to weep when he found he must separate himself from his children. He was a kind father, but the queen was mistress ; he therefore agreed to whatever she proposed. " Get up early to-morrow morning," he said, " and take your three daughters wherever you think fit."

While they were thus plotting together, the Princess Finette, who was the youngest daughter, listened at the keyhole, and when she discovered the design of her mother and father, she set off as fast as she could to a great grotto, at a considerable distance from where they lived, which was the abode of the Fairy Merluche, who was her godmother.

Finette had carried with her two pounds of fresh butter, some eggs, milk, and flour to make a nice cake for her godmother, so that she might be well received. She began the journey bravely enough, but the farther she went the more weary she grew. The soles of her shoes became worn completely through, and her pretty little feet became so sore that it was sad to see them. At length, quite tired out, she sat down on the grass and cried. A beautiful Spanish horse came by, saddled and bridled. There were more diamonds on his housings than would have bought three cities, and when he saw the princess he stopped and grazed quietly beside her.

Presently, bending his knee, he appeared to pay her homage, upon which, catching hold of the bridle, she said, " Gentle Hobby, wouldst thou kindly carry me to my fairy godmother ? Thou wouldst do me a great service, for I am so weary that I feel ready to die ; but if thou wilt assist me on this occasion I will give thee good oats and hay and a litter of fresh straw to lie upon."

The horse bent almost to the ground, and young Finette jumping upon him, he galloped off as lightly as a bird. He stopped at the entrance to the grotto, as if he had known where to go, and, in fact, he knew well enough, for it was Merluche herself, who, having foreseen her god-daughter's visit, had sent him to meet her.

As soon as Finette entered the grotto, she made three low curtseys to her godmother, raised the hem of her gown, kissed it, and said, " Good-day, godmother, how are you ? I have brought some butter, flour, and eggs, to make you a cake after our country fashion."

" You are welcome, Finette," replied the fairy. " I know well enough what brought you here. You overheard the king and queen planning how they might lose you, and you would avoid this misfortune. Well, you have only to take this skein of thread ; it will never break. Fasten one end of it to the door of your house, and keep the other in your hand. When the queen has departed, you will easily find your way back by following the thread."

The princess thanked her godmother, who gave her also a bag filled with fine dresses, all of gold and silver. Having embraced her, she placed her on the handsome horse, and in two or three minutes he carried Finette to the door of her parents' cottage.

She entered the house softly, and, hiding the bag under her bolster, went to bed, without appearing to be aware of anything that had happened.

At break of day the king woke his wife, saying, " Rise, madam, it is time to make ready for your journey."

The queen got up directly, took her thick shoes, a short petticoat, a white jacket, and a stick. She called her eldest daughter, who was named Fleur, her second, who was named Belle, and Finette.

" I have been thinking all night," she said, " that we ought to visit my sister, who will be glad to see us. We may feast and laugh as much as we like there."

Fleur, who was in despair at living in a desert, replied, " Let us go, madam, wherever you please ; provided I may walk somewhere, I do not object."

The two others said the same, and, having taken leave of the king, all four set off together. They went so far that Finette feared her thread would not be long enough, for they had covered many leagues. She walked always behind the others, drawing the thread cleverly through the thickets.

When the queen thought that her daughters could not find the way back, she entered a thick wood, and said, " Sleep, my little lambs, I will be like the shepherdess who watches over her flock for fear the wolf should devour them."

The three girls, lying down on the grass, were soon fast asleep, and the queen left them there, believing she should never see them again. Now Finette had shut her eyes but had not gone to sleep.

Having aroused her sisters, she related the whole story. They began to cry and begged her not to leave them, promising to give her beautiful dolls, a child's set of silver plate, and all their other toys and sweetmeats.

" I am quite sure you will do no such thing," Finette answered, " but I will behave as a good sister should, for all that." With these words she rose, and followed the thread with the two princesses, so that they reached home almost as soon as the queen.

The princesses knocked at the door—rap, rap.

" Who is there ? " cried the king.

" Your three daughters : Fleur, Belle, and Finette."

The queen trembled. " Don't open the door," she exclaimed, " it must be their ghosts, for it is impossible they could find their way back alive."

The king, who was as great a coward as his wife, called out, " It is false, you are not my daughters," but Finette said quickly, " Papa, I will stoop down and you can look at me through the hole made for the cat, and if I am not Finette I consent to be whipped."

The king agreed to this, and, as soon as he saw Finette, opened the door. The queen pretended to be delighted, and explained that she had come home to fetch something, but that most certainly she would have returned. They pretended to believe this story, and went up to the hayloft in which they slept.

" Now, sisters," said Finette, " you promised me a doll ; please give it to me."

" Thou mayst wait for it long enough, little rogue," they replied. " Thou art the cause of our father's caring so little for us," and thereupon, snatching up their distaffs, they beat her as if she had been so much mortar.

When they had beaten her as much as they chose, they let her go to bed, but the wounds and bruises kept her awake, and she heard the queen say, " I will take them in another direction, much farther, and I am sure they will never return."

When Finette heard this plot, she rose very softly to pay her godmother a second visit. She took two hens and a cock from the fowl-house, and wrung their necks; also two rabbits that the queen was fattening on cabbage for a coming feast. Putting them all into a basket, she set off, but had not gone a league, groping her way and quaking with fear, when the Spanish horse, snorting and neighing, came up at a gallop. She was terribly frightened, thinking some soldiers were about to seize her. Seeing the beautiful horse all alone, she jumped upon him, delighted to travel so comfortably, and in a very short time they arrived at her godmother's.

After the usual greetings Finette presented her godmother with the hens, the cock, and the rabbits, and begged the help of her good advice, the queen having vowed she would lead them to the end of the world.

The fairy told the princess not to worry, and gave her a sack full of ashes. " Carry this before you," she said to her, " and shake it as you go along. You will walk on the ashes, and when you wish to return, you will have only to follow your footmarks, but do not bring your sisters with you. They are spiteful and filled with envy, and if you bring them back, I will never see you again."

Finette took her leave, carrying with her, by the fairy's orders, a number of diamonds in a little box, which she put into her pocket. The horse was ready in waiting, and carried her home as before.

At daybreak the queen called the princesses and said, " The king is not very well ; I dreamed last night that I ought to gather some flowers and herbs that grow in a certain country some way off. They will completely cure him, therefore let us go without delay."

Fleur and Belle, who never dreamed their mother intended to lose them again, were much grieved at these tidings and set out sadly on their long journey. Finette, who never said a word, kept behind, and shook her sack of ashes with such wonderful skill that neither the wind nor the rain hurt them.

At length the queen, feeling perfectly certain that her daughters could not find their way home again, and seeing one evening that they had fallen asleep, left them and returned home.

As soon as it was light, and Finette found that her mother had gone, she awoke her sisters. " We are alone," said she, " the queen has left us."

Fleur and Belle began to cry ; they tore their hair and beat their faces with their hands, exclaiming, " Alas, what will become of us ? "

Finette was the best-hearted girl in the world, and again had pity on her sisters. " See now to what I expose myself," said she, " for when my god-mother gave me the means to return, she forbade me to take you, and de-clared that, if I did so, she would never see me again."

Their parents were greatly surprised at the return of the princesses. They talked about it all night long, and Finette heard them invent a new plot, and arrange that the next morning the queen should again take her daughters on a long journey.

Finette ran to wake her sisters. " Alas," she cried, " we are undone. The queen is going to lead us into some wilderness and leave us there. For your sakes I have offended my godmother and dare not go to her for advice."

They were in sad trouble and asked one another, " What shall we do, sister ? What shall we do ? "

At length Belle exclaimed, " Why should we worry ourselves ? Old Merluche does not possess all the wit in the world—some other folks may have a little. We have only to take plenty of peas with us and drop them along the road as we go, and it will be easy to trace our way back."

Fleur thought the idea capital, and both loaded themselves with peas, filling all their pockets ; Finette, instead of peas, carried her bag of fine clothes and the box of diamonds, and as soon as the queen called they were ready to go.

" I dreamed last night," she began, " that in a country which need not be named, there are three handsome princes who are waiting to marry you. I intend to take you there in order to see if my dream is true."

The queen went first and her daughters followed, dropping the peas without any care, as they made sure of being able to find the way home. This time their mother went farther than she had ever gone before, but during one dark night she left them and reached home weary, but happy to have got rid of so great a burden as her three daughters.

When they tried to retrace their steps there were no signs nor paths to be seen. Immense flocks of pigeons dwell in that country, and they had eaten up all the peas. The girls, seeing that they were lost, began to cry, and scream with grief and terror.

*The fairy told the princess not to worry*

After being two days without food, Fleur said to Belle, " Sister, hast thou nothing to eat ? "

" Nothing," she replied.

Fleur put the same question to Finette, who answered, " Nor have I, but I have just found an acorn."

" Give it to me," cried one.

" Give it to me," cried the other, and each insisted on having it.

" An acorn will not go far among three people," Finette pointed out, " let us plant it and there may spring up a tree that will be of service to us."

The elder sisters consented, although there seemed small chance of a tree growing where none was to be seen. The lost girls could find only cabbages and lettuces, on which they lived. Had they been very delicate, they must have died a hundred times. They slept almost always in the open air, and every morning and evening they took it in turns to water the acorn, saying aloud, " Grow, beautiful acorn, grow ! "

The acorn increased in size so rapidly that they could see it grow. When it had reached some height, Finette never failed to climb the tree twice a day, and one morning, while she was nearly at the top, Belle said to her sister, " I have found a bag which our sister has kept hidden from us. What can there be inside ? "

" She told me it contained some old lace she had got to mend," replied Fleur.

" I believe it is full of sugar plums," said Belle, who had a sweet tooth.

In order to find out the truth, she opened the bag, which did contain a quantity of old lace belonging to the king and queen, but hidden beneath were the clothes the fairy had given her and the box of diamonds.

" Well, now," exclaimed the second sister, " was there ever such a sly rogue ? We will take out all the things and put some stones in their place."

This they did, and Finette rejoined them without discovering their trick, for she never dreamed of decking herself out in a desert ; she thought of nothing but the oak, which speedily became the finest oak that ever grew.

One day, when she had climbed up, and her sisters as usual asked if she could see anything, she exclaimed, " I can see a large mansion, so fine that I want words to describe it ; the walls are of emeralds and rubies, and the roof is of diamonds, and covered with golden bells and weather-cocks that whirl about as the wind blows."

" Thou art not speaking the truth," they cried, " it cannot be as fine as thou sayest."

" Believe me," replied Finette, " I am no story-teller ; come and look for yourselves, my eyes are quite dazzled."

Fleur climbed up the tree, and, having seen the mansion, could talk of nothing else. Belle, who had a great deal of curiosity, climbed in her turn, and was as much enchanted as her sisters by the sight.

" We must certainly go to this palace," they said, " perhaps we shall find some charming princes who will be only too happy to marry us."

They talked the whole evening long on this subject, and lay down to sleep on the grass ; but when Finette appeared to be in a sound slumber, Fleur said, " I'll tell you what we should do, sister ; let us get up and dress ourselves in the fine clothes which Finette has brought."

" You are in the right," replied Belle. So they got up, curled their hair, powdered it, put patches on their cheeks, and dressed themselves in the beautiful gold and silver gowns all covered with diamonds.

Finette, not knowing of her wicked sisters' theft, picked up her bag, with the intention of dressing herself, and was vastly distressed to find nothing in it but flints. At the same moment she saw her sisters shining like suns. She wept, and complained of the trick they had played on her, but they only laughed and joked.

" Is it possible," she cried, " that you will take me to the palace without making me as fine as you are ? "

" We have barely enough for ourselves," returned Fleur. " You shall have nothing but blows if you weary us with your cries."

" But," exclaimed Finette, " the clothes you have on are mine ; my godmother gave them to me. You have no claim to them."

" If thou sayest more about it," they cried, " we will knock thee on the head and bury thee, without any one being the wiser."

Finette did not dare anger them; she followed slowly, walking some short distance behind, as if she were only her sisters' servant. The nearer they came to the mansion the more wonderful it appeared to them.

"Oh," cried Fleur and Belle, "how we shall enjoy ourselves! What grand feasts we shall have! We shall dine at the king's table; but Finette will have to wash the dishes in the kitchen, for she looks like a servant. If any one asks who she is, we must be sure not to call her our sister."

The lovely and sensible Finette was in despair at being so ill-treated.

On reaching the building, they knocked at the gate, which was opened by an ugly old woman.

"Unfortunate wretches!" she cried, "what brought you here? Know ye not that this is the Ogre's Castle, and that all three of you would make hardly enough for his breakfast? But I am more good-natured than my husband. Come in. I will not eat you all at once. You shall have the comfort of living two or three days longer."

On hearing these words, the sisters ran away, hoping to escape, but one of the woman's strides was equal to fifty of theirs. She caught them quickly, one by the hair, the others by the nape of the neck; and carried them under her arm into the house, throwing them all three into the cellar, which was full of toads and adders, and strewed with bones.

Now the woman wished to keep the princesses for herself. So, hearing her husband coming, she popped them quickly under a large tub, out of which they could look only through a hole.

"Look ye, I smell fresh meat," the giant said suddenly; "where is it?"

"Thou dost always fancy thou smellest fresh meat," his wife replied; "it is thy sheep which have just passed by."

"Oh, I am not mistaken," he said, "I smell fresh meat, and shall hunt everywhere for it."

"Hunt," said she, "thou wilt find nothing."

"If I do, and thou hast hidden it from me, I will cut thy head off."

Frightened by this threat, she replied, "Be not angry and I will tell thee the truth. Three young girls came here to-day, and I have got them safe. I am old and want rest; thou seest our fine house is very dirty, that our bread is badly made, and thy soup now rarely pleases thee. These girls know how to do everything, and they will be my servants."

The giant left the cellar, ordering his wife to bring the girls before him. He asked them what they could do, and the princesses, although almost dead with fright, answered that they could sweep and sew and spin well; that they could make nice stews, and as for bread, cakes, and patties, people for a thousand leagues round sent for them.

"Aha," said he, "set these good housewives to work, but," to Finette, "after you have lighted the fire how do you know the oven is hot enough?"

"My lord," she replied, "I throw in some butter which I taste with my tongue."

"Very well," said he, "light the fire then."

The oven was as large as a stable, and Finette made a great fire. Presently the giant, who was waiting for his new bread, asked if the oven was hot enough.

"You shall see, my lord," replied Finette, throwing in a piece of butter. "It should be tasted with the tongue, but I am too short to reach it."

" I am tall enough," he said, and, stooping, thrust his body so far in that he could not recover himself, and was burned to death.

The princess could not feel sorry for this accident, which was a very lucky one for them, but the shock proved too much for the old woman, who swooned away and never recovered. Thus they were set free from both their enemies, and no longer had any reason to be afraid.

With great glee and laughter they mounted upon the roof and amused themselves by ringing the golden bells. They ran into all the apartments, which were of pearls and diamonds, and the furniture was so costly that they were ready to die with pleasure. They laughed, they sang, they wanted for nothing. They found corn, sweetmeats, and fruit in abundance. The two elder sisters went to sleep in beds of brocade and velvet.

" Behold us," exclaimed Fleur next morning, " richer than our father was when he had his kingdom, but we want company, and no one will venture here. This mansion, no doubt, is considered an evil place. We must go to the nearest city and show ourselves in our fine clothes ; many people will be glad to make friends with real princesses."

After dressing, they informed Finette they were going for a walk, and that she must stay at home and cook, and wash, and clean the house, so that on their return they might find everything in nice order ; if not, she should be well beaten. Poor Finette, whose heart was full of grief, remained alone in the house, sweeping, cleaning, washing, without resting, and crying all the time.

Shortly afterwards her sisters returned, laden with Portugal oranges, preserves, and sugar.

" Ah," they exclaimed, " what a splendid ball we have been to ! How crowded it was ! The king's son was amongst the dancers ; we have had a thousand compliments paid to us. Come, take our shoes off and clean them ; that is your business."

*" I am tall enough," he said, stooping*

Finette obeyed, and when by accident she let drop a word in the way of complaint, they flew at her and beat her shamefully. Next day, the elder sisters went out again, and returned with an account of new wonders.

One evening, as Finette sat in the chimney corner, on a heap of cinders, not knowing what to do, she looked at the cracks in the chimney, and saw in one of them a little key, so old and so dirty that she had the greatest trouble to clean it. Then she discovered it was made of gold, and thinking a golden key ought to open a beautiful box, she ran all over the castle, trying it in all the locks, and at length found it fitted that of a casket which was a masterpiece of art.

On opening the casket, she discovered clothes, diamonds, lace, linen, and ribbons, worth immense sums of money. She breathed not a word of her good luck to her sisters, but waited for their departure next day. As soon as they were out of sight, she dressed and adorned herself, till she looked more beautiful than the sun and moon together.

Thus arrayed, she went to the ball where her sisters were dancing, and, although she wore no mask, she was so changed for the better that they did not know her. Directly she appeared a murmur ran through the room ; some of the guests were full of admiration, others of jealousy. She was asked to dance, and surpassed all the other ladies in grace as much as she did in beauty.

The mistress of the house came up, and, making a low curtsey, asked her her name, that she might always remember with pleasure the name of such a beautiful person. Finette replied civilly that her name was Cendron. There was not a gentleman who did not wish to dance with Cendron, nor a poet who did not make verses on Cendron.

Fleur and Belle, who never saw their sister but with face begrimed with soot from the chimney, and altogether dirty, had so lost all idea of her beauty that they did not know her in the least, and paid their court to her with the rest.

When the ball was nearly finished, Finette hastened away, returned home, undressed quickly, and put on her old rags before her sisters arrived. " Ah, Finette," they exclaimed, " we have just met a young princess who is perfectly charming. She is not a scarecrow such as thou art : her skin is white as snow, with a crimson richer than the roses ; her teeth are pearls, her lips coral ; she wore a splendid gown all covered with gold and diamonds. How beautiful, how lovely she is ! "

" So was I," said Finette, in a low voice, " so was I."

" What dost thou mutter there ? " asked her sisters, and she replied, in a still lower tone, " So was I, so was I."

This little game continued to be played for some time.

One evening, Finette had danced more than usual, thus not going away until a later hour. Wishing to make up for lost time and arrive home before her sisters, she walked so fast that she lost one of her slippers, which was of red velvet covered over with pearls. She tried to find it in the road, but the night being dark her search was in vain, and at last she entered the house one foot shod, the other not.

Next day, Prince Cherie, the king's son, going out hunting, saw the slipper. He had it picked up, looked at it, admired its small size and dainty shape, turned it over and over, took care of it, and carried it home. From that day he could eat nothing ; he became thin, his skin turned yellow, and he looked sad and miserable.

The king and queen, who were devoted to him, sent in every direction for the choicest game and the best sweetmeats. They were less than nothing to him. He looked at it all, without saying a word in reply to his mother when she spoke to him. At last they sent everywhere, even to Paris, for the most skilful doctors.

When these learned men arrived, they watched the prince for three days and three nights without losing sight of him, and finally concluded that all the time his thoughts were fixed on some unknown lady, and that, unless she was found, he would never get better. The queen, on hearing this, caused the most beautiful ladies of the court to be brought into his apartment, but he did not even look at them.

At length, in despair, his mother exclaimed, " My dear son, thou wilt kill me with sorrow. Tell me for whom thou art grieving, and thou shalt marry her, even though she be but a simple shepherdess."

The prince, taking courage from this promise, showed her the slipper and replied, " Behold, madame, the cause of my misfortune. I found this little, soft, delicate, pretty slipper as I went to hunt, and I will never marry any one but the woman who can wear it."

" Well, my son," said his mother, " do not afflict yourself. We will have the damsel sought for."

She hastened with this information to the king, who showed great surprise. However, he ordered a messenger to declare, with sound of drum and trumpet, that all single women should come to try on the slipper, and that she whom it fitted should marry the prince.

They hurried in crowds to try on the slipper, but not one could get it on, and the more they came in vain, the greater was the prince's sorrow.

Fleur and Belle dressed themselves one day so grandly that they were astonishing to look at.

" Where can you be going ? " asked Finette.

" We are going to the great city," Fleur replied, " to try on the slipper the king's son has found, for if it should belong to either of us the prince will marry her, and then my sister or I will be a queen."

" And why should not I go ? " asked Finette.

" Thou art a pretty simpleton, truly," they cried in scorn, " go and water our cabbages, thou art fit for nothing better."

Finette thought she would put on her finest dress, and take her chance with the rest, for she had a slight idea that she would be successful. The chief difficulty was, that she did not know the way, for the ball at which she had danced was not given in the great city. However, she proceeded to dress, putting on a gown of blue satin covered with stars in diamonds. She had diamonds also in her hair, so that with all these jewels she moved in a blaze of light.

On opening the door, she was much surprised to find the pretty Spanish horse which had carried her to her godmother's dwelling. She patted him, saying, " You are most welcome, my little Hobby. I am greatly obliged to my godmother."

The Spanish horse knelt down and she mounted upon him like a nymph ; he was all covered with golden bells and ribbons, while his housings and bridle were priceless. He galloped off gaily, his bells going " ting, ting, ting."

Fleur and Belle, hearing the sound, turned and saw the rider, but what was their astonishment at that moment ? They knew her to be both Finette and Cendron.

" Sister," cried Fleur, " I am sure this is Finette Cendron."

While they were thus talking over the matter Finette arrived at the palace. The moment she appeared everybody thought she was a queen. The guards presented arms, the drums beat, and the trumpets sounded a flourish ; all the gates were flung open, and those who had attended the ball went before her, crying, " Room, room, for the beautiful Cendron, the wonder of the world."

She entered in this state the prince's apartment. He cast his eyes on her, and was so pleased with her beauty that he hoped her foot might be small enough to wear the slipper. She put it on instantly, and produced its fellow, which she brought on purpose. Shouts arose of " Long live the princess who will be our queen."

The prince arose from his couch and came to kiss her hand. He was handsome and charming, and he paid her a thousand pretty compliments. His parents, being informed of the event, came in all haste, and the queen, taking Finette in her arms, called her her daughter, her darling, and her little queen. She gave her some splendid presents, to which the king added many more. They fired the guns ; violins, bagpipes, every sort of musical instrument was set playing—nothing was talked of but dancing and rejoicing. The king, the queen, the prince, all begged Finette to consent to the marriage taking place at once.

" No," she replied, " I must first tell you my history," which she did in a few words.

When it was learned that she was a princess born, there was another burst of joy, but their happiness was soon clouded. It appeared that the prince's father was the person who had turned Finette's parents out of their kingdom, and she refused to marry the prince until they had been restored. For the sake of his son, the king promised that this should be done.

Meanwhile, Belle and Fleur arrived at the palace. The first news to greet them was that Cendron had fitted on the slipper. They hardly knew what to do or say ; they resolved to return without seeing her ; but Finette, hearing that they had come, insisted that they should enter. Instead of frowning, and punishing them as they deserved, she rose to meet them, embraced them tenderly, and presented them to the queen, saying, " Madame, these are my sisters ; they are very amiable, and I beg you will love them."

They were so confused at Finette's kindness that they could not utter a word. She promised that they should return to their own kingdom, which the prince would restore to their family. At these words they threw themselves on their knees before her, weeping for joy.

The wedding was the most splendid that ever was seen, Finette wrote to her godmother, and put the letter, with many valuable presents, on the back of the pretty Spanish horse. She begged her to tell the king and queen of their good fortune, and that they were quite free to return to their kingdom.

# THE NEST BUILDERS

*by* R. I. G. GOODCHILD

THERE was a time when birds were most unwise,
  And slept at night beneath the starry skies.

At length the Eagle said to all the rest,
" We need some genius to design a nest.

Who shall be teacher we must first decide."
" The Magpie !  Magpie ! " all in chorus cried.

The Magpie took some sticks and laid them flat ;
" Observe, good nest-builders begin like that."

At this the wood-pigeon impatient grew :
" Down and across.   I see ! " and off she flew.

Some others waited longer and they found
How nests are warmly lined and shaped quite round.

Then they too flew away ;  they thought it slow,
For they had learned all that they wished to know.

Till now but few remained to learn how best
To make a strong and warm and cosy nest.

The tits and wrens saw how to build a roof
To keep the nest both warm and waterproof ;

To build with leaves and moss and lichens green,
So wisely that their home is rarely seen.

When next you take a walk in building-time
Just prove the truth of what I've told in rhyme.

# HOW KING ARTHUR CLAIMED HIS INHERITANCE

## by STUART CAMPBELL

IN the long, long ago, there were many small kings reigning over different parts of Britain. The greatest was named Uther Pendragon. His infant son, Arthur, was given to the wizard Merlin to care for and he charged Sir Hector and his wife to rear the babe as if he were their own son.

Following the death of King Uther, Britain was for many years a land of unrest. The barons were jealous to think they were to be ruled over by a child prince whom they had never seen, and many plotted to become king in his stead.

All this trouble Merlin had foreseen, and he took great care to keep secret the prince's whereabouts. Even Sir Hector and his wife were unaware that their foster child was the heir to the throne.

Sir Hector was true to his trust, and Arthur was treated in exactly the same way as the knight's own son, Kay. The two boys shared everything equally, and were trained together in the manly exercises of knighthood.

When Arthur was grown near to manhood, Merlin knew it was time for the young king to claim his heritage.

The magician visited the Archbishop of Canterbury, and bade him summon all the barons and gentlefolk of the realm to London at Christmas-tide. When they were all gathered together, Merlin promised that a miracle should reveal the new king.

On Christmas morning, all went into London's greatest church to mass. When they came forth, there stood in the churchyard something which had not been there before. This was a huge block of stone, upon which stood an anvil of steel. Imbedded in the anvil was a naked sword, with its point projecting beyond.

Written in gold upon the stone were these words :

" Whosoever pulleth out the sword from this anvil, he shall be known as the rightful king of all Britain."

All the people stared at the stone and its inscription, and many tried to draw out the sword, in order to prove themselves king. But no one could even stir it.

" He who shall withdraw the sword is evidently not here," said the Archbishop, after all had tugged at the handle. " Yet no doubt he shall appear at the proper time. My counsel is that ten knights shall be chosen, men of fair fame, who shall guard this sword until the rightful possessor shall present himself."

This suggestion was approved by all.

Then a proclamation was sent forth, that every man in the kingdom should try to draw the sword from its setting, and a great tourney was arranged for New Year's Day.

Sir Hector heard the proclamation, and he set out at once for London, taking with him his son Sir Kay, who had just been made a knight, and also his foster-son, the young Arthur.

Now Sir Kay had meant to take part in the tourney, but when the party drew near to the arena where the jousting was to take place, the young knight found that he had left his sword at their lodging. He begged Arthur to go back and fetch the weapon.

" Gladly I will," said Arthur, hurrying off.

But all the folk had gone to see the knights at their combats, and Arthur found the house locked up. He felt deeply worried at this, for without his sword Sir Kay could not take part in the jousting, and Arthur knew that his foster-brother was eager to prove his knighthood.

Then a thought suddenly struck Arthur.

" My brother must have a sword to-day," he said, " so why should I not ride to the churchyard and take that which sticks through the anvil there ? "

There were no knights on guard over the stone this day, for they were at the tourney. So Arthur dismounted from his horse and approached the anvil.

He took the sword by the handle and tugged, and the weapon came out of the anvil with ease.

Arthur at once rode with the sword to Sir Kay, who at first glance knew it to be the one from the stone. He showed it to his father, and said, " Sir, here in my hand is the sword from the anvil. Therefore I must be king."

But when Sir Hector questioned him, he learned that Arthur had given Sir Kay the sword.

" And how got you the sword ? " Sir Hector asked the youth, who told how he had drawn it from the anvil.

" Then you must be the ruler of Britain," declared the knight. " No man could have drawn forth the sword except the rightful king. Let me see you replace the blade in the anvil, and pull it out once more."

When Arthur had thrust the sword into its setting again, first Sir Hector and then Sir Kay tried to pull it forth. But although they strove with all their might, they could not move it. Then Arthur took the handle, and drew it clear.

HOW KING ARTHUR CLAIMED HIS INHERITANCE

He took the sword by the handle and tugged, and the weapon came out of the anvil with ease *(Page 320)*

THE STORY OF TRISTRAM

"Isoult," said Sir Tristram, as they were parting, "I promise you faithfully that I shall remain your
true knight, for all the days of my life" (*Page* 331)

Sir Hector realised that his foster-son must be the son of Uther Pendragon, and his successor to the throne.

The good knight told Arthur that he was not his real father, but had taken charge of him at the request of Merlin. Arthur was grieved to learn this, for he had come to love those who had brought him up so tenderly.

"If I am indeed king," he told Sir Hector, "I shall never forget my gratitude to you, and to the lady whom I have always believed to be my mother. Whatever you may ask of me, I will not fail to give it you."

Sir Hector led Arthur to the Archbishop, and announced how the youth had pulled the sword from its setting. The news caused such great excitement that the tourney was interrupted, and all thronged to the churchyard.

There Arthur put the sword back into the anvil, and once again all the barons and knights tried in vain to pull it forth. When they had tired themselves, Arthur advanced, and for the third time it yielded easily to his hand.

Some of the nobles, jealous that a youth should reign over them, wished to try their strength again. But the people would not allow it.

"We will have Arthur for our king!" they cried. "He has fulfilled the test."

Before long, therefore, Arthur was crowned King of All Britain. From all over the country lords and knights came to pay homage to the new king, and Arthur set right the many wrongs which had been done since his father King Uther had died.

His foster-brother, Sir Kay, was made Seneschal of England, and the people rejoiced to think that they had so wise a king to rule them.

*Arthur at once rode with the sword to Sir Kay*

## HOW ARTHUR GAINED EXCALIBUR

ONE day, very early in King Arthur's reign, a squire appeared at the court, leading a horse. On the horse was the squire's master, a knight, who had been mortally wounded by a knight dwelling in the forest nearby.

The squire knelt before King Arthur, asking for vengeance on the man who had slain his master.

At once one of the court, a youth of about King Arthur's own age, came forward.

" Sire," he begged, " pray give me the order of knighthood, so that I may ride forth against this strange knight."

Arthur was reluctant to let so young a champion risk combat on his behalf ; but Griflet persisted in his request.

He bade Griflet kneel before him, touched him lightly upon the shoulder with his sword, and thus made him a knight.

Sir Griflet donned his armour, and rode off to do battle.

The pavilion of the strange knight stood near a well. His horse was tethered near, already saddled and bridled, while his spear and shield hung from a neighbouring tree.

Sir Griflet rode forward and struck the shield with the butt of his spear, so that it fell to the ground with a clatter.

" Why did you knock down my shield, fair knight ? " demanded a gruff voice, as an armoured figure strode from the pavilion.

" Because I wish to ride a course with you," answered Griflet.

" That would be foolish," said the strange knight, " for you are young, and far beneath me in skill and strength."

" None the less," replied Sir Griflet, " I challenge you."

" So be it, then," the other answered.

He took his arms and mounted, and the two rode to opposite ends of the clearing. Then they charged upon each other with levelled spears, and at the first onset Sir Griflet and his horse were overthrown and the young knight sorely wounded.

The strange knight dismounted and helped Sir Griflet into his saddle again, then bade him return to the court.

King Arthur was angry at the defeat of his champion, and next morning he himself set out alone to encounter the knight of the well. But Merlin, the magician, suspected the young king's purpose, and he followed to guard Arthur's safety.

Arriving at the well in the forest, Arthur challenged the strange knight, just as Sir Griflet had done.

A great battle ensued between the king and the knight. Both had their lances shattered, and were dismounted from their horses. They continued to fight on foot, but in the end Arthur was betrayed by his sword. In guarding a blow from his enemy, he found the blade snap in half.

" Yield yourself as conquered, else you must die ! " cried the knight.

" I would die rather than admit defeat," retorted Arthur.

His foe raised his sword to strike, but Merlin was at hand to save his master. The magician threw a spell upon the knight, so that he stood as if turned to stone, with his arm in the air.

While the knight stood thus, unable to move or speak, Merlin lifted his master in his arms, and carried him to a cave in the forest, where dwelt a hermit.

Here Arthur's wounds were tended, so that after three days he was able to ride away with Merlin.

" Alas," declared the king as they rode, " I have now no sword at my side in case of need."

" No matter, sire," replied Merlin. " There is one close at hand, which perhaps I can obtain for your use."

Turning aside, they soon reached the edge of a deep, wide lake. In the middle of the lake, Arthur saw an arm appear above the surface of the water, holding aloft a sword.

" See, there is the sword of which I spoke," cried Merlin. " And yonder is the Lady of the Lake, who will tell you how to gain the sword."

A maiden approached King Arthur and curtseyed to him.

" Tell me," said Arthur, " what sword is it that the arm holds above the water there ? I wish it were mine, for I have no sword."

" Sir Arthur, King of All Britain," replied the maiden, " that sword is mine. If you will promise me a gift when I shall ask it of you, you may row out in yonder boat and take the sword and its scabbard."

Arthur hastened to accept her terms, for he was eager to possess the sword. He and Merlin alighted from their horses, which they tied to a tree. Then they entered the magic boat and rowed out into the lake.

As soon as Arthur took the sword by the hilt, the hand and arm vanished beneath the water.

When they were mounted again, Arthur examined the sword. It was of finest steel, and its handle was set with precious stones. Merlin told him that the sword was named Excalibur, which means " Cut Steel."

" Which do you like better," asked Merlin, " the sword or its scabbard ? "

" The sword," replied Arthur.

" Then you are unwise," Merlin told him. " The scabbard is worth far more than the sword, for it has magic properties. While you have the scabbard girt upon you, you shall lose no blood. Therefore keep the scabbard always with you."

This, then, is how King Arthur came by his sword, Excalibur, which was to serve him well in many an adventure. And Merlin's warning about the scabbard was to prove true, for whereas Arthur never suffered hurt when it was by his side, evil was to befall him when it was stolen from him.

When King Arthur returned to the court, all were glad to see him safe. Some wondered that the king should risk his life as he had done, but all rejoiced that their ruler was so brave a knight.

# A SAILOR'S SONG OF THE SEA

## by BARRY CORNWALL

THE sea ! the sea ! the open sea !
The blue, the fresh, the ever free !
Without a mark, without a bound,
It runs the earth's wide regions round ;
It plays with the clouds, it mocks the skies,
Or like a cradled creature lies.

I'm on the sea ! I'm on the sea !
I'm where I would ever be,
With the blue above, and the blue below
And silence wheresoe'er I go,
If a storm should come and awake the deep
What matter, I shall float and sleep.

I love oh ! How I love the ride
On the fierce, foaming, bursting tide,
When every mad wave drowns the moon,
Or whistles aloud his tempest tune,
And tells how goeth the world below.
And why the south-west blasts do blow.

I never was on the dull, tame shore,
But I loved the great sea more and more
And back I flew to her billowy breast,
Like a bird that seeks its mother's nest,
And a mother she was and is to me,
For I was born on the deep blue sea.

And I lived, in calm and strife,
Full fifty summers a sailor's life,
With wealth to spend and power to range,
But never have sought nor sighed for change ;
And Death, whenever he comes to me,
Shall come on the wild and heartless sea.

# The Story of SIR TRISTRAM

## by STUART CAMPBELL

AT the time when the chivalrous King Arthur ruled over England, there reigned in Lyonesse a king named Meliodas. For his queen, Meliodas had married a beautiful and gracious lady named Elizabeth, who was the sister of King Mark of Cornwall.

The king and queen were very happy together, and their joy was great when they were presented with an infant son. But, alas, a shadow was soon to fall across their happiness.

In Lyonesse there dwelt a woman who hated the king and queen, and she plotted evil against them.

One day the king went hunting alone in the forest, and presently he saw a hart in front of him. He at once pursued the beast, but actually the hart was the woman who hated him, for she possessed the power to change her form at will. The enchantress lured King Meliodas on, until he came to an old castle. Here the servants of his enemy fell upon him and made him captive.

When Queen Elizabeth missed her lord, she was frantic with anxiety lest ill had befallen him. Taking with her only a single lady-in-waiting, she ran into the forest to seek the king.

She travelled so far that she became utterly exhausted, and fell to the ground in a swoon. When she opened her eyes once more she knew that she was dying.

Bidding her lady-in-waiting stoop, she gave her a last message for King Meliodas, telling him that she would carry her love for him even to the grave. Her last request was that her infant son might be named Tristram, which means born in sorrow, and soon afterwards the noble queen passed away.

A little later the lady-in-waiting was found by a party of courtiers who were hunting the forest for their king, and these carried her back to the palace, together with the dead queen.

Because of the queen's sacrifice the king was released from his prison, the enchantment being broken. When he returned home he was grief-stricken to learn the queen's fate. Long he mourned for her, and gave all his love to his son whom he christened Tristram according to Elizabeth's wish. After seven years, however, King Meliodas married again and had other children.

Knowing that Tristram was heir to the throne of Lyonesse, his stepmother became jealous of the boy on account of her own son.

So great did her jealousy grow that she tried to poison Tristram, but her wickedness recoiled upon herself. For instead of Tristram drinking from the poisoned goblet, her own son did so, and was dead within a minute.

Although her child had been slain by her own plotting, the queen laid the blame to Tristram, and sought yet again to kill him. Once more she prepared a goblet of poison, and placed it on a table where the boy would be likely to take it.

It so chanced, however, that King Meliodas had been out riding in the heat of the day, and he came home very thirsty. As soon as he entered he espied the goblet and seized it to drink.

When the queen saw what he was about to do, she rushed forward and snatched the goblet from him.

" Why did you do that ? " asked King Meliodas in surprise.

Then he noticed the look of guilt on her face, and at the same time recalled the strange manner in which her son had died.

" False traitress," he cried, drawing his sword, " you shall die unless you tell me what is wrong with this drink ! "

His sternness made the queen confess what she had done, and at once King Meliodas called his barons and lords together, to decide what should be the punishment for so wicked a woman.

In accordance with the laws of those times it was judged that the queen should be burned at the stake.

When the day of execution came, and the queen was tied to the stake with faggots piled around her, all ready to light, the young Tristram approached his father and knelt at his feet.

" Sire," he said, " I have a boon to ask you."

" Whatever the boon may be, it shall be granted," replied the king, glad to think that his son had been spared to him.

" Then I ask you to let my stepmother live," begged the boy.

" That is a strange request for you to make, when she tried her utmost to kill you," King Meliodas said.

He tried to dissuade Tristram from his purpose, but the boy insisted. And because he had given his promise, the king could not do otherwise than agree.

" Very well, then," he said, " you may decide the queen's fate as you will."

So Tristram went to where the queen stood among the faggots, with men awaiting only the king's command to set fire to the pile. Telling the servants what his father had commanded, Tristram himself cut loose the ropes which bound his stepmother, and told her she was free.

Never again did the queen dwell with King Meliodas, though after many years Tristram persuaded his father to forgive her for her wrongs.

Because of his mercy towards her, the queen's hatred of Tristram turned to love ; but for fear of new plots against his son, King Meliodas made up his mind to send the boy away from the court.

For this purpose the king picked out a man of gentle breeding, named Gouvernail, who had great learning and was also skilled in the use of arms.

With Gouvernail as tutor, Tristram was sent into France, where he applied himself both to study and to knightly exercises. He soon excelled at jousting and the chase, while as a harpist he was superior to any other in France.

In this way he grew to manhood, and when at last the time came for him to return to Lyonesse, his father was filled with pride that Tristram had grown so strong and gifted.

## SIR TRISTRAM FIGHTS FOR CORNWALL

NOW the uncle of Tristram was King Mark of Cornwall. And at the time when Tristram returned home to his father it so happened that King Mark was greatly troubled.

For many, many years, Cornwall had been paying tribute to King Anguish of Ireland ; but owing to wars and famine, King Mark had been unable to find money to pay the tribute.

King Anguish now sent an ambassador to Cornwall, demanding that payment should be made. Calling his barons and knights together, King Mark asked what should be done.

After many hours in council a reply was given to the ambassador.

King Mark told the messenger to say that no tribute would be paid at present, but that if King Anguish would send a champion, a Cornish knight would meet him in combat, to decide whether or not the money should be provided.

When the ambassador brought him the message, King Anguish was very angry. He summoned to him Sir Marhaus, who was the queen's brother, a very famous warrior and a Knight of the Round Table.

"And now, Sir Marhaus," said King Anguish, when he had told of King Mark's challenge, " I pray that you will act as Ireland's champion."

"Willingly will I do so," answered Sir Marhaus, who was ever ready to take up arms.

Taking with him his favourite charger, he boarded a ship and reached the Cornish coast near to Tintagel.

King Mark learned of his arrival with dismay, for so far he had been unable to find a knight worthy to do battle on his behalf. When they knew the name of King Anguish's champion the followers of King Mark feared to face him, so great was his renown.

For weeks Sir Marhaus remained in his ship, each day sending word to King Mark that he should either produce a champion or pay the tribute. Heralds travelled throughout Cornwall, but no knight came forward.

Someone suggested that King Mark should send to the court of King Arthur, to beg the aid of Sir Lancelot of the Lake, who was reputed to be the greatest knight living. But others pointed out that both Sir Marhaus and Sir Lancelot were Knights of the Round Table, and thus could not enter into contest with each other.

At last the news of King Mark's dilemma reached Lyonesse, and Tristram was filled with shame that his uncle could find no one to fight for him. He went straight to seek his father, King Meliodas.

" Sire," he said, " I grieve for the disgrace which has come upon my uncle. If you will give me leave, I will myself go to Cornwall and ask King Mark to make me knight, so that I may be his champion."

" You shall do as your courage urges you, my son," answered the king, who was sad to think of the risks, but proud to see the boy's brave spirit.

So Tristram made all speed to reach Cornwall, where his uncle almost wept with joy to learn the reason of his coming. He at once gave his nephew the order of knighthood, then sent word to Sir Marhaus that he now found one worthy to meet him in combat.

Sir Tristram was given the best horse that King Mark could find in his kingdom, and provided with arms and armour of the finest quality. Then the young knight and his horse embarked in a boat, which was to carry him to an island where the battle was to take place.

Sir Marhaus was astounded to see the youth of his opponent, when he himself was so renowned a warrior.

At the signal both knights couched their lances and rode at each other with thundering hoofs. Sir Marhaus soon found that he had a doughty foe in spite of his youth, who gave as good as he took.

In the end it was Tristram's youth that told, because he did not tire so fast as Sir Marhaus. At last Tristram's sword swept down, cutting through his opponent's helmet and into his brain. As Sir Tristram tugged to free his weapon, a piece of the blade broke off to remain in the wound.

Sir Marhaus then set sail as fast as he could for Ireland. King Anguish received his brother-in-law with sorrow, and summoned his own surgeons to attend him. But in spite of all they could do, Sir Marhaus died.

His sister, the queen, was deeply angered against the unknown knight who had slain him, and to her the surgeons took a piece of steel which they had found in the brain of Sir Marhaus. This the queen kept always with her, for she knew that if she ever found the sword from which this fragment had broken, she would know her brother's slayer, and might be avenged upon him.

## THE FAIR ISOULT

SIR TRISTRAM himself had not got off lightly in his combat with Sir Marhaus. He had been wounded by a spear thrust early in the fight, and had lost so much blood that he had to sit down as Sir Marhaus ran to his ship.

The loyal Gouvernail hastened to his side as quickly as he could, and carried his master to the mainland, where he was borne to the castle of Tintagel.

Here he was nursed for a month with every attention, but he got no better, and seemed likely to die. For the point of the spear which pierced him had been tipped with poison.

At last a wise old woman came to the castle, and told King Mark that Sir Tristram would never be healed unless he went to Ireland. For that was the country where the poison was brewed, and there would be found the antidote.

King Mark at once provided a ship to carry Sir Tristram across the Irish Sea, taking every care for his comfort on the voyage.

Attended by the faithful Gouvernail, and taking with him his beloved harp, Sir Tristram set sail and duly anchored off the coast of Ireland, close to the castle where dwelt King Anguish. Gouvernail carried his master ashore, and took lodgings at a humble cottage.

Sitting up in his bed, Sir Tristram spent many hours each day playing on his harp, and news of his presence soon reached the king.

King Anguish ordered that the unknown harpist should appear before him, and Sir Tristram was conveyed to the castle on his bed.

The king and queen asked how he came to be hurt, and what was his name. Sir Tristram thought it wise not to reveal his true identity, because it was the queen's brother whom he had slain in combat.

"I come from the country of Lyonesse," he said, "and my name is Tristram. These wounds were suffered in a battle that I fought for the sake of a lady in distress."

"Truly, Tristram, you shall have all the help that my country can give you," promised King Anguish. "Even though I and my people are mourning the loss of the noblest knight in the world. His name was Sir Marhaus, and he was a Knight of the Round Table." The king then recounted how Sir Marhaus had been mortally wounded while fighting the champion of the King of Cornwall, and Sir Tristram expressed his deep sorrow at such a loss.

Having taken a great liking for the strange youth, King Anguish invited him to stay as his guest at the castle, and put him in the care of his daughter, Isoult the Fair. Isoult was skilled in the use of herbs and medicines, and she quickly discovered the nature of the poison which was troubling Sir Tristram. She applied a healing balm and soon the knight was well again.

Sir Tristram became devoted to his fair nurse and readily accepted the invitation to prolong his visit.

He taught Isoult to play the harp, and composed many lays in her honour. Then a period of jousting began, and Sir Tristram performed so valiantly that Isoult suspected that he must be a man of high station and proved knighthood.

The king and queen never tired of the company of the youth they knew as Tristram, while Isoult's love for him grew stronger every day.

One day while their guest was absent, the queen and Isoult wandered into his chamber and saw his sword lying upon the bed. The queen took the weapon in her hand and drew it from its scabbard. The first thing she noticed was that there had been a piece broken out of the edge of the blade, a foot or so from the point.

At once the queen remembered the piece of steel which had been found in the brain of her brother, Sir Marhaus.

Her suspicions awakened, she hurried to her own room, and from a coffer took the piece of steel she had so carefully guarded. She matched the fragment to the gap in the sword's edge and behold, it fitted exactly.

"Ah!" cried the queen in anger, "so Tristram is the traitor knight who slew my brother."

Gripping the sword tightly, she ran to where she knew the guest to be, and would have thrust him through had not a knight prevented her.

Prevented from taking her vengeance thus, the queen went to the king and told him what she had discovered.

King Anguish was grieved to think that the knight he liked so well was the slayer of Sir Marhaus, and bade the queen leave him to deal with the matter. He found Sir Tristram ready armed, and waiting to mount his horse.

In honour the king could not attack a guest, so he gave Sir Tristram permission to leave Ireland unmolested, asking only whether the youth was really the one who had killed Sir Marhaus.

Tristram then explained that he was the son of King Meliodas of Lyonesse, and that he had twisted his own name round in case he should be recognised in Ireland. He recounted how he had acted as champion for his uncle, King Mark of Cornwall, and had overcome Sir Marhaus in fair conflict.

"You have done nothing unworthy of a true knight," said the king, "yet for my queen's sake, I cannot longer entertain the one who killed her brother."

Sir Tristram thanked King Anguish for all the kindness that he had shown to him, and as a last favour begged that he might be allowed to say farewell to the fair Isoult.

*Sir Tristram told the maiden that he must journey to Ireland*

The king readily gave him leave to do so, and Sir Tristram went to the maiden and told her all that he had told King Anguish. He told her, also, how the wise woman had said that he would only be made whole if he journeyed to the country where the poison on the spear was made.

Isoult was stricken with sorrow at his departure, and wept in his arms.

" Isoult," said Sir Tristram, " I promise you faithfully that I shall remain your true knight, for all the days of my life."

" And I," replied Isoult, " promise to wed no one within the next seven years, unless first you give your consent."

They exchanged rings to seal their promises, and then Sir Tristram rode to where the ship lay which was to convey him back to Cornwall.

## SIR TRISTRAM DEMANDS ISOULT FOR ANOTHER

WHEN Sir Tristram reached Cornwall once more, he was greeted everywhere with gladness.

So popular did the young knight become that he soon made an enemy, who was no other than his uncle, King Mark. The king was a very jealous man, and it seemed to him that his subjects thought more of Sir Tristram than of himself.

So King Mark sought a way in which he could rid himself of his nephew. By trickery, the king got Sir Tristram to promise to fulfil a mission on his behalf, the nature of which he did not explain until the pledge had been given. Then he asked Sir Tristram to return to Ireland as his ambassador, in order to request the hand of the fair Isoult in marriage. The accounts which his nephew had given of her beauty had made King Mark eager to wed Isoult, and at the same time he thought that this time Sir Tristram might be killed in revenge for the dead Sir Marhaus.

Sir Tristram's heart was heavy, for he himself loved Isoult dearly. But he could not go back on his knightly word, so he prepared for the voyage.

Accompanied by a gallant company of knights, he set sail for Ireland. But as soon as they were well out to sea, a tempest sprang up, which bore their ship back to the coast of England.

The ship was forced to shelter in a bay, and Sir Tristram found that he was close to Camelot, where King Arthur held his court. The young knight therefore went ashore to pay his respects to the famous king.

To his surprise, Sir Tristram found that King Anguish was also at Camelot, having been summoned there by King Arthur.

Anguish was accused of having foully slain a cousin of Sir Lancelot of the Lake. In those days, the only way to meet such a charge was to engage in combat with a relative of the murdered man, and King Anguish was unhappy at the prospect. For the family to which Sir Lancelot belonged held many famous warriors, while the king was growing old.

Sir Tristram recalled the kindness which King Anguish had shown him when he was a guest in his castle, and he now offered to act as the king's champion in battle, if only Anguish would grant him two things.

In the first place, King Anguish must swear that his quarrel was a just one, in that he had no hand in the knight's murder. The second request would be made after the fight, if Sir Tristram was the victor.

King Anguish at once swore that he was guiltless of the slaying, and also gave his word to grant Sir Tristram's second request, whatever it might be.

The conflict took place next day, and Sir Tristram speedily overcame the valiant knight who opposed him. Then he and King Anguish took their leave of King Arthur and sailed for Ireland in company.

When she learned how Sir Tristram had fought for the king, the queen forgave the youth for the death of her brother, and he was right royally entertained. The fair Isoult was overjoyed to think that her lover had returned to her so soon.

At length King Anguish asked Sir Tristram why he had not made the other request that was his due.

" Sire," answered Sir Tristram, " since you recall the matter, I must ask my boon. What I desire is that you shall give me your daughter, the fair Isoult. Yet I ask it not on my own behalf, but that she may be wedded to my uncle, King Mark of Cornwall."

" But why is this ? " demanded the king. " I would give my kingdom to have you wed her instead."

" If I did so, sire," said Sir Tristram, " I should break my vows of knighthood, for I gave my promise that I would secure her for King Mark."

Isoult wept upon learning her unhappy fate, but without delay, preparations were made for her departure.

Thinking to cure her daughter of her vain love for Sir Tristram, the queen made a magic potion, which she entrusted to Isoult's maid, Bragwaine.

" On the day of the wedding," said the queen, " you must see that both King Mark and Isoult drink from this flask. It is a love potion, and when they have drunk together, they will love each other dearly all their days."

Bragwaine promised to obey these instructions, and took the flask aboard the ship with her. But it so happened that she placed it on a table in the cabin, and here it was seen by Sir Tristram and Isoult.

" Why," cried Sir Tristram, " what kind of drink is this that your maid is keeping to herself, Isoult ? "

He opened the flask and tasted the contents, then offered it to Isoult. Thus they drank the magic potion between them, and the plans of the queen were set at nought.

When Bragwaine found what had occurred, she kept it secret to herself that the drink had possessed magic properties.

Cornwall was safely reached, and Sir Tristram surrendered Isoult to his uncle, according to his vow.

# SOFTLY BLOW, THOU WESTERN BREEZE

*by* JOHN LEYDEN

SOFTLY blow, thou western breeze,—
Softly rustle past the sail ;
Soothe to rest the furrowy seas,
 Before my love, sweet western gale.

Where the wave is tinged with red,
 And the russet sea-leaves grow,
Mariners, with prudent dread,
 Shun the shelving reefs below.

As you pass through Jura's sound,
 Bend your course by Scarba's shore,—
Shun—oh, shun the gulf profound
 Where Corrovrekin's surges roar !

If, from that unbottomed deep,
 With wrinkled form and wreathed train,
O'er the verge of Scarba's steep,
 The sea-smoke heaves his snowy mane ;

Oh, then, unwind his oozy coils,
 Sea-green sisters of the main !
And, in the gulf where ocean boils,
 Th' unwieldy, wallowing monster chain.

Softly blow, thou western breeze—
 Softly rustle past the sail ;
Soothe to rest the furrowed seas,
 Before my love, sweet western gale.

# " YELLOW "

### by NED BOOTH

IT was a magnificent winter day ; an overnight fall of two inches of fresh snow had put the crust-covered hills into absolutely perfect condition for ski-ing.

Tommy Holmwood and a school chum, Don Evans, who were spending the Christmas holidays together at the former's home, stood at the top of a high hill looking over the snow-covered lake far below, and at the other smooth hilltops surrounding it that, save for a single grim circumstance, had made of the place a veritable skier's paradise.

" I'm mighty glad you told me to bring the old skis along with me last night," Evans declared. " I'm a raw beginner, as you can see, but with a week or two in this sort of country, I'll expect to pick up some of the wrinkles—don't you think ? "

" Of course you will, Don . . . you've taken all these hills we've tried this morning in good style ; confidence is the great thing—and practice, of course . . ."

" Sure . . . it's another of those things that's easy when you know how, isn't it ? "

Holmwood laughed. " I guess you're right there. . . . Look, there go the others down to the woods on the flat." He looked at the watch on his wrist. " It's time to eat already . . . hasn't the morning gone quickly ? We'll let ourselves down there on a couple of these easy slopes and join them. . . ."

" Just a moment, Tom . . . I've got to take up a hole on this strap." Evans knelt, and fussed with the harness on one of his skis.

" I say, Tommy," he continued, as he rose and pulled his gloves over his numbing fingers once more, " is Bayne always as quarrelsome as he was this morning about the hockey business yesterday ? What was the fuss about, anyhow . . . ? "

" Oh, I refereed a game and he wasn't satisfied about a decision . . . thought I favoured his enemies. We don't always pay much attention to Jimmy when he tries to start things . . . he says a great deal more than he means."

" I see . . . still, he got pretty nasty, don't you think ? "

" Well, what do you suppose I'd better do ? . . . beat him up next time he starts a row ? " Holmwood was laughing good-naturedly.

" You know best, Tommy . . . but ' Yellow ' is a dirty word to use to a chap, I always think . . ."

" I suppose it is . . . Jimmy's a good sort really, though, when you get to know him. There's no ' Yellow ' in him, I can tell you. He's only comparatively a tenderfoot at the ski game, yet you see he's afraid of no hill about the lake . . . come on and we'll get down . . ."

Instead of a run over the edge of a single steep hill that would have put them quickly at their objective in the woods on the flat at the lake-side, they made the descent in two or three comparatively easy grades, and reached the lunching-place without fall or mishap. Bayne and the other boy of the party, Art Nevins, had already a small fire alight and a hot lunch was in preparation in a jiffy. . . .

Lunch over, the four climbed, fish-tail fashion, up slope after slope, until all were again at the top of one of the exceedingly high and steep hills that lay about the lake in the hollow.

" Come on, Tommy ! " Bayne challenged. " Come with me over this one—there's a peach of a jump in the middle of it. You haven't taken a decent hill to-day ! " Jimmy pranced about joyously until he came to a windswept patch of crust where his skis missed their hold, tangled together, and let him down with a tremendous whack at the very crest of the hill, where he lay helpless a moment, in danger of taking the steep slide in a much less dignified position than he had contemplated.

" Come on, old woman ! " he insisted, when he had managed to scramble back to a better foothold. " Come on ! What's the matter with you ? "

" Nothing's the matter . . . go ahead when you want to. I'm not taking that hill just now."

" Well, 'pon my word, Holmwood, I don't know what's come over you ! . . . That hockey stuff yesterday, and now this ! Here, Art, come on ; you're not scared, too, are you . . . ? "

" Aw, lay off that stuff, Jimmy, you get too fresh ! Forget it, I tell you. Don't mind him, Tommy. Here, come on, then, if you want to land on your neck . . . I can stand it, if you can ! " Nevins lined up beside the impatient Bayne, the two made a slithering start over the icy brow of the hill, and disappeared instantly from view.

As Bayne passed Holmwood he called aloud : " Yellow ! "

There was silence for a moment after their departure. Tommy saw the flush on Evans' skin grow deeper than the vigorous exercise of the morning would account for . . . a slow grin crept over his own face as he realised the sentiments of the other.

" Don't mind Jimmy, Don . . . he acts like a kid sometimes ! Pay no attention . . ."

He watched Don shake his head as though dismissing an unpleasant thought from his mind, then turn around to gaze at the lovely country spread about them once more.

Millions of diamonds sparkled everywhere on the snow's surface and on the weighted limbs of the dark evergreens everywhere. Far away on the horizon a cloud of smoke marked the location of the city they had come from. Otherwise there was not a single cloud to mar the perfect clearness of the day.

Don drank in great breaths of the clear, cold air. " This is great, Tommy, eh ? I'm sorry Dad and Mother had to be away from home at the holidays, but I wouldn't like to miss this visit with you. If every day's as good as this first one, it'll make history, I tell you."

" Fine, Don ; this is a great place to ski ; you'd expect it to be all tracked up with people. It would, too, only it has a bad name ; the lake has no visible inlet or outlet, and there is always an open place over there at the foot of the cliff." He pointed across to where a black spot on the lake's level surface showed open water.

" The water boils up over there—they think it is the inlet—and several times people ski-ing here have fallen in and disappeared. The bodies have never been found, and no one who has ever fallen in has ever come out."

" That's nice . . . it must be a good place to keep away from ; let's go over and have a look at it."

" Sure, that's good Irish advice ; I was just going to suggest that . . ."

With no worse mishap than an innocent fall or two for Don, they descended the slopes again to the lake. Crossing it at a safe distance from the open water, they turned aside and climbed the bank a little way, where they stood looking down at the dark water swirling and eddying about angrily at the lake edge.

A few feet back from the open water the shore rose sharply in an almost perpendicular cliff, perhaps thirty or more feet in height, with sheer face toward the lake.

" Odd, isn't it ?—you'd think that cliff was made for a ski-jump take-off. There's a corking hill above it, too, but you'd land plump in the water if you took it ! It's a queer thing, too . . . the best hill here—the one the professionals use when they come out—lies up there ! "

He pointed to a tremendous rise farther along the lakeside. " There's a wonderful jump in the middle of it, and after the jump—if you're lucky —you run right on down here along the lake, along the top of that cliff, and so on down to the level of the ice."

Don Evans, watching the evil-looking swirl of black water, listened, fascinated, to the description of the big ski-run.

" Maybe so, but I'd feel much safer a long piece away from the top of that cliff, either coming over or running along it," he remarked.

An hour later Holmwood and his companion, after trying out a score of moderately steep hills and a very modest jump or so, found themselves high up at the take-off for the big jump and the long run down toward the lake shore and across the cliff top that Tommy had described to Evans as they stood together near the open water.

It was getting along in the afternoon, and they ought soon to be starting for the suburban street-railway terminus, whence a car would take them to the city again.

" I wonder where the fellows have got to ? . . . I hope Jimmy has found a hill fast enough to suit him." Tommy began to search the hilltops about the lake, and the lower levels as well, for Bayne and Nevins.

Don first noticed a movement of some sort on a hill farther along and on the same side of the lake as theirs, and in a moment, far off, the two saw Bayne and his companion come out of a bit of wood and stand, apparently talking together, near the edge of the hill.

Suddenly Holmwood came to a position of rigid intentness, his gaze fixed unswervingly on the distant pair.

" By jingo, Don," he exclaimed tensely, " they are right on the take-off for the run that I showed you going over the cliff ! Neither of them has been out here very much, though I've told them plainly about the danger there. They probably don't know that's the run."

He moved nervously toward the brow of the hill on which they were standing.

" Surely to goodness Jimmy won't start down that . . . he's in a humour to-day to do any fool thing ! He wouldn't know what he was in for until he shot over the cliff ! It's too far to call to him . . ."

Holmwood turned anxiously toward Evans, who watched his nervous fidgeting at the crest of the high hill, but made no suggestion. Tommy realised the futility of anything the boy could possibly say or do.

Suddenly one of the distant figures took half a dozen running steps, and was over the crest of the hill, headed straight down toward the treacherous menace below. In the same instant, with an unintelligible cry to Don, Holmwood shot over the edge of the great take-off before them, and started downward at lightning speed toward the big jump and the long run crossing the cliff top.

It was the action of impulse. What he hoped to do, he could not have said, but long before he reached the jump, he knew ! With the incredibly quick mental action said to be experienced by drowning men, Tommy knew that he must reach the cliff top before Jimmy did. Just what he might do there would depend . . . the two hills were probably of about equal length so far as he knew, but there was the jump in his.

*" They are right on the take-off for the run going over the cliff ! "*

Three times before, on other days, had Tommy taken the big hill—though none of the others knew of it—and only at the third attempt had he been able to keep his feet and finish the long slide across the cliff top. Now the jump was rushing at him. There must be no fumble this time. . . . If he missed, Jimmy might . . .! He put the thought from him and crouched slightly for the big leap.

The snow surface was faultless . . . he rose from the edge smoothly, in a long, bird-like flight ; the tails of his skis dropped a little as they ought, and in an instant the slanting surface of the landing came leaping up at him.

He came down in perfect form, though with heart in mouth, and in an instant that first peril was behind him, and he was rushing at express-train speed down an avenue of evergreens and on for the top of the cliff.

As Tommy burst out of the woods into the clearing above the cliff, Jimmy also raced into the open, at right angles to him, crouching slightly on his skis, rushing unconsciously straight for the cliff edge and the waiting terror below . . .

What happened next was entirely without calculation on the part of either, and of unbelievable quickness.

Holmwood crouched low, instinctively bracing himself for the crash that he saw coming . . . his weight was as great as Jimmy's, and the chances of broken bones would be even.

Less than ten feet from the cliff's edge, and at terrific speed, he crashed into the other, a terrible body blow that hurled each from his course and threw the two far apart.

Minutes passed, and Tommy lifted his head and looked dazedly about him. He lay alarmingly close to the brow of the big drop. Jimmy was sitting up on the snow, gazing at him with a ghastly-white face, in which pain and bewilderment and wrath were oddly mingled.

"Tommy . . . you did that on purpose! Why? . . ."

"You're right on the cliff over the open water, old man . . . you mistook the hill . . ."

Jimmy's eyes dilated widely in pure fright. "Good-night . . . then you saved me from . . ."

Late in the evening of the same day, Tommy Holmwood underwent what he would have confidentially described as a very unpleasant experience —almost as bad, probably, as that of that afternoon.

Mr. and Mrs. Bayne sat with him in the library of their city home, and tried to express to him as plainly as their over-full hearts would let them, something of their admiration at his plucky piece of work in the afternoon out at the lake. Their son had not failed to do full justice to the happenings of the day.

*At terrific speed he crashed into the other*

Upstairs in Jimmy's room were the others of the quartette.

Jimmy lay on the bed, propped high with pillows, and with a bandaged foot placed well up. In the flying tumble following the terrific collision with his friend at the top of the cliff, one of Jimmy's skis had been swung around and ligaments about an ankle were badly torn. That was the total of injury done. The other party to the adventure had got off scot free.

" It was the coolest piece of work I ever saw done, gang . . ."

" Yes, and, you blighter—you called him ' Yellow ' twice to-day ! " reminded Nevins.

" Did I really ? . . . he won't mind—he knows me."

" But look, fellows," exclaimed Don Evans, " why was it Tommy took no big hills all afternoon, then suddenly went over the biggest of all ? . . . Is he really an expert at the game ? "

" An expert ! I'll say he is ! No one in the city can beat him. Look here . . . come close . . . I'll tell you why he stuck to the small hills . . ." Jimmy beckoned them nearer him, and talked with lowered voice for several moments.

" Ah, go on ! " cried Nevins, drawing back. " Your trouble in your foot's gone to your head ! "

Evans sat back with a puzzled expression on his face.

" That's right, I tell you," Jimmy insisted. " I know Tommy better than you do, Art ! I tell you he saw that Don here was a greenhorn at the game, and he stayed on the small hills that a beginner could take so Don wouldn't feel cheap or second-fiddle or whatever you like to call it ! That's the kind of a guy Holmwood is ! "

---

# THE PIGS

### by JANE TAYLOR

" DO look at those pigs as they lie in the straw,"
   Willy said to his father one day ;
" They keep eating longer than ever I saw,
   Oh, what greedy gluttons are they ! "

" I see they are feasting," his father replied,
   They eat a great deal, I allow ;
But let us remember, before we deride,
   'Tis the nature, my dear, of a sow.

" But were a great boy, such as you, my dear Will,
   Like them to be eating all day,
Or be taking nice things till he made himself ill,
   What a glutton, indeed, we might say ?

" If plum-cake and sugar he constantly picks,
   And sweetmeats and comfits, and figs,
We should tell him to leave off his own greedy tricks,
   Before he finds fault with the pigs."

# CHOOSING A NAME

*by* MARY LAMB

I HAVE got a new-born sister :
I was nigh the first that kissed her.
When the nursing-woman brought her
To papa, his infant daughter,
How papa's dear eyes did glisten !
She will shortly be to christen ;
And papa has made the offer,
I shall have the naming of her.

Now I wonder what would please her—
Charlotte, Julia, or Louisa ?
Ann and Mary, they're too common ;
Joan's too formal for a woman ;
Jane's a prettier name beside ;
But we had a Jane that died.
They would say, if 'twas Rebecca,
That she was a little Quaker,
Edith's pretty, but that looks
Better in old English books ;

Ellen's left off long ago ;
Blanche is out of fashion now.
None that I have named as yet
Is so good as Margaret.
Emily is neat and fine ;
What do you think of Caroline ?
How I'm puzzled and perplexed
What to choose or think of next !
I am in a little fever
Lest the name that I should give her
Should disgrace her or defame her—
I will leave papa to name her.

# MRS. MOSS

### by MRS. J. H. EWING

"I REMEMBER," said Mrs. Overtheway, " old as I am, I remember distinctly many of the unrecognised vexations, longings, and disappointments of childhood. By unrecognised, I mean those vexations, longings, and disappointments which could not be understood by nurses, are not confided even to mothers, and through which, even in our cradles, we become subject to that law of humanity which gives to every heart its own secret bitterness to be endured alone. These are they which sometimes outlive weightier memories, and produce life-long impressions disproportionate to their value ; but oftener, perhaps, are washed away by the advancing tide of time,—the vexations, longings, and disappointments of the next period of our lives. These are they which are apt to be forgotten too soon to benefit our children, and which in the forgetting make childhood all bright to look back upon, and foster that happy fancy that there is one division of mortal life in which greedy desire, unfulfilled purpose, envy, sorrow, weariness, and satiety have no part, by which every man believes himself at least to have been happy as a child.

"My childhood on the whole was a very happy one. The story that I I am about to relate is only a fragment of it.

"As I look into the fire, and the hot coals shape themselves into a thousand memories of the past, I seem to be staring with childish eyes at a board that stares back at me out of a larch plantation, and gives notice that ' This House is to Let.' Then, again, I seem to peep through rusty iron gates at the house itself—an old red house, with large windows, through which one could see the white shutters that were always closed. To look at this house, though only with my mind's eye, recalls the feeling of mysterious interest with which I looked at it fifty years ago, and brings back the almost oppressive happiness of a certain day, when Sarah, having business with the couple who kept the empty manor, took me with her, and left me to explore the grounds whilst she visited her friends.

" Next to a companion with that rare sympathy of mind to mind, that exceptional coincidence of tastes, which binds some few friendships in a chain of mesmeric links, supplanting all the complacencies of love by in-tuition, is a companion whose desires and occupations are in harmony, if not in unison, with one's own. That friend whom the long patience of the angler does not chafe, the protracted pleasures of the sketcher do not weary, because time flies as swiftly with him whilst he pores over his book or de-voutly seeks botanical specimens through the artist's middle distance ; that friend, in short—that valuable friend—who is blessed with the great and good quality of riding a hobby of his own, and the greater and better quality of allowing other people to ride theirs.

" I did not think out all this fifty years ago, neither were the tastes of that excellent housemaid, Sarah, quite on a level with those of which I have spoken ; but I remember feeling the full comfort of the fact that Sarah's love for friendly gossip was quite as ardent as mine for romantic discovery ; that she was disposed to linger quite as long to chat as I to explore ; and that she no more expected me to sit wearily through her kitchen confidences, than I imagined that she would give a long afternoon to sharing my day-dreams in the gardens of the deserted manor.

" We had ridden our respective hobbies till nearly tea-time before she appeared.

" ' I'm afraid you must be tired of waiting, Miss Mary,' said she.

" ' Tired ! ' I exclaimed, ' not in the least. I have been so happy, and I am so much obliged to you, Sarah.'

" Need I say why I was so happy that afternoon ? Surely most people have felt—at least in childhood—the fascination of deserted gardens, unin-habited houses, ruined churches. They have that advantage over what is familiar and in use that undiscovered regions have over the comfortable one that the traveller leaves to explore them, that the secret which does not con-cern me has over the facts which do, that what we wish for has over what we possess.

" If you, my dear, were to open one of those drawers, and find Nurse's Sunday dress folded up in the corner, it would hardly amuse you ; but if, instead thereof, you found a dress with a long stiff bodice, square at the neck, and ruffled round the sleeves, such as you have seen in old pictures, no matter how old or useless it might be, it would shed round it an atmosphere of delightful and mysterious speculations. This curiosity, these fancies, roused by the ancient dress, whose wearer has passed away, are awakened equally by empty houses where some one must once have lived, though his place knows him no more. It was so with the manor. How often had I peeped through the gates, catching sight of garden walks, and wondering whither they led, and who had walked in them ; seeing that the shutters behind one window were partly open, and longing to look in.

" To-day I had been in the walks and peeped through the window. This was the happiness.

" Through the window I had seen a large hall with a marble floor and broad stone stairs winding into unknown regions. By the walks I had arrived at the locked door of the kitchen garden, at a small wood or wilderness of endless delights (including a broken swing), and at a dilapidated summer-house. I had wandered over the spongy lawn, which was cut into a long green promenade by high clipt yew-hedges, walking between which, in olden times, the ladies grew erect and stately, as plants among brushwood stretch up to air and light.

" Finally, I had brought away such relics as it seemed to me that honesty would allow. I had found half a rusty pair of scissors in the summer-house. Perhaps some fair lady of former days had lost them here, and swept distractedly up and down the long walk seeking them. Perhaps they were a present, and she had given a luck-penny for them, lest they should cut love. Sarah said the housekeeper might have dropped them there ; but Sarah was not a person of sentiment. I did not show her the marble I found by the hedge, the acorn I picked up in the park, nor a puny pansy which, half-way back to a wild heartsease, had touched me as a pathetic memorial of better days.

" Properly speaking, I was not at home just then, but on a visit to my grandmother and a married aunt without children who lived with her. A fever had broken out in my own home, and my visit here had been prolonged to keep me out of the way of infection. I was very happy and comfortable except for one signal vexation, which was this :

" I slept on a little bed in what had once been the nursery, a large room which was now used as a work-room. A great deal of sewing was done in my grandmother's house, and the sewing-maid and at least one other of the servants sat there every evening. A red silk screen was put before my bed to shield me from the candle-light, and I was supposed to be asleep when they came upstairs. But I never remember to have been otherwise than wide awake, nervously awake, wearily awake. This was the vexation. I was not a strong child and had a very excitable brain ; and the torture that it was to hear those maids gossiping on the other side of the dim red light of my screen I cannot well describe, but I do most distinctly remember. I tossed till the clothes got hot, and threw them off till I got cold, and stopped my ears, and pulled the sheet over my face, and tried not to listen, and listened in spite of all. They told long stories, and made many jokes that I couldn't understand ; sometimes I heard names that I knew, and fancied I had learnt some wonderful secret. Sometimes, on the contrary, I made noises to intimate that I was awake, when one of them would rearrange my glaring screen, and advise me to go to sleep, and then they talked in whispers, which was more distracting still.

" One evening—some months after my ramble round the manor—the maids went out to tea, and I lay in peaceful silence watching the shadows which crept noiselessly about the room as the fire blazed, and wishing Sarah and her colleagues nothing less than a month of uninterrupted tea-parties. I was almost asleep when Aunt Harriet came into the room. She brought a candle, put up my screen (the red screen again !) and went to the work-table. She had not been rustling with the work things for many minutes when my grandmother followed her, and shut the door with an air which seemed to promise a long stay. She also gave a shove to my screen, and then the following conversation began :

" ' I have been to Lady Stutfield's to-day, Harriet.'

" ' Indeed, ma'am.' But my aunt respectfully continued her work, as I could hear by the scraping of the scissors along the table.

" ' I heard some news there. The manor is let.'

" I almost jumped in my bed, and Aunt Harriet's scissors paused.

" ' Let, ma'am ! To whom ? '

" ' To a Mrs. Moss. You must have heard me speak of her. I knew her years ago, when we were both young women. Anastatia Eden, she was then.'

" I could hear my aunt move to the fire, and sit down.

" ' The beautiful Miss Eden ? Whom did she marry at last ? Was there not some love-affair of hers that you knew about ? '

" ' Her love affairs were endless. But you mean Mr. Sandford. She treated him very ill—very ill.'

" There was a pause, while the fire crackled in the silence ; and then, to the infinite satisfaction of my curiosity, Aunt Harriet said :

" ' I've forgotten the story, ma'am. He was poor, was he not ? '

" ' He had quite enough to marry on,' my grandmother answered, energetically ; ' but he was not a great match. It was an old story, my dear. The world ! The world ! The world ! I remember sitting up with Anastatia after a ball, where he had been at her side all the evening. We sipped hot posset, and talked of our partners. Ah, dear ! ' And here my grandmother heaved a sigh ; partly, perhaps, because of the follies of youth, and partly, perhaps, because youth had gone, and could come back no more.

" ' Anastatia talked of him,' she continued. ' I remember her asking me if " her man " were not a pretty fellow, and if he had not sweet blue eyes and the greatest simplicity I ever knew but in a child. It was true enough ; and he was a great deal more than that—a great deal more than she ever understood. Poor Anastatia ! I advised her to marry him, but she seemed to look on that as impossible. I remember her saying that it would be different if she were not an acknowledged beauty ; but it was expected that she would marry well, and he was comparatively poor, and not even singular. He was accomplished, and the soul of honour, but simple, provokingly simple, with no pretentions to carry off the toast of a county. My dear, if he had been notorious in any way, I believe it would have satisfied the world, and he would have had a chance. But there was nothing to talk about, and Anastatia had not the courage to take him for himself. She had the world at her feet, and paid for it by being bound by its opinion.'

" Here my grandmother, who was apt to moralise, especially when relating biographies of young ladies, gave another sigh.

" ' Then why did she encourage him ? ' inquired Aunt Harriet ; who also moralised, but with more of indignation and less of philosophy.

" ' I believe she loved him in spite of herself ; but at the last, when he offered, she turned prudent and refused him.'

" ' Poor man ! Did he ever marry ? '

" ' Yes, and very happily—a charming woman. But the strange part of the story is, that he came quite unexpectedly into a large property that was in his family.'

" ' Did he ? Then he would have been as good a match as most of her admirers ? '

" ' Better. It was a fine estate. Poor Anastatia ! '

" ' Serve her right,' said my aunt, shortly.

" ' She was very beautiful,' my grandmother gently recommenced. She said this, not precisely as an excuse, but with something of the sort in her tone. ' Very beautiful ! How stately she did look that night, to be sure ! She did not paint, and her complexion (a shade too high by day) was perfection by candlelight. I can see her now, my dear, as she stood up for a minuet with him. We wore hoops, then ; and she had a white brocade

*I can see her now as she stood up for a minuet with him*

petticoat, embroidered with pink rosebuds, and a train and bodice of pea-green satin, and green satin shoes with pink heels. You never saw anything more lovely than that brocade. A rich old aunt had given it to her. The shades of the rosebuds were exquisite. I embroidered the rosebuds on that salmon-coloured cushion down-stairs from a piece that Anastatia gave me as a pattern. Dear me ! What a dress it was, and how lovely she looked in it ! Her eyes were black, a thing you rarely see, and they shone and glittered under her powdered hair. She had a delicately curved nose ; splendid teeth, too, and showed them when she smiled. Then such a lovely throat, and beautifully-shaped arms ! I don't know how it is, my dear Harriet,' added my grandmother, thoughtfully, ' but you don't see the splendid women now-a-days that there were when I was young. There are plenty of pretty, lively girls (rather too lively, in my old-fashioned judgment), but not the real stately beauty that it was worth a twenty miles' drive, there and back, just to see, at one of the old county balls.'

" My aunt sniffed, partly from a depressing consciousness of being one of a degenerate generation, and of a limited experience in the matter of county balls ; partly also to express her conviction that principle is above beauty.  She said :

" ' Then Miss Eden married, ma'am ? '

" ' Yes, rather late, Mr. Moss ; a wealthy Indian merchant, I believe.  She lost all her children, I know, one after another, and then he died.  Poor Anastatia !  It seems like yesterday.  And to think she should be coming here ! '

" My grandmother sighed again, and I held my breath, hoping for some further particulars of the lovely heroine of this romance.  But I was disappointed.  My uncle's voice at this moment called loudly from below, and Aunt Harriet hurried off with a conscious meritoriousness about her, becoming a lady who had married the right man, and took great care of him.

" ' Supper, ma'am, I think,' she said, as she left the room.

" My grandmother sat still by the fire, sighing gently now and then, and I lay making up my mind to brave all and tell her that I was awake.  In the first place (although I was not intentionally eavesdropping, and my being awake was certainly not my fault), I felt rather uneasy at having overheard what I knew was not intended for my hearing.  Besides this, I wanted to hear some more stories of the lovely Mrs. Moss, and to ask how soon she would come to the manor.  After a few seconds my grandmother rose and toddled across the room.  I made an effort, and spoke just above my breath :

" ' Granny ! '

" But my grandmother was rather deaf.  Moreover, my voice may have been drowned in the heavy sigh with which she closed the nursery door.

" The room was empty again ; the glare of the red screen was tenderly subdued in the firelight ; but for all this I did not go to sleep.  I took advantage of my freedom to sit up in bed, toss my hair from my forehead, and clasping my knees with my arms, to rock myself and think.  My thoughts had one object ; my whole mind was filled with one image—Mrs. Moss. The future inhabitant of my dear deserted manor would, in any circumstances, have been an interesting subject for my fancies.  The favoured individual whose daily walk might be between the yew hedges on that elastic lawn ; who should eat, drink, and sleep through the commonplace hours of this present time behind those mystical white shutters !  But when the individual added to this felicitous dispensation of fortune the personal attributes of unparalleled beauty and pea-green satin ; of having worn hoops, high heels, and powder ; of countless lovers, and white brocade with pink rosebuds ;—well might I sit, my brain whirling with anticipation, as I thought : ' She is coming here : I shall see her ! '  For though, of course, I knew that having lived in those (so to speak) pre-historic times when my grandmother was young, Mrs. Moss must now be an old woman ; yet, strange as it may seem, my dear, I do assure you that I never realised the fact.  I thought of her as I had heard of her—young and beautiful—and modelled my hopes accordingly.

" Most people's day-dreams take, sooner or later, a selfish turn.  I seemed to identify myself with the beautiful Anastatia.  I thought of the ball as one looks back to the past.  I fancied myself moving through the *minuet de la cour*, whose stately paces scarcely made the silken rosebuds rustle. I rejected *en masse* countless suitors of fabulous wealth and nobility ; but when it came to Mr. Sandford, I could feel with Miss Eden no more. My grandmother had said that she loved him, that she encouraged him, and that she gave him up for money. It was a mystery ! In her place, I thought, I would have danced every dance with him ; I would have knitted for him in winter, and gathered flowers for him in the summer hedges. To whom should one be most kind, if not to those whom one most loves ? To love, and take pleasure in giving pain—to balance a true heart and clear blue eyes against money, and prefer money—was not at that time comprehensible by me. I pondered, and (so to speak) spread out the subject before my mind, and sat in judgment upon it.

" Money—that is, golden guineas (my grandmother had given me one on my birthday), crowns, shillings, sixpences, pennies, halfpennies, farthings ; and when you come to consider how many things a guinea judiciously expended in a toy-shop will procure, you see that money is a great thing, especially if you have the full control of it, and are not obliged to spend it on anything useful.

" On the other hand, those whom you love and who love you—not in childhood, thank God, the smallest part of one's acquaintance.

" I made a list on my own account. It began with my mother, and ended with my yellow cat. (It included a crusty old gardener, who was at times, especially in the spring, so particularly cross that I *might* have been tempted to exhange *him* for the undisputed possession of that stock of seeds, tools, and flowerpots which formed our chief subject of dispute. But this is a digression.) I took the lowest. Could I part with Sandy Tom for any money, or for anything that money would buy ? I thought of a speaking doll, a miniature piano, a tiny carriage drawn by four yellow mastiffs, of a fairy purse that should never be empty, with all that might thereby be given to others or kept for oneself : and then I thought of Sandy Tom—of his large, round, soft head ; his fine eyes (they were yellow, not blue, and glared with infinite tenderness) ; his melodious purr ; his expressive whiskers ; his unutterable tail.

" Love rose up as an impulse, an instinct ; it would not be doubted, it utterly refused to be spread out to question.

" ' Oh, Puss ! ' I thought, ' if you could but leap on to the bed at this moment I would explain it all to our mutual comprehension and satisfaction. My dear Sandy,' I would say, ' with you to lie on the cushioned seat, a nice little carriage, and four yellow mastiffs, would be perfection ; but as to comparing what I love—to wit, you, Sandy !—with what I want—to wit, four yellow mastiffs and a great many other things besides—I should as soon think of cutting off your tail to dust the doll's house with.' Alas ! Sandy Tom was at home ; I could only imagine the gentle rub of the head with which he would have assented. Meanwhile, I made up my mind firmly on one point. My grandmother was wrong. Miss Anastatia Eden had not loved Mr. Sandford.

" Smash ! The fire, which had been gradually becoming hollow, fell in at this moment, and I started to find myself chilly and cramped ; and so lay down. Then my thoughts took another turn. I wondered if I should

grow up beautiful, like Mrs. Moss. It was a serious question. I had often
looked at myself in the glass, but I had a general idea that I looked much
like other little girls of my age. I began gravely to examine myself in detail,
commencing from the top of my head. My hair was light, and cropped on
a level with the lobes of my ears ; this, however, would amend itself with
time ; and I had long intended that my hair should be of raven blackness,
and touch the ground at least ; ' but that will not be till I am grown up,'
thought I. Then my eyes : they were large ; in fact the undue proportions
they assumed when I looked ill or tired formed a family joke. If size were
all that one requires in eyes, mine would certainly pass muster. Moreover,
they had long curly lashes. I fingered these slowly, and thought of Sandy's
whiskers. At this point I nearly fell asleep, but roused myself to examine
my nose. My grandmother had said that Mrs. Moss's nose was delicately
curved. Now, it is certainly true that a curve may be either concave or
convex ; but I had heard of the bridge of a nose, and knew well enough
which way the curve should go ; and I had a shrewd suspicion that if so
very short a nose as mine, with so much and so round a tip, could be said
to be curved at all, the curve went the wrong way ; at the same time, I
could not feel sure. For I must tell you that to lie in a comfortable bed,
at an hour long beyond the time when one ought naturally to be asleep, and
to stroke one's nose, is a proceeding not favourable to forming a clear judgment on so important a point as one's personal appearance. The very
shadows were still as well as silent, the fire had ceased to flicker, a delicious
quietude pervaded the room, as I stroked my nose and dozed, and dozed
and stroked my nose, and lost all sense of its shape, and fancied it a huge
lump growing under my fingers.—The extreme unpleasantness of this idea
just prevented my falling asleep ; and I roused myself and sat up again.

" ' It's no use feeling,' I thought, ' I'll look in the glass.'

" There was one mirror in the room. It hung above the mantelpiece.
It was old, deeply framed in dark wood, and was so hung as to slope forwards
into the room.

" In front of the fire stood an old-fashioned, cushioned armchair, with
a very high back, and a many-frilled chintz cover. A buffet lay near it. It
was here that my grandmother had been sitting. I jumped out of bed, put
the buffet into the chair that I might get to a level with the glass, and climbed
on to it. Thanks to the slope of the mirror, I could now see my reflection
as well as the dim firelight would permit.

" ' What a silly child ! ' you will say, Ida. Very silly, indeed, my dear.
And how one remembers one's follies ! At the end of half a century, I recall
my reflection in that old nursery mirror more clearly than I remember how
I looked in the glass before which I put on my bonnet this evening to come
to tea with you : the weird, startled glance of my eyes, which, in their most
prominent stage of weariness, gazed at me out of the shadows of the looking-
glass, the tumbled tufts of hair, the ghostly effect of my white nightdress.
As to my nose, I could see absolutely nothing of its shape ; the firelight just
caught the round tip, which shone like a little white toadstool from the gloom,
and this was all.

" ' One can't see the shape, full face,' I thought. ' If I had only another
looking-glass.'

" But there was not another. I knew it, and yet involuntarily looked round the room. Suddenly I exclaimed aloud, ' Mr. Joseph will do ! '

" Who was Mr. Joseph ?—you will ask. My dear Ida, I really do not know. I have not the least idea. I had heard him called Mr. Joseph, and I fancy he was a connection of the family. All I knew of him was his portrait, a *silhouette*, elegantly glazed, and framed in black wood, which hung against the nursery wall. I was ignorant of his surname and history. I had never examined his features. But I knew that happily he had been very stout, since his ample coat and waistcoat, cut out in black paper, converted the glass which covered them into an excellent mirror for my dolls.

*Thanks to the slope of the mirror I could now see my reflection*

" Worthy Mr. Joseph ! Here he was coming in useful again. How much we owe to our forefathers ! I soon unhooked him, and climbing back into the chair, commenced an examination of my profile by the process of double reflection. But all in vain ! Whether owing to the dusty state of the mirror, or to the dim light, or to the unobliging shapeliness of Mr. Joseph's person, I cannot say, but turn and twist as I would, I could not get a view of my profile sufficiently clear and complete to form a correct judgment upon. I held Mr. Joseph, now high, now low, I stooped, I stood on tiptoe, I moved forward, I leant backward. It was this latest manœuvre that aggravated the natural top-heaviness of the chair, and endangered its balance. The forelegs rose, my spasmodic struggle was made in the wrong direction, and I, the armchair, and Mr. Joseph fell backwards together.

" Two of us were light enough, and happily escaped unhurt. It was the armchair which fell with such an appalling crash, and whether it were any the worse or no, I could not tell as it lay. As soon as I had a little recovered from the shock, therefore, I struggled to raise it, whilst Mr. Joseph lay helplessly upon the ground, with his waistcoat turned up to the ceiling.

" It was thus that my aunt found us.

" If only Mr. Joseph and I had fallen together, no one need have been the wiser ; but that lumbering arm-chair had come down with a bump that startled the sober trio at supper in the dining-room below.

" ' What *is* the matter ? ' said Aunt Harriet.

" I was speechless.

" ' What have you been doing ? '

" I couldn't speak ; but accumulating misfortune was gradually over-powering me, and I began to cry.

" ' Get into bed,' said Aunt Harriet.

" I willingly obeyed, and Aunt Harriet seated herself at the foot.

" ' Now, think before you speak, Mary,' she said quietly, ' and then tell me the truth. What have you been doing ? '

" One large tear rolled over my nose and off the tip as I feebly began—

" ' I got into the chair—'

" ' Well ? ' said Aunt Harriet.

" ' —to look in the glass.'

" ' What for ? ' said Aunt Harriet.

" Tears flowed unrestrainedly over my face as I howled in self-abasement—

" ' To look at the shape of my nose.'

" At this point Aunt Harriet rose, and turning her back rather abruptly, crossed the room, and picked up Mr. Joseph. (I have since had reason to believe that she was with difficulty concealing a fit of laughter.)

" ' What have you had this picture down for ? ' she inquired, still with her back to me.

" ' I couldn't see,' I sobbed, ' and I got Mr. Joseph to help me.'

" My aunt made no reply, and still carefully concealing her face, restored Mr. Joseph to his brass nail with great deliberation.

" There is nothing like full confession. I broke the silence.

" ' Aunt Harriet, I was awake when you and Granny were here, and heard what you said.'

" ' You are a very silly, naughty child,' my aunt severely returned. ' Why don't you go to sleep when you are sent to bed ? '

" ' I can't,' I sobbed, ' with talking and candles.'

" ' You've got the screen,' said Aunt Harriet ; and I cannot tell why, but somehow I lacked courage to say that the red screen was the chief instrument of torture.

" ' Well, go to sleep now,' she concluded, ' and be thankful you're not hurt. You might have killed yourself.'

" Encouraged by the gracious manner in which she tucked me up, I took a short cut to the information which I had failed to attain through Mr. Joseph.

" ' Aunt Harriet,' I said, ' do you think I shall ever be as beautiful as Mrs. Moss ? '

" ' I'm ashamed of you,' said Aunt Harriet.

" I climbed no more into the treacherous armchair. I eschewed the mirror. I left Mr. Joseph in peace upon the wall. I took no further trouble about the future prospects of my nose. But night and day I thought of

Mrs. Moss. I found the old cushion, and sat by it, gazing at the faded tints of the rosebuds, till I imagined the stiff brocade in all its beauty and freshness. I took a vigorous drawing fit ; but it was only to fill my little book with innumerable sketches of Mrs. Moss. My uncle lent me his paint-box, as he was wont ; and if the fancy portraits that I made were not satisfactory even to myself, they failed in spite of cheeks blushing with vermilion, in spite of eyes as large and brilliant as lamp-black could make them, and in spite of the most accurately curved noses that my pencil could produce. The amount of gamboge and Prussian blue that I wasted in vain efforts to produce a satisfactory pea-green, leaves me at this day an astonished admirer of my uncle's patience. At this time I wished to walk along no other road than that which led to my dear manor, where the iron gates were being painted, the garden made tidy, and the shutters opened ; but above all the chief object of my desires was to accompany my grandmother and aunt in their first visit to Mrs. Moss.

" Once I petitioned Aunt Harriet on this subject. Her answer was—

" ' My dear, there would be nothing to amuse you ; Mrs. Moss is an old woman.'

" ' Granny said she was so beautiful,' I suggested.

" ' So she was, my dear, when your grandmother was young.'

" These and similar remarks I heard and heeded not. They did not add one wrinkle to my ideal of Mrs. Moss : they in no way whatever lessened my desire of seeing her. I had never seen my grandmother young, and her having ever been so seemed to me at the most a matter of tradition ; on the other hand, Mrs. Moss had been presented to my imagination in the bloom of youth and beauty, and, say what they would, in the bloom of youth and beauty I expected to see her still.

" One afternoon, about a week after the arrival of Mrs. Moss, I was busy in the garden, where I had been working for an hour or more, when I heard carriage wheels drive up and stop at our door. Could it be Mrs. Moss ? I stole gently round to a position where I could see without being seen, and discovered that the carriage was not that of any caller, but my uncle's. Then Granny and Aunt Harriet were going out. I rushed up to the coachman, and asked where they were going. He seemed in no way overpowered by having to reply—' To the manor, Miss.'

" That was to Mrs. Moss, and I was to be left behind ! I stood speechless in bitter disappointment, as my grandmother rustled out in her best silk dress, followed by Aunt Harriet and my uncle, who, when he saw me, exclaimed—

" ' Why, there's my little Mary ! Why don't you take her ? I'll be bound she wants to go.'

" ' I do, indeed ! ' I exclaimed, in Cinderella-like tones.

" ' But Mrs. Moss is such an old lady,' said Aunt Harriet, whose ideas upon children were purely theoretical, and who could imagine no interests for them apart from other children, from toys or definite amusements—' What could the child do with herself ? '

" ' Do ! ' said my uncle, who took a rough and cheery view of life, ' why, look about her, to be sure. And if Mrs. M. is an old lady, there'll be all the more Indian cabinets and screens and japanned tables, and knicknacks, and lapdogs. Keep your eyes open, Miss Mary ; I've never seen the good lady or her belongings, but I'll stake my best hat on the japan ware and the lapdog. Now, how soon can you be dressed ? '

" Later in life the selfish element mixes more largely with our admirations. A few years hence, and in a first interview with the object of so many fancies, I should have thought as much of my own appearance on the occasion, as of what I was myself to see. I should have taken some pains with my toilette. At that time, the desire to see Mrs. Moss was too absorbing to admit of any purely personal considerations. I dashed into the nursery, scrubbed my hands and face to a raw red complexion, brushed my hair in three strokes, and secured my things with one sweep. I hastily pocketed a pincushion of red cloth, worked with yellow silk spots, in the likeness of a strawberry. It was a pet treasure of mine, and I intended it as an offering to Mrs. Moss. I tied my hood at the top of the stairs, fastened my tippet in the hall, and reached the family coach by about three of those bounds common to all young animals.

" ' Halloa ! ' said my uncle, with his face through the carriage door. ' You've not thanked me yet.'

" I flung my arms round his starched neckcloth.

" ' You're a darling ! ' I exclaimed, with an emphatic squeeze.

" ' You're another,' he replied, returning the embrace upon my hood.

" With this mutual understanding we parted, and I thought that if Mrs. Moss were not certain to fulfil my ideal, I should have wished her to be as nearly like Uncle James as the circumstances of the case would permit. I watched his yellow waistcoat and waving hands till they could be seen no longer, and then I settled myself primly upon the back seat, and ventured upon a shy conciliating promise to be ' very good.'

" ' You're quite welcome to come, child,' said Aunt Harriet ; ' but as I said, there are neither children nor playthings for you.'

" Children or playthings ! What did I want with either ? I put my arm through the loop by the window and watched the fields as they came and vanished, with vacant eyes, and thought of Mrs. Moss. A dozen times had I gone through the whole scene in my mind before we drove through the iron gates. I fancied myself in the bare, spacious hall, at which I had peeped ; I seemed to hear a light laugh, and to see the beautiful face of Mrs. Moss look over the banisters ; to hear a rustle, and the scraping of the stiff brocade, as the pink rosebuds shimmered, and the green satin shoes peeped out, and tap, tap, tap, the high pink heels resounded from the shallow stairs.

" I had dreamed this day-dream many times over before the carriage stopped with a shake, and Aunt Harriet roused me, asking if I were asleep. In another minute or so we were in the hall, and here I met with my first disappointment.

" To begin with I had seen the hall unfurnished, and had not imagined it otherwise. I had pictured Mrs. Moss in her beauty and rose brocade, the sole ornament of its cold emptiness. Then (though I knew that my grandmother and aunt must both be present) I had really fancied myself the chief character in this interview with Mrs. Moss. I had thought of myself as rushing up the stairs to meet her, and laying the pincushion at her green satin feet. And now that at last I was really in the hall, I should not have

*I had thought of myself laying the pincushion at her green satin feet*

known it again. It was carpeted from end to end. Fragrant orange-trees stood in tubs, large hunting pictures hung upon the walls, below which stood cases of stuffed birds, and over all presided a footman in livery, who himself looked like a stuffed specimen of the human race with unusually bright plumage.

" No face peeped over the banisters, and when we went upstairs, the footman went first (as seemed due to him), then my grandmother, followed by my aunt, and lastly I, in the humblest insignificance behind them. My feet sank into the soft stair-carpets, I vacantly admired the elegant luxury around me, with an odd sensation of heartache. Everything was beautiful, but I had wanted nothing to be beautiful but Mrs. Moss.

" Already the vision began to fade. That full-fed footman troubled my fancies. His scarlet plush killed even the thought of rosebuds, and the streaky powder upon his hair seemed a mockery of the *toupée* I hoped to see, whose whiteness should enhance the lustre of rare black eyes. He opened the drawing-room door and announced my grandmother and aunt. I followed, and (so far as one may be said to face anything when one stands behind the skirts of two elders) I was face to face with Mrs. Moss.

" That is, I was face to face with a tall dark old woman, with stooping shoulders, a hooked nose, black eyes that smouldered in their sunken sockets and a distinct growth of beard upon her chin. Mr. Moss had been dead many years and his widow had laid aside her weeds. She wore a dress of *feuille-morte* satin, and a black lace shawl. She had a rather elaborate cap with a tendency to get on one side, perhaps because it would not fit comfortably on the brown front with bunchy curls which was fastened into its place by a band of broad black velvet.

G.T.B.

M

" And this was Mrs. Moss ! This was the end of all my fancies ! There
was nothing astonishing in the disappointment ; the only marvel was that
I should have indulged in so foolish a fancy for so long. I had been told
more than once that Mrs. Moss was nearly as old as my grandmother. As
it was she looked older. Why—I could not tell then, though I know now.

" My grandmother, though never a beauty, had a sweet smile of her
own, and a certain occasional kindling of the eyes, the outward signs of a
character full of sentiment and intelligence ; and these had outlasted youth.
She had always been what is called ' pleasing,' and she was pleasing still.
But in Mrs. Moss no strength, no sentiment, no intellect filled the place of
the beauty that was gone. Features that were powerful without character,
and eyes that glowed without expression, formed a wreck with little to recall
the loveliness that had bewildered Mr. Sandford—and me.

" There is not much more to tell, Ida. This was the disappointment.
This is the cause of my dislike for a certain shade of *feuille-morte* satin. It
disappointed me of that rose brocade which I was never to see. You shall
hear how I got through the visit, however. This meeting which (like so
many meetings) had proved the very reverse of what was hoped.

" Through an angle of Aunt Harriet's pelisse, I watched the meeting
between my grandmother and Mrs. Moss. They kissed and then drew back
and looked at each other, still holding hands. I wondered if my grandmother
felt as I felt. I could not tell. With one of her smiles, she bent forward and,
kissing Mrs. Moss again, said,

" ' God bless you, Anastatia.'

" ' God bless you, Elizabeth.'

" It was the first time Mrs. Moss had spoken, and her voice was rather
gruff. Then both ladies sat down, and my grandmother drew out her pocket-
handkerchief and wiped her eyes. Mrs. Moss began (as I thought) to look for
hers, and not finding it, called ' Metcalfe ! ' on which a faded little woman,
with her forefinger in a faded-looking book, came out from behind some
window curtains and, rummaging Mrs. Moss's chair with a practised hand,
produced a large silver snuff-box, from which Mrs. Moss took a pinch, and
then offered it to Granny, who shook her head. Mrs. Moss took another
and a larger pinch. It was evident what made her voice so gruff.

" Aunt Harriet was introduced as ' My daughter Harriet,' and made a
stiff curtsey as Mrs. Moss smiled, and nodded, and bade her ' sit down, my
dear.' Throughout the whole interview she seemed to be looked upon by
both ladies as a child, and played the part so well, sitting prim and silent
on her chair, that I could hardly help humming as I looked at her :

> ' Hold up your head,
> Turn out your toes,
> Speak when you're spoken to,
> Mend your clothes.'

I was introduced, too, as ' a grandchild,' made a curtsey the shadow of Aunt
Harriet's, received a nod, the shadow of that bestowed upon her, and got out
of the way as soon as I could behind my aunt's chair, where coming unexpectedly upon three fat pug dogs on a mat, I sat down among them and
felt quite at home.

" The sight of the pugs brought Uncle James to my mind, and when I looked round the room, it seemed to me that he must be a conjuror at least, so true was everything he had said. A large India screen hid the door ; japanned boxes stood on a little table to correspond in front of it, and there were two cabinets having shallow drawers with decorated handles, and a great deal of glass, through which odd teacups, green dragons, Indian gods, and Dresden shepherdesses were visible upon the shelves. The room was filled with knicknacks, and here were the dogs, no less than three of them ! They were very fat, and had little beauty except as to their round heads, and black wrinkled snouts, which I kissed over and over again.

" ' Do you mind Mrs. Moss's being old, and dressing in that hideous brown dress ? ' I asked in a whisper at the ear of one of these round heads. ' Think of the rosebuds on the brocade, and the pea-green satin, and the high-heeled shoes. Ah ! ' I added, ' you are only a pug, and pugs don't think.' Nevertheless, I pulled out the pincushion, and showed it to each dog in turn, and the sight of it so forcibly reminded me of my vain hopes, that I could not help crying. A hot tear fell upon the nose of the oldest and fattest pug, which so offended him that he moved away to another mat at some distance, and as both the others fell fast asleep, I took refuge in my own thoughts.

" The question arose why should not Mrs. Moss have the pincushion after all ? I had expected her to be young and beautiful, and she had proved old and ugly, it is true ; but there is no reason why old and ugly people should not have cushions to keep their pins in. It was a struggle to part with my dear strawberry pincushion in the circumstances, but I had fairly resolved to do so, when the rustle of leave-taking began, and I had to come out of my corner.

" ' Bid Mrs. Moss good-day, Mary,' said my grandmother ; and added, ' the child has been wild to come and see you, Anastatia.'

" Mrs. Moss held out her hand, good-naturedly. ' So you wanted to see me, my dear ? ' said she.

" I took my hand out of my pocket, where I had been holding the pincushion, and put both into Mrs. Moss's palm.

" ' I brought this for you, ma'am,' I said. ' It is not a real strawberry ; it is emery ; I made it myself.'

" And the fact of having sacrificed something for Mrs. Moss made me almost fond of her. Moreover, there was an expression in her eyes at that moment which gave them beauty. She looked at my grandmother and laid her hand on my head.

" ' I lost all mine, Elizabeth.'

" I thought she was speaking of her pincushions, and being in a generous mood, said hastily,

" ' When that is worn out, ma'am, I will make you another.'

" But she was speaking of her children. Poor Mrs. Moss ! She took another huge pinch of snuff, and called, ' Metcalfe.'

" The faded little woman appeared once more.

" ' I must give you a keepsake in return, my dear,' said Mrs. Moss. ' The china pug, Metcalfe ! '

" Metcalfe (whose face always wore a smile that looked as if it were just about to disappear, and who, indeed, for that matter, always looked as if she were just about to disappear herself) opened one of the cabinets, and brought out a little toy pug in china, very delicately coloured, and looking just like one of my friends on the mat. I fell in love with it at once, and it was certainly a handsome exchange for the strawberry pincushion.

" ' You will send the child to see me now and then, Elizabeth ? ' said Mrs. Moss as we retired.

" In the end Mrs. Moss and I became great friends. I put aside my dream among the ' vain fancies ' of life, and took very kindly to the manor in its new aspect. Even the stuffed footman became familiar, and learnt to welcome me with a smile. The real Mrs. Moss was a more agreeable person than I have, I fear, represented her. She had failed to grasp solid happiness in life, because she had chosen with the cowardice of an inferior mind ; but she had borne disappointment with dignity, and submitted to heavy sorrows with patience ; and a greater nature could not have done more. She was the soul of good humour, and the love of small chat, which contrasted so oddly with her fierce appearance, was a fund of entertainment for me, as I fed my imagination and stored my memory with anecdotes of the good old times in the many quiet evenings we spent together. I learnt to love her the more heartily, I confess, when she bought a new gown and gave the *feuille-morte* satin to Mrs. Metcalfe.

" Mrs. Metcalfe was ' humble companion ' to Mrs. Moss. She was in reality single, but she exacted the married title as a point of respect. At the beginning of our acquaintance I called her ' Miss Metcalfe,' and this occasioned the only check our friendship ever received. Now I would, with the greatest of pleasure, have addressed her as ' My Lord Archbishop,' or in any other style to which she was not entitled, it being a matter of profound indifference to me. But the question was a serious one to her, and very serious she made it, till I almost despaired of our ever coming to an understanding on the subject. On every other point she was unassuming almost to nonentity. She was weak-minded, to the verge of mental palsy. She was more benevolent in deed, and more wandering in conversation, than any one I have met with since. That is, in ordinary life. In the greenhouse or garden (with which she and the head gardener alone had any real acquaintance) her accurate and profound knowledge would put to shame many professed garden botanists I have met with since. From her I learnt what little I know of the science of horticulture, and with her I spent many happy hours over the fine botanical works in the manor library.

" And so I became reconciled to things as they were, though to this day I connect with that shade of *feuille-morte* satin a disappointment not to be forgotten.

.      .      .      .      .      .      .      .      .      .

" It is a dull story, is it not, Ida ? " said the little old lady, pausing here. She had not told it in precisely these words, but this was the sum and substance of it.

Ida nodded. Not that she had thought the story dull, so far as she had heard it, and whilst she was awake ; but she had fallen asleep, and so she nodded.

Mrs. Overtheway looked back at the fire, to which, indeed, she had been talking for some time past.

" I was wrong," she thought. " It is a child's story, but the moral is more for me than for her. Perhaps it was too foolish, even to tell—the unreasoning, wilful folly of childhood ; and yet, would that unreasoning, wilful folly belong to childhood alone ! Alas ! my grown-up friends, are there now no passionate, foolish longings, for which we blind ourselves to obvious truth, and of which the vanity does not lessen the disappointment ? Do we not still toil after rosebuds, to find *feuilles-mortes ?* "

No voice answered Mrs. Overtheway's fanciful questions. The hyacinth nodded fragrantly on its stalk, and Ida nodded in her chair. She was fast asleep—happily asleep—with a smile upon her face.

The shadows nodded gently on the walls, and like a shadow the little old lady stole quietly away.

*She was fast asleep—happily asleep—with a smile upon her face*

When Ida awoke, she found herself lying partly in the arm-chair, and partly in the arms of Nurse, who was lifting her up. A candle flared upon the table, by the fire stood an empty chair, and the heavy scent that filled the room was as sweet as the remembrance of past happiness. The little old lady had vanished, and, but for the hyacinth, Ida would almost have doubted whether her visit had not been a dream.

" Has Mrs. Overtheway been long gone, Nursey ? " she asked, keeping her eyes upon the flowerpot.

" Ever so long ! " said Nurse, " and here you've been snoring away, and the old lady's been downstairs, telling me how comfortably you were asleep, and she's coming again to-morrow evening, if you're good."

It was precisely twelve minutes since Mrs. Overtheway left the house, but Nurse was of a slightly exaggerative turn of mind, and few people speak exactly on the subject of time, especially when there is the opportunity of triumphing over some one who has been asleep before bed-time. The condition of Ida's being good was also the work of her own instructive fancy, but Ida caught eagerly at the welcome news of another visit.

" Then she is not angry with me for falling asleep, Nursey ? I was so comfortable, and she has such a nice voice, I couldn't help it ; I think I left off about the pugs. I wish I had a pug with a wrinkled black snout, don't you, Nursey ? "

" I'm sure I don't, Miss Ida. My father kept all sorts of pigs, and we used to have one with a black snout and black spot, but it was as ugly as ugly could be ! and I never could fancy the bacon would be fit to eat. You must have been dreaming, I'm sure ; the old lady would never tell you about such rubbish, I know."

" It's pugs, not pigs, Nursey ; and they're dogs, you know," said Ida, laughing. " How funny you are ! And indeed she did tell me, I couldn't have dreamt it ; I never dreamt anything so nice in my life."

" And never will, most likely," said Nurse, who was very skilful in concluding a subject which she did not want to discuss, and who was apt to do so by a rapid twist in the line of argument, which Ida would find somewhat bewildering. " But, dear Miss Ida," she continued, " do leave off clutching at that chair-arm, when I'm lifting you up, and your eyes'll drop out of your head if you go on staring like that."

Ida relaxed the nervous grasp, to which she had been impelled by her energy on the subject of the pugs, let down her eyebrows, and submitted to be undressed. The least pleasant part of this ceremony may be comprised in the word curl-papers. Ida's hair was dark, and soft, and smooth, but other little girls wore ringlets, and so this little girl must wear ringlets too. To that end, her hair was every night put into curl-papers, with much tight twisting and sharp jerking, and Ida slept upon an irregular layer of small paper parcels, which made pillows a mockery. With all this, however, a damp day, or a good romp, would sometimes undo the night's work, to the great disgust of Nurse. In her last place, the young lady's hair had curled with a damp brush, as Ida well knew, and Nurse made so much of her own grievance, in having to use the curl-papers, that no place was left for Ida's grievance in having to sleep upon them. She submitted this night therefore, as other nights, in patience, and sat swinging her feet and accommodating her head to the sharp tugs, which always seemed to come from unexpected quarters. Perhaps, however, her mind may have been running a little upon grievances, which made her say :

" You know, Nursey, how you are always telling me I ought to be thankful for having things, and not having things, and——"

" I wish you'd talk sense, and not give way with your head so when I pull, Miss Ida," retorted Nurse, " having things, and not having things ; I don't know what you mean."

" Well, you know, Nursey, the other day when I said I didn't like bread and treacle, treacled so long before, and soaked in, and you said I ought to be thankful that I had bread and treacle at all, and that I hadn't a wooden leg, and to eat anything I could get, like the old sailor-man at the corner ; well, do you know, I've thought of something I *am* so thankful for, and that is that I haven't a red screen to my bed."

# THE BAILIFF'S DAUGHTER
# OF ISLINGTON

TRADITIONAL

THERE was a youth, and a well-beloved youth,
And he was a squire's son;
He loved the bailiff's daughter dear
That lived at Islington.

Yet she was coy, and would not believe
That he did love her so;
No, not at any time would she
Any countenance to him show.

But when his friends did understand
His fond and foolish mind,
They sent him up to fair London,
An apprentice for to bind.

And when he had been seven long years,
And never his love could see,
"Many a tear have I shed for her sake,
When she little thought of me."

Then all the maids of Islington
Went forth to sport and play,
All but the bailiff's daughter dear;
She secretly stole away.

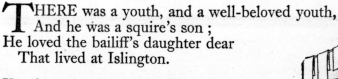

She pulled off her gown of green
And put on ragged attire,
And to fair London she would go
Her true love to inquire.

And, as she went along the high road,
The weather being hot and dry,
She sat her down upon a green bank,
And her true love came riding by.

She started up with a colour so red,
Catching hold of his bridle rein,
" One penny, one penny," she said,
" Will ease me of much pain."

" Before I give you a penny, sweetheart,
Pray tell me where you were born ? "
" At Islington, kind sir," she said,
" Where I have had many a scorn."

" I prythee, sweetheart, tell to me,
Oh tell me whether you know
The bailiff's daughter of Islington ? "
" She is dead, sir, long ago."

" If she be dead, then take my horse,
My saddle and bridle also,
For I will to some far country,
Where no man shall me know."

" Oh stay, oh stay, thou goodly youth,
She standeth by thy side ;
She is here alive, she is not dead,
And ready to be thy bride."

# THE POET'S ADVENTURES

*by* VICTOR HUGO

## CHAPTER I

### THE POET PUZZLED

COLD and penniless, Pierre Gringoire, who thought himself a poet, wandered through the darkening streets of Paris on the 6th of January, 1482. It was the Feast of Fools and all the city was making holiday. Coming at last to the Place de Grève he hastened towards the bonfire which blazed magnificently in the middle. A large assemblage of people formed a circle round it.

. . . . . . . . . . .

" Cursed Parisians ! " said he to himself ; for Gringoire, like a genuine dramatic poet, was addicted to soliloquies ; " there they are, shutting me out from the fire ! And yet I am in need of a comfortable chimney-corner."

On looking more closely he perceived that the circle was much larger than it needed to have been, had the persons composing it been desirous of warming themselves at the king's fire ; and that the assemblage of spectators was not drawn together solely by the beauty of the hundred blazing faggots. In an extensive space left open between the crowd and the fire there was a young female dancing.

Whether this young female was a human being, or a fairy, or an angel, Gringoire, sceptical philosopher and satirical poet as he was, could not at the first moment decide, so completely was he fascinated by the dazzling vision. She was not tall, though she appeared to be so from the slenderness and elegance of her shape. Her complexion was dark, but it was easy to divine that by daylight her skin must have the beautiful golden tint of the Roman and Andalusian women. Her small foot too was Andalusian. She danced, whirled, turned

*Having nothing better to do, Gringoire took it into his head to follow the gipsy girl*

round, on an old Persian carpet, carelessly spread on the pavement ; and every time her radiant face passed before you as she turned, her large black eyes flashed lightning.

Every eye was fixed upon her, every mouth open ; and in truth, while she was thus dancing, what with the sound of the tambourine, which her two plump exquisitely shaped arms held above her head, her bodice of gold without folds, her spotted robe which swelled with the rapidity of her motions, her bare shoulders, her finely turned legs which her petticoat now and then discovered, her black hair, her eyes of flame, she was a supernatural creature.

" Verily," thought Gringoire, " it is a salamander, a nymph, a goddess, a bacchanal of Mount Menalæus ! " At that moment one of the tresses of the salamander's hair got loose, and a piece of brass which had been fastened to it dropped to the ground. " Ha ! no," said he, " 'tis a gipsy ! " The illusion was at an end.

She began dancing again. She picked up from the ground two swords, which she balanced on their points upon her forehead, and made them turn round one way, while she turned the other. She was in fact a gipsy, neither more nor less.

The girl at length paused, panting with her exertions, and the people applauded with enthusiasm.

" Djali ! " said the Bohemian, and up started a pretty little white goat, a nimble, lively, glossy creature, with gilt horns, gilt hoofs, and a gilt collar, which Gringoire had not yet perceived, and which had, till then, been lying at the corner of the carpet watching her mistress dance. " Djali," said the girl, " it is your turn now ; " and seating herself, she gracefully held the tambourine before the animal. " Djali," continued she, " what month are we in ? " The goat raised her fore-leg and struck one stroke upon the tambourine. It was actually the first month. The crowd applauded. " Djali," said the girl, turning the tambourine a different way, " what day of the month is this ? " Djali again raised her little gilt hoof, and struck six blows upon the instrument. " Djali," continued the Egyptian, again changing the position of the tambourine, " what o'clock is it ? " Djali gave seven blows. At that moment the clock of the Maison-aux-Piliers struck seven. The people were astounded.

" There is sorcery at the bottom of this ! " said a sinister voice in the crowd. It was that of a bald man, who never took his eyes off the Bohemian. She shuddered and turned away ; and thunders of applause burst forth and drowned the morose exclamation. They had the effect of effacing it so completely from her mind that she continued to question her goat.

" Djali, show me what Master Guichard Grand Remy, captain of the city pistoleers, does in the Candlemas procession." Djali raised herself on her hind-legs, and began bleating and walking with such comic gravity, that the whole circle of spectators roared with laughter at this parody upon the interested devotion of the captain of the pistoleers.

" Djali," resumed the girl, emboldened by the increasing applause, " show me how Master Jacques Charmolue, the king's attorney in the ecclesiastical court, preaches." The goat sat down on her rump, and began bleating and shaking her fore-paws in such a strange way, that, in gesture, accent, attitude, everything excepting bad French and worse Latin, it was

Jacques Charmolue to the life. The crowd applauded more loudly than ever.

"Sacrilege! profanation!" ejaculated the bald man. The gipsy turned round once more. "Ah!" said she, "it is that odious man!" then, lengthening her lower lip beyond the upper, she gave a pout that seemed to be habitual to her, turned upon her heel, and began to collect the donations of the multitude in her tambourine. Silver and copper coins of all sorts and sizes were showered into it. She came to Gringoire, who so readily thrust his hand into his pocket that she stopped. The poet, fumbling in his pocket, found the reality, that is, nothing. The graceful girl stood still before him, looking at him with her large eyes, and holding out her tambourine. Big drops of perspiration started from Gringoire's brow. If he had had Peru in his pocket, he would certainly have given it to the dancer : but Gringoire had no Peru there, and besides, America was not yet discovered. An unexpected incident luckily relieved him.

"Wilt thou begone, Egyptian grasshopper?" cried a sharp voice, issuing from the darkest corner of the Place. The young girl turned about in alarm. It was not the voice of the bald man ; it was the voice of a female, a devout and spiteful voice. This exclamation, which frightened the gipsy, excited the merriment of a troop of boys who were strolling near the spot. "'Tis the crazy woman in Roland's Tower," cried they, with shouts of laughter ; "'tis Sacky who is scolding. Perhaps she has had no supper. Let us run to the city larder and see if we can get something for her!" And away they scampered to the Maison-aux-Piliers.

Meanwhile, Gringoire had taken advantage of the girl's agitation to sneak off. The shouts of the boys reminded him that he had not supped either. He thought that he too might as well try his luck at the larder. But the young rogues ran too fast for him : when he arrived, everything was cleared away ; there was not a scrap of any kind left.

It is not pleasant to be obliged to go to bed without supper, and still less agreeable to have no bed to go to as well as no supper to eat. So, having nothing better to do, Gringoire took it into his head to follow the gipsy girl at all hazards.

He therefore walked pensively on after the girl, who quickened her pace, and made her pretty little goat trot along by her side, when she saw the shopkeepers retiring to their houses.

The streets, meanwhile, became every moment darker and more deserted. The curfew had long since rung ; and it was only at rare intervals that a passenger was met on the pavement, or a light seen at the windows. Gringoire, in following the Egyptian, had involved himself in that inextricable labyrinth of lanes, and alleys, and cross-ways, surrounding the ancient sepulchre of the Holy Innocents, and which resembles a skein of thread entangled by a playful cat.

He had, by this time, begun to attract the notice of the young girl : she had more than once turned her head and looked at him with some uneasiness ; nay, she had stopped short and taken advantage of a ray of light issuing from the half-open door of a bakehouse, to scrutinise him attentively from head to foot. Gringoire had seen her, after this survey, pout her lip as she had done before, and then she passed on.

This pretty grimace set Gringoire about inquiring what it might denote. It certainly conveyed an expression of disdain and dislike. He began, in consequence, to hang his head, as if to count the stones of the pavement, and to drop farther behind, when, on reaching the corner of a street into which she had turned, he was startled by a piercing shriek. The street was extremely dark; a wick steeped in oil, burning in an iron cage at the foot of the Blessed Virgin, at the angle of the street, nevertheless enabled Gringoire to distinguish the Bohemian struggling in the grasp of two men, who were striving to stifle her cries. The poor little goat, terrified at this attack, drooped her head, presented her horns, and bleated.

*Quasimodo dealt him a back-handed blow that sent him reeling*

"Watch! watch!" shouted Gringoire, boldly advancing. One of the men who held the girl turned upon him. It was the formidable visage of Quasimodo, the hunchback bell-ringer of Notre Dame and new Pope of Fools. Gringoire did not run away, neither did he advance another step. Quasimodo went up to him, and dealt him a back-handed blow, that sent him reeling three or four yards and stretched him sprawling upon the pavement; then, darting back, he caught up the young girl, and bore her off across one of his arms like a silken scarf. His companion followed, and the poor goat ran after the three, bleating in a most plaintive manner.

"Murder! murder!" cried the unfortunate gipsy girl.

"Halt, scoundrels, and let the wench go!" suddenly roared, in a voice of thunder, a horseman who came dashing along out of the next street. It was the captain of the archers of the king's ordnance, armed cap-a-pie, and his drawn sword in his hand. He snatched the Bohemian out of the grasp of the stupefied Quasimodo, laid her across his saddle, and, at the moment when the formidable hunchback, recovering from his surprise, would have rushed upon him to regain his prey, fifteen or sixteen archers, who followed close at the heels of their captain, came up armed with quarter-staves. It was part of a company of the king's ordnance, which did the duty of a counter-watch, by the order of Messire Robert d'Estouteville, keeper of the provosty of Paris.

Quasimodo was surrounded, seized, and bound. He bellowed, he foamed, he kicked, he bit; and had it been daylight, no doubt his face alone, rendered doubly hideous by rage, would have sufficed to scare away the whole detachment; but night disarmed him of his most formidable weapon, his ugliness. His companion had disappeared during the struggle.

The Bohemian gracefully raised herself upon the officer's saddle. Clapping her two hands upon his shoulders, she looked at him intently for a few moments, as if charmed with his handsome face, and grateful for the seasonable succour which he had afforded her. Then, giving a sweeter tone than usual to her sweet voice, she inquired, " What is your name, sir ? "

" Captain Phœbus de Chateaupers, at your service, my dear," replied the officer, drawing himself up to his full height.

" Thank you," said she; and while the captain was turning up his whiskers *à la bourguignonne*, she slid down the horse's side to the ground, and vanished with the swiftness of lightning.


## CHAPTER II

### SEQUEL OF INCONVENIENCES

GRINGOIRE, stunned by his fall, was extended on the pavement before the good Virgin at the corner of the street. By degrees he came to himself. At first he was floating for some minutes in a kind of dreamy reverie, which was rather soothing, though the aerial figures of the Bohemian and her goat were coupled with the weight of the ungentle fist of Quasimodo. This state was of short duration. A painful sensation of cold in that part of his body which was in contact with the pavement suddenly awoke him and recalled his mind to the surface. " Whence comes this cold ? " said he sharply to himself. He then perceived that he was nearly in the middle of the kennel.

" Hang the hunchbacked Cyclop ! " muttered he, and attempted to rise, but he was so stunned and bruised, that he was forced to remain where he was. His hand, however, was at liberty. He held his nose and resigned himself to his fate.

All at once he was assailed by an annoyance of a totally different kind.

A party of boys, of those little bare-legged savages, who have in all ages padded the pavement of Paris by the name of *gamins*, ran towards the spot where Gringoire lay, laughing, and whooping, and hallooing, and caring very little whether they disturbed the neighbourhood or not. They were dragging after them something like an enormous bag; and the mere clattering of their wooden shoes would have been enough to wake the dead. Gringoire, who was not absolutely dead, propped himself up a little to see what was the matter.

" Halloo ! Hennequin Dandeche !—halloo, Jehan Pincebourde," they bawled at the top of their voices, " old Eustache Moubon, the ironmonger at the corner, is just dead. We have got his paillasse and are going to make a bonfire of it ! "

So saying, they threw down the paillasse precisely upon Gringoire, close to whom they had stopped without seeing him. At the same time, one of them took a handful of straw, and went to light it at the Virgin's lamp.

" 'Sdeath ! " grumbled Gringoire, " I am likely to be hot enough presently ! "

Between fire and water he was certainly in a critical situation. He made a supernatural effort, the effort of a coiner who is going to be boiled and strives to escape. He raised himself upon his feet, threw back the paillasse upon the urchins, and hobbled away as fast as he was able.

" Holy Virgin ! " cried the boys, " 'tis the ironmonger's ghost ! " and off they scampered in their turn.

The paillasse was left in possession of the field of battle. Belleforêt, Father Le Juge, and Corrozet relate, that on the following day it was picked up with great pomp by the clergy of the quarter, and carried to the treasure-house of the church of St. Opportune, where the sacristan, down to the year 1789, made a very handsome income with the grand miracle performed by the statue of the Virgin at the corner of the Rue Mauconseil, which had, by its mere presence, in the memorable night between the 6th and the 7th of January, 1482, exorcised the spirit of Jehan Moubon, which, to play the devil a trick, had when he died maliciously hid itself in his paillasse.

## CHAPTER III

### THE BROKEN JUG

AFTER running for some time as fast as his legs would carry him, our poet stopped short, in the first place for want of breath, and in the next collared, as it were, by a dilemma, which just occurred to his mind.—" It seemeth to me, Master Pierre Gringoire," said he to himself, clapping his finger to the side of his nose, " that you are running about like a blockhead. The young rogues were not a whit less afraid of you than you of them. It seemeth to me, I tell you, that you heard their wooden shoes clattering off to the south, while you are scudding away to the north. Now, either they have run away, and then the paillasse, which they have no doubt left behind in their fright, is precisely the hospitable bed, for which you have been running about ever since morning, and which the Virgin, blessed be her name ! miraculously sends to reward you for having composed in honour of her a morality accompanied by triumphs and mummeries : or, the boys have not run away ; in that case they have set fire to the paillasse ; and a good fire is the very thing you want to warm, to dry, and to cheer you. In either case, a good fire, or a good bed, the paillasse is a gift of Heaven. It was perhaps for this very reason that the Virgin at the corner of the Rue Mauconseil caused the death of Jehan Moubon ; and it is stupid of you to run your legs off in this manner, like a Picard from a Frenchman, leaving behind what you are seeking before you. You are a fool for your pains."

He turned, and, with eyes and ears on the alert, strove to steer his way back to the lucky paillasse, but in vain. His course was incessantly checked by intersections of houses, blind alleys, spots where several streets terminated, and where he was forced to pause in doubt and hesitation, more perplexed and more entangled in the intricacies of those dark narrow lanes and courts than he would have been in the maze of the Hôtel de Tournelles itself.

At length a kind of reddish light which he perceived at the extremity of a long narrow lane helped to cheer his spirits. " God be praised ! " said he, " yonder it is. Yonder is my paillasse burning ! "

Before he had proceeded many steps down the long lane, which was sloping and unpaved, and which became more and more muddy the farther he went, he perceived something that had a most extraordinary appearance. Here and there, all the way along it, crawled a number of indistinct and shapeless masses, proceeding towards the light at the bottom of the lane.

Nothing makes a man so adventurous as an empty pocket. Gringoire continued to advance, and soon came up with the hindmost of these strange figures, which was leisurely wriggling itself along after the others. On a near approach, he perceived that it was only a wretched cripple in a bowl, who was hopping along upon both hands. At the moment when he was passing this species of spider with human face, it accosted him in a lamentable tone : " *La buona mancia, signor ! la buona mancia !* "

" The devil fetch thee," said Gringoire, " and me along with thee, if I know what thou meanest ! " And he walked on.

He overtook another of these moving masses. This was a cripple too—a man who had suffered such mutilation in legs and arms that the complicated system of crutches and wooden legs by which he was supported gave him the appearance of a walking scaffold. Gringoire, who was fond of lofty and classic comparisons, likened him in imagination to the living tripod of Vulcan.

This living tripod took off its hat to him as he passed, but held it up under Gringoire's chin, like a barber's basin, at the same time bawling in his ear, " *Señor caballero, para comprar un pedaso de pan !* "

" This fellow," said Gringoire, " seems to be talking too ; but 'tis an odd language, and he must be cleverer than I am if he understands it."

He would have quickened his pace, but, for the third time, something obstructed the way. This something, or rather this somebody, was a little blind man, with Jewish face and long beard, who, rowing on in the space around him with a stick, and towed by a great dog, sang out with nasal twang and Hungarian accent, " *Facitote caritatem.*"

" Come," said Pierre Gringoire, " here is one at last who speaks a Christian language. I must have a most benevolent look for people to ask charity of me, in this manner, in the present meagre state of my purse. " My friend," continued he, turning towards the blind man, " it is not a week since I sold my last shirt, or, as you understand no language but Cicero's, *Vendidi hebdomade nuper transitâ meam ultimam chemisam.*"

This said, he turned his back on the blind man, and pursued his way. At the same time, however, the blind man quickened his pace, and in a trice, up came the two cripples, in great haste, with a tremendous clatter of bowl and crutches upon the pavement. All three, jostling each other at the heels of poor Gringoire, opened upon him at once.

" *Caritatem !* " sang the blind man.

" *La buona mancia !* " sang the man of the bowl.

The other cripple joined in the concert with, " *Un pedaso de pan !* "

Gringoire stopped his ears. " O tower of Babel ! " exclaimed he.

He began to run for it. The blind man ran. The man of the bowl ran. The man with wooden legs ran. Presently he was surrounded by halt, and lame, and blind, by one-armed and one-eyed, and lepers with their hideous sores, some issuing from houses, others from the adjoining courts, and others from cellars, howling, bellowing, yelping, hobbling, rushing towards the light, and bedraggled with mire, like snails after a shower.

Gringoire, still followed by his three persecutors, and not knowing what to think of the matter, walked on in some alarm amidst the others, turning aside, and passing the cripples on crutches, stepping over the heads of those in bowls, and entangled in this crowd of limping, shuffling wretches, like the English captain who found himself suddenly surrounded by a prodigious host of land-crabs.

The idea occurred to him to try to return. But it was too late. The whole legion had closed behind him, and his three mendicants stuck to him like bird-lime. He proceeded, therefore, propelled at once by this irresistible tide, by fear, and by a dizziness, which made the whole scene appear to him like a horrible dream.

At length he reached the extremity of the lane. It opened into a spacious place, where a thousand scattered lights flickered in the confused haze of night. Gringoire pursued his way into it, hoping by the lightness of his heels to escape from the three infirm spectres who stuck so closely to him.

" *Onde vas hombre?* " cried the cripple upon crutches, throwing them down, and running after him on two as goodly legs as ever stepped upon the pavement of Paris. At the same moment the other cripple, standing bolt upright upon his feet, clapped his heavy bowl cased with iron upon Gringoire's head, by way of cap ; and the blind man stared him in the face with a pair of flaming eyes.

" Where am I ? " cried the affrighted poet.

" In the Cour des Miracles," replied a fourth spectre, who had joined them.

" Miracles, upon my soul ! " rejoined Gringoire, " for here are blind who see and lame who run."

A sinister laugh was their only answer.

The poor poet cast his eyes around him. He was actually in that dreaded Cour des Miracles, into which no honest man had ever penetrated at such an hour, a magic circle, in which the officers of the Châtelet and the sergeants of the provost, who ventured within it, were disposed of in a trice ; the haunt of thieves ; a hideous wen on the face of Paris ; a sewer disgorging every morning and receiving every night that fetid torrent of vice, mendicity, and roguery, which always overflows the streets of great capitals ; a monstrous hive, to which all the drones of the social order retired at night with their booty ; the hospital of imposture, where the gipsy, the unfrocked monk, the ruined scholar, the blackguards of all nations, Spaniards, Italians, Germans, of all religions, Jews, Christians, Mahometans, idolaters, covered with painted wounds, beggars by day, transmogrified themselves into banditti at night ; immense robing-room, in short, whither all the actors of that eternal comedy which theft and murder are performing in the streets of Paris, resorted at that period to dress and to undress.

It was a spacious area, irregular, and ill-paved, like all the open places of Paris in those days. Fires, around which swarmed strange-looking groups, were blazing here and there. All was bustle, confusion, uproar. Coarse laughter, the crying of children, the voices of women, were intermingled. The hands and heads of this multitude, black upon a luminous ground, were making a thousand antic gestures.

A dog which looked like a man, or a man who looked like a dog, might be seen from time to time passing over the place on which trembled the reflection of the fires, interspersed with broad ill-defined shadows. The limits between races and species seemed to be done away with in this city, as in a pandemonium. Men, women, brutes, age, sex, health, disease, all seemed to be in common among these people. They were jumbled, huddled together, laid upon one another ; each there partook of everything.

The faint and flickering light of the fires enabled Gringoire to distinguish, in spite of his agitation, all round the immense place a

*He was surrounded by halt, and lame, and blind*

hideous circumference of old houses, the decayed, worm-eaten, ruinous fronts of which, each perforated by one or two small lighted windows, appeared to him in the dark like enormous heads of old hags ranged in a circle, watching the witches' sabbath rites and winking their eyes. It was like a new world, unknown, unheard of, deformed, creeping, crawling, fantastic.

Gringoire—more and more terrified ; held by the three mendicants as by three vices ; deafened by a crowd of other faces bleating and barking around him—the unlucky Gringoire strove to rally his presence of mind, and to recollect whether it was Saturday or not. But his efforts were vain : the thread of his memory and of his thoughts was broken, and, doubting everything, floating between what he saw and what he felt, he asked himself this puzzling question : " If I am, can this be ? if this is, can I be ? "

At this moment a distinct shout arose from amidst the buzzing crowd by which he was surrounded : " Lead him to the king ! lead him to the king ! "

" Holy Virgin ! " muttered Gringoire—" the king of this place !—why, he can be nothing but a goat."

" To the king ! to the king ! " repeated every voice.

He was hurried away. The rabble rushed to lay hands on him, but the three mendicants held him fast in their grip, tearing him away from the others, and bawling, " He is ours ! " The poet's doublet, previously in wretched plight, was utterly ruined in this struggle.

While crossing the horrible place, the vertigo which had confused his senses was dispelled. He had taken but a few steps before a conviction of the reality flashed upon him. He began to become used to the atmosphere of the place. The Cour des Miracles was in fact nothing but a tavern, but a tavern for ruffians, quite as much stained with blood as with wine.

Around a great fire which burned upon a large circular hearth, and the flames of which rose among the red-hot bars of a trevet unoccupied at the moment, sundry crazy tables were placed here and there at random; for the waiter had not deigned to study geometrical symmetry in their arrangement, or to take care at least that they should not intersect each other at too unusual angles. On these tables shone pots flowing with wine and beer, and round these pots were grouped a great many jolly faces, empurpled by the fire and by drink. Here a man, with huge paunch and jovial phiz, was whistling, the while he took off the bandages from a false wound, and removed the wrappers from a sound and vigorous knee, which had been swathed ever since morning in a dozen ligatures.

A large dog was seated on his haunches, looking at the fire. Young children were present at these orgies. A stolen boy was crying bitterly. Another, a stout fellow, about four years old, was sitting on a high bench, dangling his legs at the table, which reached up to his chin, and saying not a word. A third was gravely spreading with his finger the melted tallow which ran from a candle upon the table. The last, a little urchin, crouching in the dirt, was almost lost in a kettle, which he was scraping with a tile, and from which he was extracting sounds that would have thrown Stradivarius into a swoon.

Near the fire stood a hogshead, and upon this hogshead was seated a mendicant. This was the king upon his throne. The three vagabonds who held Gringoire led him before the hogshead, and for a moment the whole motley assemblage was silent, excepting the kettle inhabited by the boy. Gringoire durst not breathe or raise his eyes.

"*Hombre, quita tu sombrero*," said one of the three fellows in whose clutches he was, and, before he knew what was meant, one of the others took off his hat—a shabby covering, it is true, but still useful either against sun or rain. Gringoire sighed.

"What varlet have we here?" asked the king. Gringoire shuddered. He raised his eyes. It was Clopin Trouillefou himself, the most rascally beggar in Paris.

Clopin Trouillefou, invested with the insignia of royalty, had not a rag more or a rag less than usual. The sore on his arm had disappeared. He held in his hand one of the whips composed of thongs of white leather, which were used by the vergers in those days to keep back the crowd. On his head he wore a cap of such peculiar form that it was difficult to tell whether it was a child's biggin or a king's crown—so much are the two things alike.

"Mark me!" cried he. "Thou art in the presence of three mighty sovereigns: myself, Clopin Trouillefou, King of Thunes, and supreme ruler of the realm of Slang; Mathias Hunyadi Spicali, Duke of Egypt and Bohemia, that sallow old crone whom thou seest yonder, with a clout round his head; and Guillaume Rousseau, Emperor of Galilee, the porpoise who is too busy with his neighbour to attend to us. We are thy judges. Thou has entered our territories without being one of our subjects; thou hast violated the privileges of our city. Thou must be punished, unless thou art a prig, a cadger, or a stroller—or, to use the gibberish of those who call themselves honest people, a thief, a beggar, or a vagrant. Art thou any of these? justify thyself: state thy qualities."

"Alas!" sighed Gringoire, "I have not that honour. I am the author——"

"Enough!" exclaimed Trouillefou, without suffering him to proceed. "Thou shalt be hanged. And quite right too, messieurs honest citizens! As you deal by our people among you so we will deal by yours among us. The law which you make for the Vagabonds, the Vagabonds will enforce with you. 'Tis your fault if it is a harsh one. It is but proper that an honest man should now and then be seen grinning through a hempen collar—that makes the thing honourable. Come, my friend, divide thy rags with a good grace among these wenches. I will have thee hanged to amuse the Vagabonds, and thou shalt give them thy purse to drink. If thou has any mummery to make, go down into the cellar; there is a capital crucifix in stone, which we picked up at St. Pierre-aux-Bœufs. Thou hast four minutes to settle the affairs of thy soul."

This was an alarming announcement.

"Well said, upon my life! Clopin Trouillefou preaches like his holiness the Pope," cried the Emperor of Galilee, breaking his pot to prop up his table.

"Most puissant emperors and kings," said Gringoire quite coolly—I never could make out how he recovered sufficient firmness to talk so resolutely—" you cannot mean what you say. My name is Pierre Gringoire; I am the poet, whose morality was represented this morning in the great hall of the palace."

"Oho! master!" said Clopin. "I was there too. But, comrade, because we were annoyed by thee in the morning, is that any reason why thou shouldst not be hung to-night?"

"I shall be puzzled to get myself out of this scrape," thought Gringoire. He made nevertheless another effort.

"I do not see," said he, "why poets should not be classed among the vagabonds. Æsop was a vagabond, Homer a beggar, Mercury a thief."

Clopin interrupted him. "I verily believe thou thinkest to bamboozle us with thy palaver. 'Sdeath! as thou must be hanged, make no more ado."

"Pardon me, most illustrious King of Thunes," replied Gringoire, disputing the ground inch by inch; "is it worth while—only one moment —you will not condemn me unheard——"

His voice was absolutely drowned by the uproar which prevailed around him. The little urchin continued to scrape his kettle with greater energy than ever; and, to mend the matter, an old woman had just placed on the red-hot trevet a frying-pan full of fat, which yelped and cackled over the fire, like a dog that has been pipe-tailed by a troop of mischievous boys.

Clopin Trouillefou appeared to be conferring for a moment with the Duke of Egypt, and the Emperor of Galilee, who was quite drunk. He then cried out sharply, " Silence, there ! " and, as the kettle and the frying-pan paid no attention to him, but continued their duet, he leaped from his hogshead, gave one kick to the kettle, which rolled away with the boy to the distance of ten paces, and another to the frying-pan, which upset all the fat into the fire. He then gravely reascended his throne, caring no more for the smothered crying of the child than for the grumbling of the hag, whose supper had gone off in a blaze.

Trouillefou made a sign, and the duke, the emperor, and the high dignitaries of the kingdom of Cant ranged themselves around him in a semi-circle, the centre of which was occupied by Gringoire, who was still held fast by his captors. It was a semi-circle of rags and tatters and tinsel, of forks and hatchets, of bare brawny arms and legs, of squalid, bloated, stupid-looking faces. In the middle of this round-table of ragamuffins Clopin Trouillefou, like the doge of this senate, like the chief of this clan, like the pope of this conclave, overawed, in the first place by the whole height of his hogshead, and in the next by a certain haughty, ferocious, and formidable look, which made his eye sparkle, and corrected the bestial type of the vagabond race in his savage profile. You would have taken him for a wild boar among domestic swine.

*He leaped from his hogshead and gave one kick to the kettle*

"Fellow," said he to Gringoire, stroking his deformed chin with his horny hand, " I see no reason why thou shouldst not be hanged. Thou seemest, indeed, to have a dislike to it, but that is natural enough ; you citizens are not used to it. You have too frightful an idea of the thing. After all, we mean thee no harm. There is one way to get out of the scrape for the moment. Wilt thou be one of us ? "

The reader may conceive what effect this proposition must have produced upon Gringoire, who saw that he had no chance of saving his life, and began to make up his mind to the worst. He caught eagerly at the proposed alternative.

" Certainly, most assuredly I will," said he.

" Thou consentest," rejoined Clopin, " to enrol thyself among the men of Slang ? "

" The men of Slang, decidedly so," answered Gringoire.

" Thou acknowledgest thyself one of the crew ? " proceeded the King of Thunes.

" One of the crew."

" A subject of the kingdom of Cant ? "

" Of the kingdom of Cant."

" A Vagabond ? "

" A Vagabond."

" With all thy soul ? "

" With all my soul."

" Take notice," said the king, " thou shalt nevertheless be hanged."

" The devil ! " ejaculated the poet.

" Only," continued Clopin, with imperturbable gravity, " thou shalt be hanged not quite so soon and with more ceremony, at the cost of the good city of Paris, on a fair stone gibbet, and by the hands of honest men. That is some consolation."

" As you say," replied Gringoire.

" There are some other advantages which thou wilt enjoy. As one of the crew, thou wilt not have to pay rates, either for lamp, scavenger, or poor, to which the honest burgesses of Paris are liable."

" Be it so ! " said the poet. " I am a Vagabond, a subject of the kingdom of Cant, one of the crew, a man of Slang, anything you please ; nay, I was all these before, august King of Thunes, for I am a philosopher ; *et omnia in philosophia, omnes in philosopho continentur*, you know."

The august King of Thunes knitted his brow. " What do you take me for, my friend ? What Hungary Jew gibberish are you talking now ? I know nothing of Hebrew."

At length King Clopin became somewhat more calm. " Knave," said he to our poet, " thou has a mind then to be a Vagabond ? "

" Undoubtedly," replied Gringoire.

" 'Tis not enough to have a mind," said his surly majesty ; " goodwill puts not one more onion into the soup. To be admitted into our brotherhood, thou must prove that thou art fit for something. Show us thy skill at picking a pocket."

" Anything you please," said the poet.

Clopin made a sign. Several of the Vagabonds left the circle, and presently returned. They brought two poles, each having a flat horizontal piece of wood fastened at the lower extremity, upon which it stood upright on the ground. Into the upper ends of these two poles the bearers fitted a cross-bar, and the whole then formed a very handy portable gibbet, which Gringoire had the satisfaction to see set up before his face in a trice. Nothing was wanting, not even the cord, which dangled gracefully from the cross-bar.

" What are they about now ? " said Gringoire to himself, while his heart sank within him. A tinkling of small bells put an end to his anxiety. It was the figure of a man, a kind of scarecrow, in a red dress, so profusely bestudded with little bells that they would have sufficed for the caparison of thirty Castilian mules, which the Vagabonds were suspending by the neck from the rope. The chatter of these thousand bells, occasioned by the swinging of the rope, gradually subsided, and at length ceased entirely with the motion of the effigy.

Clopin pointed to a crazy stool placed under the figure. " Get upon that ! " said he to Gringoire.

Gringoire mounted the stool, and, after some oscillations of head and arms, recovered his centre of gravity.

" Now," continued the King of Thunes, " cross thy right leg over the left and stand on tiptoe."

" *Morbleu !* " cried Gringoire, " then you absolutely insist on it that I shall break some of my limbs ? "

Clopin shook his head. " Hark ye, my friend, thou talkest too much for me. In two words this is what thou hast to do. Thou must stand on tiptoe as I tell thee, so as to reach the pocket of the figure. Thou must take out a purse that is in it, and if thou canst do this without making any of the bells speak, 'tis well : thou shalt be a Vagabond. We shall then have nothing to do but to baste thee soundly for a week or so."

" *Ventre Dieu !* " exclaimed Gringoire. " And if the bells should give mouth in spite of me ? "

" Why, then thou shalt be hanged ; dost thou comprehend me ? "

" Not at all," answered Gringoire.

" Well then I tell thee once more. Thou must pick the pocket of that figure of a purse, and if a single bell stirs, while thou art about it, thou shalt be hanged. Dost thou understand that ? "

" I do," said Gringoire. " And then ? "

" If thou art clever enough to prig the purse without setting the bells a-chattering, thou art a Canter, and shalt be soundly thrashed every now and then for a week."

" But what better shall I be ? Hanged in one case, beaten in the other ? "

" And a Canter ! " rejoined Clopin, " a Canter ! Is that nothing ? It is for thy own benefit that we shall beat thee, to enure to blows."

" Many thanks to you ! " replied the poet.

" Come, bear a hand ! " said the king, stamping upon his hogshead, which sounded like a big drum. " To thy task, knave ! And recollect, if I hear but a single bell, thou shalt change places with that figure."

The crew applauded Clopin's words, and ranged themselves in a circle round the gallows, with so pitiless a laugh that Gringoire saw he amused them too much not to have to fear the worst from them. The only hope he had left was the most precarious chance of succeeding in the ticklish task imposed upon him. Before he set about it, he addressed a fervent prayer to the effigy which he was going to rob, and which he would have softened as easily as the Vagabonds. The myriad of bells with their little copper tongues, seemed to him so many gaping jaws of serpents, ready to bite and to hiss.

" Oh ! " said he aside, " is it possible that my life depends on the slightest vibration of the smallest of these bells ? " He tried the effect of a last effort on Trouillefou. " And if there should come a gust of wind ? "

" Thou shalt be hanged," replied the King of Thunes, without hesitation.

Finding that there was neither respite, nor reprieve, nor any possible evasion for him, he went resolutely to work. Crossing his right leg over the left, and raising himself on tiptoe, he stretched out his arm ; but, at the moment when he touched the effigy, he found himself tottering upon the stool which had but three legs : he lost his balance, mechanically caught at the figure, and fell plump on the ground, stunned by the fatal jingle of the thousand bells of the figure, which, yielding to the impulsion of his hand, at first turned round upon itself, and then swung majestically between the two poles.

"*Sacré!*" cried he as he fell, and he lay like one dead, with his face towards the ground. He heard, however, the horrid chime above his head, the diabolical laugh of the Canters, and the voice of Trouillefou, who said, "Pick up the varlet, and hang him out of hand."

He rose. They had already taken down the effigy to make room for him. The Vagabonds made him once more mount the stool. Clopin stepped up to him, put the rope about his neck, and patting him on the shoulder : "Farewell, my friend!" said he. "Thou canst not escape now, even with the devil's luck and thine own."

He stopped short, as if a sudden thought had occurred to him. "Wait a moment!" said he, "I forgot. It is customary with us not to hang a blade, till the women have been asked whether any of them will have him. Comrade, this is thy last chance."

Gringoire breathed once more. It was the second time that he had come to life within the last half-hour. He durst not, therefore, place much reliance upon this reprieve.

Clopin again mounted his hogshead. "This way, gentlewomen!" cried he. "Is there any among you who will have this knave? Come forward and see! A husband for nothing! Who wants one?"

Gringoire, in this wretched plight, looked far from tempting. The female mumpers showed no eagerness to accept the offer. The unhappy man heard them answer one after another, "No, no, hang him, and that will be a pleasure for us all."

Three of them, however, stepped forward from among the crowd to take a look at him. The first was a strapping broad-faced wench. She closely examined the deplorable doublet and the threadbare frock of the philosopher. She shrugged her shoulders. "Queer toggery!" grumbled she. Then turning to Gringoire : "Where is thy cloak?"—"I have lost it," answered he. "Thy hat?"—"They have taken it from me."—"Thy shoes?"—"They are nearly worn out."—"Thy purse?"—"Alas!" stammered Gringoire, "I have not a *denier* left."—"Hang then, and be thankful!" replied the wench, turning on her heel and striding away.

The second, an old wrinkled hag, dark, and hideously ugly, walked round Gringoire. He almost trembled lest she should take a fancy to him. At length she muttered to herself, "He is as lean as a carrion," and away she went.

The third was young, fresh-looking, and not ill-favoured. "Save me!" said the poor poet to her in a low tone. She surveyed him for a moment with a look of pity, cast down her eyes, twitched her petticoat, and stood for a moment undecided. He narrowly watched all her motions. It was the last glimmer of hope. "No," said she at last ; "no ; Guillaume Longjoue would beat me," and she rejoined the crowd.

"Comrade," said Clopin, "thou art unlucky." Then standing up on his hogshead, "Will nobody bid?" cried he, imitating the manner of an auctioneer, to the high diversion of the crew. "Will nobody bid? once, twice, three times!" and then turning to the gallows, with a nod of the head, "Gone!"

At that moment cries of "La Esmeralda! La Esmeralda!" arose among the Vagabonds. Gringoire shuddered, and turned the way from which the clamour proceeded. The crowd opened and made way for a bright and dazzling figure. It was the gipsy girl.

"La Esmeralda!" ejaculated Gringoire, struck, amidst his agitation, at the sudden manner in which that magic name connected his scattered recollections of the events of the day. This extraordinary creature appeared by her fascination and beauty to exercise sovereign sway over the Cours des Miracles itself. Its inmates of both sexes respectfully drew back for her to pass, and at sight of her their brutal faces assumed a softer expression. With light step she approached the sufferer. Her pretty Djali followed at her heels. Gringoire was more dead than alive. She eyed him for a moment in silence.

"Are you going to hang this man?" said she gravely to Clopin.

"Yes, sister," replied the King of Thunes, "unless thou wilt take him for thy husband."

Her lower lip was protruded into the pretty pout already described.

"I will take him," said she

"I will take him," said she.

Gringoire was now thoroughly convinced that he had been in a dream ever since morning, and that this was but a continuation of it. The noose was removed, the poet was dismounted from the stool, on which he was obliged to sit down, so vehement was his agitation.

The Duke of Egypt, without uttering a word, brought an earthenware jug. The gipsy girl handed it to Gringoire. "Drop it on the ground," said she to him. The jug broke into four pieces.

"Brother," said the Duke of Egypt, placing a hand upon the head of each, "she is thy wife. Sister, he is thy husband. For four years. Go."

# BEING NEIGHBOURLY

### *by* LOUISA M. ALCOTT

"WHAT in the world are you going to do now, Jo?" asked Meg, one snowy afternoon, as her sister came clumping through the hall, in rubber boots, old sack and hood, with a broom in one hand and a shovel in the other.

"Going out for exercise," answered Jo, with a mischievous twinkle in her eyes.

"I should think two long walks this morning would have been enough. It's cold and dull out, and I advise you to stay, warm and dry, by the fire, as I do," said Meg, with a shiver.

"Never take advice; can't keep still all day, and not being a pussy-cat, I don't like to doze by the fire. I like adventures, and I'm going to find some."

Meg went back to toast her feet, and read *Ivanhoe*, and Jo began to dig paths with great energy. The snow was light; and with her broom she soon swept a path all round the garden for Beth to walk in when the sun came out, and the invalid dolls needed air. Now the garden separated the Marches' house from that of Mr. Laurence; both stood in a suburb of the city, which was still country-like, with groves and lawns, large gardens and quiet streets. A low hedge parted the two estates. On one side was an old brown house, looking rather bare and shabby, robbed of the vines that in summer covered its walls, and the flowers which then surrounded it. On the other side was a stately stone mansion, plainly betokening every sort of comfort and luxury, from the big coach-house and well-kept grounds to the conservatory, and the glimpses of lovely things one caught between the rich curtains. Yet it seemed a lonely lifeless sort of house; for no children frolicked on the lawn, no motherly face ever smiled at the windows, and few people went in and out, except the old gentleman and his grandson.

To Jo's lively fancy, this fine house seemed a kind of enchanted palace, full of splendours and delights, which no one enjoyed. She had long wanted to behold these hidden glories, and to know the "Laurence boy," who looked as if he would like to be known, if he only knew how to begin. Since the party, she had been more eager than ever, and had planned many ways of making friends with him; but he had not been lately seen, and Jo began to think he had gone away, when she one day spied a brown face at an upper window, looking wistfully down into their garden, where Beth and Amy were snowballing one another.

"That boy is suffering for society and fun," she said to herself. "His grandpa don't know what's good for him, and keeps him shut up all alone. He needs a lot of jolly boys to play with, or somebody young and lively. I've a great mind to go over and tell the old gentleman so."

The idea amused Jo, who liked to do daring things, and was always scandalising Meg by her queer performances. The plan of "going over" was not forgotten; and when the snowy afternoon came, Jo resolved to try what could be done. She saw Mr. Laurence drive off, and then sallied out to dig her way down to the hedge, where she paused and took a survey. All quiet; curtains down at the lower windows; servants out of sight, and nothing human visible but a curly black head leaning on a thin hand at the upper window.

"There he is," thought Jo; "poor boy! all alone, and sick, this dismal day! It's a shame! I'll toss up a snowball, and make him look out, and then say a kind word to him."

Up went a handful of soft snow, and the head turned at once, showing a face which lost its listless look in a minute, as the big eyes brightened and the mouth began to smile. Jo nodded, and laughed, and flourished her broom as she called out:

"How do you do? Are you sick?"

Laurie opened the window and croaked out, as hoarsely as a raven:

"Better, thank you. I've had a horrid cold, and been shut up a week."

"I'm sorry. What do you amuse yourself with?"

"Nothing; it's as dull as tombs up here."

"Don't you read?"

"Not much; they won't let me."

"Can't somebody read to you?"

"Grandpa does, sometimes; but my books don't interest him, and I hate to ask Brooke all the time."

"Have some one come and see you, then."

"There isn't any one I'd like to see. Boys make such a row, and my head is weak."

"Isn't there some nice girl who'd read and amuse you? Girls are quiet, and like to play nurse."

"Don't know any."

" You know me," began Jo, then laughed, and stopped.

" So I do. Will you come, please ? " cried Laurie.

" I'm not quiet and nice ; but I'll come, if mother will let me. I'll go and ask her. Shut the window like a good boy, and wait till I come."

With that Jo shouldered her broom and marched into the house, wondering what they would all say to her. Laurie was in a little flutter of excitement at the idea of having company, and flew about to get ready ; for, as Mrs. March said, he was " a little gentleman," and did honour to the coming guest by brushing his curly pate, putting on a fresh collar, and trying to tidy up the room, which, in spite of half a dozen servants, was anything but neat. Presently there came a loud ring, then a decided voice, asking for " Mr. Laurie," and a surprised-looking servant came running up to announce a young lady.

" All right, show her up ; it's Miss Jo," said Laurie, going to the door of his little parlour to meet Jo, who appeared, looking rosy and kind, and quite at ease, with a covered dish in one hand and Beth's three kittens in the other.

" Here I am, bag and baggage," she said briskly. " Mother sent her love, and was glad if I could do anything for you. Meg wanted me to bring some of her blanc-mange ; she makes it very nice ; and Beth thought her cats would be comforting. I knew you'd shout at them, but I couldn't refuse, she was so anxious to do something."

It so happened that Beth's funny loan was just the thing ; for, in laughing over the kits, Laurie forgot his bashfulness and grew sociable at once.

" That looks too pretty to eat," he said, smiling with pleasure as Jo uncovered the dish and showed the blanc-mange surrounded by a garland of green leaves and the scarlet flowers of Amy's pet geranium.

" It isn't anything, only they all felt kindly and wanted to show it. Tell the girl to put it away for your tea ; it's so simple, you can eat it ; and being soft, it will slip down without hurting your sore throat. What a cosy room this is ! "

" It might be, if it was kept nice ; but the maids are lazy, and I don't know how to make them mind. It worries me, though."

" I'll right it up in two minutes ; for it only needs to have the hearth brushed, so—and the things stood straight on the mantelpiece, so—and the books put here, and the bottles there, and your sofa turned from the light, and the pillows plumped up a bit. Now, then, you're fixed."

And so he was ; for, as she laughed and talked, Jo had whisked things into place, and given quite a different air to the room. Laurie watched her in respectful silence ; and, when she beckoned him to his sofa, he sat down with a sigh of satisfaction, saying gratefully :

" How kind you are ! Yes, that's what it wanted. Now, take the big chair, and let me do something to amuse my company."

" No ; I came to amuse you. Shall I read aloud ? " and Jo looked affectionately towards some inviting books nearby.

" Thank you ; I have read all those, and, if you don't mind, I'd rather talk," answered Laurie.

" Not a bit ; I'll talk all day if you'll only set me going. Beth says I never know when to stop."

" Is Beth the rosy one who stays at home a good deal, and sometimes goes out with a little basket ? " asked Laurie with interest.

" Yes, that's Beth ; she's my girl, and a regular good one she is, too."

" The pretty one is Meg, and the curly-haired one is Amy, I believe ? "

" How did you find that out ? "

Laurie coloured up, but answered frankly :

" Why, you see, I often hear you calling to one another, and when I'm alone up here, I can't help looking over at your house, you always seem to be having such good times. I beg your pardon for being so rude, but sometimes you forget to put down the curtain at the window where the flowers are ; and, when the lamps are lighted, it's like looking at a picture to see the fire, and you all round the table with your mother ; her face is right opposite, and it looks so sweet behind the flowers, I can't help watching it. I haven't got any mother, you know," and Laurie poked the fire to hide a little twitching of the lips that he could not control.

The solitary, hungry look in his eyes went straight to Jo's warm heart. She had been so simply taught that there was no nonsense in her head, and at fifteen she was as innocent and frank as any child. Laurie was sick and lonely, and, feeling how rich she was in home-love and happiness, she gladly tried to share it with him. Her brown face was very friendly, and her sharp voice unusually gentle, as she said :

" We'll never draw that curtain any more, and I give you leave to look as much as you like. I just wish, though, instead of peeping, you'd come over and see us. Mother is so splendid, she'd do you heaps of good, and Beth would sing to you if *I* begged her to, and Amy would dance ; Meg and I would make you laugh over our funny stage properties, and we'd have jolly times. Wouldn't your grandpa let you ? "

" I think he would, if your mother asked him. He's very kind, though he don't look it ; and he lets me do what I like pretty much, only he's afraid I might be a bother to strangers," began Laurie, brightening.

" We ain't strangers—we are neighbours ; and you needn't think you'd be a bother. We *want* to know you, and I've been trying to do it this ever so long. We haven't been here a great while, you know, but we have got acquainted with all our neighbours but you."

" You see, grandpa lives among his books, and don't mind much what happens outside. Mr. Brooke, my tutor, don't stay here, you know, and I have no one to go round with me, so I just stop at home and get on as I can."

" That's bad ; you ought to make a dive, and go visiting everywhere you are asked ; then you'll have lots of friends, and pleasant places to go to. Never mind being bashful ; it won't last long if you keep going."

Laurie turned red again, but wasn't offended at being accused of bashfulness ; for there was so much goodwill in Jo, it was impossible not to take her blunt speeches as kindly as they were meant.

" Do you like your school ? " asked the boy, changing the subject, after a little pause, during which he stared at the fire, and Jo looked about her well pleased.

" Don't go to school ; I'm a business man—girl, I mean. I go to wait on my aunt, and a dear, cross old soul she is, too," answered Jo.

Laurie opened his mouth to ask another question; but remembering just in time that it wasn't manners to make too many inquiries into people's affairs, he shut it again, and looked uncomfortable. Jo liked his good breeding, and didn't mind having a laugh at Aunt March, so she gave him a lively description of the fidgety old lady, her fat poodle, the parrot that talked Spanish, and the library where she revelled. Laurie enjoyed that immensely; and when she told him about the prim old gentleman who came once to woo Aunt March, and, in the middle of a fine speech how Poll had tweaked his wig off, to his great dismay, the boy lay back and laughed till the tears ran down his cheeks, and a maid popped her head in to see what was the matter.

*" We ain't strangers—we are neighbours "*

"Oh! that does me lots of good; tell on, please!" he said, taking his face out of the sofa cushion, red and shining with merriment.

Much elated with her success, Jo did "tell on," all about their plays and plans, their hopes and fears for father, and the most interesting events of the little world in which the sisters lived. Then they got to talking about books; and to Jo's delight she found that Laurie loved them as well as she did, and had read even more than herself.

"If you like them so much, come down and see ours. Grandpa is out, so you needn't be afraid," said Laurie, getting up.

"I'm not afraid of anything," returned Jo, with a toss of her head.

"I don't believe you are!" exclaimed the boy, looking up at her with much admiration, though he privately thought she would have good reason to be a trifle afraid of the old gentleman if she met him in some of his moods.

The atmosphere of the whole house being summerlike, Laurie led the way from room to room, letting Jo stop to examine whatever struck her fancy ; and so at last they came to the library, where she clapped her hands and pranced, as she always did when especially delighted. It was lined with books, and there were pictures and statues, and distracting little cabinets full of coins and curiosities, and Sleepy-Hollow chairs, and queer tables and bronzes ; and, best of all, a great, open fireplace, with quaint tiles all round it.

" What richness ! " sighed Jo, sinking into the depths of a velvet chair, and gazing about her with an air of intense satisfaction. " Theodore Laurence, you ought to be the happiest boy in the world," she added impressively.

" A fellow can't live on books," said Laurie, shaking his head as he perched on a table opposite.

Before he could say any more, a bell rang, and Jo flew up, exclaiming with alarm : " Mercy me ! it's your grandpa ! "

" Well, what if it is ? You are not afraid of anything, you know," returned the boy, looking wicked.

" I think I am a little afraid of him, but I don't know why I should be. Marmee said I might come, and I don't think you're any the worse for it," said Jo, composing herself, though she kept her eyes on the door.

" I'm a great deal better for it, and ever so much obliged. I'm only afraid you are very tired talking to me ; it was *so* pleasant, I couldn't bear to stop," said Laurie gratefully.

" The doctor to see you, sir," and the maid beckoned as she spoke.

" Would you mind if I left you for a minute ? I suppose I must see him," said Laurie.

" Don't mind me. I'm as happy as a cricket here," answered Jo.

Laurie went away, and his guest amused herself in her own way. She was standing before a fine portrait of the old gentleman when the door opened again, and, without turning, she said decidedly : " I'm sure now that I shouldn't be afraid of him, for he's got kind eyes, though his mouth is grim, and he looks as if he had a tremendous will of his own. He isn't as handsome as *my* grandfather, but I like him."

" Thank you, ma'am," said a gruff voice behind her ; and there, to her great dismay, stood old Mr. Laurence.

Poor Jo blushed till she couldn't blush any redder, and her heart began to beat uncomfortably fast as she thought of what she had said. For a minute a wild desire to run away possessed her ; but that was cowardly, and the girls would laugh at her ; so she resolved to stay, and get out of the scrape as best she could. A second look showed her that the living eyes, under the bushy gray eyebrows, were kinder even than the painted ones ; and there was a sly twinkle in them, which lessened her fear a good deal. The gruff voice was gruffer than ever, as the old gentleman said abruptly, after that dreadful pause : " So you're not afraid of me, hey ? "

" Not much, sir."

" And you don't think me as handsome as *your* grandfather ? "

" Not quite, sir."

" And I've got a tremendous will, have I ? "

" I only said I thought so."

" But you like me, in spite of it ? "

" Yes, I do, sir."

That answer pleased the old gentleman ; he gave a short laugh, shook hands with her, and putting his finger under her chin, turned up her face, examined it gravely, and let it go, saying, with a nod : " You've got your grandfather's spirit, if you haven't his face. He *was* a fine man, my dear ; but, what is better, he was a brave and honest one, and I was proud to be his friend."

" Thank you, sir," and Jo was quite comfortable after that, for it suited her exactly.

" What have you been doing to this boy of mine, hey ? " was the next question, sharply put.

" Only trying to be neighbourly, sir ; " and Jo told how her visit came about.

" You think he needs cheering up a bit, do you ? "

" Yes, sir ; he seems a little lonely, and young folks would do him good perhaps. We are only girls, but we should be glad to help if we could, for we don't forget the splendid Christmas present sent us," said Jo eagerly.

" Tut, tut, tut ; that was my boy's affair. How is the poor woman ? "

" Doing nicely, sir ; " and off went Jo, talking very fast, as she told about the Hummels, in whom her mother had interested richer friends than they were.

" Just her father's way of doing good. I shall come and see your mother some fine day. Tell her so. There's the tea-bell ; we have it early, on the boy's account. Come down, and go on being neighbourly."

" *I shouldn't be afraid of him, for he's got kind eyes* "

" If you'd like to have me, sir."

" Shouldn't ask you if I didn't ; " and Mr. Laurence offered her his arm with old-fashioned courtesy.

" What *would* Meg say to this ? " thought Jo, as she was marched away, while her eyes danced with fun as she imagined herself telling the story at home.

" Hey ! why, what the dickens has come to the fellow ? " said the old gentleman, as Laurie came running downstairs, and brought up with a start of surprise at the astonishing sight of Jo arm-in-arm with the redoubtable grandfather.

" I didn't know you'd come, sir," he began, as Jo gave him a triumphant little glance.

" That's evident by the way you racket downstairs.  Come to your tea, sir, and behave like a gentleman ; " and having pulled the boy's hair by way of a caress, Mr. Laurence walked on, while Laurie went through a series of comic evolutions behind their backs, which nearly produced an explosion of laughter from Jo.

The old gentleman did not say much as he drank his four cups of tea, but he watched the young people, who soon chatted away like old friends, and the change in his grandson did not escape him.  There was colour, light and life in the boy's face now, vivacity in his manner, and genuine merriment in his laugh.

" She's right ;  the lad *is* lonely.  I'll see what these little girls can do for him," thought Mr. Laurence, as he looked and listened.  He liked Jo, for her odd, blunt ways suited him ;  and she seemed to understand the boy almost as well as if she had been one herself.

If the Laurences had been what Jo called " prim and poky," she would not have got on at all, for such people always made her shy and awkward ; but finding them free and easy, she was so herself, and made a good impression.  When they rose, she proposed to go, but Laurie said he had something more to show her, and took her away to the conservatory, which had been lighted for her benefit.  It seemed quite fairy-like to Jo, as he went up and down the walks, enjoying the blooming walls on either side—the soft light, the damp, sweet air, and the wonderful vines and trees that hung above her —while her new friend cut the finest flowers till his hands were full ;  then he tied them up, saying, " Please give these to your mother, and tell her I like the medicine she sent me very much."

They found Mr. Laurence standing before the fire in the great drawing-room, but Jo's attention was entirely absorbed by a grand piano.

" Do you play ? " she asked, turning to Laurie respectfully.

" Sometimes," he answered modestly.

" Please do now ;  I want to hear it, so I can tell Beth."

So Laurie played, and Jo listened, with her nose luxuriously buried in heliotrope and tea roses.  He played remarkably well, and didn't put on any airs.  She wished Beth could hear him, but she did not say so ;  only praised him till he was quite abashed, and his grandfather came to the rescue.  " That will do, young lady ;  too many sugar-plums are not good for him.  Going ?  Well, I'm much obliged to you, and I hope you'll come again.  My respects to your mother.  Good-night, Doctor Jo."